Praise for
When Every Breath Becomes a Prayer

"When Every Breath Becomes a Prayer *delves deep into the heart of love, life, and relationships. When faced with profound suffering, how do you move on, heal, and live a life of joy? Susan Plunket expertly guides you on a courageous and spiritual journey of soulful self-exploration.*"

—**Debra Oakland,** founder of Living in Courage, and international bestselling coauthor of *Unwavering Strength Volume 2*

"When Every Breath Becomes a Prayer *beautifully tells the story of a mother and her teenage daughter as they travel the landscape of heartbreak and betrayal—accompanied by a wise, funny, and loyal sisterhood— and arrive, at last, on a luminescent shore. With her penetrating eye, Jungian psychologist Susan Plunket takes us on journey deep into the heart of the feminine psyche, where we come to feel the scorching truth of Jung's famous words: "'Love is not a choice. You're captured.'"*

—**Nancy Fleisher Johnson,** PhD, clinical psychologist

"*Susan Plunket has written a magical book, full of heart. She speaks eloquently to those of us who know there is more to life than meets the eye, and to those of us who are searching for that something 'more.'* When Every Breath Becomes a Prayer *is a beautiful story of mysticism, heartbreak, and love.*"

—**Charmayne Kilcup PhD,** soul healer and author

"*It's so refreshing to see spiritual truths woven into the pages of a novel rather than confined to the self-help shelves. Susan Plunket's faith and expertise come through in the most compelling form: story. She wisely understands the power of story and that it is the fastest path to transformation.*"

—**Tammy Letherer,** intuitive healer, writer and author of *Hello Loved Ones, My Health in My Hands* and *Real Time Wreck*

"When Every Breath Becomes a Prayer *is captivating and compelling storytelling that teaches us how to claim the gift in the grit. A vividly rich novel that you can just sink your whole being into, and characters you can get comfy with who are willing to authentically reveal their inner worlds, reminding us 'You don't face off with the dark. You find the light in it.'"*

—**Pollyanna Blanco,** educator, dancer, and author of *In Rhythm With Your Soul: Breakthrough the Barriers to Being Creative, Face Your Daimons and Dance!*

"At once heart wrenching and heart soaring, When Every Breath Becomes a Prayer *is a wise tale of spirit and grace that offers a gentle hand to draw you forward, toward that hallowed space of love beyond love."*

—**Carrie E. Ruggieri,** psychologist

"When Every Breath Becomes a Prayer *is a truly unique novel that tenderly explores the sensitivities of suffering, love, loss, and friendship. This captivating book takes us on a journey of discovery that encourages personal nurturing and self-acceptance as it views the raw pain of human experience through timeless spiritual and scientific insights."*

—**Jo-Anne Brown,** holistic wellness practitioner and coauthor of the **Nurtured Woman book** series

"When Every Breath Becomes a Prayer *is a beautifully crafted novel. As a specialist who works with adolescents and their families, I found this powerful book not only clinically accurate, but also deeply moving in its portrayal of a family finding meaning and transcendence through heartache, laughter, and love."*

—**Monica L. Creelman,** PhD

"Susan Plunket's breadth of knowledge as a Jungian psychologist, her words as poetry, and her presence as a spiritual being, shine through on every page of her brilliant novel When Every Breath Becomes a Prayer, *as well as its powerful message of how suffering can transform our lives."*

—**Christen Daniel,** MA, intuitive healer and psychotherapist

WHEN EVERY BREATH
BECOMES A PRAYER

SUSAN PLUNKET

Creative Director: Anthony J.W. Benson, injoicreative.com
Cover Design: Anthony J.W. Benson, Shannon Whealy
Book Design: Anthony J.W. Benson, Shannon Whealy
Typesetting: Anthony Sclavi
Cover Artwork: © Richard George Davis
Author Photo: Susan Bowlus
Edited by: Sheridan McCarthy

Printed in the United States of America

ISBN-10: 0985715251
ISBN-13:978-0-9857152-5-0

Library of Congress Control Number: 2015948547
Published by: Deeper Well Publishing, deeperwellpublishing.com
For press inquiries, email publicity@deeperwellpub.com

For Ana, Brandon and Lucy

CONTENTS

ACKNOWLEDGEMENTS

When I told Anthony J.W. Benson I was afraid of letting go of this book, which had been in my hands alone for more than two years, that I was afraid to let it set sail into the world, he reassured me with the words: "I will be at the helm to navigate the journey and there will be wondrous hands on deck to help." He spoke the truth. He has been at the helm to navigate the journey with his knowledge, talent, grace and wisdom, all of which he applied to every facet of creating a book from this manuscript, everything from creating the cover art and coming up with the title, to choosing type face and creating a marketing plan. I am so grateful to you Anthony J.W. Benson. And also true to his word, the hands on deck have been wondrous. Among those wondrous hands were those of editor Sheridan McCarthy. I thank you Sheridan for your perfect care in creating the more than ten thousand thoughtful line edits to make this work more comprehensible.

Cyndi Dale, *When Every Breath Becomes a Prayer* would not exist but for your inspiration. The idea to do it came through you and it was your positive energy which set me on this course. I wish I could do something equally beautiful for you. You are, in Anthony's words, a "wondrous being."

This book would have not have made it from the yellow pads on which I wrote it and onto my computer, if not for the tech savvy Anastasia Khadivi. For your technical skill, and for your just all around brilliance, I thank you and thank you yet again.

And then there are all those in realms invisible to us who helped me. I join my palms before my heart and bow to each of you on the inner planes for your support, and for at times, actually pouring the words into my ear. Thank you. My gratitude to each of you is boundless.

Susan Plunket
New York City

GREENWICH VILLAGE

I love evening light, Georgina thought as she stood on the corner of Fifth Avenue and Tenth Street looking up at the building across the way. Counting up nine floors, she tried to see into the windows of her own apartment. About all she could make out were the silk drapes floating in the breeze. The light changed, halting the stream of traffic, and she stepped into the street.

As she entered the building, the light vanished into the white marble walls and floors of the lobby, and this cool oasis absorbed the cares of the day that had collected in her hair and clung to her arms and legs, cares that at times, even invaded her organs. Georgina listened to people's pain for a living. Smiling, the new doorman reached for her bag. She declined his offer. It only held two trout and a lemon. In a few weeks, he'd know everyone's names, the old renters and the new condo owners alike. Georgina was a renter. While she waited for the elevator, she heard the church bells on the corner ring six times. Good, she thought. *I can feed Olive and spin her around the block before Emma arrives.*

The phone was ringing when she opened the front door of her apartment, to be greeted by a dog wagging not just her tail, but her whole back end. Georgina bent to caress Olive's warm brow. "How is it that, even if I walk through this door twenty times a day, you always go totally insane with joy?" She let the phone go to voice mail while she knelt to kiss Olive's forehead and revel in her love. Olive was a rescue, only eleven weeks old when they first carried her shivering into their home, but the gift had always been all theirs. Now at nearly thirteen years old, Olive was so much a part of the family they couldn't remember a time when they hadn't had her.

"I'm going to be half an hour late," she heard Emma say. "A former Olympic athlete has died, and I have to check a couple of the details in the obit we have on file."

Georgina walked across the room and picked up the phone. "Take your time. I'm just coming in." She slipped off her striped espadrilles and went barefoot into the kitchen. Setting the bag on the counter, she took Olive's sweet potato and chicken out of the refrigerator. The refrigerator was just the right size now. It had been too small when Kate was still at home. She was always angling for some big energy-gobbling monster with double doors. But now Kate was married and living far away in Okinawa. At first Georgina hadn't known how she would face all the suppertimes alone without her. But she'd gotten used to solitude. She set Olive's dinner down next to her water bowl.

With no need to rush now, she went to her room to lie down on her yoga mat. She always left it spread out on the floor next to her bed, its light blue looking like a piece of sky. Resting her feet and legs up against the wall, she tried to drop into that still place inside herself—until a tongue smelling of sweet potatoes started licking her face. "Okay, let's go for a walk."

Georgina had lived in Greenwich Village since the seventies. Her daughter, Kate, had grown up in this very apartment. But the fact was, she'd never given up the hope of returning to Woodstock and living in an actual house on the Mill Stream. The sweet smell of grass in the morning and the sound of trees whispering their secrets to one another overhead at dusk were more in harmony with her psyche than the urban melody of horns, sirens, and jackhammers. And she missed the stars in the night sky. She'd grown up in starlight and moonlight, chanting the same words each evening of her childhood, standing under the open sky in the garden behind their house at firefly time: "I see the first star, and the first star sees me. God bless the first star, and God bless me." How she had loved those moments, waiting for the first star to appear.

To Georgina all light was a living luminous being, caressing everything as it accompanied her like a friend throughout the day. Dreaming of a garden and reading by the stream she'd swum in as a child, Georgina had kept in regular touch with a Woodstock Realtor for years. Despite this, she went on practicing psychology in Greenwich Village decade after decade. Sometimes a voice in her head told her that this was a defeat.

She was just setting the table when Emma sailed through the front door, her summer skirt rustling around her. "I could murder a gin and tonic."

"Coming up. There are pistachios on the table, but don't give Olive any. She's had enough."

Emma leaned over the kitchen counter, sipping her drink and watched Georgina squeeze a lemon over the frying trout, then drizzle melted butter on it, and finally sprinkle it with almond slivers. "So who died?" Georgina asked.

"I don't want to talk about work tonight," Emma said. Georgina raised her eyebrows just the tiniest bit as she lifted a whole fish onto each plate. Emma took the plates from her hands and carried them to the table at the dining room end of the large living room. Georgina followed with saffron risotto and asparagus.

They ate in silence, concentrating on their food, as was their custom. Only after they had set their forks down, to pause before salad, did Georgina, sensing Emma's mood, choose what she thought was a safe subject. "The thing with apartments is that you either have one exposure or another. There's no real relationship to light."

"Oh, please," Emma said, picking up the last few almond slivers with her fingers. "You have both southern and western light. You can see pink and blue sunsets from your bedroom windows."

"But an apartment is not a house."

"I don't know why you have a grudge against apartments. Freestanding houses aren't even eco-friendly. But if you're on about moving to a small town again because there are no roses overhanging your door, no rippling stream heard through an open window, I'll take this apartment." Emma reached for a plate, and Georgina passed her the salad.

"You know I treasure this apartment. It's held me through all my good and bad times. But I feel cut off from the beauty of the earth here. Anyway,

I can't leave my practice and start up in a small town."

"I don't buy it," said Emma. "Why can't you start up in a small town? You're finally divorced from Colin. I thought that radical simplification of your life would have set you free." Georgina grated Parmesan cheese over her salad and waited for Emma to say something mean about Colin, but Emma disappointed her.

"You keep saying, 'I can't leave New York.' What if that's just a story you're telling yourself. What if it isn't true?"

Georgina was thrown by Emma's question. "So you think I'm lying to myself?"

"Calm down," Emma said. Then she wiped her fingers on her napkin and picked up her salad fork.

"No, but maybe you're right. Maybe I don't know what I want. Maybe I've lost my path. Anyway, probably nobody in a small town even sees a psychologist."

"Well, not because they don't need to," said Emma. "Pass the bread." Emma ripped off a piece of baguette and dipped it in olive oil. "And if you really feel you've lost your path, good for you."

"What do you mean?" Georgina asked.

Emma blotted her lips before answering. "If you're lost, isn't that the best time to search for a new path?"

"You mean actually pick up and move?"

"I don't know. Maybe your path will lead you to an idyllic village filled with light or maybe to something deeper inside yourself." Emma helped herself to more salad. "What happened to the girl I knew in college who quoted Walt Whitman to me?"

Georgina looked perplexed. "Loaf and invite the soul," Emma reminded her.

Georgina let the familiar words sink into her heart. "That approach to life takes more courage than I have in me anymore," she said. "In fact I don't know how anyone can choose to be born at all. It's the bravest act I can imagine."

Emma reached for the wine and refilled both of their glasses. She wanted to roll her eyes. "Oh, stop taking it all so seriously. Why not have a cosmic giggle about it?"

"About what?" Georgina asked.

"About us being here at all, hurling through space on this big rock," Emma said. "It's remarkable that we even exist."

Georgina wasn't in a giggling mood. "Were you drinking at the office before you came over?"

"Oh, lighten up," Emma said.

Georgina couldn't lighten up. Why did Emma have to mention Colin? It pissed her off. "And what about death?"

"What do mean, 'What about death?'" Emma said.

"While we're rolling around on this rock, aren't we constantly trying to forget that death waits for us all in the end?"

"Not me. I prefer to live every day with the awareness of death on my shoulder," Emma said. "And besides, aren't you always telling me there is no death, that the soul's eternal?" They bent their heads over their salads. When they'd finished, Georgina asked, "Espresso?"

"Make mine a double. Do you have any chocolate to go with it?"

Tougher and more practical than Georgina, Emma had lost both of her parents in a car accident when she was seven. Even before they were buried, she'd started reading the encyclopedia. *I'm alone now*, she'd reasoned. *There's no one to take care of me. I'd better teach myself something so I can get a job.* Despite her Bostonian great-aunt taking her in and raising her, Emma had still felt the need to complete her task. By age twelve she'd read all twenty-six volumes, *A* through *Z*. She'd also replaced her fear with a will of steel. That the nature of life is impermanence was a truth she'd had to metabolize early. Her survival had depended on it. Though Georgina agreed with Emma about the nature of life, she'd never even opened an encyclopedia, and her will was more like a flexible branch than a rod of steel. Still, the two women had been friends since they'd met in college and discovered their mutual infatuation with Whitman and Yeats.

Emma had accompanied Georgina through heartbreak, two divorces, the deaths of both her parents, and the near loss of Kate. And Georgina had watched as Emma wrote obituaries for the *Times* year after year, telling the stories of people's lives, trying to make sense of senseless deaths.

"Shall we do the dishes before I go?" Emma asked. She took a last sip of her espresso, then popped a raspberry and a piece of Toblerone in her mouth.

"No, leave them. It's late." *Emma* didn't argue. She let out a moan as she stood up, and her hand went to her back.

"What's with your back?" Georgina asked.

"I sit too much."

"It's not just that, Emma."

Emma gathered up her things to leave. "Don't say it. I already know you believe that every ailment has its origins in our emotions."

"Yes, I do. Physical pain begins with the mistaken belief that we're not loved."

Georgina walked Emma to the elevator. To make sure she had the last word, Emma waited until the elevator doors were closing before she said, "How did we ever become friends?"

Georgina went back into her apartment and locked the front door. She carried their cups into the kitchen and pulled on the rubber gloves with the fancy cuffs that Kate had given her. She began to question herself. *What if Emma's right, and the story I'm telling about myself isn't true? None of my partners ever shared my dream of living in a house in a small town. Maybe that made it easy for me. None ever even saw home as a sheltered place in which to dream, a refuge from the world. None was interested in the play of light either.*

Her last husband, Colin, had gone so far as to tell her, "It isn't the fifties anymore, Georgina. No one sits on a swing on a big front porch, drinking lemonade. The world has bigger problems now. You're dreaming a dream that no longer exists. Air conditioning and television finished off small-town social life even before computers came along."

"You weren't even born yet in the fifties," she'd reminded him as she stubbornly continued to dream her dream. And besides, small-town life did exist. Her sister, Julia, lived in a small town that was still a small town— well, just outside one, on a hillside covered with lily of the valley and wild roses, in a house built in the 1700s. She didn't want Julia's life entirely, just the small-town part and a sheltering home.

On her own again, with no husband anymore to tell her where she couldn't live, Georgina had made a life for herself and Olive. Olive had been Kate's dog. But ever since Kate married Finn, Olive had lived with Georgina.

At the thought of Kate, a sigh escaped her heart. Even now, thinking back to the time when she'd nearly lost her daughter made Georgina break into a sweat. For a time both she and Kate had been completely lost in a dark wood, but Kate had survived. And together they'd learned the big lessons. Pain is a part of life, but how you meet your pain is a choice. Nothing is ever done *to* you. It is done *for* you, to wake you up, force you to grow, even against your will. At some point in their journey, they'd stopped asking: Why do I have to endure so much pain? And they realized the important question was: What has this pain come to teach me? The answer had arisen from the place where all wisdom is born—out of the crucible of heartbreak.

At sixteen and seventeen, Kate had learned that life requires each of us to walk into the fire and that even the worst things, the most difficult times, harbor a blessing somewhere inside them. "There's no way around it, just living breaks your heart," Georgina whispered to herself as she scrubbed the trout pan. She knew she should turn the water off while she scrubbed, but she loved the sight and feel of water, and it gave her such pleasure as it moved over the pan. She reached up and turned the faucet off.

Colin leaving her the day she returned from her mother's funeral had brought Georgina to her knees. But it was nearly losing Kate that had torn her heart half out of her body. *Will I still be if I lose her?* she'd asked herself each day for a year. You can love your child more than your life and still be unable to secure her safety. Georgina thought she'd be anxious about Kate forever. But now, with Kate married and living thousands of miles away in Okinawa on the South China Sea, far from her watchful eye, she even managed to sleep through most nights. Though rare, there were still times when she awoke in a sweat, panicked that Kate was lying dead on a train track. There had been months of insomnia and standing guard when Kate was sixteen and seventeen. Then, it had been unsafe to sleep as she lay on the floor of Kate's bedroom on a makeshift foam mattress, swamped with terror.

Georgina had still been married to Colin when Kate's nightmare began. While she lay on the floor in Kate's room, keeping guard, he slept peacefully in their big bed under a down cloud, dreaming his own dreams, not wanting to know that the castle walls had been breached, that the enemy already had his heel on her throat.

Georgina gave up on the pan and left it soaking in the sink. She peeled off her hot-pink rubber gloves with the leopard cuffs and switched off the kitchen light. "Thank God I had friends," she said to herself. Emma, Carrie, and Selma were as different from one another as earth, air, and fire. The fourth corner had been held by her sister, Julia, who flowed over the landscape of Georgina's life like a gentle stream. These four women had been her safety net when her life capsized, her eyes when fear had blinded her. Georgina tried to stop her mind from winding back in time to Kate's near death. But tonight it got away from her and pushed her like a fish carried backward in a stream, back to old conversations.

Hard-boiled Emma had been the most vocal. "Colin's not in this battle with you," she'd told Georgina in the earliest days of Kate's illness. "He has a choice. He could step up and lend his strength, but he doesn't."

"Where is his compassion for Kate?" Georgina had asked. "He's been with us since Kate was six years old."

"Don't you see that he resents Kate?"

When Emma said this, Georgina had looked at her as if this was a new and terrible idea. "It's like he's moved to a cold abyss inside himself where he's devoid of compassion, even of feeling," Georgina said. "I don't recognize him anymore."

"He hasn't moved to a cold abyss," Emma said. "That's his natural habitat." Emma had disliked Colin from the beginning. The feeling had been mutual.

Georgina pushed that long-ago conversation out of her mind and washed her face. Then she brushed her teeth, avoiding looking at herself in the mirror. She'd never been comfortable with mirrors. Now it was worse. Would the wrinkled face of an old woman be looking back at her? Was fifty-six considered an old woman these days? She wasn't sure. *Well at least I don't have to manage the tension between Emma and Colin anymore*, she reminded herself. It was so quiet in the apartment now. No Colin, and even no Kate. She flicked the bathroom light off, walked into her bedroom, and turned on her bedside lamp. This pottery lamp from Morocco had been a gift from her friend Carrie when Georgina married Cyrus, Kate's father. Like Georgina and Cyrus, Carrie was a psychologist. But she partnered with horses to treat her patients. Carrie's lamp had spread its light across the pages of hundreds of novels since Colin had left. The lamp and the novels had been the bulwark that kept her loneliness at bay even as she'd worried: *Am I going to spend the rest of my life just getting by reading novels?*

Still raking over the terrifying years with Kate and her own breakup with Colin, Georgina unzipped her creamy linen circle skirt and let it drop into a puddle around her feet. *I'd like to let the past drop off me just like this skirt,* she thought. Fortunately, Carrie, Emma, and Selma had stood by her through that time. But Carrie and Emma had disagreed about the reasons for Colin's lack of empathy for Kate. What was it Carrie said in Colin's defense that had so enraged Emma? Something about his own mental health terrifying him so much he couldn't do anything but distance himself from Kate's pain. When Carrie said that, Emma railed at her, telling her to stick to horse therapy and accusing her of making excuses for Colin's savagery toward Kate. Georgina bent to pick her skirt up off the floor and laid it on the chair next to her dresser. Carrie had argued back with Emma, explaining that Kate's suffering must have shaken Colin to his core. And so to survive, he had to invent a distorted image of himself as heroic.

When she heard that, Emma lost it: "Heroic? That talking snake, he's the very opposite." Then she accused Carrie of having a thing for Colin. But Carrie hadn't let go. "Maybe he spins it that he's the one who's been betrayed and ignored," she said. "That way he can abandon Georgina and Kate, quietly and without guilt."

At that point Emma threw up her hands. Then Georgina had stepped in. "You're too generous to him," Georgina told Carrie. "He could have come to me to renew his courage. Even as I was struggling to assure Kate of her worthiness to exist, I attempted to lend him my strength."

"But he turned his back on them," Emma said. "Then he had an affair and lied about it." This remark finally silenced Carrie, but Emma didn't stop. "For God's sake, the man burned the house down and poisoned the well." Emma's image had stuck in Georgina's mind for days after that long- ago conversation. Why was she carried back to all this tonight, she wondered. Still, her thoughts held her in the past.

And Colin hadn't left quietly. He'd raged openly, berating and blaming Kate for her depression and slamming his fist into doors, frightening and wounding her further as she struggled to survive. He worked himself into such a rage that it was a relief when he finally did leave. Even so, Georgina nearly fell to pieces once he was gone. Grief settled over her like a snowdrift. She'd thought they'd grow old together, that he'd be the one to close her eyes when she died. Or she would be there to comfort him at his death, to walk him to the edge. And he took so much when he left. *That's over now*, Georgina reminded herself. *I'm probably just thinking about him because Emma brought him up at dinner. Damn Emma.* Once reminded of Colin, Georgina's every thought carried her to him. She took her favorite pair of white pajamas out of her drawer, then shut it a little too hard.

Georgina turned back the covers and looked over at what had been Colin's side of the bed for the twelve years of their marriage. His bedside lamp had now been dark for more than six years.

Before she discovered his affair and witnessed his cruelty toward Kate, Georgina had viewed their marriage as a safe, deep harbor that would shelter them all their lives. She'd taken refuge in him, and she'd loved him. She'd loved the singularity of his face, the lilt in his laughter, his English accent. That love left him with a claim on her. How had he stopped loving her? "Was it little by little that you stopped loving me?" she said to his pillow. "Or all at once, in the middle of an ordinary day?" *If only he wasn't so damn funny and smart and sexy*, she thought. Kate had disagreed about the sexy, but he was. "A heartless person can never be sexy," Kate told her and Selma about a year after Colin left. Selma had come by with blueberries that hot afternoon. She was one of Georgina's oldest friends. Georgina poured her an iced tea.

"No, he was cute and sexy," Selma said holding up her hand, palm out, as if to stop Kate. "At least until he started talking and exposing how self-centered he is."

"Sexy? No way. He's Dr. Jekyll and Mr. Hyde," Kate said. "No. He's not even as human as the evil Mr. Hyde." Then, pausing, Kate gathered her long dark hair up in her hands and twisted it into a knot on the top of her head to cool off her neck. Georgina could still picture her doing it. It had stayed up without a single thing to hold it in place. "The intuitive you love, the one from Minnesota," Kate continued, "who compared Colin to Gollum, got it right. He is like Gollum: a distorted, driven, self-obsessed being carrying on an incessant conversation with himself. How else can you explain the depth of his self-involvement, his cruelty to my mother, his secret affair, and then bailing on us when we were hanging over a cliff? That's when he stomps on our fingers and walks away? What kind of person does that?" Kate asked, not really wanting an answer.

"He's all locked up inside," Selma told her. "And he's not a strong man." You could hear the South in Selma's speech even though she'd lived in New York City for more than fifty years. At eighty she was still living her life at a dead run, but the cadence of her speech was round and slow. Speaking privately to Georgina, Selma confided: "That boy's as low as a snake." The daughter of a black sharecropper, raised in Georgia before civil rights, Selma heard the same thing from her daddy each morning as she left to walk the three miles along the dirt road to the colored school: "Stay in your place." Selma could have been bitter but she wasn't. "Bitterness is a prison you build for yourself," she told Kate. Selma hoped Kate would pass up the cup of bitterness, chew on her anger at Colin until she could digest it, and let it go.

"You're right, Selma," Kate said. "He's not strong or a man. He's a little mouse, always looking for cheesy gossip about other people to nibble on to amuse himself and fill that empty place inside where his heart should have been. No point in being bitter about a mouse."

Sometimes Georgina still got angry at herself for ever having subjected Kate to Colin's cruelty. How could she have let him lay claim to her? It made her doubt her judgment. She turned off Carrie's lamp and lay her head down on the white pillowcase, imagining she was back in the nineteenth century in a large well-run country home where the white sheets were hung outside on the line to dry and always smelled of sunlight, wild lavender, and the sea. Thinking about a slower, quieter time made Georgina feel safe. Even now, years later, she was still grateful for anything that secured her a good night's sleep after that time of terror over Kate. She'd never forget the lessons it had taught her or the friends who had stuck by her.

Olive lay on the bed at her feet, her golden-haired belly rising and falling in her sleep. Georgina sat up and leaned forward to kiss her good-night. Olive's eyelashes had once been reddish gold. They were all white now. Then Georgina did the same thing she did every night. She closed her eyes, placed her palms over her heart, and fell asleep listing all the things for which she felt gratitude, beginning with Kate's life.

BY THE SOUTH CHINA SEA

"Use the funnel technique," Kate's professor once told the class. "It gathers your readers in and brings their focus to where you want to begin." Now, half a world away from New York City, sitting on a deserted beach on the shore of the South China Sea, pen and paper in hand, Kate knew where she wanted to begin. She just wasn't sure anyone would want to be funneled there. She looked out over the water and thought. *Some truths are too hard to hear. Most of us prefer to spare ourselves the sight of the suffering of others as we try to arrange our lives so we don't get our own hearts broken.* "Well, that's impossible," Kate heard herself say in answer to herself.

Looking up from the blank paper on her lap, she gazed out across the water as a slender native boy in a red loincloth dove from his canoe into the turquoise sea. He couldn't be more than eighteen. Was this his true path, already set, to dive below the surface and bring up treasure? Was he living out his ordained pattern? And was she as she sat on the deserted beach, waiting for that timeless sacred part of herself to speak?

"Just put the pen on the page and trust what emerges," her mother had texted earlier that day. "Take the plunge."

"That sounds like the Fool in the tarot who just steps off the cliff into the unknown," Kate typed back.

"Not exactly," Georgina wrote. "It's more like taking your first steps, on faith, in order to find the hidden path."

But will people want to follow a hidden path to where everything went completely black? Kate wondered. It wearied her heart to think of that time. And she missed her mother. New York City seemed a million miles away. But she was married to Finn now.

They'd been together since they were seventeen. Just when the worst nightmare of Kate's life was ending, Finn walked into the party she was secretly throwing in her father's apartment while he and his new wife were in Paris. She hadn't seen Finn since they were eleven years old in middle school. Back then they'd been seated at the same math table when she'd offered him some friendly advice. "If you don't start doing your homework, you're going to fail," Kate told him as she flipped first one of her braids then the other to the back of her shoulders. As a reward for this advice, at lunchtime the next day when Kate and her friends walked by, he called out: "Hey girl, this is for you!" and picked up a plant from in front of a Korean deli and smashed it on the sidewalk. Dirt splashed on the girls' bright-colored Pumas and up their legs. And his prank brought the school principal down on the whole class: "You can all thank Finn for the fact that there'll be no out-lunch for the any sixth-grader for the next two weeks."

"You've made yourself very unpopular, and you're still going to fail math," Kate told him later when the dismissal bell sounded.

"And some girls just don't know when to stuff it," Finn called to his friend Mo as he snatched Kate's blue math notebook out of her arms and bolted through the door.

Seventeen and just back from prep school the day of Kate's party, Finn was all grown up. Sort of. At least he was a lot taller. From that night on, they were together. Something clicked and came alive between them, out at their edges; and like two magnets, they stuck. They didn't pause to ask, "Who will I be if I let myself love you?" Had they been older, say twenty, they might have taken it slower. But they were seventeen, so they sailed ahead, opening the world wide for one another. They were at the age when just touching something can make it spring to life with a blinding beauty.

At age eleven at their math table, they'd represented two different poles of being. Kate was practical and aware of the necessity of doing well within the corporate world of middle school. Finn was living out his desire to express his freedom despite the cost. Since then each had been confronted by the opposite necessity.

Now they were twenty-three, married, and living in Okinawa. After attending the Defense Language Institute in Monterey, Finn had been stationed here. Kate joined him a month later, once he'd found a house for them in a grove of palm trees a short drive from the base. While Finn was at the base or on a mission, Kate worked on her graphic novels. A single drawing could take days. She was disciplined about writing and drawing. But not infrequently she had to remind herself that creativity can't be commanded. It belongs to the unbound part of oneself.

Still staring out at the sea, watching for the boy in the red loincloth to resurface, Kate reached into her bag for a box of Raisinetes and popped a few in her mouth. "You have to draw your story," her editor told her. "It'll help other teens cope when they're hopeless, depressed, and suicidal." She did want to draw and write that nightmare—that time when everything had gone completely dark—even just as a way to contain it, take control of it, and make sense of it. *But how do I put in all those people my mother collected to help*, she asked herself. *The psychics, the Irish mystic, the Reiki master, and the archangel channel, the energy healers and the Life Between Life regression therapists?* And then there was the pain to remember, the begging for death to end her suffering. Where would the courage come from to draw that?

Kate didn't even consider including the "possession by a dark shaman from her bloodline" explanation that she knew her mother believed was the cause of the mental breakdown and crushing suicidal depression she had survived as a teenager. Maybe she should just stick to the four psychologists and the five psychiatrists and the image of herself hanging from the Highline. Even now at twenty-three, it was still hard to think about it.

Kate lay back in the warm sand, closed her eyes, and listened to the waves breaking on the shore. The sun felt hot on her bare legs. Her neck was damp under her long thick hair. Her mind loosened in the heat. *The human psyche is like the ocean or the sky*, she thought. *As deep and invisible as the depths of the ocean and as vast inside of us as the starry heavens are outside.* She squinted her eyes open and looked up at the sky, then closed them again and continued her reverie. *Not a single star is visible when the sun is out, but they're there all the same, shining down on us. Our unconscious is like the stars in the daytime. You can't see it, but you know it's there, exerting influence, shaping your choices.* She tried to remember: How had her confrontation with her unconscious begun? When had the terror taken hold of her? When had she started to feel that something was after her? When did she first wonder if maybe the something that wanted to kill her was something inside herself? Had it been some invisible entity that no longer had a physical human body and wanted hers? She knew that was what her mother believed. Her mind drifted back to the August before eleventh grade. Yes, that was when the waking nightmare had become reality, sweeping away all her childhood innocence in one swoop, pushing her out of the eternal world of the child into the adult world of time. All the magic of childhood had disappeared by that hot day on Pier Forty at the beginning of eleventh grade. Kate had thrown up that day as she bent over to remove her soccer cleats after practice. She was the five-foot-two, 100-pound captain of her high school varsity team. Muscle and bone were all there was to her after the summer she'd spent at Vogelsinger Soccer Camp in North Amherst.

"Yacking on the field after the first practice. Way to go captain. Beautiful," her high school teammate Jenny chided. Rinsing the vomit from her mouth, Kate felt compelled to slip off the yellow captain's armband. *If you're not perfect, you don't get to wear it* was the thought that jumped out at her from a scary little corner of her mind. *You're not good enough,* a voice in her head told her. At some point that idea slipped into place and became a fact to her: *I'm not good enough.*

I feel like I can touch that day, that moment in time, as if it was now, this second, Kate thought. *The past and the present are both happening together, piled on each other like bits of paper on a pointed spindle attached to a small square of wood on someone's old-fashioned desk. Time isn't spread out in a line. It's all stacked up on itself, all happening at once. At twenty-three, lying by the South China Sea, I'm also still my sixteen-year-old self throwing up by the soccer field in New York City. Had the future already happened when I was sixteen? Had my twenty-three-year-old self been with me back then; only then, I just didn't remember the future?* "It's easier for humans to remember the past than to remember the future," her mother had often told her.

Though Kate admired her mother, she couldn't swallow all her ideas. But what she wouldn't give now to slip into her bed and cuddle up to her, feeling the soft white cotton, inhaling the sweet scent of her pajamas. Orange peels and vanilla, that's what Georgina smelled like. How many times during that nightmare period, when everything had gone dark, had Georgina taken a shaking and shivering Kate in her arms, led her to the fireplace, and built a blazing fire behind the owl andirons. The light and heat of the fire guarded by the two indestructible iron owls had restored them, if only momentarily, to the hope that they were safe in their castle. *I can still touch those moments when I clung to my mother for life. I never want to go back there. But those moments are here too, a living part of me. That suffering is part of this happiness. I'll draw those owl andirons. That's where I'll start. Later I'll figure out where they fit in the story. Good*, she thought. *I have a way to begin.*

Kate sat up and dug in her canvas bag for her phone. "Hi, Finn."

"Hey, girl. Do you want me to pick up anything on the way home?"

"No, I got it. I'll stop at the PX so we can make tacos."

"Great—see you soon, baby."

Brushing the sand off her white short shorts, Kate fished in her pocket for the keys to her old American Chevy. Okinawa was like a big used car lot for American cars, at least around the air force base. Finn had taught her to drive when she'd first arrived. He'd been a patient teacher, and she'd discovered the pleasure of it. After the bitter prayer that had been her stepfather's attitude toward her, Finn had reentered the atmosphere of her life like an incandescent being bearing, at long last, hope. He made her see again how remarkable existence was. She'd completely forgotten. Her stepfather had tried to destroy her. Finn called her soul back into being.

Even at seventeen she'd known Finn was one of the good guys, despite her sixth-grade first impression of him. He was kind and generous. Well, except for maybe last night when she'd been in the middle of writing, and he'd called her cell phone from his while taking a shower to say the shampoo bottle was empty and could she bring him a new one. She smiled to herself. She'd not only brought him a new one but had climbed right in the shower with him. She shivered with pleasure at the memory.

Kate put the key in the ignition and took one last look at the sea before starting the engine. The boy in the red loincloth was climbing back into his boat with his net bag full of oysters. She smiled through the car window at him as if he could see her happiness at his success.

It was freezing in the PX after the warmth of the beach and the heat of the car. She'd just collect the cheese, tomatoes, ground beef, tortillas, limes, beer, avocados, chips, salsa, and Popsicles, and hope she didn't bump into any of the other wives who would want to talk. Even when she wasn't chilled, small talk wasn't her thing. But when the space opened for a real conversation, she never declined the invitation. Then she was willing to reveal herself and to invite the other to do the same. It was only in the form-without-content exchanges where she became a clam.

Finn was a lighter sort: willing, but not necessarily looking for opportunities to chew the fat. And he was sensitive to her need to be silent at times. He made the space for it. He knew how to wait.

Oops, there was Lydia, three customers ahead of her in the checkout line. Hopefully, she wouldn't turn around. Lydia was a friend, really a friend, but this just wasn't the moment for Kate. It had been Lydia who'd first approached her when she'd arrived on the island, introduced her to the other wives, and shepherded her through the early days, seducing Kate with her soft beauty, her South Carolina accent, Southern cooking, and sundresses. *What's wrong with me?* Kate thought. *Why do I hang back? I love Lydia.* Lydia didn't notice Kate. She was busy charming the cashier. Just as well. Kate waited her turn, paid, walked back outside, stowed her bags on the floor of the back seat, and slipped inside the silent warmth of her car.

STREET FAIR

"Yes, it'll be completely anonymous. So will you do it?" Emma asked. Georgina thought about it as they strolled through the street fair on Grove and turned south on Bedford at a table holding rock-and-roll LPs from the sixties. Selma gave Emma a look meant to silence her.

"What?" Emma said.

"Stop pressuring Georgina to dredge up that business about the little hussy who stole her husband," Selma said.

"Nobody stole Georgina's husband, Selma. He fell for a younger woman because he was insecure and afraid of getting old," Emma said. "And by the way, nobody under eighty uses the word hussy."

"It's okay, Selma. It's old news now," Georgina said.

"So you'll do it?" Emma asked.

"Yes, I'll do it. How many women is she planning to interview for this article? Did all the marriages end because of affairs?" Georgina asked.

Selma stopped at a table covered with beaded purses from the twenties, not to look at the purses, but because a friend of hers from the runners' club was selling them.

"We've lost Selma," Georgina said. The narrow, winding streets were filled with shoppers bargaining and debating with themselves over whether they really needed the things they were holding. Emma climbed up the steps of a brownstone and craned her neck to see if she could spot Selma in the sea of people. Despite the crush, this was the best street fair in New York. It wasn't just the same tables full of iPhone cases, socks, sunglasses, and watermelon in plastic cups. This was West Village neighborhood artists and sellers with unusual collections. Selma could be talking to any one of a hundred people she knew.

Selma had lived in New York in the same apartment on West Tenth Street since the late fifties. It was stuffed with all kinds of things because it was hard for Selma to throw anything out. She'd been one of twelve children on the Georgia farm where she was raised. Her mother had given birth to fourteen babies, but two had died before they reached their first year. With only six forks, the family had to eat in shifts. Georgina guessed Selma was near eighty now, but she would never tell her age. She was uninterested in mirrors, and age was her only vanity, unless you counted her sleek runner's body without an ounce of fat on it.

When Georgina was in trouble, Selma was always the first in. When her father died, when her mother died, when Kate walked close to death, when Colin left her, Selma was right there telling her, "Pull up your socks, girl. Like my mama used to say, 'You've got to pull up your socks.'"

"I see Selma over there," Emma said pointing from the top of the brownstone steps. "Let's get her. I'm starving, and my feet hurt. I want to go to that place on Hudson with the red awning and the outdoor tables." Georgina nodded her assent and silently followed Emma through the crowd to Selma. Within a few minutes, the three friends were sitting outside under the awing and sharing a bottle of Chianti and a thin-crust pizza with artichokes on it.

When she got home, Georgina kicked off her shoes in her foyer and wished she hadn't agreed to be interviewed about Colin's affair. Why had she given in to Emma's pressure? Emma was a bully. She'd tell her that tomorrow. The writer wasn't even that close a friend of Emma's. Or maybe it wasn't that Emma was a bully. Maybe she'd agreed because she did want to review that period of her life. It was the only time a man had ever left her. Up until then she'd done the leaving. At least the article was for *Psychology Today*, so the author wouldn't be able to spin things to make it too sensational.

She turned on the water in the bath, sprinkled in three drops of wild-orange oil, then went to check her email. The woman had wasted no time in sending her the interview questions. Emma must have hopped right on it as soon as she got home, unless she'd already texted her from the restaurant. Probably that was it. Georgina read over the questions the interviewer would be asking her when they met:

How did you discover your husband was having an affair?

What was your reaction?

Did you confront him?

Had you had any inkling of it before you found out?

What else was going on in your life at the time?

Did you have children?

Are you divorced now?

Was the divorce a result of his affair?

Georgina unzipped her bright cotton circle skirt and let it drop to the floor with a soft thud. She liked doing that. *The questions aren't very creative*, she thought. *But they're definitely intrusive. So how did I discover Colin was having an affair?* She walked into the bathroom, leaned over, and turned off the water in the tub. Scrolling her mind back six years, she thought about the question. It was Olive, really, who'd found Colin's little spiral notebook with the top part of its spiral caught on the chair cushion. Colin always carried one in his back pocket to jot down ideas for his novel. Georgina had put a pack of six of them in his Christmas stocking. It was one of those, the yellow one, that Olive pulled from the cushion and was chewing on the day Georgina returned from her mother's funeral. Colin hadn't gone with her to the funeral. That should have been a clue things weren't right, given her an "inkling," as the interviewer called it. She stepped into the bath and heard Colin's sonorous voice in her head telling her, "I'll stay in New York and take care of Olive. You and Kate go to your mother's funeral." That's what he'd said in the soft voice of an adulterer. So they'd gone alone without him. Yes, it was that day, the day she got back from the funeral. They'd been talking in their living room. Then Colin said he was leaving to go and write in his studio. "But I just got back. Don't you even want to hear about my mother's funeral?" *I think that's what I said.* He'd been hard. "I need to go and write," he said getting up and moving toward the door. "And I'll probably spend the night in my studio." He pulled the door closed without kissing her good-bye. That's when Olive jumped onto the chair where he'd just been sitting and began chewing on something. She walked over to see what it was—Colin's little yellow notebook. She took it out of Olive's mouth and went to the front door, but the elevator had already carried Colin off. She flipped through it.

Georgina leaned back in the hot water and rested her head against the back of the tub. What she'd read had stunned her. On every little page of that little pocket-size notebook was written a tarot question about Liz. "How does Liz feel about me after last night? What does it mean that she took my suggestion to have the red velvet cake? How does she compare me to Ron (her husband of less than a year)? Does it mean anything that she smiled at me by the copy machine at noon today? Where will our relationship be by spring?"

On and on the questions went, each more juvenile than the last, each about Liz, this young girl in his office. Was she really reading this? Colin had spoken to her of Liz as the twentysomething, newly married Stepford wife with the big breasts that his fifty-year-old boss had a crush on. But it wasn't his fifty-year-old boss; it was fifty-year-old Colin who was obsessed with Liz.

Standing in the foyer by the front door that day, holding that little yellow notebook with its bent spiral, a new idea entered her thoughts. Colin didn't rent that studio to write. It was his lover's hideaway. He'd been lying two months earlier, when, just as they finished putting the lights on the Christmas tree, he told her: "By the way, I've rented a studio on Eleventh Street to have a quiet place to write. I didn't think you'd mind. It's just temporary until I finish the book." She did mind. It felt like a punch in the stomach, and she asked, "What does this mean?"

"Nothing," he said. Some part of her knew he'd just blown up the landscape of their life, and she sank into a chair by the fireplace. "Let's finish decorating the tree tomorrow," she said.

The next day when she and Kate were out shopping for stocking stuffers, they bought that pack of little notebooks for Colin. They'd even debated about spiral versus bound and chosen spiral because they were easier to write in and the perfect size to slip into his back pocket.

Yes, that's how she'd found out about his affair. She'd read it in his own handwriting on the day she got back from her mother's funeral, in a notebook she bought for him and put in his Christmas stocking.

Georgina reached up and turned on the faucet to add more hot water to her bath. Did she really want to share all this with a stranger writing an article on extramarital affairs? It didn't hurt anymore, but she did look like a blind fool even to herself as she recalled the details. Why had she let Emma pressure her to do this interview? *I'm a wimp*, she thought.

Next question: What was your reaction? She lay back in the bath again. What is any woman's reaction when she discovers reality isn't what she thought, that the man she loves is obsessed with someone else? Some variety of devastation and some attempt to absorb the new order of things. Once, I filled his mind. Now thoughts of a girl called Liz fill it. Learning that he'd secretly rented a studio and only informed her after the fact was gut wrenching. Finding the notebook was a stab directly to the heart. What was my reaction? What did I do? I stood there, feeling my thighs turn to cement, too heavy to even move, and I read Colin's chicken scratch in that notebook over and over to be sure I wasn't mistaking it. When I was finally able to move my cement legs, I dragged them into my bedroom, opened my closet door, and dropped the notebook into my cowgirl boot.

Did I confront him? No. He called, a couple of hours after I'd stowed that notebook in my boot, to ask if I'd found it because he needed it for his workouts. He said his trainer had given him some routines, and he'd written them down in the yellow notebook. The only workouts she'd found in there were his mental gymnastics over how Liz felt about him. "Well, maybe I lost it at the gym then," he said and hung up. To this day, years later, she'd never told him she had it. She still didn't understand why she hadn't thrown it in his face when he asked if she'd found it. Next question.

Did we have children? Yes, I had a teenage daughter, Kate, who was his stepdaughter, whom he had at one time loved. And what was going on at the time? Kate was depressed and suicidal, and she wanted to die to end the pain. I was terrified for her life. I was in awe of how much pain she endured and how hard she fought to live. Colin made everything worse. He wanted to send her away to boarding school to "grow up." He was cruel to her, and to my shame, I didn't tell him to leave. So thank God for you, Liz. You rescued us from him, though I didn't realize it at the time. I'm grateful to you. You can have him. Georgina shivered as she remembered her shame. She added more hot water to the tub until it reached up to her earlobes when she lay back.

Last question: Yes, we are divorced; and no, it wasn't because of his affair. It was because he was emotionally abusing my child. Even the hot water couldn't take away the chill of this thought. Georgina climbed out of the bath and wrapped herself in a big white towel.

TYPHOON

"I want you to come over and spend the night, Kate." Lydia was insistent. "A typhoon is bearing down on Okinawa, and with Finn off island, you'll be better off here. And Myrna's made fried chicken, black-eyed peas, and corn fritters."

"It's very tempting, Lydia, but I'm all prepared for the storm, and it'll be a good time to get some work done."

"Listen to me, darlin'. You haven't experienced a typhoon on Okinawa yet. It can be pretty harrowing. And there's not going to be any power soon, so working on your computer for long won't be an option."

"I have lots of drawing to do, and working by candlelight might be fun."

"You're so stubborn. Have it your way. But if you get scared, and we still have cell service, call me."

"I will. Thanks, Lydia."

Kate never knew exactly where Finn went on his missions. He respected the military code. His flights were secret, and he kept it that way. Kate checked her computer. "Stay inside," all the websites warned. The palm trees in front of their stucco house were already bent over nearly to the ground in the wind. The largest one hanging over the driveway was leaning toward her car. Kate backed away from the windows and took her laptop to the bedroom to check for more news of the typhoon's path.

She'd been scared before, much worse than this. This storm was outside of her. This was nature kicking up her heels. *I can go through this alone,* she assured herself as she hunkered down on her bed. *I'm bulletproof.* That other storm that had raged inside her when she was sixteen and seventeen—that one she hadn't been able to handle alone. That storm had dismembered her. Like some terrifying demon, it had dragged her into hell, past the edge of her sanity, and nearly taken her life.

That storm had been unnatural, spooky, inexplicable as it tore through her body and mind, ripping her apart like a giant prehistoric winged monster. The material that had burst forth from some dark level of the unconscious had swamped her, possessed her, and thrown her down into a deep pit. She'd hit rock bottom. Being alone in a typhoon could never be as bad as that. Having been to that hell made her unbreakable. Nothing would ever be worse. Hadn't she already faced the blood-red eyes of the three-headed Cerberus? That thought and the memory of her mother's voice allowed her to be calm. "Dark things happen," Georgina had told her. "We have to endure the suffering, and if we can, strength and wisdom will take root in us."

A crash made Kate jump. Her car horn started blaring. She walked out to the living room and looked through the window at the driveway. Their big palm tree was lying across the hood of her old Chevy, its roots torn out of the ground. It made her sad to see the tree uprooted, its life ended. Just minutes ago it had been alive, conscious, breathing, waving its worried fronds around with the other trees. Now it was dead, just like that. *How long can a car horn go until it stops blowing?* she wondered. The graceful palm tree couldn't even have a quiet, peaceful death. She retreated to her bedroom. Suddenly blackout—no cell phone, no lights, no power at all.

Alone in the sweet confinement of her dark bedroom, she listened to the typhoon rage outside her windows. *Good time to draw and write*, she told herself. Candles, matches, notebooks, pens were all assembled on the table by her bed. She felt around for the matches and lit nine candles. Then she picked up the drawing of the fire and the owl andirons she'd begun for her graphic novel—the one about her breakdown. What does a teen descending into depression and madness need to know? What could she show them to help explain the terror, the denial, the struggle to keep from killing yourself when that's all you can think of to end the pain?

You can survive it. When you're in hell, just keep walking. Hadn't that been Virgil's advice to Dante? "You'll be stronger because of the battle," she said out loud. A momentary doubt flickered through her. Would her old enemy insomnia reach out and take her in its clutches this stormy night as she sat alone on a tropical island? The wind was picking up. She could hear it whistling through the palms trees surrounding her house, circling like a wild animal closing in. It wasn't the soft rustling of silk she fell asleep to most nights. Tonight the wind was a ferocious battle cry. Let it roar! She would never fall to pieces again. She would sit with her fear and hold together, and she would do it as she had so many nights, by drawing. Keeping your hands busy when you're anxious is good. That way you can't dig holes in your head or pick at your skin.

As a teenager she had survived the desire, the wish, the intense longing for death as an end to unbearable mental suffering. For herself, she would have been long dead; but for love of her mother, she had withstood the torture. She had endured agony herself to spare her mother the agony of her death. Nothing less than love could have stayed her hand. She knew now that there is no greater power on earth. But how could she communicate that to other teens who might need to hear it? What if they felt that there was no one who loved them? How could they find the strength to love themselves and know that it would carry them through? How would she put that in a graphic novel?

Kate let her mind roam backward through her teen years to the day she burned her finger with her curling iron, deliberately holding it between the two hot rods and squeezing. That was the autumn after her sixteenth birthday, not long before the night she told her mother, "If I stay in eleventh grade in this high school, I'm going to start drinking."

"What?" Georgina asked.

"I'm so depressed. I don't sleep. I'm jumping out of my skin all the time. I want to hurt myself. I have hurt myself." As Georgina heard this, all the muscles of her face went slack, and she sank down on the foot of Kate's bed. Kate had been working on a Spanish project when Georgina came in to say good-night, and Georgina had to move some of the papers aside to make room to sit on the bed.

"I'm scared all the time, terrified of something I can't see, something that's threatening me."

"Terrified of what? What's threatening you?"

"I don't know. I can't fall asleep at night. I'm afraid something bad will happen if I'm not awake and on guard."

Georgina stared at Kate, unable to comprehend what her daughter was saying. "What will happen if you're not awake?"

Kate looked back at her mother, longing to be understood, longing for her mother to make her feel safe. "I don't feel like myself. Something or someone is drawing near, and it wants to hurt me. Or to make me hurt myself."

"Who would want to hurt you?"

"I don't know. Something is happening to me. When I was little, like in kindergarten, I never wanted to be anybody else but me, even in my next life. I don't feel that way anymore, Mom."

"Is this about being adopted?" Georgina asked.

"No—maybe partly. I've felt sorrow clinging to my edges since I was old enough to realize that my birthday was the day my birth mother gave me away. But this is something else. Something worse."

Kate had always known she was adopted, but when she was little, she thought everyone was. "Isn't everyone adopted?" she asked Georgina one night at story time when she was three.

"Some people are and some aren't," Georgina explained.

"But you are, aren't you, Mom?" Kate asked.

"No."

"I came from here," three-year-old Kate insisted, laying her little head on Georgina's belly.

"How do you deal with not being wanted by the person who gives birth to you?" Sixteen-year-old Kate asked Georgina. "People telling you things like 'Your birth mother just couldn't raise a baby—she didn't have the resources. It was a bad time in her life.' None of those excuses cuts it. They make it worse. Plenty of poor people don't give their babies away. Is there a bigger rejection than being given away the moment you're born?"

"Oh, my darling girl," Georgina said, taking Kate in her arms and holding her close.

"How can I—or any adopted child—understand, absorb, forgive being unwanted by her own mother at the moment of coming to earth?" Kate said. She lay her head against Georgina's warm neck. "I know I have to heal that wound in order to be whole, but what I'm feeling now is more than that," she whispered, her breath on her mother's throat.

Georgina's head was spinning as she listened to her teenage daughter. "When did it become more?" She released Kate from her embrace so she could see her face.

"A few months ago, I started noticing that I was having thoughts that didn't feel like mine. Bad thoughts about myself."

"Like what?"

"That I don't belong in the world, that I should die, that I'm not good enough, that I'm somehow deformed. Why else was I given away? I must be deformed, subpar, otherwise she wouldn't have given me away."

"Oh, Kate." Georgina pulled Kate into her arms again and held her next to her heart.

"I used to want to ask my birth mother, 'Why didn't you keep me? Do you think of me? Do you remember me on my birthday? Do you wonder what I look like? Do you regret giving me away? Do you miss me? Do you know how old I am?' Do you think she thinks of me as her daughter on Mother's Day?"

"I'm sure she does, Kate. She carried you inside her for nine months. A woman doesn't forget that."

"I hate her," Kate said.

Georgina listened and felt her insides turn to jelly. Then Kate said, "But this voice in my head isn't about her. It feels like it's someone else who wants to kill me." Kate looked at Georgina and saw she was white with fear.

"My darling. Oh, my darling girl." Georgina rocked Kate in her arms.

"I'm afraid to sleep. I have to be on guard. I'm bending out of shape to keep going."

"What do you mean, 'bending out of shape'? What are you doing?"

"Twice I walked too close to the subway tracks as the train entered the station. I came so close to jumping. Some voice in my head kept telling me I should do it."

"My God." Georgina's heart wrenched, and her throat went dry.

"It's all right, Mom. Now while I wait for the subway, I make myself read *The Girl with the Dragon Tattoo* to drown out that threatening, alien voice that is taking over my brain, telling me I'm worthless."

"It's not all right. You're done with the subway."

"Mom, it's not just the subway. Whatever it is, it's either going to kill me somehow or push my soul out and take my body for itself."

"That's not going to happen." From that moment Georgina was galvanized and terrorized. Why hadn't she known sooner? How had Kate come so close to leaving this earth? How had she missed the signs? Georgina felt her heart crack inside her chest. How could this be happening?

Because Kate was by nature so silent as a child, Georgina had called her "my little clam." When she was about five, Kate dreamed she was being chased down Fifth Avenue by giant clams. Georgina told her she, Kate, was the clams, that they were an aspect of herself. Kate didn't understand that back then.

Georgina sat at the bottom of Kate's bed, unable to speak. To fill the silence and drive away the terror, Kate started talking. "I can't concentrate on my homework. And I can't sleep. I'm afraid to let my guard down. It feels like something monstrous is after me. If I sleep, it'll get me." Concentrating on her Spanish project had taken every bit of strength Kate had. Nightmares and lack of sleep left her exhausted and jumpy. She'd hidden all this from Georgina, hoping she could deny it even to herself. If she didn't talk about, didn't admit to it, just clammed up, maybe it would go away. That hadn't worked.

When Georgina, still holding Kate in her arms, kissed the top of her head, Kate broke down again and poured out her dream of the previous night. "My numbers are going down. I can't stop them. If they keep going down, I'll die. You're there in my dream. You're trying to keep my numbers up, but I'm afraid you won't have the strength, that you'll get tired. There's no one to help you."

The dream was terrifying in its simplicity. Its meaning was not lost on either of them. Kate watched as her mother absorbed it and tried to stay calm so as not to frighten her. It was too late for that. A dark shadow was moving over their lives. Kate desperately wanted her mother to grasp the compass with both hands and help her find a path through this hell. Would she have the strength? Their lives changed that night with the telling of that dream. Now Kate wasn't alone with this anymore, trying to pretend it wasn't happening. She had an ally. Whatever it was, would they be strong enough to fight this monster off?

In the following days Kate got more scared as Georgina lost her voice and stopped working. She watched her mother try not to shake with heartbreak and fear. Once, walking into the living room, she saw Georgina paralyzed, staring at the words "Kate's network" on her computer screen. *What if I die? Will she still have to see "Kate's network" on her computer? I have to survive or I'll kill her*, Kate told herself.

High school ended for Kate the night she told her mother her numbers dream. She couldn't eat or sleep. Her eyelids were heavy, but no matter how heavy they got, they wouldn't stay shut. She'd lie exhausted, yet vigilant and wired, her head bleeding and burning from her digging at it without even knowing she was doing it until she felt the blood running down her face and neck. *What am I trying to dig out of my head?* she asked herself.

They consulted five different psychiatrists in the hope that some medication would help end Kate's suffering. Nothing worked—not Klonopin, or Xanax, or Valium, or Ambien, or Seroquil, or Remeron, or six different antidepressants. Some made her loopy, but none put her to sleep or stopped the digging and terror. Loopy, she'd stumble into the bathroom before bed to put in her night retainer so her teeth would be straight. What a joke. But she wore it anyway because she might live through this, and it was one of the few normal things left in her sleepless, terrified life.

Sometimes in the middle of the night, she'd get out of bed and do the elliptical until she dripped with sweat, hoping to knock herself out. But nothing shut down her mind or stopped the terror. Her scalp felt like it was full of bloody pools of self-hatred. She'd sit in bed shaking, too scared to let go, watching Olive sleep. Sometimes relief would come for an hour or two, and then she'd realize she was awake again, back in the waking nightmare instead of the dream nightmare.

In her dreams someone was always trying to kill her: usually one man, but sometimes he split himself into several men or changed his shape into a type of reptile. He could turn himself into wild animals and strange half-human creatures or suddenly appear and disappear. Kate created strategies for coping. Would it be a 2:50 a.m. game of Club Penguin or an episode of *Ugly Betty* while playing Bejeweled to keep her hands busy? Nothing worked for long. The only time she felt safe was when she leaned in bed against Georgina's heart, listening to it beat while Georgina held her hands to keep her from digging her head. She knew her stepfather, Colin, disapproved of this. "Kate's not a baby, Georgina. You don't have to hold her." Kate knew he had no compassion for her suffering. He seemed to have turned into someone else. His jealousy was so naked. If only he understood this was nothing to be jealous of. If just once he'd come in and put his arms around both of them and told them he was there for them, things might have turned out differently. But he never did. He left them alone in their terror. After a while there were no day and night and then no separate days. All time rolled together in waves of endless fear and pain. And then, after more than a year, it ended: not all at once, but the tide turned. What turned it? Kate didn't know for sure. Was it the healers and shamans and mystics and exorcists her mother had worked with or something else, maybe therapy or all their prayers? She didn't know. But somehow she had survived.

All that was over now. *After living through that, I can easily sleep through a typhoon*, Kate thought. But she didn't want to sleep, not yet. Instead she wrote and drew what she remembered of that time. It had taken the distance of six years to revisit it. But she was there now. She held her sketchbook so the candlelight fell across the white paper. Somehow they had found their way through the dark to the light. Yes, it was about finding the light in the dark. Now how to convey that to teens suffering as she had? It was probably the last thing they wanted to hear.

WAS IT A POSSESSION?

"Why do you still have dinner with Cyrus even though Kate's grown up," Emma asked.

"It's too early in the morning for such a complicated question, Emma." Georgina tucked the phone between her neck and shoulder so she could pull the covers up. Then she lay back on the propped-up pillows and took a sip of coffee.

"So how was it?" Emma asked.

"He was funny as usual, but he looked tired. And he misses his movie dates with Kate and Finn since they got stationed in Okinawa."

"I don't know why you two ever split up. He's smart, funny, gorgeous, generous."

"Really, Emma. Do we have to go down that avenue at eight in the morning?"

Emma barreled ahead anyway. "Remember that time you were in graduate school, just before your wedding, and you came home with a necklace and told Cyrus you'd charged it at Tiffany's for eight thousand dollars, and he told you it was perfect with your thrift store wedding dress."

"Of course I remember. Why are you bringing that up now?"

"Not a man in a million would react like that when the two of you were just graduate students," Emma said. "And he didn't even seem relieved when you told him you were kidding, that it was only rhinestones."

"He's enchanting, but he enchants only to disappoint. Unfortunately it took me ten years to figure that out."

"You mean how he's married to his work?" Emma said.

"He's still completely driven now at fifty-eight."

"You must have seen how driven he was even at twenty-four."

"I didn't want to see it. He was the most exotic and exciting man I'd ever met. That's all I knew."

"Well, you had your magic carpet ride."

"For a time."

Born in Teheran to a wealthy family, but with the gray-blue eyes of more Northern Iranians, Cyrus was both exotic and enchanting. The Russian guys working in the hardware store downstairs from their graduate school apartment nicknamed him Omar, after Omar Sharif. Whenever Georgina went in for picture hangers or nails or tape, they flirted with her and called after her as she left: "Say hello to Omar."

Cyrus and Georgina married downtown at City Hall while they were interns. Living and breathing various psychological models and theories, they shared a passion for psychology as well as for one another. Georgina was already a hard-core admirer of Jung. Cyrus was open to any approach that helped the patient. Even as an intern, what had marked him as special was his extraordinary compassion for each person he worked with.

"I got the feeling that Cyrus never approved of your marriage to Colin," Emma said.

"That's true. When Colin left me, Cyrus told me, 'Well, what did you expect marrying a former client?'"

"How did you answer that?"

"I reminded him it was four years after Colin stopped coming to me that I'd met him again at a reading at the Strand. But Cyrus said, 'That's irrelevant—therapeutic relationships are for life even if the person has a dozen therapists after you.'"

"What did you say?"

"I told him he was wrong. 'Life's more complicated than that, less black and white. Besides, I don't meet anybody besides clients. Maybe next I'll marry my new client. He used to be a bank robber.'"

"What did Cyrus say to that?"

"He laughed and said, 'At least he'll bring in money.'"

"You were a fool to let go of Cyrus and then settle for Colin."

"I've got to get up and walk Olive. I'll talk to you later."

"You always get off the phone when you don't like what I'm saying."

"Stop."

"Go skitter off then."

Georgina pulled on her jeans and leashed up Olive. The park was already busy, but Georgina barely noticed. Her thoughts were still on Cyrus. *I have Cyrus to thank for Kate. Adopting a baby was his idea.* She remembered how he'd taken her in his arms the day they were looking at country houses. They'd been married about five years by then, and he was already the chief of psychology at the hospital. After looking at four or five places, the Realtor took them to a farm near Millbrook. "I love it. We could have baby chicks here and baby pigs and baby ducks," she told Cyrus.

"Georgina," he said, "why don't we forget the farm and the baby chicks and piglets and ducklings and just adopt a baby."

"Really?"

"Yes, really."

They both wanted a girl, but neither of them had any idea how to go about adopting. Luckily, their friend Irwin did have some ideas. He knew of an adoption agency in San Antonio, Texas.

Holding Kate in her arms as a baby and toddler was the happiest time of Georgina's life. Holding Kate in her arms when she was sixteen and begging for death to end the pain was the most unhappy time of Georgina's life. Kate was a brave warrior. She fought to live with all her might, and Georgina and Cyrus fought alongside her, ripping the invisible monster from Kate's psyche and flesh, digging it out of her mind. Georgina's single purpose had been to save her child from death or possession by this dark force, this energy from some lower vibrational world that was trying to harvest the spark of light in Kate's heart. Georgina believed that dark entities, having cut themselves off from Source in their grab for power, needed to feed on the divine energy in human hearts in order to sustain themselves. Cyrus had said, "Get a grip, Georgina. You sound like you're describing the dementors from the Harry Potter books."

But psychology and psychiatry were failing Kate. And the other resources in the field were good and great. A shaman from Peru, an energy healer from Minnesota, an Irish mystic, and an archangel channel from Australia had each separately told her that a corrupt energy with a predator consciousness was trying to possess Kate, drive her soul out, and take over her body or kill her and absorb the spark of the Divine in her heart. Each healer cleared what they could of the demon's energy, but the battle was Kate's. She must hold fast. She was of Mayan descent, and there were shamans in her bloodline. One energy healer explained to them that Kate's eighth chakra was wide open because she was next in line for the shamanic power and that was one reason she was susceptible to this corrupt being who had tried to slip in and take over her body. Cyrus scoffed at this explanation, telling Georgina that Kate was clinically depressed and suicidal. But he wasn't there the day the thing looked at Georgina through Kate's eyes and spoke through Kate in a voice that wasn't Kate's. She doubted that even Jung would have called it Kate's own shadow—maybe an archetypal shadow but not her personal shadow. And it threatened Georgina, telling her in a chilling voice, "You're going to be sorry." The memory still haunted her.

Georgina left the park having barely noticed she was there. She didn't like to let that happen. She apologized to Olive. *I'll take a hot shower when I get home and shake off these old memories and send them down the drain,* she said to herself.

The possession scenario might have been too weird and frightening even for Georgina except for the dream she had during Kate's darkest time. In the dream she and Kate were falling through the air, into worlds of blackness. They were clinging to one another as they fell downward. A man with long black hair, claws for hands, a demonic face, and a tail like a whip was pursuing them. He wanted Kate. Suddenly, he was upon them and had ahold of Kate. Georgina reacted, grabbing for him and shredding him, burning her hands on his surface, which was more like scales than skin. He came at them again and again, lacerating Kate's body, trying to open a passage into her near her heart. The three of them tumbled over and over each other in their downward descent, falling through worlds, the beast holding fast to Kate as she twisted and turned to evade his grasp while his knifelike fingers slashed her. Georgina went for his hair and yanked it when she saw him trying to enter through the top of Kate's head. She dragged the man-beast out of Kate and hurled him away, watching as he seemed to be sucked backward. She begged and prayed for the light to come and take him before he could attack again.

Kate looked dead, her body translucent, as Georgina lifted her in her arms and flew to a mountaintop where she laid Kate across her lap. She sat and sewed up her daughter with green thread in all the places where the monster had torn her. Sewing and sewing, she worked, leaving no wound open, especially near her child's heart. Light began to reenter Kate as Georgina sewed, but it was wobbling around, and Kate's roots had torn loose. She was no longer connected to the earth. Georgina grabbed for her own taproot and tore it up the middle, splitting it, and then tied it to Kate, securing her to this world. "Close she came to leaving this earth," came a voice from somewhere in space. "Close she came to leaving this earth." Georgina sat on the mountaintop and wept over the body of her wounded child. Again she heard the voice. "Bright souls are hunted by powerful lower vibrational entities who want to keep all human souls separate from Divine Source. She has survived the attack."

Georgina had awakened from the dream in a sweat and sat up in her makeshift bed on Kate's floor. Kate was sitting up in bed too, staring straight ahead, her face a mask. Georgina called her name, and Kate turned to meet her mother's eyes in the dark. "Close your eyes. Rest now," Georgina told Kate as she crawled into bed beside her and kissed her forehead, rocking her to sleep.

Maybe the tide had turned. Frightening as it was, perhaps the dream portended Kate's release from the demon that had been trying to possess her. Georgina prayed as she'd never prayed in her life while she rocked Kate in her arms all through that long night. And her prayers were answered.

Before stepping into the shower, Georgina adjusted the water temperature. Maybe the warm water running over her back and down her body would wash away that old nightmare. Looking out through the slender white stripes on the clear shower curtain, she stared at the sun falling across the sea-glass floor of her bathroom, setting it alight. She rinsed the shampoo out of her hair and reached for a towel. But the memory of the nightmare still clung to her. Something about it had always bothered her. You don't face off with the dark. You find the light in it. But that's not what had happened in the dream. They hadn't asked it what it had come for. They had driven it off. She dried herself quickly.

The dream had terrified her, and the morning after it, she had called Cyrus so she wouldn't have to hold it alone. Colin had already left them by then. "Emma insists the demon from the dream who is trying to kill Kate is Colin," she told Cyrus. "She says he was always doing mean things to hurt and humiliate her, that he was a psychic vampire, and I turned a blind eye. That thought tortures me. Did I turn a blind eye?"

"Emma may be right, or she may have her own issue with Colin." Cyrus could have piled on and judged her, but he didn't. He remained calm and rational and fair, even compassionate. He reminded her of her own belief system about demons: that they come to teach us, and when we have heard them and embraced them, they transform into allies.

"But some thoughts stick in my brain and I can't shake them," Georgina told him. "I hurt myself over and over again with them. Like, why did I ever marry him?"

"I'm not the one to talk to about that choice," Cyrus reminded her. "But you're the dream expert. Use this dream to help yourself. Aren't you always saying we should go out to meet our dreams on a field between conscious and unconscious? Sit and trust the intuition that comes to you."

"I'm trying, but sometimes I feel so hopeless."

"You have sat with grace, Georgina, no matter what has been thrown at you. You have to hold on now, for Kate's sake. Keep searching in the dark until you find the light in it. Hold on to your own beliefs."

"But I'm afraid. I don't know how we'll ever survive this."

"When you don't know what else to do, sit down and surrender to the situation. Accept it as best you can. That's what Jung would have told you. Your dream shows you how courageous you have been. How courageous Kate is. It shows you how fearlessly you have fought for our daughter's life, how you have sewn up her wounds and prayed for her own soul to return to her body. Even though I don't take your possession theory literally, I do believe in the power of dreams to give us a symbolic picture of the psyche. Let's hope the worst is over." Then Cyrus paused before adding, "But we don't know what yet may come."

"Sit down and don't worry. We don't defeat the dark—we must find the light in it. That's the task." Georgina repeated this to herself over and over after they hung up that day. *You are not in control here. Not man, but some timeless essence is in command*, she reminded herself. *Our will and intention must give way to the inscrutable design of the divine matrix.* That was what she believed.

So they sat still, huddled together, she and Kate, and Kate survived. There were those who stood by her: Cyrus, her sister, Julia, and her friends Selma and Emma and Carrie. None of them slept beside her on the floor in Kate's room or took Kate's hands in their own when she shook and dug holes in her head. But she felt their presence holding her up like an invisible web of light with the intention of keeping her and Kate from falling into complete darkness.

Georgina shivered and realized she had been lost in the past and was still wrapped in a wet towel. She put on a warm robe, made herself some tea, and curled up in her favorite chair.

For a long time she had been afraid that the nightmare would come back again, that fault lines etched into Kate's psyche from the experience would open, and she could become vulnerable again. They'd survived Kate's sixteenth and seventeenth years. By her eighteenth birthday, they understood that nothing would ever again be as bad as those earlier years. But even now, six years later, the thought of writing about what they had been through frightened Georgina. She didn't want to awaken any sleeping demons. But she knew that sometime she must face down this fear. And so must Kate. Setting her teacup down, she picked up a fine-point, black felt-tip pen, uncapped it, and opened her journal to a new page. The final healing—for both of them—would be in the writing. *Journal writing is the warrior path*, she told herself. *How can I expect Kate to do what I myself cannot?*

I'm afraid of the pain of recounting this. And afraid of awakening some sleeping demon. I realize now that Kate's sixteen-year-old hormones and her brain chemistry and her spiritual openness all made her vulnerable to the dual attacks of depression and dark energies that wanted to break her connection to the Divine and steal her spark of Godhood. I know dark entities are also part of the Divine and come to test us, but it's hard to remember that when it's happening. What seems certain now is that at twenty-three, she's solid again. She's not spinning or wobbly. Best of all, Finn came along and made her want to live just as she was emerging from the nightmare that had been her life. He made her want to put down her own roots into the earth again. For love of me, she fought her demon. But Finn was the treasure at the bottom of her suffering, the one who called her soul back into being.

Colin never understood any of that. He fled in fear and distracted himself with an infatuation. He missed the life lesson that might have changed him forever. When he abandoned us in our time of need, he snuffed out his own light. As I lay on Kate's floor at night praying for her life, praying for some medication to work or for some divine intervention, Colin had already moved into his fantasy world of new love. I'm not a religious person, but I prayed to Mary, as a fellow mother, begged her really, for Kate's life. Day and night I whispered to her, and when my fear was so great that it swallowed my voice and I couldn't make a sound, I thought the prayers in my head. It was more than a month before my voice came back. I was not even able to croak like a frog. There was only dry silence. I guess Colin felt I had nothing left to offer him, so he dusted off his sandals and moved on as his therapist had advised him to do. My foot's asleep, and I need to cook some sweet potatoes for Olive, so I'll stop writing even though I didn't get very far. At least I've made a start.

Georgina capped her pen and put it down. As she reread what she'd written, she saw that she'd veered off into writing about Colin. Even now, years later, she couldn't keep her consciousness on that scary time of Kate's possession for too long. But then, that's the nature of consciousness. The mind drifts down its own stream, catching here and there, snagged by leaves and sticks among the rocks. Then, freeing itself, it leaps up from the gurgling brook to alight on the branch of an overhanging tree, only to dive down again to the silty bottom of the stream before resurfacing to soar up on the back of a lark into the sky.

The mind can't stick on one thing. Georgina had rattled herself even with that little bit of revisiting those years. She wanted to hear her sister's voice. Julia's calm would make the terror go away. She picked up the phone.

DREAMING OF MONTEREY

Kate awoke to silence. The typhoon was over. She'd been dreaming they were still in Monterey, and she was riding on the back of Finn's motorcycle. They'd had an apartment off base and had gone everywhere on that motorbike.

"Motorcycle accidents are where all the hearts come from for heart transplants," Georgina had told them.

"We always wear helmets," Finn lied.

Monterey was romantic and lonely for Kate. While Finn spent his days up at the Presidio, she read Steinbeck and walked around the wharf and Cannery Row, making sketches. Evenings and weekends, they'd hop on the motorbike and head to Pebble Beach or along the coast to Carmel. With Kate holding onto Finn's waist, they'd speed up and down the hills above the ocean. But why was she dreaming of Monterey now? If she were having breakfast with Georgina, they'd puzzle over that question. Georgina delighted in decoding a dream the way her sister, Julia, delighted in solving crossword puzzles.

Kate put on a cotton kimono, the one with big red flowers on a pale blue background. Then she padded down the hall to the kitchen, thanked the stove gods that she had a gas stove, and put the kettle on. While she waited for the water to come to a boil, she looked out and saw the large palm still lying across the hood of her car. The horn must have blown itself out during the night. At least none of the other palm trees seemed to have been uprooted.

The kettle whistled, and Kate made herself a pot of tea. Drinking out of the small handleless cups that had come with the teapot was one of her little daily pleasures. She rolled her cup between her palms after each sip while she thought her morning thoughts. This tea set had been her first purchase on arriving on Okinawa. The smell of the small local shops reminded her of stores in Chinatown back in New York.

Kate carried her cup with her into the bedroom to retrieve her sketchbook and see if she'd done any good work the night before. Not bad. Her graphic novel was beginning to take shape. Each of the panels drawn on the page held a piece of the story of her old numbers dream: the one that had awakened her mother from denial of what was happening to Kate. Sharing that nightmare with Georgina had also been the end of high school for Kate and the official acknowledgement of her suicidal depression. Kate shivered as she looked at the panel depicting her mother's face as she absorbed the meaning of the dream. Looking back at her from the drawing were Georgina's familiar almond-shaped eyes under curved brows, her shoulder-length blond hair, and the soft line of her lips. Yes, Kate had captured the terror in those almond eyes.

"Dreams can see around corners and into the future," Georgina had told her when she was still a child. "They can warn of events before they happen, as they describe the inner situation of the dreamer." They both knew what Kate's numbers dream meant. It was a clear message from Kate's unconscious, and they took it seriously. The dam broke the night Kate told her mother that dream. She had been secretly living with thoughts of suicide for weeks, but she couldn't hide her pain anymore to protect her mother—she needed her too much. Moving her long hair aside that night, she showed Georgina the pits she'd dug in her head to feel physical pain in the hope it would give her relief from her psychic agony. Physical pain was so much easier to bear than mental pain.

Kate tightened the belt on her kimono and poured herself some more tea. At the time of her numbers dream, she was angry, believing that her father had replaced her with a young wife. She hadn't spoken to him for five months. But Georgina had insisted on calling Cyrus. They needed his help. "You're his child too," Georgina reminded her. Kate remembered herself as a skinny, shrunken, terrified, shaking, bleeding mess when Cyrus walked in that night. Unlike her mother, whose face was a movie screen of her emotions, her father, a Persian aristocrat, habitually wore a mask of impenetrable reserve. He sat down beside her and took her cold, shaking hands in his warm ones. He made no mention that she'd cut him off for five months, and if he noticed her bloody scalp, he didn't comment. Speaking softly, he reassured her. "Kate, together we'll get through this. You're not alone. Your mother and I will do everything we can to help you feel safe again."

Kate was sixteen at the time. Her parents had divorced when she was four. Now here she was suspended between their love and strength. Would they be enough to hold her through this? "I don't want her hospitalized in a psychiatric inpatient unit," Cyrus told Georgina. "Can you manage here? I can come evenings to relieve you."

"I agree. I want her home where I can be with her all the time. While Kate's suicidal, I don't trust anyone with her life but us."

"She needs twenty-four-hour-a-day supervision; she must never be left alone," Cyrus cautioned Georgina.

Colin listened to this discussion from across the room. *How will this affect my life?* he wondered.

Georgina glanced over at him and asked herself, *Will Colin help us?* He hadn't yet bailed on them, and Kate still thought of him as one of the pillars supporting her. They didn't know he was already crumbling.

That was the evening the nightmare became official. Despite her fear, at least now Kate wasn't alone in it any more. She needed strategies to get through the worst moments. To try to drive the alien and suicidal thoughts out of her head, she watched *Gilmore Girls* reruns, curled up next to Georgina in bed. When they'd seen all seven seasons multiple times, they moved on to *Grey's Anatomy*, gorging on five or six episodes at a go. Their video watching was punctuated by Georgina grabbing Kate's hands to keep her from digging more holes in her head. Then there were the repair sessions when Georgina put Neosporin on all the bloody pits. For months Kate couldn't put a brush to the battlefield of her scalp. If she wasn't digging, she was shaking or raging. Sleep vanished from her life. Georgina removed all scissors, curling irons, and glass picture frames from Kate's room after she sliced her arm in a rage one morning with a shard of glass. "I suppose she's trying to drive out the demon," Colin threw over his shoulder as he walked out the door for work that morning. He didn't take a single day off to help them. Kate shuddered remembering that time in her life.

She had remembered enough for now. She put her work down. The drawings were good, powerful, but a painful reminder. Drawing had been a form of salvation back then. It had kept her hands engaged. Holding a calligraphy pen, her fingers danced and swept across the paper, commanding her attention. Like little friends, her drawings took on a life of their own. She'd known intuitively that when she was freaking out, drawing could help. "When you create an image for an emotion, you take control of that emotion, you objectify it, and then it can't possess you," Cyrus explained to her when she told him she was drawing constantly. The images she created kept her from yielding to whatever was trying to destroy her. Writing and drawing became the warrior path for her. It felt as if not just the drawings, but her journal itself was alive, a being who would listen to her thoughts without judging them. It never rejected or critiqued what she told it. It listened with acceptance.

She no longer kept a journal. *Maybe I should*, she thought pulling herself back to the present moment and getting up to check out the damage in the refrigerator that had been down for more than twelve hours. Finn would be back soon, and they had plans to go out tonight for their favorite local food: Okinawan soba, hot noodles in a pork soup, and tonkatsu, a breaded fried cutlet. Hopefully, the restaurant had its own generator. Maybe over on that part of the island, they hadn't even lost power. She didn't know what was going on outside her own house.

The fridge wasn't the wreck she'd expected. It was still cool inside, so she shut the door again and decided to forget it for now. Maybe the power would be back on soon. She made herself some more tea, curled up in her favorite chair, and allowed her thoughts the freedom to roam into the past. When had she first gotten interested in drawing? She'd created a character called Boxy one Christmas when she was about seven and drawn a whole cartoon story about him as a present for Colin. She'd wanted so much to please him. At first she'd even attempted to imitate his style of drawing. Colin was a writer, but Kate at age six told him he was doing the wrong job. "You should be a cartoonist," she said looking up at him. They spent hours together drawing when she was little and cuddling together on the couch watching DVDs of *The Simpsons*, *Family Guy* and *Monty Python* while Georgina saw evening patients. But that was way before everything went wrong.

The phone made Kate jump. Cell service was definitely back on. "Kate, thank God. Is Finn with you? Are you okay?"

"All good, Mom, and Finn'll be back later today. What's Olive barking at?" Kate asked.

"The people in 8B are giving a party tonight, so there's lots of strangers in the hall. What have you been up to alone in a typhoon, my darling girl?"

"Working on the graphic novel about my breakdown."

"That's brave of you. Do you remember that you started a blog during that time? You called it *Panicking Girl*. You had followers all over the world," Georgina reminded her.

"Yeah, I remember when I wrote in it how annoying Colin was, and he said, 'Great, now teenagers in Romania know I'm annoying.'"

"Annoying—you were being kind. That was the beginning of his period of pathological jealousy, when he was projecting all the childhood rage he felt for his sister onto you. It was a bit more than annoying."

"Still, do you ever miss him, Mom?"

"Not ever. I went down the wrong path when I married him. He wasn't right for me, nor I for him. A relationship is supposed to be a vessel for alchemical change, for growth. We failed each other."

"Mom, I don't want to hear about vessels for alchemical change. What went wrong with him? Was it all because of my breakdown?"

"No. Your breakdown just revealed to me who he really was. And it showed me that, like a fool, I had let myself become subservient to his needs."

"You're too hard on yourself, Mom."

"I try to stop my self-recrimination by telling myself that most girls of my generation were instilled with the idea that they must keep the peace at all costs, and be good and nice and cooperative. What lethal, stupid, soul-murdering thinking that is."

"You didn't instill me with that thinking."

"That thinking sets girls up to be preyed upon, to be victims, subservient to men."

"Did your mom expect you to sacrifice yourself to keep the peace?" Kate shifted the phone to her other ear.

"My mother's generation thought that was the right message to give their daughters. Otherwise I don't think I would have ever tolerated the way Colin treated me once the infatuation was over."

"You mean once he started bullying you with his two paid helpers?" Kate asked. Georgina was silent, so Kate continued. "Those two were such fixtures in our daily life with Colin. Remember, Mom, I used to say Colin was like a Whack-a-Mole with you. Anytime you disagreed with him, he'd whack you over the head with an opinion he'd gotten from either Alexandra or Lars. He treated their opinions as facts. It was as if his tarot reader and his therapist were at all our family dinners, speaking through him like he was their mouthpiece."

"I hated that he forced their point of view down my throat. And I remember you sticking up for me at the dinner table and telling Colin he was treating me like the mole in that game. I'd never even heard of that game, but I knew what you meant. Naturally he was outraged at the accusation."

"Bullies don't usually admit they're bullies, Mom." Kate set her cup on the counter and walked outside with her phone for a closer look at the damage in her yard. "And Colin was a weak, scared bully who could only hold himself up with his two human crutches. It might be fun to draw that scene. I could draw their heads stuck in his armpits to support him, their mouths open and dispensing their propaganda. And I'll make Colin's legs especially spindly."

"I'd love to see that drawing. Funny, in the last dream I had of him, he was in a wheelchair, holding a baby."

"You still dream of him?"

"Rarely."

"So what's it mean?"

"Just what it looks like, I guess: that he has no strength in his legs to support himself, or he's crippled."

"And the baby?"

"Himself, I think."

"Do you ever feel any compassion for him, Mom?" Kate asked. She was staring at the exposed roots of the palm tree that lay across the hood of her car.

"Sometimes, even though he could be very cruel, I still feel sorry that he missed out on getting his life right. He wasted too much energy being angry."

"So you don't ever regret that he's gone?" Kate let her eyes roam over her garden to peruse the damage. A gentle breeze stirred the palms over her head, baptizing her with water droplets as she made her way around the grounds.

"Never. He got to be like a pair of shoes I'd outgrown but just kept wearing out of laziness. He'd become too small for me. We weren't bringing one another alive anymore. I was just playing it safe by staying with him. And I wasn't letting myself see how intense his jealousy of you had gotten."

Georgina hated thinking about how she'd sat there paralyzed the night Colin had screamed at Kate and tried to put his fist through her closet door. She knew she'd forever regret her inability to protect her daughter in that moment. *Regret is such a little word, but it causes so much agony. It gets its roots so deep in you that you just can't dig it out, and each time you stumble across the memory of it, the mental pain grabs you again and drags you to that place of self-hatred.* These were Georgina's thoughts, but all she said was, "What I regret is not the loss of him, but how I let him treat you."

"Let it go, Mom. What was it the archangel channel told you—'Bless the past and let it go'? I love you, Mom."

"Love you too, sweet-pea girl."

"Talk to you soon."

"Oh, Kate, don't forget I'm going to visit Julia this weekend, so if you want to reach me, use my cell not my land line."

"Okay, Mom."

"'Bye, sweetheart."

STEALING AWAY

Georgina hung up the phone and climbed into bed. It was morning for Kate across the world in Okinawa, but nighttime in New York. Talking about Colin with Kate had awakened memories of him, and they were stretching out and trying to take over her mind. She turned away from these thoughts and fell asleep and into a dream.

Colin was getting into a boat, like a gondola, with one of Georgina's clients, a beautiful and exotic girl who had been raised in her father's harem in Morocco. Like Colin, she had been terribly wounded in childhood. But unlike him, she had a heart as big as the sky. They stood still in the boat together. She wore a kaftan. A black cape hung from his shoulders. In one hand he carried a wand that appeared to have the power to make the boat move. Georgina, half hidden among the trees along the water's edge, watched unseen as they stole away together in the dark. Her guts wrenched at the sight of them floating out onto the smooth, glassy surface of the black water as if gliding over a vast unconscious. Wasn't he supposed to be her one? When did he get with this woman? Where were they stealing away to? Why was he leaving her?

Georgina awoke from the dream and tried to see the clock in the dark. Her abdomen was in knots, the old familiar pain from back when she'd discovered Colin's affair. It was only 1:00 a.m. She lay there in the dark and remembered that he was already gone. *I am only dreaming what is true, what has already happened. He did sneak away.*

The pain had begun even before she'd known he was leaving her. Just when Colin was due home from work each evening, Georgina's insides tightened and burned like she'd ingested some acid or poison. Then once he was in the apartment near her, she felt her energy drain out, as if he had a big red hose stuck in her intestines and was siphoning off her life force.

Her friends had weighed in on the situation with clarity. Emma said, "Cut the cord to him. He's a psychic vampire." Selma, the wise and patient crone in her life, told her, "He's making you sick, girl. Heartache over him is knotted into your intestines. What else is all this abdominal pain about?" Georgina didn't answer her, but she thought about it. What the pain was about for her, was her own shadow, her own demons and neuroses. That's what she believed was knotted into her intestines. And only she could meet them, talk to them, and find out what they wanted. If she did, maybe they would become her allies. Maybe they were only trying to communicate using the mechanism of pain.

But even her most gentle friend, Carrie, thought the pain was about Colin and warned her that Colin was without compassion for others. Georgina and Carrie shared an appreciation for all the beings of the natural world. They went through infatuations and fell in love with everything from crystals and moss to elephants and mountains. One of them would take something up and ignite the other. It was Georgina who got Carrie into crystals when they were supposed to be studying for their PhD exams. "Crystals are first-dimensional beings," Georgina said to Carrie, pulling a piece of rose quartz and an amethyst out of her pocket in the library one morning. So after graduate school, when Carrie told her she was renting out her Soho apartment and moving back to Rhode Island, Georgina was angry. Carrie was even understanding about that, just as she understood that Colin was jealous of her relationship with Georgina. Georgina wanted to listen when her friends warned her about Colin. She wanted to face her fear of being alone. But she didn't. Instead, she got sicker and lost more weight. Somehow, in her mixed-up mind, that seemed less difficult than facing the melancholy prospect of having her morning coffee every day for the rest of her life without him.

Only her sister, Julia, hadn't offered an opinion on Colin. She counseled

Georgina to follow her heart and not mind what other people thought of her husband. They couldn't know all the spoken and unspoken agreements made during her marriage. That was surprising coming from Julia, who had never been close to Colin. But Julia was perhaps too tolerant, too passive. She did, however, say, "Love shouldn't hurt, Georgina," as they'd sat in the sterile waiting room of yet another gastroenterologist. Like the other doctors, this one too said it was anxiety and gave Georgina a prescription to ease the gut wrenching. At times the little green pills helped, but she knew they weren't addressing the root cause of her pain. Looking back, she must have known without knowing that Colin had already betrayed her. The unconscious, unbound by time and space, knows long before we do. Her body had been trying to tell her she was in a situation she couldn't stomach. Maybe Selma was right: heartache was knotted into her intestines. It took her longer than she wanted to admit before she finally heeded her body's warning. Her intestines had already discerned the situation while her conscious mind was still denying it.

Georgina tried again to read the hands on her bedside clock in the dark. It looked like 2:00 a.m. *I've got to get back to sleep*, she thought as she lay there wide awake. *I'll do some sweeping breaths. That'll calm my mind.*

🍀

Over a panini and iced coffee the next day, Georgina confided her dream to Emma.

"That dream is no surprise," Emma said. "The only curious thing is why you're dreaming of him sneaking off now, after all this time. I told you back then that Colin was a black magician who would shatter your heart." Emma poured cream into her iced coffee. Georgina watched it spiral down the glass until Emma picked up her spoon and gave it a stir.

"You pushed your broken heart down into your guts. But your guts couldn't handle all that denial, heartache, and betrayal, so you lived with burning pain for two years."

Georgina looked up at the striped awning above them. "Please stop, Emma."

"Well you're the one who brought up your dream."

Trying again to derail Emma, Georgina said, "You must have been making it up, years ago, when you told me you were Episcopalian. Episcopalians aren't usually this pushy. And I've never once seen you make a lime Jell-O mold salad with shredded cabbage inside it."

"Don't try being funny to get me off the subject, Georgina. This is serious. You know your body used to react if you even thought of Colin after he left."

"Do you think I don't know that the body reacts to every thought we think, to every dream we dream, to every word we speak?"

"You know for your clients, but for yourself . . . ? I wonder." Emma tossed her napkin down on the table, nearly knocking over her iced coffee.

"My mistakes are more apparent to me with each passing year. I get it. I messed up. Seeing how Colin was treating Kate blew out all the circuits in my heart. I not only didn't secure her safety—I put her in harm's way. You don't have to remind me." Tears of shame and regret gathered behind her eyes.

"You were in denial about him, Georgina, longer than was good for you—or Kate. But it's not a sin."

"Well, thank God for that."

Georgina glanced away and saw a daddy longlegs climbing up the wall next to their outdoor table. Emma followed her gaze, picked up her heavy white cotton napkin, and whacked the spider.

"Why did you do that?"

"Oh, come on. It was just a spider."

"It wasn't just a spider. It was a spider living its life until you ended it. You don't have to kill things just because they walk into your line of vision. That spider was a sentient being made of the same star stuff as you and me. If you thought of that spider as a little cow, would you have killed it?"

"Spare me your Carl Sagan lecture."

"You're missing the point, Emma. It's not only about killing things. It's about our attitude toward everything on the planet. We're not the top of the heap with rights over every other form of being in creation. We're all made of the same elements, and so are our houses and tables and shoes, even your napkin. There's spirit in all things."

"I hope you don't go around espousing this philosophy to your clients, or you won't have any left." Emma beckoned the waiter. "Calm down. I know you're all wound up and ranting because of that dream. Now tell me, how are Kate and Finn?"

Walking back to her office after lunch, Georgina replayed their conversation. What if she had listened sooner? Colin kept her on a pedestal for so long, she'd grown used to it and didn't want to give it up. She knew the danger involved in being idealized: it's an out-of-balance situation that can't last. The opposite feeling is naturally evoked in the name of balance. Then the idealization had ended—and Colin began finding fault with her. Down she'd tumbled, like every other idealized creature. She'd given up so much of herself to live inside that relationship. It had gone on so long she'd lost the ability to even see what was missing in her life. How had she let that happen? The enticement had been so strong. It was as if they'd inhabited a secret world.

Emma, Selma, Carrie, and Julia all saw that she had lost her way by staying with Colin way before she did. Her mother used to quote a saying to her and Julia when they were in high school and dating someone she didn't like: "Love is blind, but the neighbors aren't." She had been blind about Colin. But for a time, he'd held her heart in his hands. Before he trod on it. The early feelings had been celestial. Could she forgive herself on those grounds? No.

The dream gnawed at her. Just when she thought she'd rehabilitated herself and was in the clear, she had to go and dream of him. What was her unconscious trying to tell her now? That particular client Colin had been stealing off with in her dream was someone Georgina had worked with for years and had immense respect for. And she was magical, like a night-blooming flower. Colin was bland by comparison and much less conscious than she. Was this strong girl who had endured so much with courage meant to represent Colin's feminine aspect or Georgina's own shadow? *Stop. You don't have to be thinking about anything to do with him. He left you.* Was she really back to needing self-talk at this stage, years after their divorce?

She unlocked her office door and let her eyes rest on the comforting, familiar figure of Ganesh sitting on the table by her chair. Kate and Finn had sent all the way to India for him the Christmas they were eighteen. He was the crown jewel of her collection of Ganeshes, the largest and most elaborately detailed, painted in oranges, blues, and golds. Like a friend, he accompanied her through each session, offering solace and lending inspiration when her own well ran dry. She looked at Ganesh and whispered a prayer for the daddy longlegs. "May he find the light and journey to his new form."

Georgina heard her client come into the waiting room and went out to greet her. For the next hour she would have some relief from herself. She would become a field of consciousness for someone else, her little self forgotten for the moment.

DRINK YOUR TEA MINDFULLY

When she heard Finn's car in the drive, Kate ran to the front door. He lifted her off her feet and kissed her, all in one motion. "I smell brownies," he said. Kate turned off the oven and put the brownies on a cooling rack. "Wait, they're too hot."

Finn nodded toward the window. "I see you've been remodeling the garden."

"Like the new look?"

"Come here," he said, taking her in his arms and carrying her into their bedroom.

An hour later they emerged from their front door in T-shirts and shorts, hopped into Finn's car, and headed across the island for their promised dinner of soba and tonkatsu. That side of the island had been less hard-hit by the typhoon. It was comforting and strange to see all the lights working, the palm trees still rooted in the earth and growing upright, people taking electricity for granted.

After they'd eaten, Finn wiped his fingers and lips and laid his napkin next to his plate. Then he looked across the table into her dark eyes. "So were you okay sleeping through the typhoon?"

"I was fine. I sketched and wrote. That old thing my mother used to say popped into my head as I was blowing out the candles: 'A mind not centered in the heart is constantly chased by fear.' So I breathed into my heart a few times and fell into a blissful sleep."

Finn put on his fake serious face. "Well, as I always say, mindfulness creates bliss."

"So drink your tea mindfully," she said, and poured him another cup.

As they neared home, Kate gazed out the car window at all the uprooted trees, and shivered. Finn glanced over at her and recognized that faraway look in her eyes. He kept quiet. He was right. Kate was thinking of her bedroom back in New York where she'd sat in bed for the better part of a year, uprooted like these palm trees, trying to stay alive. It had been a high-wire act, keeping her balance during that internal storm. To endure the strangling terror, she'd held on to an India ink pen and focused on moving it over the paper, wrangling her fear, trying to capture it in one form after another as it shape-shifted. A pen seemed such a little weapon to defend oneself with against a giant tidal wave of terror. But it wasn't. Her pen and book and drawings had given her the beginning of a sense of control, allowing her to see the inside of her head and to hope. Her old wounds had healed, but sometimes she could still feel a pulsing in her psyche, as if the fear and depression might creep back in like a couple of sneaky thieves in the night. Maybe the typhoon had shaken her up a little, or maybe drawing and writing about that period of her life had stirred her up.

"You're awfully quiet," Finn said as he pulled into their driveway and parked next to Kate's Chevy, still buried under the fallen palm tree.

"Hmmm."

"All right, my little clam. I can see when you're shut tight." Kate slid across the front seat toward him, opened her mouth wide, and closed her lips over the ripe fruit of his neck. He smelled pure.

Later as they snuggled in bed, Kate's head on his shoulder, her mind drifted away again to a time before Finn was in her life. She shuddered as she counted the number of psychologists and psychiatrists she'd seen back then. After trying numerous people, they finally found Dr. Mann. He at least didn't make her more anxious than she already was. She'd been taken to him twice a week, first by her mother and then later, when she'd started to recover a bit, by Ben, an NYU student her mother hired to accompany her.

"Kate can't leave the apartment alone right now," her mother explained to Ben during the interview.

"I had a friend who went through that in high school," Ben told them.

"Good, then you know a little about anxiety and agoraphobia." Georgina decided to omit mention of the more esoteric causes of Kate's panic.

"My friend used to vomit right on the doorstep if his parents tried to push him to go out."

Kate took Ben in with all her senses and decided to trust him. "That happened to me when I tried to go to the grocery store alone a few days ago," she said.

For the next eight months, if Kate had to go out and Georgina wasn't available, Ben accompanied her. During her therapy sessions, he sat in the waiting room, eating trail mix and looking for food deals on his phone. On the days her mother took her, she sat in the waiting room playing Bejeweled in the hope of alleviating some of her own fear. She'd read online that if you played for forty-eight minutes a day, it helped lift your depression. It was something about how it balanced your right and left hemispheres. Kate also played sometimes to keep her fingers busy. The game was crack. She was glad she didn't have a lot of homework to do—or any, since she had left high school. Bejeweled took as much concentration as she was capable of.

During one of her first sessions with Dr. Mann, he did guided imagery with her. After instructing her to close her eyes and then relaxing her into a semihypnotic state, he directed, "Look around. Where are you?"

"I'm in some past century. I'm a slave girl in rags, and I'm pulling a heavy load of stone. Maybe it's ancient Egypt."

"What are you feeling?"

"I'm tired and hot and thirsty and afraid. I hate being in rags and being oppressed. I hate being a slave."

After they ended the meditation, Dr. Mann told Kate, "You feel enslaved by the heavy burden of your misery and feelings of worthlessness."

"I hate being a burden to my mother, and I hate struggling to live so as not to kill her, when all I want is to die to end the pain."

"Trying to survive so as not to destroy your mother is another form of slavery," Dr. Mann said. "You're not even free to die."

When Kate told Georgina about his interpretation, Georgina asked her what she thought. "All I deserve is rags and to be enslaved because I'm worthless." Georgina hugged her and said into her hair, "Feelings can change."

Dr. Mann was helpful for a time, but after several months, Kate felt herself clamming up. The sessions became strained and painful. She felt like he had an agenda to talk about her father, and she resented it, feeling her own narrative was being swallowed. So she asked Georgina to find a new therapist. Both her parents interviewed people. Some turned out to have been supervised by Cyrus, or their kids had gone to school with Kate. Some were just anxious messes themselves or too inexperienced. Finally, they settled on Dr. Jonas on Washington Square Park. After Kate's first session, Georgina asked Kate what she thought of her. "I like her all right, but I don't think she's very smart and she's kind of a hippie with big ugly feet and she wears sandals."

"Big ugly feet—huh. She can't help that. But why do you think she isn't very smart?"

"It's a feeling I get from her, like she's skating along the surface and being a technically okay therapist but not letting anything touch her. I don't feel the click with her."

"Do you want to find someone else?"

"I'll give her a chance. We've only had one session." And she went on seeing Dr. Jonas for the better part of a year until Georgina heard that she wore those sandals year-round and put her feet up on a hassock in Kate's face every session. "Who sticks their feet in a client's face?" Georgina said to Cyrus.

"Forget her feet. The point is, is she helping Kate?" Cyrus asked.

Kate had just begun seeing Dr. Jonas when Colin, gripped by jealousy and anger over the loss of Georgina's attention, started going nuts. "He came into my room last night waving his anger around until he got so worked up he punched my closet door with his fist," Kate told Dr. Jonas.

"What was he so angry about?" Dr. Jonas asked.

"He was ranting that I was ruining his life by taking all my mother's attention and I should just grow up. I should take care of myself and let them have their life back. He said I was selfish, and he didn't care if I wanted to kill myself. That lots of people feel like that when they're teenagers, and they deal with it. Then he slammed his fist into the door and hurt his hand."

"What did you do?"

"I sat there shaking. I'd never seen him yelling like that with a red face.

He's usually so in control. He's kind of a control freak really, obsessively rearranging his CDs and comic book collection, putting each comic in its own plastic slip. He'd never attacked me so openly before. He's more of a sniper. Or he puts you in a deep freeze to let you know you're garbage."

"How does he do that?"

"Like when my mother bought me my first high heels, black suede from Steve Madden, for my sixteenth birthday, and the plan was for all of us to go out to dinner to celebrate. I loved those shoes. I didn't know yet that the tidal wave of suicidal depression was coming for me, but I'd started to feel off, bad about myself in some way. The high heels made me feel pretty and feminine. I couldn't wait to wear them out. I modeled them for Colin one evening. Cold as ice, he ignored the high heels and said, 'I'm not coming out to dinner to celebrate your birthday. I don't feel like it.' There was so much intention to hurt and humiliate me in his tone that I couldn't bear to stand there in my new shoes. I slipped them off and left them there on the floor like two black dead geese with broken necks. He was smiling. His plan to cooly destroy me had begun, only I didn't know it. I still thought he was on my side."

"He was gloating that he'd crushed you."

"I think so."

"And the night he punched the door, where was your mother?"

"Sitting next to me on my bed. Silent and frozen. I kept wanting her to protect me, to stop him somehow, but she didn't. She must have been in shock too. I'd never felt unsafe with her before. I wanted my father."

"What happened then?"

"When Colin hit the door with his fist and hurt his hand, he said: 'Shit, now you've made me hurt my fucking hand.' And he walked out."

"Then what?"

"My mother put her arms around me, but I wanted to just end it all. There was no longer any safety in her presence, or anywhere."

"Did she go and speak to him?"

"No. She stayed and held me and told me it would be all right, but I didn't see how."

"Did you tell your mother how you felt?" Dr. Jonas leaned farther forward in her chair as she listened to Kate.

"She said she was so sorry for not stopping him, for not protecting me."

"But she left you feeling unsafe." Dr. Jonas leaned back in her chair again, and Kate relaxed a bit.

"Your stepfather seems to prefer blaming others to looking at himself."

"He doesn't want to look at himself. He wants to stay angry."

A month after the door-punching incident, she told Dr. Jonas that Colin had left the day they got back from her grandmother's funeral and that Olive had found his little yellow notebook stuck in the chair cushion. "My mother's stunned, and Olive is grieving over Colin too. Her liver enzymes are elevated to ten times what they should be. The vet couldn't figure out why, so my mom hired a dog psychic, who told us it was grief."

"What a mess that man left behind him," Dr. Jonas said. There was an expression of disgust on her face, which surprised Kate.

"Now he's a cliché, enjoying his greener, thirty-years-younger pastures," Kate said. "He always told us he was authentic, not one to follow the crowd. He was no sparrow flying in a flock. He was an eagle, and eagles fly alone."

"But he turned out to be sparrow after all," Dr. Jonas said.

Kate had almost forgotten about Dr. Jonas and her big feet and sandals. They might be fun to draw if she decided to include her in the graphic novel. She lifted her head off Finn's shoulder and looked at his face. He was asleep. *There's not a lie in him, not a mean bone in his body*, she thought. *He couldn't be more opposite to Colin.* She nestled back into his shoulder and lost herself in her past again.

Dr. Jonas had been okay, maybe too heavy handed, not aware enough of the more mysterious aspects of life. After seeing her for a year, Kate wanted a break. She needed a rest to metabolize it all. Then after a half year off, she announced to Georgina that she'd find her next therapist herself on ZocDoc.

Her choice turned out to be the best of the bunch. He was helpful, and they made each other laugh, even over the hard things. In her first session, he asked Kate about her mother. Kate described Georgina to him as a hybrid. "She's always seeking new oxygen through meditation or some other form of consciousness raising, but then she also loves watching those old-fashioned BBC crumpet shows like *Downton Abbey* where you see the housemaids dropping the down cushions on the floor to fluff them up." The following week when Kate walked into her session and was about to sit on the sofa, he stopped her. "Oh, let me," he said, grabbing a pillow and dropping it on the floor to fluff it before placing it behind her back. She was definitely going to include that sequence in her graphic novel.

When Kate told Georgina about this incident, she laughed out loud. "He's wild, but he's listening to you." After that they referred to him as "Wild Man." It had been a couple of years since Kate had even thought of Wild Man. He might have been her last therapist, for this lifetime anyway. Tonight, from halfway across the earth, she sent him a silent thank-you for his sense of humor and for the help he'd given her when she was a teenager in trouble.

Finn's eyelids fluttered at a dream scene. Kate lifted the manual he'd been reading off his chest and closed it after folding back the corner of the page. Then she kissed his dreaming face and turned off the light. "Thank God for you Finn," she whispered. Lying there in the dark, listening to the sound of the palm trees overhead, Kate imagined them to be elegant ladies rustling their silk gowns as they moved through a ballroom.

GEORGINA IS A SELF-WILLED LAMB

"I dreamed of Colin two nights ago. He was a magician stealing away in a boat with a girl," Georgina told Selma. Selma was a night owl and loved talking on the phone into the wee hours. She'd never mastered email, calculating that with the number of years she had left, she could probably get along without it. "Emma called and told me you dreamed of 'that ass,' as she put it," Selma said. Selma was up front when she knew a thing. She didn't wade into a conversation slowly, feeling out the temperature first.

"Of course she did."

"Oh, let it go. She worries about you, that's all. So why do you think you're dreaming of him now?"

"I don't know. Somehow he penetrated my psyche again." Then Georgina remembered she'd looked at Facebook for the first time in months just a day or so before that dream. Colin had never been on Facebook, but Alexandra, his tarot reader, regularly posted. "Unless Alexandra's post stirred up memories of him. Maybe seeing that brought back all the frustration of those times when he used his two paid helpers to dominate me."

"You mean the tarot reader and his therapist?" Selma asked. "I remember you complaining that he treated Lars like his Svengali."

"Yes, Alexandra and Lars, my two nemeses. I should have turned tail and run when he started therapy with Lars."

"Maybe so."

"I was a fool, still telling myself the wrong story about us—the one where we were meant to be—still telling myself that Alexandra wasn't that intrusive and that she was helping Colin. But adding Lars into the mix made life hell."

"I remember how he used them as leverage against you to get his way. Emma and I used to talk about how you and Colin never made decisions together, how he made his decisions with those two and informed you. It drove Emma crazy." Picturing Selma and Emma talking about her marriage made Georgina angry, and it was embarrassing. But why wouldn't they talk about it? They were her friends, and what they saw worried them. And it's not as if Emma hadn't told her to her face what she thought.

"Did it drive you crazy too?" Georgina asked. Though Emma had been vocal about Colin, Selma hadn't said much.

"I knew you'd come to your senses sooner or later. You'd see he didn't trust himself and needed those two crutches. One day it would be a drop too much, and the water barrel would just tip over, as my mama used to say." Georgina tried to find relief from her embarrassment by picturing a water barrel tipping over outside Selma's childhood Georgia farmhouse. She couldn't see how too much water could make a water barrel tip over, but she didn't doubt that it had been Selma's mama's expression.

Not really wanting to have this conversation but unable to stop herself, Georgina said, "Nothing could be decided until Colin consulted Alexandra. Nothing was too trivial for him to run to her with: 'Should I buy the silk boxers or the cotton ones? Do the elliptical for twenty minutes or thirty? Go on holiday with Georgina or just take the time off to work on my novel?'"

Georgina felt her heartbeat rising like thunder and wanted to somehow swallow back her words.

"You must have had your reasons for putting up with their interference," Selma said. Georgina could shut the conversation down right here. Was Selma giving her an out or inviting an explanation? She could take it either way. She plunged forward. "Initially, it was interesting hearing what they had to say, especially Alexandra, since she's psychic."

"Interesting to hear her point of view about what?"

"In the beginning, Colin asked Alexandra mostly about his sister and his parents. He wanted advice about how to get his parents to deal fairly about finances with him and his sister. You must remember him complaining about how his sister was squatting in their parents' multimillion-dollar carriage house on a private mews in Notting Hill Gate. And Alexandra did have some good suggestions."

"I remember meeting his sister once, back in the nineties, when she visited New York," Selma said.

"That was the last time he spoke to her."

"Didn't he accuse her of being a fire-breathing dragon sitting on her stolen treasure, or something, the night she flew back to London?" Selma asked.

"He lived to regret that comment. She made such a meal of it, telling their parents what a beast he was. That was a big problem he had. He was always lighting fires with his verbal micro-aggression."

"Fire-breathing, thieving dragon doesn't sound that micro," Selma said.

"He was afraid his parents would leave everything to her—the house in Notting Hill Gate, the art, and all the stock."

"Do you think they will?"

"Who can tell? Their lives don't make sense to me. After fifty years in London, they move to Florida. His mom hates Florida. She loves London and misses her friends and her mews house, and she knows her daughter is taking it over." This turn in the conversation was good. The spotlight was off Georgina's relationship with Colin and onto his family. Georgina relaxed as she recovered her grip.

"Why doesn't Colin's mom go back to London and stake her claim and tell her daughter to get her own place? I enjoyed her so much the time we all had dinner at the Blue Water Grill for one of Colin's birthdays. I found her smart and charming," Selma said.

"She is smart and charming, but she's full of fear. She can't go back to London because Colin's father wants to be in Florida, and she's afraid of him. And her daughter may not be a dragon, but she is a bully and a hoarder, and Colin's mom is afraid of her too."

"I remember you always trying to help Colin with his anger at his family." Selma was turning the conversation back to her and Colin. *Should I head this off at the pass?* Georgina wondered. She couldn't do it.

"We talked about it ad nauseam. That's what was so infuriating. I listened to him for years on this subject, and then he'd ask Alexandra and do exactly as she advised. It was the three of us in our marriage. But Alexandra was the one with all the power because she was psychic, and therefore 'closer to the unconscious' than I was as a mere psychologist. At least that's how Lars explained it to Colin."

"I never realized that Lars supported Colin's relationship with Alexandra."

"Colin would even ask her questions for Lars and report back."

"That's a little unusual for a therapist, to get assistance from a client."

"It wasn't a therapeutic relationship," Georgina said. "Colin treated his sessions with each of them like a class or mentorship. He recorded every word each of them spoke, and then later transcribed all the recordings and organized them in three-ring binders using several systems, like the date of the session, the subjects covered in the session, specific concepts within a session, and people discussed in the session. He kept a lot of information on different people. He was a snoop, really, though he said he was just trying to understand the psyche."

"So that's why Kate used to call him J. Edgar Hoover," Selma said. "He didn't keep a notebook on you, did he?"

"Of course he did, and one on Kate and one on his sister and on each of his parents and on his bosses and various friends. He'd become obsessed for a period of time with one person or another. He kept one on Emma for a while because he hated her and wanted to end my friendship with her. You were spared, though. Unless he hid it from me. He'd even ask Alexandra about people's sex lives, and she'd tell him. Nothing was over the line for those two. Then he'd run to Lars, and they'd discuss Alexandra's information, and Lars would analyze it. Colin and Lars examined everyone in Colin's life. The only person they never analyzed was Colin himself."

"Hold on," Selma said. "My neighbor's at the door. I'll be right back."

Georgina waited for Selma and wondered why she was sharing all this now. It made her look like such a fool that she'd put up with it. But the horse was not only out of the barn, but he was also galloping across the fields, willy-nilly, dragging all the dirty laundry behind him.

"What did your neighbor want at this hour?" Georgina asked. This might be an opportunity to shut the conversation down.

"I wasn't going to tell you yet, but he's teaching me email, and I left him a note to stop by when he got home tonight, because I touched the wrong button, and the damn thing won't type anymore."

"Good for you, Selma. Well done."

"I've got to get in the game. But never mind that now. What I was going to say was that I remember you had a lot of arguments after Colin started seeing Lars, but you never said it was this bad. Did you read those notebooks he kept on people?"

"Do you really want to hear this old story, Selma?"

"If you're worried I'm judging you for staying with that talkin' snake, I'm not. I know he had his charms. Now that you've started, I'd like to hear the whole story. I want to understand what happened. So did you read those notebooks he kept on people?"

"Some of them. Colin would print particular sections he wanted me to read, but what he really liked was to read out loud to me excerpts from his and Lars's sessions about how I was failing him as a partner. Then there were times he was so excited, he was nearly wetting himself, and nothing would do but for him to play me the actual recording of what Lars had said. He didn't realize how cruel it was. My protests never stopped him. He'd just plow ahead until I got angry and left the room. 'You can't take it personally, Georgina,' he'd call after me, 'or you won't grow.' I wanted to explode."

"You never told me this at the time," Selma said.

"I was too embarrassed. I felt like a fool. I didn't want you and Emma to know how bad it was."

"Come on, girl, don't put that on your plate. I knew you almost twenty years before you even met Colin. If Irwin had still been alive, he'd have sorted this out sooner. I feel as if I let you down, not seeing that Colin was emotionally abusing you."

"I let myself down, Selma. I let Colin and Lars make me feel inferior. Those two thought with their heads and felt superior to people like us who think with our hearts. They couldn't comprehend my way of being. Feeling the poignancy of life didn't interest them. Feeling anything to the quick frightened Colin and probably Lars too."

Selma didn't say anything for a minute, then asked, "Remember how Irwin used to quote Camus—'live to the point of tears'? He often used that expression when he was describing you, Georgina."

"Of course I remember. That advice would have been unfathomable to Colin and Lars. They didn't let things touch them. They dined on judging others." Georgina didn't like that she was getting so negative. She was being the judgmental one, and it felt bad. *If you're going to continue talking about this, stick to the facts and leave your judgments out of it*, she reprimanded herself.

"I do remember you telling me you were surprised that when Lars died, Colin wouldn't go to his memorial service," Selma said.

"Colin had been seeing Lars for ten years by that time. He just cut off his feelings for Lars after he died, like he was removing a dead limb and tossing it in the junk heap." That was a fact. She wasn't painting Colin as any worse than he was. "Of course he still had Alexandra, who was even more of a fixture. She was around the entire fifteen years we were together, since before we were married. Kate called them Colin's two paid friends and nicknamed Lars 'Desperado' because he was so rickety and needy of Colin's adulation."

"I knew those two bothered you, but never this much. You kept it on the down low, girl."

"The worse thing was when Lars said vicious things about Kate, which Colin used as more ammo against me."

"Like what?"

"The most unforgivable thing he ever told Colin was that Kate had to be allowed to kill herself if that's what she wanted. She was sixteen years old! Who says something like that? Lars had never even had a child." Georgina felt herself getting angry. "How could Colin even listen to that, let alone repeat it to me? I began to hate them both. Let's not go there now. It's late, Selma. We don't have to drag all this up."

"Yes, we do. Now what else was going on in those so-called therapy sessions between Colin and Lars?"

"Very little therapy. Picture the scene, Selma. Colin and Lars sitting together in Lars's sun-drenched office, Colin stretching out and lapping up every word like a thirsty cat, and recording it too, and letting Lars know he would later transcribe his pearls and file them under multiple categories in his three-ring binders. And Lars holding forth for his appreciative audience of one, knowing that his every word was being taped, to be later transcribed. Lars's pet peeve was of course how unfair I was to Colin and how badly I failed at recognizing Colin's genius and superior nature. In one sentence he could manage to savage me and pat Colin's ass at the same time." Colin would certainly have disputed this, but Georgina didn't care; this was her version. She knew she would probably feel bad tomorrow for trashing them to Selma, but she didn't want to stop.

"Do you think Lars was in love with Colin?"

"Kate once asked me the same thing. No, I don't think so, but he did appreciate Colin drinking in his every word. What an unfair waste it was. Instead of helping Colin with his massive rage or his terror of his father or his pathological jealousy of his sister, Lars supported Colin's projections onto others, especially onto Kate. Colin even frequently slipped and called Kate by his sister's name."

"What did Lars tell Colin about you?" Georgina could feel Selma moving toward the heart of her humiliation. But she went along with her.

"Mainly, that I didn't give him enough attention or appreciate him enough. Some of his choice comments will stick in my mind forever. It's ludicrous, really, thinking back on it, but it made me so angry at the time. One of his classic forms of telling Colin to leave me was to refer to Jesus's attitude when his word wasn't heard. 'If Georgina doesn't appreciate you, isn't giving you enough attention, dust off your sandals and move on.' He told Colin that more than once."

"You never told me that. Did you ever tell Emma?"

"No. She already hated Colin."

"Lars doesn't sound like much of a therapist."

"One of Lars's favorite styles was to compare me to Colin. He'd tell Colin, 'You're special—is Georgina special? No. She's not even Jane to your Tarzan.'"

"Colin Tarzan? He was sexy in a wire-rimed glasses sort of way, but Tarzan? You're putting me on, girl."

"And Lars would say things like, 'Is Georgina wise or beautiful or spiritual? No. She's hypersensitive. She neglects you. You have too much investment in her, and she's not worth it. She's a pain in the neck. You have these brilliant ideas, and she dismisses them. Perhaps you have to drop her. She should endure your rage rather than bend out of shape. Tolerating her inability to tune in to you is heroic on your part, Colin. You are the seer.'"

"Whoa, girl! Colin a seer? You're making this up."

"I wish. Then Lars would continue, 'Is Georgina a seer? No. She doesn't have the capacity to see. You are exceptional Colin. Is Georgina exceptional? No. She's asleep. She's a self-willed lamb. Distance yourself. Through your insight you liberate people, while Georgina is stuck in ignorance.' And this comment really took the cake: 'Colin, you are the awakened one.' Kate nearly choked laughing when she heard Colin play the recording of that bit."

"We could have made a play out of this," Selma said.

Georgina could sense she was trying to lighten things up, ease Georgina's humiliation. "Maybe you and Emma could have, but for me it was one exercise in frustration after another."

"Do you blame Lars for the end of your marriage?"

"Lars did me a favor. I had gotten into a dark wood. I was sleepwalking in a marriage that didn't fit any more. I just didn't know it." As she heard herself say this, Georgina realized how much she meant it.

"But he didn't do Colin any favors," Selma said.

"I wouldn't have believed it if I hadn't heard the recordings and read the transcripts. I would have assumed Colin was making it up or just exaggerating. But he wasn't."

"I'm sorry you couldn't tell me this when it was happening."

"Maybe things would have ended sooner with Colin if I had told you. I just wasn't ready to face how weird it was, because I knew that would be the end, and I wasn't yet ready for it to end. I was still building up my courage, which became irrelevant because he dumped me."

"Let it go now."

"We'd better say good night," Georgina said. "It's nearly two a.m. Good luck with the email. I'm proud of you, Selma. Let me know when you get your keyboard unstuck."

"Good night, girlfriend."

FIRST YOU SMELL THE ORANGE

"Hey, Mom, if you're there, pick up. Hello . . . come to the phone. It's your daughter."

"Hi, honey. What's up?"

"I'm stuck. I'm sitting here staring down at my drawing table. But working on this graphic novel is kind of excruciating," Kate said.

"Which one?"

"The one about my teenage breakdown." Kate hated even saying the words. Her free hand went involuntarily up to scratch her head.

"The one I've been encouraging you to write?"

"You and my editor," Kate said. "If I could somehow jump over the darkness of the depression, the crippling anxiety, the insomnia and shaking and agoraphobia and panic, and get to the redemption, I think I could do it."

"It doesn't work like that in art or life, Kate."

"But does anybody want to hear about all the suffering?"

"All creatures suffer, Kate. What you've endured is what makes you, you."

"You really believe all creatures suffer?"

"If you want to take Buddha's word for it, they do."

"He said that?"

"Think about it. At every moment there's the potential for trauma, for accidents, for bad news, for loss, for the death of someone we love. Human life—all life really—is precarious. And then there's old age and death, which are frightening to most of us."

"You're right."

"But despite the catastrophe of the human condition, most of us find the courage to carry on," Georgina said.

"What was it you used to quote to me from Rilke, the thing about the dragons?" Kate asked.

"'Perhaps all the dragons of our lives are princesses who are only waiting to see us once beautiful and brave. Perhaps everything terrible is in its deepest being something helpless that wants help from us.'" Georgina didn't know how she'd recalled it.

"That's the message I want to convey in this graphic novel. That's what I want to get across to teens who are in the agony of depression. They must look it in the teeth. And I believe that about our dragons and demons and neuroses—they do come to us to help us wake up. If we can face them and ask them why they've come, and we have the courage to listen to them and love them, our love will transform them. But God, what guts it takes. I guess that's why I work a bit and then get blocked by my own fear."

"Would it help to look back at the blog you wrote during that time of terror? Maybe it'll help you see the path you took through the dark so you can share it." Georgina knew this was asking Kate to summon up a lot of courage. She started biting her cuticle without realizing it.

"I'll look for it. It's on my computer somewhere."

"What's all that racket?" Georgina asked.

"Some men are here removing the palm tree that crashed onto the hood of my car during the typhoon. I better go, Mom, and find out how much I owe them."

"'Bye, sweetheart."

After she paid the men, and they drove off with her fallen tree, Kate opened her laptop and began searching her files for her old blog. There it was: *Panicking Girl*. She clicked on a random entry, written when she was sixteen.

What's happening to my life? What are these alien feelings that cause a blackness to seep into my heart and creep over me until there is nothing left of living but fighting off creeping dark to survive? From this distance in the future, the voice from her past sounded like it could never have been her. Yet she recognized it. That creeping blackness had lived out its appointed season. And she had survived and returned to the living.

At sixteen, she'd started the blog in desperation, hoping to share what she was feeling, to find a kindred soul out there somewhere in cyberspace who could understand. It turned out that she had lots of company all over the world, suffering from despair, depression, insomnia, and panic, and not only teens either. People of all ages had met the creeping blackness, and they wrote back to her.

Some days she made multiple entries to catalog the terrifying changes that were eating up her life. Other days her hands shook so much it was hard to type. She kept her blog up every day, faithfully, for a year, until she didn't want to be "panicking girl" anymore. Then she closed it down and had never looked at it since, until now. She clicked on another entry.

Depression is a black and slimy snake twenty feet long coiled around you, making escape impossible. Its tongue is dark and long, and it licks your face and chest, spreading a cold black mist over your heart so awful that you beg the snake to strangle you and be done with it.

Kate closed her laptop and walked all the way across the room and nearly out the door. Grabbing a hair elastic off a door knob as she passed it, she swept her long hair up into a ponytail and secured it. Her sixteen-year-old voice echoed through her. That cold black feeling of depression had been agony. She didn't want to conjure it up now; better to leave it in the past. She stared out the window at the little pieces of palm fronds still lying on the hood of her car, but she didn't see them. Back when she was sixteen, her blog had been a lifeline back and forth between her and other people all over the world who were also jumping out of their skin. Teenagers in Venezuela, France, Russia, Brazil, Iceland, Romania, and all over the US had followed her. In three days, she'd had a thousand hits.

"I think you should keep a journal too, for your private use," Georgina had suggested to her. "Separate from your blog." But when they went to purchase a journal, Kate told Georgina, "What I need is an artist's book. I need to draw my feelings. Maybe that way I can learn how to relate to them."

Week after week Kate drew her despair in black shapes on the white pages. The pain was cold and slithery, but it could be sharp too, like being stabbed with a thousand shards of glass all over your face and head and body. In less than two weeks, she'd filled the 190 pages of that first book. All the drawings were black and sharp. Somewhere in the second book, the spiky, fragmented designs had begun to curve, and softer patterns emerged, but still the lines were heavy and black and disconnected. She was still blown apart. *This is myself I'm drawing. I'm a bunch of disconnected black pieces.* Whenever Kate started to dig holes in her head, Georgina put the pen in her hand and opened the book. Kate drew as a way to wrestle with her terror and anguish and stop digging.

The digging was something she frequently blogged about. While blogging, her hands were busy typing instead of digging. *What is it about digging into my scalp that makes me feel better, no matter how much it hurts later? Sometimes I don't even know I'm doing it until I feel the burning or see the blood. I pick away in hopes that in one pick I'll be able to cut through my skull and take a deeper look into my head to reveal all the layers of emotion that I have locked up unexpressed.*

Digging, bleeding, blogging, drawing, shaking, insomnia, terror, therapy, trying one medication after another, searching for an escape from the fierce desire to take her own life: that was her life at age sixteen and seventeen, happiness forgotten, her former self utterly lost, her innocence obliterated.

After pages and pages of heavy, black lines in every drawing, one day the color blue appeared mixed in among the black. Kate remembered not wanting to let Georgina see this. She hadn't wanted her to comment on it or feel hope and be disappointed. The pressure of her mother's hope for the end of Kate's suffering would be too much. But she'd wondered to herself if the blue wasn't a tiny herald of something positive in the sea of blackness that was her psyche. Had the transformation begun? Were these dark dragons taking on a new aspect by being recognized and acknowledged? Could she hold the space for a new relationship to them and possibly for the birth of a stronger self?

Just after Kate began the blog, Georgina succumbed to pressure from Colin to homeschool her, in order to stop his repeated suggestions to send

Kate away to boarding school. Georgina tried to structure something for Kate. *As if I could have survived even a day in boarding school in my condition*, Kate thought as she overheard Colin having a go at her mother one night. Georgina hadn't known that Kate knew Colin wanted her sent away. But Kate, though depressed, suicidal, and a clam, had ears to hear and eyes to see. And what she saw was her stepfather pressuring and criticizing her mother for her inattention to his needs. He was blind to Kate's condition, except for the way it impacted him.

So homeschooling began. Trying to concentrate and do the homework Georgina assigned made Kate so anxious she took to wearing a wool cap pulled down over her ears to keep from digging more pits in her head. She had to do the homework to keep Colin's pressure off her mom. She forced herself to read *The Scarlet Letter* and answer the eleven questions Georgina had typed on the paper. Concentrating was hard; many days she shook too much to even hold a book. How could a person read with a twenty-foot snake wrapped around her body, squeezing her so she couldn't move and hissing in her face at the same time she was being pursued by a man intent on murdering her? How could she possibly concentrate on *The Scarlet Letter*? Reading was irrelevant. But she forced herself for Georgina's sake. And she realized that before this blackness, she might have loved the writing in this book. She might have, surely would have, appreciated the way Hawthorne constructed a sentence, the exact words he chose. But not now. At least she could identify with Hester. *I have a letter pinned to my breast too*, she thought. *I'm an outcast like Hester. I live apart from all others. I don't participate in society, have friends anymore, go to school, or even leave the apartment. I may as well be shunned.* Depression does cause a kind of shunning. Who wants to be around someone wearing their shadow on their breast? Everyone pulls away.

Kate dreaded Colin's return from work each evening. His brand of cruelty was not unlike that of Hester's sadistic husband. Kate shuddered, remembering all this. She clicked on another blog entry.

Colin hates me now. The temperature in the room drops twenty degrees when he walks in exhaling his disapproval. I hate hearing him ask my mom why I'm not better yet. Why I have to keep on inconveniencing him by being a mess. And two nights ago he completely lost it and screamed that there's nothing wrong with me, I'm just selfish. He made me want to kill myself. After his rant I looked suicide in the face and weighed the cost. What would it solve? It would kill the slithery evil snake and stop the cold black pain. It would stop the digging and insomnia and panic. It would stop the inhuman voice in my head that wants control over me. It would free my soul from my messed-up body. But it would kill my mother.

Kate took a few deep breaths before reading any more. It still frightened her to remember that time. She could feel her shoulders hunching up toward her neck and her back and jaw muscles tightening. She pulled her ponytail tighter and stared at her own words on the screen.

If only Colin would lay off my mom and open his eyes and help us in this battle. Why isn't he with us? When did his evil twin take over? Why did he stop loving me? Because I got depressed and suicidal? What happened to the idea of love standing by you through thick and thin?

That blog post got more than five hundred hits in less than an hour, as kids from around the world shared similar feelings about their parents and stepparents.

Kate knew her mother's friends had confronted her about Colin's lack of compassion and support. Emma told Georgina straight out to break with him, that he was hurting Kate. Selma was surprised how weak and selfish he'd turned out to be, and Carrie had repeatedly murmured, "I'm stunned by his lack of compassion." All three of Georgina's friends had early on marked Colin down as self-involved, but none of them had envisioned this level of cruelty.

When Julia asked Georgina how Colin was handling Kate's suffering, Georgina had no defense for him—there was none. He hadn't shown up for this fight. He'd not only abandoned them at the precipice, but he'd ignited the landscape with his rage. Georgina told Kate that Colin was missing a karmic opportunity to grow, that it was his loss. But it was their loss too, and Kate knew it. He himself blamed his lack of compassion on his stock excuse: "bad childhood." There would be no help from him. They just hadn't expected all the abuse his fear and jealousy unleashed. He had no idea that acknowledging his dragons was the way to become whole.

Kate shivered, rolled her shoulders to shake off the tension, and clicked on another blog entry.

When I start to shake, I know anxiety is coming for me, and once that paralyzes my chest and my heart and lungs and they freeze with fear, I know depression will follow like a slithering monstrous serpent to finish me off. If I notice my hands shaking in the morning as I try to pour a glass of orange juice, I know it's going to be a bad day, worse than just shaking and darkness and digging. Sometimes I have to pound on my bad knee, the one with the torn MCL from playing soccer. I pound over and over until the pain gets so bad it breaks the grip of my panic and depression. The physical pain displaces the far worse mental pain. Physical pain is so much easier to cope with than mental pain. It's cut and dried, and there can be an end to it. It's more controllable than the unstoppable black slitheriness of depression. But then I remember to draw the slithering, and it calms down.

This entry got more hits than anything Kate had yet posted. Girls and young women from all over the world shared their stories of cutting, burning, starving, picking their skin, and pulling their hair out in the hope of breaking the grip of their self-hatred, depression, frozen rage, and desire for death to end their suffering. The outpouring had awed her. In response, she'd asked them if they would draw the pain for her to share with all of them. She told them how it helped her to draw. Then she posted all their artwork in an online gallery. Each piece was powerful and beautiful in its agony.

Kate looked at the time on her computer. She'd been lost in this world of her past for more than two hours. She got up, stretched, and made herself a grilled cheese and tomato sandwich and ate it sitting on her front steps in the sun, still not fully back in the present.

When and how had the pain started? At soccer camp, the summer of her sixteenth birthday? Or before? Every summer since age nine she'd been away from Georgina. Then suddenly at sixteen, she wanted her mother, desperately. At first she didn't know what was happening to her. She was antsy, shaky, sleepless, and feeling out of control all the time, on the soccer field and off it. That autumn she'd pushed herself into eleventh grade and varsity soccer anyway. But the depression and anxiety kept growing in her until she begged Georgina to change her school, hoping that would be some kind of solution.

Kate stood up, went back inside, carried her plate to the sink, and ran it under hot water. But the memories kept coming, like when she told her mother she had to leave her high school, or she'd start drinking. Georgina listened and removed her from her gifted high school and put her in a private school. She lasted at the new school only from December 8 until February 11 when she'd collapsed under the pressure of intruding suicidal thoughts and crippling anxiety. She had never returned to any high school again. Even in those few weeks at her new school, she struggled working hard and making friends. Changing schools was a valiant effort to fight off the tidal wave moving toward her, but it failed. She'd left the sure road. Something was going to die: either her depression, self-loathing, and anxiety, or . . . The depression had moved more and more steadily over her, the voice in her head relentlessly telling her how worthless she was, that she should just jump onto the subway tracks instead of going to school. She bent more and more out of shape in her struggle to survive. Standing outside the turnstile until she could see the train entering the station was one way to outwit the voice. Reading, getting lost, if she could, in another world at the subway station had been another—until reading became impossible.

Kate dried her plate and put it on the dish rack. Then she let herself remember how her father had come up with strategies to help her control her bad thoughts. One evening, not long after her high school career ended forever, Cyrus came over. He sat down next to her on the couch and pulled an orange out of his bag. "I want to teach you a technique called 'first you smell the orange.' We use it in the hospital to help depressed patients. You hold the orange in your hand, and a hundred percent of your focus has to be on the orange, so there isn't room for any other thought. When you feel a bad thought coming for you, bring your focus back to the orange. Can you do that?" Kate nodded, and Cyrus continued. "Then smell the orange. Keep coming back to the orange like you would a mantra in meditation. Don't let your mind drag you down some other path." Kate had never meditated or used a mantra, but she didn't want to interrupt her father. And she was willing to try anything. "Then peel the orange with attention. Breathe in the aroma. Hold your focus. Keep at it. Don't let your mind defeat you. You can control what you think about. Now let's practice." Cyrus handed her an orange and took her through the steps. It was hard to concentrate, and she didn't believe it could stop the terrible onslaught of negativity sweeping over her. How could concentrating on an orange defeat a twenty-foot snake and an evil being intent on killing her? But she tried, more for her father's sake than her own. Cyrus was calm and patient, and if he feared for her life, which he most certainly did, he didn't let her see it. And his orange technique helped, up to a point. She shared it on her blog, and other kids wrote back to say it helped them too, sometimes. At least it was a better technique than pounding her knee. Kate knew Georgina was grateful for Cyrus's help, especially because Colin was being so difficult. Where did Colin go? Had he just stopped loving them because it was too hard now? Did love just break?

Kate glanced at the kitchen clock. Finn would be home in an hour. She pulled her mind out of the past and back into the present. Right now she'd put all of her focus on surprising Finn with his favorite dessert, a graham cracker crust, peanut butter and chocolate pie. Exhaling the past, she breathed in from the soles of her feet and swept the breath right up through her whole body to the crown of her head before sweeping it back down and exhaling out the soles of her feet. Then she reached up into the cupboard for the box of graham crackers.

STANDING ON A PLATFORM IN SPACE

Georgina's door lady handed her an envelope. "Your ex just dropped this off for you. What does that little shit want after all this time?" None of the other door people would have spoken to her like that. Tough and cutting and standing just under five feet tall, Marie reminded Georgina of a French concierge. A gaggle of women in the building flocked around when she was on the door, and like women gathered at the well to fill their water jugs, they gossiped about who was pregnant, whose husband was having an affair, the best way to peel a peach. Georgina wasn't part of Marie's flock. These past few years, she would have cramped their style.

"It looks like a piece of my mail that went astray," she said, ignoring Marie's comment about Colin as she followed Olive into the elevator. Georgina hung up Olive's leash and put some water on for coffee. Her first client today wasn't until one thirty, so there was plenty of time to write in her dream journal. She'd scribbled down a few words on awakening just to get ahold of her dream by the tail so she could go back later and climb up the body to get ahold of it by the throat.

The kettle whistled, and Georgina waited thirty seconds before adding the steaming water to the freshly ground coffee beans at the bottom of her small French press. Then she poured heavy cream into a tiny glass bottle that held exactly one ounce. It looked like a miniature, old-fashioned milk bottle. She delighted in using it because it held just the right amount of cream for one cup of coffee. Cyrus had found it for her when they were first married. She sat down with her coffee and her dream journal, but the dream was gone. Even her scribbled notes didn't help. Dreams were like that. This time the tail had slipped out of her grasp.

Dreamwork was Georgina's favorite part of being a psychologist. "A dream is a gift from the wisest, most ancient part of oneself," she explained to clients. "To ignore the gift can evoke the vengeance of fate." Georgina knew from experience that dreams bring us knowledge of our unconscious motives. They warn us about what's coming, long before it happens. Sometimes she immediately understood the symbols the unconscious sent her, and sometimes it was only later that she'd know what a dream was preparing her for.

Just before everything went dark for Kate, Georgina dreamed she was in outer space, standing alone on a wooden platform. The platform was like a basketball court but had no walls or ceiling. It was a polished wooden platform floating in the vastness of space. Alone there, looking out into the starry heavens, she was stunned to see the earth way out in front of her, suspended like a jewel, silent and still. It looked just as beautiful as in the NASA photos, a blue-and-white orb hanging in the darkness, reflecting light. But if she could see the earth like this, where was this platform she was standing on? As she stared at it in the distance, suddenly the earth flipped upside down, astounding her. Why had her unconscious placed her on a space platform and showed her this image of the earth flipping upside down? What was it trying to tell her? *Is my world about to turn upside down?*

Within six months of that dream, Kate was hanging onto life by a thread, and Colin had both his lying feet out the door. That dream had been the warning shot, the opening gambit from her unconscious alerting her that, yes, her world was about to turn upside down. It heralded what was to come. Not long after it, the dreams of fighting against ancient clawed and fire-breathing creatures began. Sometimes the creatures had scales like reptiles and were half human or humanlike beings, creatures who'd gone to the dark side. Sometimes she couldn't see them at all; she just knew they were there. Whatever form they took, they were trying to possess Kate.

91

Could these really be my dreams? she wondered. *They seem more like scenes from* The Lord of the Rings *or the dreams of a teenager who plays violent science fiction video games.*

"I can't understand the meaning of my own dreams anymore," Georgina had told Carrie during one of their Sunday afternoon phone calls in that period. The calls had become their habit after Carrie moved back to Rhode Island. "It's unbearable not to be able to take Kate's pain away," Georgina said. Carrie understood suffering; she always had. She was born with that understanding.

"Suffering that we don't understand is the only unbearable suffering," Carrie said in her gentle way.

"I want to save her from this," Georgina said.

"We can't save anyone. You can only accompany her through this. Hold her through it. And she'll save herself."

"She's only sixteen. How can she save herself? Everything in our lives has broken apart—Kate, our family, my marriage, my practice, her health and mine, our finances, the normal rhythm of a day, of a week. I don't even know what season it is. Kate said yesterday that she got an email that Insomnia Cookies is having a back to school special. I'd had no idea it was autumn. Did I think it was still spring?"

"She'll come through this, Georgina. You have to hold on, and so does Kate."

"She sees no one. All her friends have vanished. Neither of us has a life."

"Life will return at the end of this."

"Thank God, I can call you. No one wants to hear how frightening this is."

"No one wants to think it could happen to their child," Carrie said.

"We don't even cook, not even scrambled eggs; we only order in. Just trying to make it through another hour alive takes everything we have."

"Aren't Selma and Emma around? Don't you speak to Julia? What does Cyrus say?"

"He's busy at the hospital, and he has a new wife. He's solid and does what he can, but he isn't living this terror night and day with us. Selma comes by with fruit and nuts, and yesterday, a big pot of marigolds. Emma emails articles on depression, suicide, possession, and panic attacks; and she calls to rant against Colin. Julia and I speak on the phone. They're trying to keep connected to us while we're blowing apart. But there are so many terrifying hours every day. If she dies—I can't even . . ."

"No one gets your terror, or how exhausting this is, but you have to embrace it. It's the only way through."

"I have no strength for anything but keeping Kate alive. I can't even summon the energy to change the sheets on our beds."

"Your strength will return. Kate will make it."

"I want to believe you." Though she was grateful for that phone call, it still haunted her.

Georgina made herself another cup of coffee, filled her clean little bottle with cream again, and sent Carrie a silent prayer of thanks for those conversations during the nightmare time with Kate. *I wish I was having coffee with her right now*, Georgina thought.

Selma, Carrie, Emma, Julia, and Cyrus had each accompanied them on their journey. Their compassion held Georgina together when she was fraying into shreds of fear, unable to take a deep breath. They all told her over and over again to "just sit still and hold Kate and don't let go." And that's what she did. They reassured her that she was a good mother and wiped away her fear that this was her fault. They reminded her that all creatures suffer and that she and her daughter would survive if they embraced the pain without resentment. Resentment was the real killer.

The terror over Kate finally ended, and Kate survived. She moved through it like a hero on a journey, seeking the heart of herself. When the danger was past, Georgina looked around. Marie was still on the door, gossiping with the same women. Little girls in pastel summer dresses still danced down the street ahead of their mothers. Teenagers with tight pants and cigarettes, driving fast cars and drinking beer, still set each other's hearts on fire. Old people still crossed the street slowly on their way to the grocery store and the post office. All this had been taking place without them even knowing what season it was. The nightmare and terror ended—not all of a sudden, but with a recognizable turning point, heralded by her dream of an epic battle and sewing Kate back together. After that dream, Kate began to seem more like herself. And Georgina stopped holding her breath so much.

But she hadn't known how they were supposed to put the pieces back together when they had come so near to the end of everything. For a long time, she was terrified of the voice in her head that whispered to her about Kate. "Close she came to leaving this earth. Close she came to leaving this earth."

"Oh my God, oh my God," she had whispered as she put the laundry in the dryer in the basement of their building. "Oh my God, oh my God," she whispered as she tied her sneakers to walk Olive. "Oh my God, oh my God," she whispered as she dug money from her wallet to pay the delivery man for their chicken cutlet sandwiches. They had lived on those sandwiches for months. It had just been too hard to think of an alternative. Holding on had taken all their might.

Georgina tried to pull her mind back to the present. She stood up and carried her coffee cup to the kitchen. *I mostly feel great*, she thought. *I've moved on from the nightmares. My foundation is strong again. And I almost never think of Colin anymore.*

But despite feeling generally good, her mind kept jumping the fence this morning and wandering into that old pasture of the past: the time when, exhausted and muddled from months of terror and no sleep, she had no idea how to rebuild her life. And she had to face that new life without a partner. It took her a long time to digest that Colin was gone, that he'd deserted her. On top of that, a few months after he left, he got in a rage and demanded divorce lawyers. "I don't know what he has to be in a rage about," Georgina said to Julia.

"He's the architect of his own misery," Julia said. "Tell him that."

"I can't tell him anything. You can't talk to someone who's in a rage."

"What did he say when you suggested mediation?" Julia asked.

"'I already have a lawyer!' he told me. Another sneaky move before we even discussed what to do. Does he think I'm going to rob him?"

"Why's he so furious? After all, he left you."

"I only know what he claims, not the real reason for his rage—which I doubt he knows either."

"So what does he claim?"

"That I deserted him emotionally and chose Kate over him."

"He's hopeless, Georgina. You're lucky to be out of it. Just try to be self-loving as you go through this divorce. Don't let him make a victim of you," Julia warned her. And Julia knew about being a victim.

Fortunately, Georgina had learned a few things about being a warrior during her battle for Kate's life. She knew she could be a tough fighter. Her strength had been tested, and it had held. Colin and his lawyer tried to dismantle her by dragging their divorce out for years. In the end, no money exchanged hands except what went into the lawyers' pockets. Finally it ended, with the last comment coming from Emma, naturally. "I warned you, Georgina, that people get posttraumatic stress disorder from dealing with divorce lawyers. They're worse than ex-husbands."

"Let the past go," Georgina said to herself as she washed and dried her bone china cup and saucer and tiny bottle. It's just that living alone gives you so much time to think.

A WOUND OPENS

"I'm craving pizza," Finn said.

"Too bad good pizza isn't one of the delights of Okinawa," Kate answered.

"I could really go for thin-crust snow-white pizza from the PIE on Fourth Avenue," he said. "Ah, the food in New York City."

"I'd love a Chipotle's black bean and steak burrito. My second choice—a burger and fries from Shake Shack," Kate said.

"If we're going for second choices, I'll take dragon rolls from Toto Sushi."

"Okay, my third choice is chicken tikka masala from Cafe Spice, with piping hot, fresh baked garlic naan to dip in the sauce," Kate said. "The way things change in New York, will any of it still be there when we get back?"

"Definitely," he told her. "So do you want to go to the A&W Root Beer drive-through?" Finn asked. Kate made a face. "Hey, babe, I'm just offering what we've got here."

"In that case, lead on," she said, taking his hand. "At least their fries aren't half bad."

Growing up in Greenwich Village with a mother not gifted with the cooking gene, she'd eaten a lot of ordered-in food: Thai, Mexican, Indian, Afghani, Persian, Chinese. One evening when Kate was about three, Cyrus called her to the table for dinner. Kate looked up from her show and said to him, "But the man didn't bring the rice yet." Engrossed in singing along to the *The Sound of Music*, Kate hadn't noticed that Cyrus had actually made saffron chicken kabobs and rose rice. Kate's remark became a family joke. Cyrus, unlike Georgina, was an excellent cook, when he had time—which unfortunately wasn't often enough for Kate to realize that dinner didn't arrive via the man who brought the rice to the front door.

Kate, as it turned out, took after Cyrus and was creative in the kitchen. Finn appreciated her talent. But he could have lived on canned soup. He loved chowder and gumbo and loaded them both with oyster crackers. He was easy that way. No fuss necessary. And he was manly. He could pull off that jaunty walk with the slight shoulder swing some guys use to let you know they're cool, but he didn't need it. His presence was enough. Finn's wasn't the manliness of Cyrus, who walked like a confident general, but a more casual strength. Finn was easy in other ways too. He could be jollied out of a bad mood if one ever got ahold of him, which was rare. He was one of those sunny people despite his own childhood abandonments. There was none of that heavy brooding and rage in Finn that had characterized Colin.

Both Kate and Finn had been adopted at birth, but Finn wore his adoption lightly, like it was just one of many things about him. Kate wore it like a defining feature that she felt deformed her. Finn was born in Kansas and adopted at birth by parents from Illinois. They divorced when he was eleven, and his mother moved to New York to be a Republican fund-raiser. That was a hard move for Finn. It felt to him like his mother had ripped the roots out of their lives. She divorced his father, took him to court, and got full custody of Finn. She sold their big white house and gave Finn's dog to the new owners. In one move, he'd lost his sheltering home, his friends, his cousins, grandmother, aunts and uncles, his dog, and his father. Finn had hated his mother for this, and he was not a hater by nature. His father reeled off into space, and Finn didn't see him again for two years after the move. When his dad told him they were getting divorced, it was the only time he ever saw his father cry.

Kate was born in San Antonio, Texas, and moved to New York City as soon as Cyrus and Georgina had the paperwork to leave Texas with her. She was one week old when she took up residence in Greenwich Village. In all fairness, childhood, at least, was easier for Finn than for Kate because he was pure white bread like his midwestern adoptive parents. Kate didn't look like Cyrus or Georgina; she was Mexican American, part Mayan Indian. Georgina was a golden-eyed blonde; Cyrus had blue eyes and dark hair. This would turn out to be more painful for Kate than they could have imagined. For one thing, everyone knew her business just by looking at them. Her dark eyes and black hair and perfectly round little face didn't match them. It hurt her that everyone, even strangers, knew she'd been given away, just by looking at her, then at Georgina and Cyrus, and then back at her.

When they first got together, Finn had told Kate that when he was nine years old, he'd met his birth mother. "My dad and I drove back to Kansas to meet her in a diner. I don't know what I expected when I walked in there. The place was pretty empty, but I spotted a woman in a booth with two little boys, younger than me, and I freaked. I just turned around and ran out of that diner as fast as I could."

"I would have run out too," Kate said.

"She kept those two boys she had after me, but she gave me away."

"How could she bring them to her first meeting with you? Did you even know she had two more kids?"

"No. But I got the message when I saw them sitting in the booth with her. I wasn't good enough to keep, but they were. I'll never see her again."

"Did you and your dad talk about it? Did you tell him how you felt?"

"No, we drove back to Illinois in silence. You're the only person I've ever spoken to about that day." Kate put her arms around him and held him tight. After a while, he asked her about her birth mother.

"All I know is that her name is Patricia. I don't want to know anything else. She gave me away. That's enough for me to know." This time it was Finn who put his arms around Kate.

Finn came off as a tough guy, but with Kate he was warm, even sweet. He was the neat one, folding their clothes and putting them in the drawers while she sat on a pile of clean laundry, writing or sketching if an idea came into her head. What Kate loved most about Finn was not his neatness or even his gentle thoughtfulness; it was his desire to do the right thing. He was one of the good guys. He still bit his nails on occasion and hated paperwork of any kind and anything resembling schoolwork, but he could break your heart with his eyes. He'd barreled into her life just as she was emerging from her prison of anxiety and depression. She'd been like a chick half hatched, not fully attached to the earth. He was strong; she was wobbly. He stuck with her anyway. He said he had a thing for wobbly chicks with long black hair and beautiful eyes.

Kate was glad he said he loved her eyes and heart when they hooked up, because months of lying in bed unable to leave the apartment alone had left her with slack, melted muscles under her skin. Finn didn't mention it. And once she started to recover, she took her wobbly self to Pilates. After a few weeks, she began to feel her old toned body under what felt like a blanket of soft flesh. She and Georgina went to yoga together and to the gym on the corner of Fourteenth and Fifth Avenue to take chick boxing. They tried boot camp, hot yoga, and Zumba, and even Pure Barre. But that nearly crippled Georgina, and she refused to take another Pure Barre class ever again. At first they were both so weak they had to drag themselves to work out. Slowly, their physical strength returned, and with it came the birth of a deeper inner power. They'd been down on their hands and knees, but they were standing now. It had been while Kate was just upright again that Finn, whom Kate hadn't seen since middle school, reappeared in her life.

Now they were married and munching fries at an A&W in Okinawa, looking out at the South China Sea. *Life can change on a dime*, Kate thought.

"Ready to go?" Finn asked. She nodded, and he started the engine.

The next day, as Kate was just finishing a drawing of herself and Georgina doing downward facing dog to depict the period of their rejoining the world after her breakdown, her computer dinged, announcing an email. Usually, she turned off the sound when she was drawing so she wouldn't be interrupted, but now that she'd heard it . . . She clicked on her iCloud account and *bang!* right between the eyes: a name she hadn't expected to see in her in-box ever again. Colin. It had been six years since he deserted them for his young but married girlfriend. Kate had had no contact with him since she was seventeen. *The delete button was made for moments like this*, she thought as her fingers drifted upward toward it. Instead, she jumped up, heart pounding, and walked across the room and out the door.

She kept walking all the way to the beach and didn't stop until she stood facing the sea. Salt water lapped against the soles of her blue Converses and then over the tops of them, drenching her laces and feet.

It surprised her that the sight of his name could still cause so much pain. What could this be? An apology? Not likely. Colin wasn't great at remorse. So what did he want? She tried to breathe and focus out on the horizon where the ocean met the sky. It was useless. Memories flooded in against her will. She saw her seven-year-old self with her black pigtails, wearing her red-and-purple striped Hannah Anderson T-shirt and jeans, sitting at the piano playing Beatles songs, Colin leaning over her to read the music, accompanying her piano with his guitar, one foot up on the piano bench beside her. "Two of us riding nowhere . . ."

"You have perfect pitch," he told her. "And you pick up the melodies and harmonies so easily. A six-year-old kid shouldn't have so much talent."

"I'm seven," she reminded him.

'I know you are," he said, giving her pigtail a light tug. He was too shy to ever sing himself. She understood, so she sang for the two of them: "Yellow Submarine," "Love Me Do," "Hey Jude," "Can't Buy Me Love," "In My Life," "All My Loving," "I Want to Hold Your Hand." He strummed along.

"I bought you a new piano book," he said one evening. "Randy Newman songs. He wrote one especially for you—'Short People.'" Kate took the book from him and placed it on the baby grand piano. The piano had been a gift from Cyrus when she was four.

Kate sang while Colin and Georgina stood together smiling.

"Of course I'm short—I'm a child," she told him as she flipped through the songbook. "I'll learn to play 'Marie' first. That's my friend's name. . . . What's a redneck?" she asked Colin. Music was one of their things, one of the ways they communicated.

After he left, Kate never touched that baby grand piano again. But she also refused to let Georgina get rid of it.

As she stood now at the edge of the South China Sea, salty tears spilled over her lower lids and slid down her cheeks. Not bothering to remove her soaking wet shoes, Kate waded deeper into the water, right up to the bottom of her shorts. It was not the sea she saw in front of her, but herself as a child of five or six at their dining room table, sitting on a stool beside Colin, their two heads bent close together over the model of a World War II Jeep they were making.

"I had this model when I was a kid growing up in London," he told Kate. "I found a replica kit online for us to do together. Have a look."

"Can we do it tonight?"

"We can make a start tonight at least," he said.

"Models are fun," Kate told him later before going to bed. "Thanks, Colin."

"Your little hands are a lot better than my big ones at gluing on the tiny pieces. I couldn't do it without you."

Georgina took a photo of them working together. Their intent faces wore identical expressions. That same year Kate said to Georgina. "Mom, can you keep a secret?"

"I think maybe I can."

"I'm planning a surprise for Colin for Christmas. I'm making him a game. It's going to be a Monopoly game, but instead of the regular places around the board, I'm drawing all the places in Colin's life. I'm calling it Colinopoly."

"Which places?" Georgina asked her, smiling.

"The house on the mews in London where he grew up and his school there, his fish and chips place, and his friend James's house in Notting Hill Gate, his tarot reader's apartment and his therapist's office, the ad agency, our house, Central Park, French Roast, the dog run—you know, all the places he goes, his barber shop, comic book store, stuff like that."

"That's going to be a lot of work, Kate, and Christmas is only three weeks away."

"I can do it."

Colin was so proud of her present that he wanted to take it to show Lars, but he couldn't because Kate's drawing of Lars seated in his therapy office pictured him tooting little farts. That same Christmas, Colin gave Kate several books on how to draw cartoons. "You should be a comic book artist," Kate told him. "You draw better than anybody."

"It's not that easy," was all he answered.

"You don't have to be afraid to try. You're really good," Kate said as if she was speaking to another child in her class.

Kate looked out over the sea and shoved the memories away. Why was he contacting her now? She turned around and slowly walked out of the clear turquoise water. Her feet were wrinkled right through her sneakers. She sat on a rock facing the water. Even as she asked herself if she would read Colin's email, she knew she would. Would it be cowardly if she called her mother and read it with her? Yes, cowardly and unfair. She got up and squeaked home in her wet sneakers.

The screen door banged behind her as she crossed the room and picked up her sketchbook. Kicking off her wet shoes and curling up in her comfy chair, she began to draw. With her full attention on the page and letting go of everything else, Kate drew Colin's face from memory: his small, intense dark eyes, his black eyebrows and hair, his high cheekbones and aquiline nose. Then she drew his wire-rimmed glasses on his face. She leaned her drawing up against the lamp and studied it. "Why did you desert me when I needed you most?" she asked him. In therapy she'd learned to question her thoughts and label them in order to control the pain they caused. First you were supposed to visualize the thought and then the feeling attached to it. Next you were supposed to sit with the thoughts and feelings and label them. Labeling helped create a distance from the pain so it wouldn't grip you and drag you off to a world of shaking, picking, and numbness. What were the feelings that just the sight of Colin's name evoked? Anxiety, fear, pain, loss, anger, sorrow? And what were the thoughts that went with these feelings? Colin was a heartbreaker, a fool, a coward, a liar, a bully, and an unconscious idiot who'd been programmed by his therapist to believe that he was the conscious enlightened one. "I loved you, you know," Kate told the Colin in her drawing. "Maybe you weren't used to the feeling of being loved so you couldn't recognize it." It still broke her heart.

Less shaky now, Kate let her thoughts roam a little freer. It was true that seeing Colin's name could still open her abandonment wound. Anger and love for him were a potion mixed together in her. She was angry at him, too, for the way he'd hurt her mother. Grief had built up around her mother's heart like a glacier when he'd left her. Of course she'd survived, but it had brought her to her knees.

And he had cared for her since she was a little girl and then abandoned her without even saying good-bye. What had she done to him to be left without even a single word, like there had never been anything between them? He'd ripped off half her insulation when she needed it the most. How could he have done that? Was he missing some part of a human heart? What did he want now? Was he finally going to explain himself or apologize or say good-bye now, after so much time?

Kate walked over to the freezer, swung open the door, and stood gazing in as if the answer to her question was in there somewhere, hiding between the frozen peas and the cookie dough ice cream. She dug out an orange popsicle, tore the paper off, and walked back over to her drawing of Colin. Objectively, he was handsome. His second generation half-Chinese Michigan-born mother had been a beauty. His Czech father not so much. She read them both in his face. Drawing Colin's face had helped push the pain back. It had objectified him. Kate took the last bite of her popsicle, then tossed the wooden stick in the wastebasket and opened her laptop.

Love fled and paced upon the mountains overhead and hid his face among a crowd of stars.

— Yeats —

A sudden shower sparkled through the evening sun. Raindrops bounced against the top windows and danced in through the screens below, wetting the sill and floor. Georgina didn't close the windows. After a lonely day, the rain carried with it a sweet relief. She had meant to take Olive to Central Park that morning. But it was still painful to go there, even after all this time. It had been her thing with Colin. Every Saturday and Sunday morning, they got in a cab on Tenth Street and rode all the way up Sixth Avenue past Bryant Park and Radio City Music Hall, right to the bottom of Central Park. Once in the park, they let Olive off leash and followed her north along the side of the skating rink and up to the carousel, then on to Bethesda Fountain. Sometimes Olive doubled back to hurry them along and got a pat on her warm brow for her trouble. They'd started this when she was barely more than a puppy and kept it up for a decade.

In the beginning, Kate was only eight and she came too. Colin or Kate would toss a tennis ball into the fountain, and Olive, and sometimes Kate also, would bound in after it. Dogs were everywhere, plunging into the lake, swimming, shaking off, chasing sticks, delighting in being dogs. It was hard not to love the world at these moments. Then they'd leave the fountain and cross the bridge over the lake into the Ramble. Its less groomed, wild, closer-to-the-oneness feel excited Olive. Emerging from the Ramble at the castle, they'd look over the great lawn before heading down to circle around it. After that, it was back to the Boathouse for coffee with real cream, hot apple turnovers for Colin and Kate, and a cinnamon scone for Georgina— each of them shared with Olive. Later, once Kate was a teen, it was just the two of them taking Olive. They'd bring their coffee to the sailboat pond and have long conversations about the esoteric and the mundane. But this was all before the time of their mutual incomprehension. This was when she could put her hand in his and say nothing, and he understood everything.

It was while sitting by the sailboat pond that Georgina and Colin planned their pilgrimage to Switzerland. "What did Jung's grandson say in his email?" Colin asked and bit into his apple turnover.

"He wanted to know which dates we'll be in Zürich so we can arrange a time to visit the house and see Jung's library and consulting room."

"What else do you want to do in Switzerland?" Colin asked her.

"Besides going up the lake to see Jung's tower, I want to hike in the mountains around Wengen, with walking sticks. Then I'd like to go down to sea level to Lake Maggiore and stay in Ascona in the same hotel where Jung stayed. And I want to have someone take a photo of us in the spot on the bridge there where Jung and Emma were photographed."

"In that picture of them you have on your desk?" he asked. Georgina nodded. "What about you?"

"I want to go to the top of the Jungfrau."

"You realize to get to the top you have to take a train six and a half kilometers through a tunnel cut in the middle of a glacier. We'll be surrounded above and below and on both sides by a thick wall of ice. Won't that be a bit claustrophobic? Remember how you felt in the pyramids," Georgina reminded him.

"It's the top of the world, Georgina. I think I'll risk it." And that settled it.

They took that train through the glacier together. But as the train rolled forward, drawing them through thick walls of ice, it was Georgina who got claustrophobic. Colin was gentle with her fear. It was the time before his anger destroyed more than they could ever have imagined. At the top of the Jungfrau, Georgina photographed him with his head in the clouds, using one of her many disposable cameras. He'd made fun of her for packing a whole suitcase full of them. The photo was brilliant, and Colin had never looked more handsome in his navy-blue sweater, standing in the snow at the top of the world. But that wasn't her favorite moment of the trip. That came when they'd been walking along the railroad tracks which ran beside Lake Zürich. They'd just had a conversation with some friendly goats and had moved on a piece when all of a sudden she saw it, there between the trees—Jung's tower. She'd had a relationship with it for so long as a place in her psyche that it astounded her to actually see it physically in the world. That moment was now etched in her heart.

Colin had seemed to enjoy the trip as much as she, except for the day he lost his glasses and got in a bad mood, until he later found them, in their case, in his suitcase, in their hotel room.

They had shared adventure, love and fear, conversation, passion, laughter, their morning coffee, and their love for Kate and Olive. She thought it would be that way for as long as they lived, that their relationship would keep renewing itself like the perennials and hedgerows in a mature English garden. But love ended. It vanished. And there was nothing left but a pile of heartbreak. What path had they trod from the sacredness of their union to get to this heap of ashes? Where had they missed a turn, gone the wrong way? Even now she wasn't sure. Maybe all along it had been the celestial plan for it to end. You know going into every relationship that it'll break your heart, one way or another. Maybe it won't be until the person dies, but the heartbreak will come eventually. In spite of that, you risk love again and again. It's not a choice.

And after his love was gone and pacing on the mountains overhead, came Colin's wild hatred of both her and Kate. He stopped seeing them as themselves, and saw only his own dark images of them. Georgina was no longer the woman he loved; she was the woman who was depriving him of love. Kate was no longer his little girl; she was the person stealing his wife from him—or worse, she was the sister who had stolen away his mother. His projections became so powerful, his anger so raw, that it would have been better had he been far away on a mountaintop. It felt to Georgina as though he'd slipped into a psychosis. But she could remember a time when everything had carried him to her. Then love ended. After that, the feeling she'd gotten from him made her physically sick. Unable to stomach it, her guts began wrenching, and she lost ten pounds. Colin was so in thrall to his two paid advisors that he didn't even notice. Lars continued to tell him to dust off his sandals and move on. Alexandra said she saw in the tarot cards the possibility of a second marriage with a younger woman.

The phone rang, interrupting Georgina's reverie. Emma wanted to know what she was up to. "Watching the raindrops and remembering our trip to Switzerland," Georgina told her.

"Really? Still?"

"I was only just thinking that if Colin and I had been more conscious of our fears, they wouldn't have gripped us so tightly."

"Wrong. Colin didn't want to be more conscious of himself. He wanted to blame other people."

"I never could explain Colin to you."

"People don't need to be explained. You experience them. Don't do this to yourself, Georgina."

"What?"

"Tangle yourself up. Keep getting lost in your own story. Leave the past behind you." Georgina could hear the impatience in Emma's voice. "Now what are we doing for Selma's birthday? I was thinking of a picnic at the Cloisters."

After they hung up, Georgina slipped back into her reverie. Sometimes on Sundays, she let herself do that. Once she'd read her eyes into tiredness and had to close them, she set her book down and let the memories come. She remembered her hand shaking as she lifted her coffee cup to her lips the morning Colin said to her, "I'm not your captive anymore, Georgina. Once, you held me prisoner in heaven, no longer. Not now that all your focus is on Kate." He was angry and his usual eloquence was missing. "Are you going to say anything, Georgina?"

"Kate could die, Colin. She needs both of us."

He threw her a look of distain. "Listen to me, Georgina. Kate needs to grow up. And you need to act like a wife." How she hated him in that moment. But she controlled herself, tried to explain why things had changed. "What I felt for you in the beginning, Colin, was an experience of the Divine. You obliterated everything else for me. I allowed you to consume me.

107

I had no will to be separate from you. But that can't last. Even if we weren't in this crisis with Kate, that experience would have ended."

She thought she saw a smile forming on his face, but it turned to a sneer when he spoke: "What happened to the woman who expounded the philosophy that unity is the true nature of reality?" Then, before she could tell him that she'd always meant the unity of all beings, her belief that we're all part of the divine whole, not only the two of them, his phone rang, and he turned his back to her and took the call.

That same evening when they were walking Olive, she tried again. "When the rapture ends, relationships can transform. It doesn't mean they're over."

"It does for me. You made the wrong choice, Georgina. You chose Kate over me." It was dusk. The leaves were blowing overhead, and there wasn't much traffic on Fifth Avenue. Georgina suddenly felt all alone in the world. She looked at him and struggled to explain. "We're the adults. We both need to choose her. She's sixteen and in the grip of a monster. It's up to us to help her."

"You're not hearing me, Georgina. You made the wrong choice."

"Please, Colin."

"I'm done. It's over. We're over." His face was hard.

"You're still looking for the symbiotic bliss of a mother-child relationship," she said. She could feel herself starting to lose it. Soon she'd say something that would make him snap. She didn't want to, but she needed to make him see that what he was asking of her was deadening for both of them. "Just because the phase of symbiotic bliss was corrupted in your relationship with your mother doesn't mean I'm supposed to provide that for you forever."

That was when he snapped, right there on the corner of Eleventh Street. "You're providing nothing anymore, Georgina, and leave my mother out of it. You're not my therapist."

It felt like he'd slapped her. She gathered herself together before speaking again, this time in a controlled voice. "I held you for years as if I was a vessel, and you never realized it." She looked into his eyes to see if he was even a little receptive. He was inexorable. She continued anyway. She didn't know what else to do. "Now the vessel has shattered as it should in order for you to hold yourself together."

"I'm not asking you to hold me, or for anything else either, Georgina. I'm done." They hadn't moved from the corner. She wanted to collapse onto the sidewalk.

He failed to mention that he was done because he had found another vessel to hold him, that he was already busy with his secret affair. And as everyone knows, forbidden fruit is the sweetest.

As long as Georgina had been his exclusively, he'd been happy. But it had cost her. Over their years together, he'd barely tolerated her friends and family.

As a little girl, Kate fed his narcissism by sharing in his interests, but as she grew and individuated herself into more of a separate being, he began to reject her. And then Kate got sick. Instead of standing by her and Georgina, he fled in anger. It was so much easier for him to turn to a new woman, not yet buried in the inevitable negativity that grows up in intimate relationships. He could merge with his new obsession into an undifferentiated ball of symbiotic bliss. Of course he'd make all manner of forever promises to her as he had once done to Georgina. Georgina was now his antibeloved, his unbeloved. He'd pulled her off the pedestal and dumped her in a ditch.

Love. It can make you believe you are a god, not separate from the highest—until it flees.

Once, sitting across from Colin in the bathtub early in their relationship, having an ordinary conversation, Georgina had seen the Divine in him. His face glowed with an otherworldly light, and the beauty of it stopped her breath. *It's as though I'm looking into the face of the Divine*, she thought. The psychologist in her knew this was a projection of her own idealized masculine. But the woman in her was having an experience of the Divine. The present had disappeared as they sat facing one another in the large old-fashioned tub. Georgina felt her awareness extend into a realm of timelessness where she floated on a vast sea in a secret world. "I feel as though I'm existing a thousand years in the past and a thousand years in the future, simultaneously, in this moment," she told him.

She could still hear Colin's sonorous voice in her head, "You've led me into the court of heaven, somewhere outside of time." That bath remained a moment of rapture, captured, a snapshot, filed in her psyche like her first sight of Jung's tower through the trees.

Their relationship had not been a choice for either of them. She had evoked within him that eternal image of woman, his anima, that which made him whole. Lars never understood this. Jung was right: love is never a choice. We're captured. Once, while driving over the George Washington Bridge, Colin turned to her and said, "You are my delight, the solace for all the bitterness of my life, the compensation for all my disappointments." They had soared high into a world of emotionally toned experience, then crashed down into the sea. No longer her captive, he walked away and left her to drown. It only remained for her to drag herself up onto the beach and survive the heartbreak.

The sun shower was over and darkness was beginning to fall by the time Georgina got up from the love seat to take Olive for her evening walk, alone.

"Anyone who takes the sure road is as good as dead."

— C. G. Jung

They were sitting under the ceiling fan playing chess when Kate told Finn about the email from Colin. "What the hell did he want? If he hurts you again, I'll trash him into a coma!"

"I think he wants to ease his conscience, or make sure he doesn't have any unfinished karma with me. He was big on karma, funnily enough. That's what his novel was about."

"Yeah, well I didn't read it, and he can take his conscience and shove off. You're not going to reply, are you?"

"I don't know. I almost hit the delete button the minute I saw his name."

"Leave it alone, Kate—blow him off like he did you. Forget you ever heard from him. It's your move." Kate stared down at the chess board but she didn't move a piece.

"When I saw the email, I had to leave the house to get away from my laptop and my feelings, but of course they came with me. Maybe a dialogue with him would be a final letting go."

"You can't work through things with a dick, Kate." Kate climbed onto Finn's lap and buried her face in his neck to breathe in his goodness. He folded her in his strong arms, and Colin was forgotten for the moment.

It must be about four in the morning, Kate thought when she realized she was awake as the sky was lightening. Finn was asleep beside her. As she slipped out of bed, she calculated the time in New York and picked up her cell phone. "Mom."

"Hi, honey, isn't it the middle of the night there?"

"Mom, I got an email from Colin today."

"Oh?"

"I'll read it to you."

Hey Kate,

I realize you'll be surprised to hear from me, but I'd like very much to talk to you. Would you be up for that?

C."

"Are you going to respond to it?"

"I don't know. I feel angry, sad, even repulsed."

"I can imagine. Let your feelings settle. You don't have to do anything until you're ready. Wait for a dream if you're not sure what you want to do."

"Right now, I'm glad I'm in Okinawa and he's in New York, or at least I assume he is. Today for the first time in ages, I thought of my old recurrent dream of him watching me being murdered and just standing there doing nothing."

"I'm sorry you had to think of that dream again. It was so powerful in its terribleness. But it gave you such clarity about how your wisest self felt about his treatment of you."

"I had that dream so many times that last year he was with us," Kate said. Georgina felt herself slipping into therapist mode. "You need a new dream now to guide you, to show you the current position of your unconscious regarding Colin. Once you have the whole picture of your feelings, conscious and unconscious, you'll know what to do."

"Finn wants me to ignore Colin's email. To him, Colin's nothing but a dung heap."

"Finn's very clear, even if you aren't."

"Mom, tell me something boring or visual to take my mind off this so I can go back to sleep."

"I was reading an article today about how the iron in our blood and

112

the calcium in our bones, even the oxygen we breathe, all came from stars that died eons ago. Even the water on our planet is older than our solar system. Apparently, ancient water molecules formed a giant gas cloud, and that cloud spawned our sun and all the planets in our solar system. Those ancient water molecules survived and ended up in our oceans and even in our bodies.

"Am I putting you to sleep yet?"

"Good night, Mom. I love you."

"Good night, treasure."

Finn stirred as Kate slipped back into bed beside him. Half asleep, he pulled her back and hips into his abdomen and draped his arm around her. His steady, even breath caressed the back of her neck, comforting her as she wondered how those ancient water molecules had survived the scorching birth process of a planet.

Kate awoke to the smell of coffee and toothpaste. Finn set her cup down beside the futon and kissed her a real kiss on the lips. "Want to take a shower with me before I go?"

"A shower, huh," she said smiling up at him.

"That's what I said, ma'am."

Drying her hair after he left, she thought about his body. He had the softest feet. She loved to run her fingers over them. And his back was perfection, long and slender and strong. He didn't like his hairy legs and believed the problem had gotten worse because he'd had to shave them for wrestling when he was in high school. She thought men should have hairy legs. It was delicious when she rubbed his hairy ones with the silky smoothness of hers.

Kate was glad for her mother's advice to slow down and wait for her unconscious to weigh in before reacting to Colin's email. It took some of the pressure off, kept her from bugging out. She tried to put Colin's intrusion into her life on the back burner. She'd try to work on her books until her unconscious spoke on the situation one way or the other. It could be days before she got the gift of a dream showing her how her unconscious felt. Meanwhile, she'd try to forget about it.

So, her mother was reading science articles again. Good. It had worried her when Georgina had lost interest in everything but novels, and had almost become a recluse after Colin left her. For nearly two years, she seemed to have no social life at all beyond her old standbys. She mostly just saw her clients, meditated, and took a lot of naps. Grief is tiring. Despite her grieving over Colin, Kate knew Georgina's psyche had been tuned in to her and would hold her through the terror no matter what. This love from her mother would stand with her forever, longer than this life.

Kate swallowed the last of her cold coffee and put the kettle on for tea. Today she would solve the problem of how to capture in a drawing the image of the earth flipping upside down. She reread her mother's dream to get the feeling right. But her mind kept going back to the unanswered email. Why should she answer it? Colin had blown out all the circuits in her mother's heart and hers.

Georgina had put a different spin on Colin's leaving. "I'm alive and I'm awake now. I was headed down the wrong path with him. I thought it was right because I could see all the way to the horizon, which made me feel safe. But I was lost, only I didn't know it." Kate had admired her mother's strength when she was dumped by Colin. Had she ever told her that? She didn't think so. "I was heartbroken and frightened at first," Georgina told Kate. "But I'm finding a new path. I'd been slowly dying on my sure road. Jung was right when he said, 'Anyone who takes the sure road is as good as dead.'"

"So there's an upside to having your world turned upside down and your heart ripped out?" Kate had asked.

"Absolutely," Georgina said, ignoring the irony in Kate's voice. "It forced me to find a new narrative for my life, to look deeper into myself. We have to leave the beaten path to meet that challenge. If you're on the sure road, the well-worn path, it's not yours. It was made by someone else."

"Still, it hurts to be left," said Kate.

"It does," Georgina agreed. "But in the end, I believe we can grow from every painful thing that comes to us—if we don't resist it. Each of our trials is a kind of gift to help us awaken to the true reality that we're all one, all part of the whole."

Kate sat replaying this old conversation, when suddenly she knew exactly how to draw the impact of the earth flipping upside down.

It was after one o'clock when she stood up to stretch and rub her back. As she bent to touch her toes, she heard her phone ringing. Lydia. *Oh shit. I forgot our lunch date.* This she was definitely going to blame on Colin's email.

"YOU'RE NOT THE FEMME
INSPIRATRICE I NEED"

Olive was lying on the living room rug in a pool of afternoon sun, all four paws twitching gently while she dreamed, probably of stalking a squirrel. Georgina sat watching her. Olive opened her eyes, rolled over, and stretched into downward facing dog. "The head must bow down before the heart," she remembered coaching Colin. "That's the point of downward facing dog." When had she tried introducing Colin to yoga—a year, or was it two years before he left her?

"Well, I can't do it," he'd snapped. "It hurts my back."

"Which means you really need it. Your body isn't just something to carry your head around."

"I'm an introverted thinking type, Georgina, and I'm English. My focus is in my own head."

"I know you're not a shallow extroverted feeling type, like me, as Lars has pointed out to you on multiple occasions."

"Let's not go down that avenue."

"Why not? We should work through this controversy about Lars and then we can let it go. There's something we're each afraid of in this that we have to face."

"We can't work it through because the problem is that you resent Lars for being Swiss."

"Are we going to argue, Colin?"

"I'm just stating a fact—you do resent Lars for being Swiss." Colin lay back on the yoga mat and covered his forehead with his arm.

"How could that possibly be true when Jung is my inspiration, and he was Swiss?" Georgina said. She knew she should walk away, yield to him as usual if she didn't want a fight, but the words flew out of her mouth before she could move her feet. "What I do resent Lars for is saying that Europeans are superior to Americans and that introverts are superior to extroverts. And what I further resent is you using being an introvert to avoid going with me to see my family this weekend." This wasn't the way she'd meant to get into it. This was too hot, too soon. She watched his body stiffen at her words. The conversation was already all over the place, each of them venting. She wanted to roll it back, slow it down, eliminate the criticism. Colin moved his arm down to cover his eyes before he spoke to her.

"All Lars advised is that I spend as much time alone as possible, because as an introvert, I'm depleted by contact with other people."

"And that's not an excuse to avoid my family and friends?" asked Georgina.

Colin sat up. His face was red. "What friends of yours do I avoid, Georgina? Carrie, the space cadet psychologist who believes horses can do therapy better than people? Or Emma, that hellcat. Admit it, you know she's a know-it-all maneating animus hound. Or maybe you mean Selma, who could star in the season finale of *Hoarding: Buried Alive*." Colin was on a roll, winding up for the knockout punch. "But I don't know why I should I be surprised at your friends when you believe trees are sending you messages and people can talk to their DNA to heal themselves."

"How unkind you are. And by the way, horses can connect with some clients where humans have failed." He threw her a withering look. She shriveled up at his contempt. "Do you never see the good in people?"

"No, Georgina, I'm a cunt, but then you know that."

"Why are you acting like this, Colin? I'm just trying to tell you it hurts me that you prefer to stay in New York and have double sessions with Lars or see Alexandra every day rather than visit my sister and her family with me."

"And I'm trying to tell you that Lars and Alexandra say I should focus on my writing." Then he stood up and faced her. And she felt threatened but didn't back down.

117

"I hate those two meddling around in our relationship, telling you what you should and shouldn't do with me."

"Look, I don't even visit my own family," he said.

"Because you've cut them off. I'd be happy to see them."

At that he walked away without answering. More and more of their conversations ended that way the last year they were together. Georgina sighed remembering this. She should have known right then it was over. Contempt finishes off a relationship faster than anything; and there it was, in her face, scorching her.

Olive rolled onto her back and wiggled, jiggling her legs in the air in a way that always made Georgina laugh. *Forget Colin and the past. Emma's right*, she told herself. *Why am I even thinking of all this now?* It must be that Colin's email to Kate bothered her more than she realized. It was an intrusion—no, more like a raid. She walked into the kitchen for a handful of almonds, and Olive paddled after her. But the memories of her brokenness were hard to shake off. They had a deft way of working their way back into her just when she thought she'd banished them. Lodging in her body, in her shoulders, in her intestines, in her heart, her stomach, her lower back, they stitched her to that old betrayal. She exhaled, ate a handful of almonds and handed one to Olive. She loved to listen to Olive chewing.

Eating hadn't helped. Her thoughts turned back to Colin. The time Colin came home from Lars armed with a lecture on the anima was a big stomachache. She felt her abdomen tighten remembering it. "I had an interesting session with Lars," he told her, walking into the kitchen while still wearing his blue down jacket. That wasn't a good sign.

"We got on the subject of the anima, a man's internalized image of the ideal feminine, his Beatrice, so to speak."

"And?" *Just breathe*, she told herself, and went on washing the dishes. She rinsed off the last plate and stood it in the drainer.

"Lars said that the external woman in a man's life, you know, his wife or partner, can spark the development of his relationship with his internalized feminine, which then sparks his creativity."

"Jung's theory," Georgina said. She squeezed out the sponge and stood it up sideways against the faucet to dry.

"According to Lars—and yes, I suppose he takes it from Jung—there are five stages of anima development in a man." Colin spoke with excitement, like he was trying to get somewhere in a hurry. Georgina felt her own heartbeat rising. "In a good relationship, the woman nurtures the development of all five stages," he said.

"Would you like some coffee?" she asked him, hoping to slow the conversation down or even derail it, sensing the approaching criticism of her.

"No." His tone was annoyed. He leaned back against the kitchen counter and folded his arms across his chest. "Lars says the stage of my anima is complicated because I long for the fourth and fifth stages. In the fourth or priestess stage, women are experienced as beautiful healers ministering to a man's needs." Georgina listened without moving. Colin's speech was pressured and fast for him. "In the fifth stage, the femme inspiratrice, a man's partner, is a magical, enigmatic, mysterious inspiration for his writing." More to avoid looking at him than to do the task, Georgina picked up a dish towel and started drying the dishes in the drainer. "But I'm spread out below that, in levels one, two, and three, with parts of me stuck in the mother complex and the substitute mother and at the prostitute level." She knew she shouldn't take any of this personally. That was fatal with Colin, and stupid, because it always hurt to take anything personally no matter who you were talking to. *Don't react. Don't assume Lars is building another case against you,* she told herself.

"Did Lars help to illuminate how you could experience the priestess and femme inspiratrice?"

"He said I'd need to be ignited by a flesh-and-blood woman." *Is that even true?* she wondered. *Jung didn't say that was necessary. Did every artist need a flesh-and-blood Beatrice? Didn't Jung mean we each need a relationship with our internal Beatrice?* Georgina hung the dish towel on the rack and spread it out to dry. *Don't take the bait,* she told herself.

"Lars feels you're not igniting me. Otherwise, I wouldn't be stuck in the mother complex and at the prostitute level."

"So once again, it's all my fault."

"You can't take it personally, Georgina," he said.

Though she knew it was a defeat, she couldn't help herself. "I agree

119

your mother complex is as big as the Empire State Building, but that's to do with your own inner feminine, Colin. Don't blame me. And as for the prostitute level, that's how you like sex best, hot and disconnected." She felt like a freight train on a roll—and she wanted to roll over him. His face was getting red right up to his ears. She knew she'd failed herself by reacting.

"Why are you getting aggressive, Georgina?"

"Because once again, you and Lars are blaming me for your creative block; when the truth is that you're immensely talented, but you're unconsciously afraid your father will kill you if you outshine him. And you hate him, and you hate your mother for never protecting you from his rage. And you hate them both for favoring your sister."

"Thank you for the insult, I mean insight," Colin said calmly. Now that she was out of control, he'd calmed down. He knew he'd won.

"All Lars is saying is that, after twelve years, I'm not able to finish my novel, and that's the same twelve years I've been with you."

"I don't care what he's saying. I'm married to you, not Lars. I don't give a fig what he thinks." She was near tears now. "What do you think? Do you even think for yourself anymore?"

"You bitch." Colin walked out and slammed the door. For once he'd lost it. She didn't gloat. She stood there wrapped in his contempt, feeling awful for both of them. He'd never used that word to her before or any word like it. It stunned her. There was life before he'd called her a bitch and life after, but the life after had a changed aspect. That moment when he called her a bitch was a turning point. It was only that one time in all their years together he'd called her any name. She knew without knowing it, that it was the end. The contempt was spoken aloud with that single word. Their mutual criticism and defensiveness had been bad enough, but now that he'd moved on to contempt, there was no going back. But she couldn't admit it to herself yet.

The buzzer rang, announcing the delivery of her pizza and pulling her back to the present. It was halfway between lunch and dinner on a Saturday afternoon, so it would do for both meals. *I've got to stop thinking about Colin and his Svengali*, she told herself. The buzzer sounded again as she picked up the intercom. Olive was already at the door, tail wagging.

Replaying these old arguments doesn't help anything. But why is he contacting Kate now? Has his consciousness shifted? He'd always had islands of awareness, but those islands had never emerged from the sea to join and form a conscious continent capable of any serious reflection on himself. Could he be seeking forgiveness for abandoning Kate when she was most in need of help? She opened her wallet and pulled out a twenty and a five for the delivery guy. Eating pizza alone isn't as much fun as sharing it. *Will I be eating my pizza alone for the rest of my life?* she wondered. She banished that melancholy thought and opened the door.

The pizza box was warm on her palm. She carried it to the table, set it down, and opened a bottle of red wine. But all the while, she was still lost in thought.

Kate's illness and Colin's desertion had been the catalysts that broke open her story. She did a lot of talking to herself back then, trying to stay calm. "I've lost my husband. I could lose my daughter. I may not earn enough money to keep living in what has been our home since Kate was born. Both my parents have just died. These are external facts. I have a choice as to how I'll react to them." As she lay awake those first nights after he left, she comforted herself with the knowledge that it's our worst moments that make us who we are. Maybe all these things carried a lesson, even a gift. In the end, she hadn't lost her daughter or her home or her work. Kate recovered. Georgina rebuilt her practice and finally stopped asking, *What happened to my life?* Then one day while making her bed, she overheard herself murmur, "Sorrow just happens. And heartbreak happens. It's part of every life. Don't make too much of it. And if you can, try to find the gift in it."

After that she was less exhausted, less depleted. And she started to re-magnetize her body and breathe life back into herself. *Find the gift in this heartbreak*, she repeated to herself every day as she walked the dog, made the bed, boiled an egg, took the laundry out of the dryer, dressed for work.

Georgina opened the box and put a slice of pizza on her plate. When she finished it, she took another slice and handed the crust of her first piece to Olive, who was sitting by the table in anticipation. *I'm still on my own*, she thought, *but that's okay. Maybe Colin was my final partner for this life, and from now til the end, I'll be single. Lots of women are.* She lifted her wine glass and toasted all the women out there on their own.

The summer that Kate and Finn fell in love, Georgina was trying to figure out how to give her soul a place to live in her new life without Colin. For a dozen years she had understood her place in the world by living along the edge where they connected. That edge gone, she had to give back her heart to herself. She'd felt lost in the world at first. Kate and Finn had made her smoothies, burritos, and chocolate chip cookies. They'd done all the grocery shopping that summer and even offered to do her laundry. Smoothies were about the only thing she could get down. The gut wrenching, that had begun even before she consciously knew Colin was leaving her, went on for two years. Pain is tiring. Unable to metabolize and digest the heartache, she pushed it down into her intestines, and they knotted in pain. *What's important now?* she'd asked herself. *Now that I am unencumbered? Where do I step? How do I harvest this pain for wisdom? How am I to understand what happened? Why did he stop loving me?* She didn't know.

Now, after years of silence, he was turning up in Kate's in-box. Georgina hoped his email wouldn't unleash more in Kate than she could metabolize. *Stop thinking about him!* She turned off her thoughts, wrapped up the rest of her pizza, and carried the empty box out to the recycling bin. Then, still holding her wine glass, she called her sister.

"I saw the doctor yesterday," Julia said. "It wasn't a urinary tract infection. I feel tired all the time, and there's a little blood in my urine. He thinks I may have bladder cancer."

"What?"

"He wants to do exploratory surgery next Wednesday."

"My God, Julia, I'm coming up. You must be in shock."

"We don't know anything for sure, Georgina. You don't have to come."

"I do have to. Have you told Charlotte and Sara?"

"Not yet, but I will. It's just that I know Sara will get on the Internet and scare herself, and I don't want my daughter scared, especially since bladder cancer is very treatable."

"I don't want you to have any kind of cancer."

"If it is bladder cancer, I'll have surgery. I'll be fine. Let's just wait and see. Anyway, I was going to call you myself today to tell you about it. In other news, Jack has started talking. Sara's thrilled. It's like he was saving up his words, and now they're spilling out."

"He's such a little Buddha. What's he saying?" Georgina asked. She knew Julia needed to change the subject.

"Mostly that he wants to play in the car. He loves to hold the steering wheel. I hope he doesn't grow up to be a race car driver."

"And Charlotte?"

"She told me yesterday that she thinks she's in love. It's a guy who lives in Vermont, an old friend from when she lived there. This is a good period in her life. She's getting over her father's death and opening out to people again. When Peter and I divorced, it was so much harder on her than on Sara. Rob's just pulling in. Let's talk tonight."

"Okay."

"I love you. And don't worry about me."

"Love you too, Julia." Only when she'd hung up the phone did Georgina realize she was crying. "No, please no, not my sister."

MEMORIAL DAY

Kate pulled her sundress over her head. "So who's going to be at this party?" she asked. She slipped first one foot then the other into her sandals before leaning over to center the straps on her heels.

"Didn't Lydia already give you the skinny?"

"No, I'm in the dog house for forgetting our lunch."

"Naughty girl. Besides my commanding officer and his wife and the guys you know, I'm not sure," he said over his shoulder as he headed to the kitchen for the bottle of Chardonnay he had chilling in the fridge. Kate dabbed a drop of lavender oil behind each ear and picked up her lip gloss. Parties still made her a little anxious.

About to buckle her seatbelt, she remembered the cookies and dashed back inside for the basket sitting on the counter. "Sorry," she said. Finn leaned across the seat and kissed her. "How about one of those cookies?"

He bit into the still warm chocolate chip cookie and started the engine.

When she first met Lydia and Spencer, she'd clammed up in their presence. They seemed worldly and glamorous for lifers in the military. Originally from South Carolina, they still carried a veneer of Southern charm. Lydia, who'd initially seemed unapproachable beyond form-without-content banter, was now a close friend. At Lydia's suggestion, they'd taken a Japanese flower-arranging class together. The scent of mums now had special meaning. Lydia admired Kate's sense of proportion and use of color, and

124

Kate, Lydia's can-do approach. Kate had a vase for each season, all gifts from Lydia, and she'd learned the proper placement of these vases in a home, depending on the time of year and the particular flower she was using. Kate looked down at the basket of cookies on her lap and wondered if maybe she should have brought flowers instead.

Finn pulled into Spencer and Lydia's circular drive and parked. He rang the doorbell and gave Kate a quick kiss to reassure her. "Hmmm, lavender." He smiled and nuzzled her neck. As usual it was Myrna, Lydia's housekeeper, who opened the door.

"Hey, Myrna." Finn said.

"Hi, Myrna. These are for the party," Kate said. Myrna took the basket from Kate's outstretched arms. Kate stepped through the door into the foyer and glanced back over her shoulder at Finn with a soft smile. Myrna pointed them toward the French doors at the back of the house. She'd been with Lydia and Spencer since their wedding and had traveled around the world with them to their various postings. Kate wasn't comfortable with people having servants, and though she liked Myrna, she felt awkward around her. Why should Myrna have to cater to Lydia and all her guests in the permanent role of underling? Myrna, like Lydia, was childless. She'd never married, though she must be close to fifty.

"I have to tell you about something I did last night," Lydia whispered into Kate's ear as she kissed her hello. Then, stepping back, she told them both, "Spencer's arranged for fireworks. He's like a kid about it." After Lydia spent the first hour of her party dutifully making each of her guests feel as if their comfort was her only concern, she took Kate's arm and led her to a swinging seat for two suspended on four chains under a green-and-white striped canopy. The swing was partially hidden by bushes of tropical flowers. Myrna appeared carrying a tray holding two sweating and spiked glasses of strawberry lemonade. Kate thanked her. Lydia launched right in, telling Kate about the lecture she'd attended the previous evening on Body Talk. At times like this, Lydia reminded Kate of Georgina, the way she'd get so excited about the next great thing that was going to cure all the ills of the world and raise everyone's consciousness at the same time. Kate could see Finn through the bushes, eating corn on the cob. He was at ease. *It's early in the season for corn on the cob*, she thought to herself. Lydia continued talking.

"I volunteered at the lecture to be the guinea pig for the demonstration. It was so relaxing—not that I understood half of what she was doing. Balancing my organs and endocrines and tapping on my head and telling me to breathe were a big part of it. According to this system, illness is created by stress, which causes imbalances and internal disharmony. Don't you love that? It's so much less terrifying than our Western approach. Spencer wants to hear nothing about it. He says it sounds like voodoo."

Kate didn't tell Lydia right away that she'd had two years of Body Talk work back in New York during her teens. Body Talk had been one of Georgina's "discoveries" as well. Georgina had even taken the first four-day course to learn to do Body Talk. Kate hoped Lydia wasn't going to try to convince her to do that. She had two graphic novels to finish and a publisher with a timetable. And even if she didn't have deadlines, she wasn't into being a healer; that was her mother's thing. She'd better nip this in the bud, or her graphic novels would end up languishing. "I know, it's great. I had some sessions when I was a teenager," she managed to blurt out when Lydia finally paused for a breath.

"And what other secrets are you keeping from me? We're going to lunch this week. You owe me after forgetting our date last week, and you're telling me all about your Body Talk sessions." Lydia rose to meet Spencer, who was striding toward them. His white linen blazer was open over a fitted navy-blue shirt. His shirt was tucked neatly into his tight white jeans, which he had cuffed above a pair of elegant brown leather tie shoes. He wasn't wearing socks. Kate hadn't seen a man this well dressed since the fabulous gay men she'd known back in Greenwich Village. He wasn't exactly strutting but moving in a way she found tremendously self-assured and appealing. After reminding Kate of their lunch date, Lydia walked off on his arm.

Kate leaned into Finn and tilted her head up to get the full effect of the fireworks. Supported by the whole length of his body behind her, she felt warm and protected. Across the lawn she saw Myrna standing alone.

On the drive home, Kate told Finn about Lydia's new obsession. "Not Body Talk! The most expensive nap I ever had," he said. Georgina had natu-

126

rally not been content for just Kate to have the experience, but she'd paid for Finn to go as well. He mocked it when the Body Talk person rebalanced all his reciprocals—shoulders, hips, elbows, wrists, knees, ankles—because she said they were all twisted out of shape as if he'd been a wrestler. Which he had. "Well, you wouldn't be in the air force, flying planes, if not for Body Talk."

"So says your mom. Maybe the nerve damage just repaired itself and that's why the feeling came back into my fingers."

"Suddenly, in three days, right after your Body Talk session, after a year of no feeling in them? Come on, Finn. Give a little credit."

"But didn't your mom give up on Body Talk?"

"Yes . . . no . . . not really. She believes for a story to stop hurting a person it must be told and heard, witnessed. After it's witnessed, it can depart. Body Talk doesn't think it's necessary for the client to tell the story for it to leave."

"Your mom's heard a lot of stories, sitting in her office all these years."

"When people find their narrative, it forges meaning from their suffering, because finding meaning allows their trauma to become part of their identity, part of who they've come to be, what makes them them. Kate dropped into silence for a moment before she added: "And every life holds traumatic experiences. It's the nature of life itself."

"But some traumas are worse than others," Finn said.

"But they all need to be told and heard in a safe place in order to release their hold on the person."

"Listening as an act of healing," Finn said.

"And listening as an act of love," Kate added. "I also think Body Talk was too much memorization for her. She's a right-brain type, if you know what I mean."

"Remember the time she put the gratitude stickers under all the liquids in the refrigerator?" Finn asked.

"That was because she'd read Masaru Emoto's water experiments about how emotions affect the molecular structure of water. At the time, Finn, even you seemed to accept that if you were grateful for the water you drank, the water would alter its molecular structure to nurture your body."

"Hey, I was an eighteen-year-old guy, living in her house, sleeping with her seventeen-year-old daughter. Was I going to question her if she wanted to believe that stickers could change the molecular structure of water?"

"It wasn't the stickers that changed it—it was the human intention behind the stickers. It was the feeling of gratitude for the water."

"Her gratitude period. That went on awhile," Finn said. "And I was politic about it."

"But you weren't so politic the time she invited us to take the tree whispering course with her. Let me see, what was it you said to her? Oh, I remember. You told her, 'I'm definitely in, just shoot me first.'"

"Hey, she cracked up."

"She laughs at anything you say."

"Okay, forget the water and the tree whispering, what about her body-dousing period? Come on, that was weird, even for her."

"I don't know, I kind of like body dousing," she teased. Finn eased into their driveway and turned off the motor.

"You don't have to body douse about this," he said, pulling her into his arms.

Later as they were falling asleep, Finn piped up. "Just one question for you. Are you planning to tell Lydia that Body Talk causes especially large bowel movements as you release your locked-up stress and emotions?"

"I think I'll let her manifest that bit of information for herself."

THE WOUND IS THE PLACE WHERE THE LIGHT ENTERS

"All right, see you at seven, and don't bring anything. I'm making my spaghetti sauce, and I have wine," Georgina said.

"But I like to contribute," Selma said.

"Not this time. I'm trying to thank you for all the support you've given Julia and me through her surgeries."

"Nothing," Selma told her.

"It was very far from nothing. See you at seven." Georgina hung up the phone but stood still.

There had been two attempts, just a few weeks apart, to remove the cancer from her sister's bladder, but it was still blocking her right ureter and causing her right kidney to swell. As a result she now had a tube in her back going directly into her kidney, which drained into a bag she wore at her side. Hopefully, this would be temporary, just until they unblocked the ureter. Maybe robotic surgery could do it, but for that she'd have to go away to a big teaching hospital hours from home. If this third surgery failed, Julia could lose her bladder. It had been bad. She was beaten up and ripped apart and tired of being touched in harsh ways, but still uncomplaining. And now she was facing another surgery in a strange, faraway hospital. Julia's daughters, her friends, Georgina, and her brothers were all stunned at this progression. Julia's husband, Rob, remained stalwart. The phone rang, making Georgina jump.

"So what are you up to on this lazy Sunday?" asked Julia.

"Reading about Chiron, the wisest of all the centaurs," Georgina told her.

"Isn't he the one who was accidentally wounded by an arrow dipped in the blood of a hydra?"

"Yes, but I'm amazed you know that, Julia."

"The kids had a book about centaurs when they were little. They got into them because of Harry Potter. So what are you learning about Chiron?" Georgina wondered if Julia really wanted to talk about Chiron or if she was having trouble getting to the reason for her call, if there was a special reason. But she answered the question without comment.

"Because Chiron was immortal he couldn't die, so he was doomed to suffer for all eternity."

"And why are you reading about him now?"

"I'm writing a paper using Chiron to illustrate Jung's archetype of the wounded healer."

"'Only the wounded physician heals'—wasn't it Jung who said that?" Julia asked.

"It was. So I hope all your physicians are wounded."

"Why does Jung say the healer has to be wounded to heal?"

"Because suffering makes us wiser and more compassionate. Most of us want our burdens lifted, but it's in bearing them that we become who we were meant to be, more aware that we're all one, more enlightened. At least that's what I think he meant."

"Ah, sort of like Rumi's idea that the wound is the place where the light enters," Julia said. "I've been thinking about that lately." More interested in poetry and mysticism than science, Julia naturally made reference to Rumi or Hafiz or Swedenborg and not infrequently to Yeats. Her references to Yeats were for Georgina's enjoyment.

"Exactly, light enters through the wound. So keep breathing in light, my darling sister. Light and love are the great healers."

"I won't mention that to my oncologist."

"But you do believe it yourself?"

"I sit on the steps every evening, absorbing the moonlight and starlight, breathing them into my organs."

"Good. I love picturing you on the steps, gazing at the stars," Georgina said before asking, "Anything new?"

"No, I'm waiting for the results of my last scan so we can make a decision about what's next. I'll let you get back to your paper. I was only checking in."

"I'm about to stop and begin cooking. Selma's coming over."

"Tell her hi for me. I appreciate all her cards."

"I will. Love you."

Julia was already the most compassionate person Georgina had ever known, so why did she have to suffer more? It wasn't fair. To distract herself, Georgina put on Bob Marley's "Is This Love." Then, singing along, she stacked up the papers and books covering her big, round pottery dining table. Julia had been with them when she and Cyrus bought it in Soho, when Kate was a baby. It had been made just outside of Florence by the Cicarelli family and fired in one large piece. Georgina loved the pomegranates and figs with their seeds bursting forth painted on the ceramic top.

The expense was a lot for them at the time, but Cyrus, unconcerned, put the $5,000 charge on their credit card. "This table is a work of art," he told her and Julia. "Is a bigger number of dollars sitting in our bank account a work of art? Can a number stir a man's soul?" Georgina rationalized buying the table in a completely different way. She considered the earth element aspect of the piece. "You're right," she said, "and besides, all three of us are air signs. This large round piece of fired earth will ground us." Georgina pictured Kate sitting at the clay table doing her homework in years to come. And Kate had grown up doing her homework and art projects at the table made of earth. But Cyrus was no longer with them by then; Colin was. It was on this table that Kate and Colin drew cartoons and built models and ate spaghetti while she worked evenings. But it had been Cyrus who provided it.

Unlike the introverted Colin, Cyrus was generous, gracious, and welcoming to people. He'd grown up in Teheran under the last shah, in the midst of his extended family in a big four-story mansion near the palace. His grandparents occupied the large, spacious ground floor with their servants as well as the cook and the chauffeur. His parents had the second floor, and his two uncles and their wives, children, and servants had the third and top floors. All the children roamed everywhere in the house and garden, their nannies in casual pursuit.

The day Kennedy was killed, Cyrus was six years old. His cousin Safinaz, who was also six at the time, saw on TV a lot of people in cowboy hats and heard that Kennedy had been shot. She ran downstairs into Cyrus's room and shook him awake. "Wake up! The Mexicans have killed Kennedy."

"Nonsense, you little donkey," Cyrus's nanny said. "The cowboys in Texas killed him." In all fairness his nanny was as old as they were young. She had been nanny to Cyrus's mother when she was a child and had spent all her life with the family.

Cyrus's childhood seemed romantic to Georgina. She loved the image of the samovar in the garden and all the family having tea among the roses. On hot summer nights, the servants carried the beds out into the walled garden, fragrant with honeysuckle, and draped them with mosquito netting. Everyone slept together under the Teheran moon, brushed by the scented breezes. At the end of summer while the family was away at their home on the Caspian Sea, the mattress man would come and cut open each mattress, remove all the stuffing, and pile it up in the center of the garden. Then, holding two wooden instruments and beating them together, he'd walk into the pile, making the stuffing swell to four times its size before pushing it all back inside each mattress and sewing it up. That had been Cyrus's life up until he left Teheran to come to the United States for college. During his freshman year the revolution happened, and Cyrus never went home again, not to the mansion in Teheran or to the house on the Caspian Sea. The rest of his family escaped through Turkey. Afraid even to tell the servants what they were doing, they took nothing with them.

Georgina and Cyrus met in graduate school just outside the library when the guy she was dating stopped to say something to him, and introduced them. Two years later Cyrus asked her to marry him. He was the most handsome, generous, and exotic man she'd ever met.

One Saturday morning when they'd been married for about a year, Cyrus drove off early to go quail shooting. He returned instead with six barn pigeons that he'd shot. He cleaned and cooked them in his own pomegranate sauce. As they sat down to dinner, listening to the Three Tenors' Rome concert, Cyrus smiled across the table at her. "I bet we're the only two people in New York City tonight, dining on squab they shot, cleaned, and cooked themselves."

"How old were you when you first went hunting?" Georgina asked him.

"Six," he said. "On that first trip as we started home after a long day, our jeep broke down on an isolated road in the mountains. Our driver couldn't find the problem. Night was falling, and we were all cold and stranded in the middle of nowhere. It grew darker and colder, and we could hear wolves howling in the distance. The howling grew closer. When the moon rose, we could see them closing in on our canvas-topped jeep. They circled at first. Then they began hurling themselves against the side of the jeep. The jeep started to rock with their assault. My uncles decided we had to shoot one of the wolves, and then the others would fall on it and eat it and leave us alone. One of the plastic windows would have to be opened enough for a gun barrel and a hand to fit through. We knew our scent would drive the hungry wolves crazy once the window was opened. I was the only child in the hunting party. I had the smallest hand. I asked if I could do it. They agreed."

"Did you get a wolf on your first shot?" Georgina asked.

"What do you think?" Georgina hated hunting but it was a part of Cyrus she'd come to accept. At least he killed them clean and ate every pheasant and duck and even pigeon he shot.

Ambitious, funny, successful, and cool under fire, Cyrus never reacted emotionally. But he knew how to even the score. Georgina had not been surprised when he assigned the patient with no nose to the intern who'd arrived two weeks late for the start of the training year. Work was almost everything to him. His identity depended on being excellent at it.

Georgina and Kate were often left on the sidelines. Luckily, Georgina had a sister and friends. Julia and her two little daughters came to New York often during the early years of her marriage to Cyrus. One Christmas she and Julia were strolling around the Village with Charlotte and Sara, then ages four and two and a half. "Let's take a cab up to Rockefeller Center and show the kids the tree," Georgina said on a whim. Three minutes later they were in the backseat of a taxi, each with a little girl on her lap, when two-year-old Sara piped up: "What are we doing in this man's car?" After they had a good laugh, Julia told her little daughter, "You're right to ask."

"She has no schema for taxis yet," Georgina said. Cyrus had been very amused by this story and used it as an illustration when teaching his graduate students how schemas are created in the brain. Now Sara was grown up with a two-year-old of her own, and Julia was sick, maybe very sick. With effort Georgina pushed that thought away. Her mind went back to Cyrus.

Georgina, Cyrus, and Kate were so close at the start, especially that first week of Kate's life in San Antonio. When they got the call that she was born, Georgina was speechless with joy. Finally managing to move her vocal cords, she didn't know what to say and asked only: "What's she like?"

"Perfect," said the voice down in Texas. "She's perfect." Meeting their baby daughter was, and would always be, the most profound moment of Georgina's life. Kate showed her storehouses of love in herself she hadn't known existed, carried her to a place of joy beyond joy, healed all the hurt she felt from her own mother. As they lay in bed that first night, Cyrus looked down at Kate's perfectly round little face asleep between them and told Georgina, "She owns my heart." Now Kate was in Okinawa, Cyrus was in Thailand on vacation with his new wife, and Georgina was setting their clay table in New York, singing along to "No Woman, No Cry," and trying not to worry about Julia. She glanced at the clock. Selma was due in an hour.

Georgina chopped the carrots and dropped them into the warm olive oil to fry before adding the sliced onions and stirring them in the black cast-iron skillet that had once been her mother's. A guy she'd dated briefly in London way before she'd met Cyrus had taught her to start her sauce with carrots because they absorbed some of the acid in the tomatoes. Cooking for Selma made Georgina happy. She loved Selma. Despite her slender runner's frame, Selma could eat.

Born and raised in Georgia before the Civil Rights Act, Selma had stories but no chip on her shoulder. They'd met through their mutual friend Irwin back in the '80s when Georgina was in graduate school. One of the first stories she heard about Selma from Irwin was that when her father was just a boy picking cotton in Georgia, he'd watched his own father hung. He'd thought all the white men had already had a drink of water, so he took a dipper full for himself. But one white man said he hadn't had a drink yet. "Wha'd' ya think you're doin', nigger?" Selma's granddaddy was twenty-six at the time, and he apologized for his mistake. But they hung him anyway, in the middle of that sweltering Georgia day as Selma's daddy, then a seven-year-old boy, watched, his terror and incomprehension unimaginable. That boy, Selma's daddy, who'd watched his father hung, grew up to be a share-cropper. Each Friday "the man" came by to tell him what he wanted done the following week. During those visits Selma hid inside behind the curtain, peeking out to watch her daddy with the man. He never took his eyes off the ground while the man spoke to him. He never dared to look up. Even if he hadn't seen his daddy hung, he might have been afraid to make eye contact. That's how it was for black people. After the war Selma's brothers saved up and bought her daddy a farm of his own so he wouldn't have to answer to the man every Friday.

Selma had never told Georgina her grandfather's story. If not for Irwin, Georgina wouldn't have known it. Selma wasn't acquainted with bitterness. When Colin left her, it was Selma who spoke directly to Georgina's heart. "It knocks you down, child. It just knocks you down, but you got to pull up your socks, as my mamma used to say."

Georgina stirred the spaghetti sauce and took a taste. Selma would be there any minute with her characteristic greeting, "So what's on the line for the lizard?" Except she was usually late, so Georgina could take her time. Hopefully, the five miles Selma ran every morning at six and the two-hour workout she did at the gym afterward would give her an appetite. At eighty, Selma was still running marathons and was competitive in her age group, usually taking the gold. Their friend Irwin always said, "She's a champion. If she'd been born a generation later, she'd have made it to the Olympics."

Selma and Irwin had been such an unlikely pair. He was a Princeton PhD in mathematics and a former RAND Corporation person who had been working there with Daniel Ellsberg when he made the decision to release the Pentagon Papers to the *New York Times*. Selma was all down to earth and smart in her bones about life, with no intellectual frills or bullshit. Irwin was an intellectual and a theoretician and a left-wing liberal. When they got together in 1958, it was still unusual to see a black and white couple strolling so openly. Selma's affair with Irwin had been over for thirty years by the time she, Georgina, and Cyrus found him dead in his Tenth Street apartment; but their friendship had never ended. Kate had just turned one when Irwin died. The plan had been for him to teach Kate tennis and the game of Go, to take her on gallery tours in Soho and Chelsea, not for him to die suddenly with no warning. If it was a hot, sticky day and life felt flat and sad, Irwin could make you feel the decency and purity of existence. He could make you fall in love with the world again.

Climbing the stairs to his fifth floor, high-ceilinged, south-facing studio, Georgina, Cyrus, and Selma had found him sitting up on his bed, leaning back against the wall, with the *New York Times* open across his lap. "He looks like he could be sleeping," Georgina said. Selma sank down to the floor. The coroner later said he'd been dead more than twelve hours, most likely of a stroke. He was seventy.

He had been part of Selma's life for more than forty years. She had dropped out of Howard University and moved to New York City and was working in the math department as a secretary at NYU when she met Irwin, a young mathematics professor. The first week he knew her, he brought her an application to college to finish her BA, and when she did that, he showed up with another application, this time for a master's degree. And he attended both graduations. The little girl who'd walked miles along a dusty Georgia road to the one-room school while the white kids rode by on their big yellow bus had become a teacher in New York City.

It wasn't only for Selma that Irwin showed up. As Georgina was about to enter the room to defend her dissertation, he schooled her: "When you go in there and stand before them, remember, it's not what you know that's important. It's your attitude about what you don't know."

It had been Irwin too, at another moment, who got it, who exactly, completely understood a simple life-altering remark she made to him. They were walking down Tenth Street, and she was pushing her cart full of groceries in front of her. "Why are you pushing that when it would be so much easier to pull it?" Irwin asked.

"Because if I pull it, I can't pretend it's a baby carriage."

"Of course, makes perfect sense." The next day he dropped by to tell her, "I have someone I want you to meet." That someone turned out to be a nine-month-old baby girl born in San Antonio who had been adopted at birth by two anthropologist friends of his. That was in November. Six months later Kate was born, and Georgina and Cyrus flew to Texas to bring her home.

Irwin had died more than twenty years ago now. "I'll never stop missing you," Georgina said to the air around her as she sliced the baguette to make garlic bread. Had he been alive, she knew he would have given her all the arguments against marrying Colin. He would have seen through him where she had failed to. And if she hadn't listened to his arguments, he would have accepted that as right too. She and Selma still celebrated his birthday every year, sitting on his steps on Tenth Street, eating chocolate and drinking champagne.

I SMELL LYDIA

"Did you know that it's your liver that decides where in your body to store your experiences and feelings? And that you must be asleep between one and three in the morning because that's the time your Wei Qi goes inside your body to help your liver process the day's stresses? You're less protected then, so you shouldn't be walking around," Lydia explained. Kate squeezed the lemon into her iced tea as she waited for Lydia's battery to run down a little. "And the small intestine is the organ of discernment, deciding what to absorb and what to let go of." They were seated outside the Officer's Club at a table with a soft white cloth, their menus suspended in front of them. Flowers in shades of pink and red spilled out of grand pots standing by each tall white pillar around the terrace.

Kate listened with as much enthusiasm as she could muster. The young waiter in his crisp white jacket approached the table. "Two Caesar salads with grilled chicken, and please take the bread off the table." Lydia smiled up at him just long enough to dismiss him before she plunged into the quantum physics underlying Body Talk. "Kate, do you realize that the whole universe and every cell and every atom and every subatomic particle contain all the information of the whole? And each particle is in communication with every other particle."

When Lydia finally paused, Kate suggested she read Gregg Braden's book *The Divine Matrix*. Lydia demanded a synopsis. "Basically he says that the universe is a dynamic web of interrelated consciousness. All sentient beings, events, even objects that are separated in space are in communication. That's how remote healing can happen." Lydia absorbed this as she opened her white cloth napkin and placed it across her lap over her lavender dress. The waiter set their salads before them and withdrew.

"My mother has been seeing an energy healer in New York City to work on her sister who lives five hours away in the country," Kate said.

"Does your aunt feel it when the healer is working on her?"

"I don't know, but it's a big comfort to my mom since she has to work in New York, and Julia's husband doesn't always want my mom there."

"Why not?" Lydia's tone bordered on outrage.

Kate wanted to soften the conversation. "He's a bit of a recluse, that's all, and he likes to be in control. He thinks taking control is being loving. So tell me about your session with the Body Talk woman." Kate took a bite of the perfectly grilled chicken in her salad.

Lydia motioned for the waiter and asked for more iced tea and lemon before diving into a description of her Body Talk session.

"Before I lay down on the massage table, she explained to me that our bodies have their own innate wisdom. And innate wisdom is in touch with universal consciousness. That's how Body Talk works—our innate wisdom gets information from universal consciousness and relays it to the healer through a sort of muscle testing. I didn't understand it all, but somehow despite that, I felt like a dry plant that was at long last being watered."

Lydia paused while the waiter set the iced tea down in front of her. She squeezed two lemon wedges into her glass. "There's a scar on my thigh from when I was riding my bike as a kid and was hit by a car. At times the pain from that accident still runs up my leg and causes back and even neck issues."

"You were hit by a car as a child?"

"Talking about it embarrasses me and makes me feel like a victim. And I didn't mention it to the Body Talk woman either until she asked what happened to me at age ten. Then I told her that's when I had to stay in the hospital for two months."

"How did it happen?"

"A smart-ass kid from my school stuck his foot out in front of my bike wheel. I swerved my bike in reaction without looking and ran right into an oncoming car."

"My God."

"When I was in the ambulance just before I passed out from seeing my thigh bone sticking out, I said to the EMT 'Please don't cut up my new jeans.' I'd finally been allowed to have jeans, and I was afraid my mother wouldn't let me get another pair."

"Oh, Lydia. What a trauma."

"According to the Body Talk woman, my spleen Qi is weak because the spleen meridian runs right through the thigh where my scar is. That's also why I worry and overthink things, because the spleen also controls how much we worry. At least according to Eastern medicine it does." Lydia still hadn't touched her salad. Kate had never seen her this excited about anything, and that was saying something. Her eyes were alight, her speech was pressured and a little desperate. A lot of Lydia's emotional history must have opened up in that one Body Talk session. Kate hoped Lydia wouldn't take it too fast, in gulps too big for her to metabolize. Lydia continued talking, unaware of Kate studying her.

"After she worked on my scar, she asked me what happened between me and my parents when I was five. Within seconds I was crying. That was when my kindergarten teacher called a meeting with my parents because I asked her how the earth and all the people came to be here. My teacher was shocked and angry and asked me if I wasn't a Christian. Mama and Daddy were furious with me over this and marched me to see the minister. You're not from the South, Kate, but in my town, little girls didn't ask those kinds of questions. That memory of my intellectual curiosity being met with anger got buried deep inside but was lying in wait for me all these years. I was told I was bad just for asking a question." The waiter was standing a few tables away, obviously waiting for them to finish. Kate set her sweating glass down on the white tablecloth. Lydia hadn't touched her lunch, and most of the people at the tables around them were already leaving.

Even though she knew emotions were held in the body, Kate wasn't sure she believed that just by bringing them up and tapping the head and heart, they'd be gone. She studied Lydia's face.

140

"A few things started to make sense to me after the session," Lydia said. "Like why I didn't stay in South Carolina and have a family like all my relatives for generations. I married Spencer right out of UVA, and we've traveled the world ever since to far-off postings. I never looked back. The session started me thinking about my early life. It made me cry."

"Oh, Lydia."

"Before I left, she did a curious thing. She massaged my diaphragm and pushed down toward my small intestines so I could release all the emotion brought up by the session, especially the painful memory from kindergarten." Lydia leaned in closer to Kate and dropped her voice. "It worked. I really released this morning, physically, I mean, from my bowel. Oh, and she had me put one hand on my left nipple and the other on my right eye while she tapped over my head and thymus gland. She said that would foster self-nurturing."

All the tables around them on the terrace were empty now. Their waiter stood beside a nearby pillar. The last group of women, in their summer dresses, with fancy pastel handbags and high heels, had clicked past half an hour ago. Still Lydia and Georgina sat talking, covered by the high canopy of palm trees. The trees lifted and lowered their fronds in the warm breeze as if they were taking deep and gentle breaths, which, Kate realized, they were. Kate observed Lydia's face. It was smoother and more clear. It reminded her of a remark Selma had once made to her mother: "You look like you just had a massage on your face."

Kate was happy for her friend. Who knew so much pain lurked beneath Lydia's smooth, friendly, oh so socially smooth exterior? But then Kate knew it was the same for all humans. *Buried pain lies under the psychic landscape in each of us*, she thought, *waiting and hoping to be released before it downloads into our physical body and makes us sick. I suppose we all believe we're not up to the mark in some way, not good enough. Maybe because many of us born in the West suffer from that myth of unworthiness caused by the wound of original sin. What a mean that idea is. How could a baby just arriving in the world already be tainted with original sin, spoiled and in need of forgiveness? It's wrongheaded.* Kate noticed that Lydia had stopped talking and was looking at her.

"Sorry, I was just thinking about the idea of original sin." But Lydia, her excitement spent, had turned her attention to her salad and was enjoying it on the now empty terrace while Kate sat opposite her in silence under the peaceful arms of the palm trees.

❧

Kate was stirring the pasta when Finn came up behind her and put his arms around her. "I smell Lydia on you."

"She had her first full Body Talk session."

"And?"

"Yes, a big bowel movement followed it."

"Stop. I don't want to picture that," Finn protested.

"Well, you started it."

"Come on, lose the pasta and walk to the beach with me."

"Why? What's up?"

"I'll tell you on the way." Kate drained the pasta and left it standing in the colander in the sink.

Finn kicked a few pebbles as they walked along the road toward the beach. Kate noticed but didn't comment. Finn rarely spoke of his parents, but something to do with them was in the air around him now. She could feel it. And he was biting his fingernails. Thinking about his parents made him jumpy. He did have a few good memories. His father, a sharpshooter in the first Gulf War, had taught Finn how to use a rifle, taken him camping and jump fishing. His mother had provided the more glamorous vacations like skiing in Switzerland, dining in Paris, visiting the London Bridge. But all that was before his parents split up and stopped talking to one another.

A couple of years after their divorce, his parents started speaking again. Finn saw it as his mother trying to use his father as muscle to control him and his father going along with it. "He's such a pussy," Finn had told Kate when they first started dating. "My mom kicks his ass out, takes him to court, steals his kid, upends his life, and he's back two years later licking her boots, siding with her against me, pretending we're still a family even though he knows she's with somebody else."

Finn had just made it through high school before the final break with

142

his mother. She was a wealthy woman, thanks to job connections through her rich Republican friends. While paying for college for all her nieces and nephews, she wouldn't pay for Finn unless he went to the college of her choice. She waited to announce this until the first week his freshman year when he was enrolled in college in New York City. Then she pulled the rug out from under him: "I've changed my mind about paying your tuition for college in New York," she told him, while secretly enrolling him in Michigan State through her connections. Was she hoping to end his relationship with Kate and gain control of him by shipping him off when it was too late for him to find another way to finance college in New York? If that was it, she'd miscalculated. He was done letting her jerk him around. No longer twelve, he could do more than stuff his pain inside, get in trouble with the principal, and eat a lot of candy. But they'd come a long way since then, in large part due to his mom accepting him as an adult and Kate counseling him to forgive and move on.

Finn stopped kicking the pebbles and wrapped his big hand around Kate's small one as they strolled seaward. It wasn't until they were standing at the edge of the sea with the water lapping right up under the soles of her sandals that he spoke. "I got an email from my mother today. She's marrying that rich Republican banker she's been dating forever. She wants us to come to the wedding." Kate breathed in the salty smell of the water.

Finn kicked off his docksiders and dropped them on a nearby rock.

"What else did she say?" Kate took off her sandals and set them on the rock beside Finn's shoes.

"She wants us in her life more. She wants this to be a new beginning. She wants to know her grandchildren." They waded into the water and felt it lapping up the backs of their calves.

"What are you going to do?"

"How about I begin my answer 'Dear Mrs. Bates'?"

"That's not over the top at all," Kate said with irony.

The night before they'd been scrolling through HBO Go looking for interesting shows and found *Bates Motel*, the prequel to Hitchcock's *Psycho*. It illuminated the relationship between Mrs. Bates and her son, showing how she drove him crazy with her manipulation. They watched for about half an hour before Kate realized Finn was jumping out of his skin, biting his nails and picking at his cuticles. She grabbed the clicker and hit "Off." That mother, Mrs. Bates, completely creeped Finn out. And that wasn't easy to do.

A sea breeze ruffled Kate's hair. She snuggled against Finn's chest. "Sometimes just hearing from our parents or stepparents can blow up the landscape," she said, turning her head up to look into his eyes. He pulled her closer and held her tight. The sun got so low it touched the water, igniting the surface. They walked in a little deeper until their knees were underwater. The sky grew darker, shutting down the day. Still they stared, transfixed at the bioluminescent water. Now they each had an unwanted email to answer. Kate sent this annoying thought back out to sea on the next retreating wave. She slipped her hand into his. "We'll probably disappoint our kids too. Maybe it's part of the plan between parents and kids so everyone has to own their stuff and grow." Finn took her head between his hands and, leaning down, kissed her lips.

NEWS REQUIRING ESSENTIAL OILS

Georgina stepped out of her bath and dabbed four drops of Balance oil on the bottom of each foot. Evening was the time when she and Colin would have shared a glass of red wine and talked over the day. Did she miss him? Still? Even when she knew it had been hopeless? Or did she just miss loving someone? She dried herself off and slipped on her robe. Her bare feet sank into the silence of the Persian carpet in the hallway between the bathroom and her bedroom. It felt good to stand there. The pain of Colin's leaving was done. But now, catching her almost off guard, was this admission: *I am lonely. But I'd be afraid to risk my heart again. And my body? Could I ever let myself be open in those ways with another man? Do I have the courage to live at that edge and be broken? But how many years can a person go on eating grilled cheese and tomato sandwiches, alone, reading novels?*

There was a man with his dog in the park that morning. He'd approached her so carefully, even gently. She didn't know how it happened, but it was so nice talking to him, even though she immediately told herself there was no physical attraction between them. Still, interacting with masculine energy felt good. He had a small brown dog. Olive was okay with them. Both dogs just stood there while they talked, mostly about the park.

In her dream the previous night, Olive had opened the bedroom window with her paws, then opened the screen too, and dropped her pink tennis ball down eight floors onto Ninth Street. It was a funny little dream. Maybe

Olive would open the way for her to meet someone. Was she sending a message out into the world with that pink tennis ball, the message that a lonely woman lived up here behind the window? She hated thinking of herself as a lonely woman. The truth was, she was just getting by. It was the time of day when one wanted a partner to share things with. When Colin first left, Selma told her, "You'll be okay. There are a lot of us out there alone." And she knew it was true. Sorrow and loneliness are a part of human life.

She let her mind unwind. It turned to a recent dream, and she hoped tonight's dream would give more of the story. In the dream she was being chased by a man. To escape from him, she hid in a doorway, and he ran right past her, but then he doubled back and walked up to her, handed her an envelope, and left. She wished now she'd opened the envelope in her dream. What message was this from her inner masculine? Being chased was such a common child's nightmare.

Once in a while a dream is so visual, so intense, that you never forget it. Her dream of the giant red-and-green pagoda floating up in the sky, perched up there on nothing, as if by magic, had been like that. As she'd gazed up at the pagoda, it had tilted to one side and begun to slide out of the blue sky, down to earth, like it was slipping down a mountain, except there was no mountain, only sky. Then she and Kate were in a cab, and the giant pagoda crashed right behind them onto the street, just missing the cab.

Georgina was puzzled at the time as to why her unconscious had chosen a pagoda to put in her dream. She knew it was a warning that something to do with a pagoda was about to fall out of the sky and crash. But what? It was so visual. She knew dreams prefer pictorial, picturesque language to colorless statements because emotionally charged images and symbols work more directly on the psyche than words can. What could a pagoda mean to her? It was ancient Chinese architecture. Her brother's wife was Chinese, but she was young and healthy. Her mother-in-law was Chinese American, but she was born in the Midwest and educated at Yale and had lived for most of the past fifty years in London. She didn't seem very Chinese to Georgina. It never occurred to her at the time that Colin, though born and raised in London, was half Chinese. He didn't look it, and with his British accent, didn't sound it either. It wasn't until a year later when he left her that she understood the message of the dream. It was her marriage that was falling out of the sky and crashing to earth. Now Colin was emailing Kate. She had better not dwell on that, or she'd never get to sleep. She put on her favorite pajamas, white with light-blue piping, and picked up her book, *Anna Karenina*. Every ten years or so, she reread it. This one was a new translation by a couple.

The next morning as she poured the water over the coffee in her small, one-person French press and tried to remember her dreams, her phone lit up. "Mom, you'll never guess what. Lydia's into Body Talk, and she's seeing a practitioner."

"So Body Talk has reached Okinawa—good. But you didn't call to tell me that. I can hear something else in you. There's music in your voice."

"I'm pregnant."

"Oh, my darling."

"You know what this means to me, Mom."

"I think I can safely say that I do." Georgina took the news in with careful joy. It was too big to approach greedily. Kate had even been too shy to open the conversion with it. "Have you been to a doctor?" Georgina asked, trying to slow her own excitement down.

"Not yet. I just did the test."

"Is Finn with you?"

"No, he's off-island on a mission. He doesn't know yet. I'll tell him tomorrow when he gets back." Georgina felt a spring open in her heart as she listened to the joy in her child's voice. "This baby will be the first blood relative I've ever seen. I'm afraid to be too ecstatic, but I feel like shouting from the rooftops or skipping down the road. It's like the sky around me has expanded and spread out; the air smells sweeter. I want to sing a hymn to existence."

"Then do, my sweet-pea girl."

"Mom, this is the most remarkable moment that I could ever imagine. I love everyone."

"A miracle is what it is," said Georgina with the pure intention of bestowing a blessing on the life beginning in Kate.

"Oh, I want to sing this miracle preparing inside me into being."

"I know, my darling girl. I want to savor your joy, too, and take it in in tiny butterfly sips to make it last."

"This is the reward for all the raggedness of my depression."

"I believe it is. Once again you'll live close to the quick, only this time it will be rapturous."

"Rapture. That's the word, Mom."

"Live your rapture, my sweetest love. Now you know how your father and I felt the first moment we saw you." Georgina's throat tightened at the memory. It had been a flood of love so vast that she was forever altered. Joy was born in her in the moment she first held infant Kate in her arms.

"I love you, Mom. I love the whole world. Ecstasy, that's what I feel— ecstasy and rapture."

"I'm over the moon for you, my darling. I'm going to send you some essential oils that support pregnancy."

"Okay, but don't overdo it. You know how Finn gets about your woo-woo stuff."

"Oils aren't woo-woo stuff. They raise the vibration of the physical body so unwanted feelings can be released."

"And that isn't woo-woo?"

"No. Anyway I thought he called it tap-tap juju stuff."

"That's what he used to call Body Talk, back in the day when you were really into it."

"Can I tell Julia you're pregnant?"

"Yes, of course. I'll tell her too. We text every couple of days, but she doesn't say much about how she's doing."

"Her latest scan was clean."

"Yes, Charlotte emailed me that," Kate said.

"It's hard to carry on from scan to scan. She wants so much to live to see her little grandsons grow up. She's not ready to give that up, which is a good sign."

"How are your energy healing sessions for her going?"

"They're intense. For backup I pray, mostly Hail Marys and my own made-up prayers. I fling them from my heart and send them off on little wings, piloting them to her with my intention."

148

"Remember your old mantra, Mom—'intention heals.'"

"I wish my prayers could hoist her up to the feet of God, who could, with a single glance, bestow his healing on her."

"I remember how you said to me when I was little that if you pray for someone, an angel goes and sits on that person's shoulder."

"That sounds more like your grandmother talking."

"I love you, Mom. I'll pray for Julia too."

"I love you, sweet-pea girl. And today I will love everything that happens."

One entire wall of Georgina's living room was covered in books. She scanned the shelf that held the ones on essential oils and pulled out her favorite. Kate would only tolerate so much interference, so she'd better choose wisely. Oils that Kate could apply to the soles of her feet or drop in her bath water would be easiest. Using a diffuser was out of the question. Georgina had investigated essential oils back when Kate was a teenager, hoping to use them to help alleviate her depression and anxiety. She'd purchased a diffuser, but Kate told her that only hippies and flower children diffused oils all over the house, and she wasn't having it in her room. So Georgina took it to her office, and her clients loved it.

Curling into her most comfortable chair with a fresh cup of coffee, Georgina opened her book. She decided on blends rather than single oils. But which blends? Hormone blends would support pregnancy by releasing emotional tension around the reproductive organs. That seemed a logical choice. She'd look for something with clary sage, lavender, bergamot, Roman chamomile, cedarwood, palmarosa, and yarrow. Two more blends would be about all Kate would accept. Maybe a grounding blend, with its soft tree energy, would be a good choice or a citrus blend that would reduce stress and promote happiness. But then, liver support blends were particularly helpful to women, so maybe a combination of lemongrass, geranium, and grapefruit oil would be good. Cinnamon oil was known to support the reproductive system, so that had to be included in one of the blends.

Rose oil was Georgina's favorite oil of all. It holds a higher frequency than any other oil on the planet. As a powerful healer of the heart, it costs more per ounce than gold. She'd sprinkled it on Kate's T-shirts when she was at her lowest point, alternating it with frankincense, which rids the body of darkness. Probably her biggest helper during Kate's depression had been myrrh, the oil of Mother Earth. Myrrh nurtures the soul's relationship with the maternal and can help heal trauma related to adoption.

Georgina closed her book and took the last sip of her coffee. Kate was pregnant. She wanted to tell someone the news. Normally she would have called Julia and her mother first, because her mother, though not fond of Georgina, had adored Kate; but her mother was dead. Julia would be thrilled but, despite the clean scan, she'd been feeling bad again this past week. Georgina didn't want to wake her if she was asleep. Maybe Carrie was between clients or Emma between meetings. She knew Selma would be out running. And Kate would want to tell Cyrus herself.

No luck. Carrie's and Emma's phones both went directly to voice mail, and this wasn't voice mail news. Georgina walked into her bedroom and looked down on Fifth Avenue. The owner of the building across the street had finally taken down the part of the last restaurant that had covered half the sidewalk for twenty years. A new French-Moroccan bistro called Claudette was coming soon. Her bird's-eye view of the work going on down there was a little pleasure Georgina enjoyed several times each day as she gazed out of her window. The arms and backs of the workmen looked strong even from seven floors up. She'd never held a muscular workingman in her arms or kissed one or even smelled one, and she wondered what it would be like.

Reluctantly, she stopped watching the men working on the street below and picked up her cup and saucer and carried them into the kitchen, where she tenderly washed and dried them. They were bone china in blue, white, and gold, a replica of Catherine the Great's wedding china. *Kate's pregnant!* Forget absorbing the news in butterfly sips; she wanted to gulp it into her singing heart and run down and tell all the workmen on Fifth Avenue—"Kate's going to have a baby!"

SERENITY

Kate chewed a fig bar as she scanned an article on *The Huffington Post* about the latest iPhone. The Tech section was usually her first click, but today she couldn't even focus on the article. She was out of sorts, peckish, even ornery. "What's up with me?" she asked herself out loud.

The package that had arrived two days ago still sat on the counter, unopened. It was essential oils, and it pissed her off. She was in the grip of some mood, but why take it out on a package? Georgina used to tell her that whenever you're in the grip of a mood, it's helpful to ask, "Where have my feelings been hurt and I haven't paid sufficient attention to them?" Involuntarily, Kate's hand went to rest on her heart. The truth was that she'd been hurt by Finn's reaction to the news that she was pregnant. He hadn't been over the moon as she'd expected. He hugged her and told her he was thrilled. But something else was in his face and voice too.

When she mentioned it to him, he said only, "I'm surprised that it happened so fast; that's all. The first month you're off the pill." Maybe that was it, but still she felt there was something more in his mind that he wasn't saying. She knew she should let it go, or she'd get constipated. *Constipation is about holding on to things we should be letting go of*, she reminded herself. Kate had always had a tendency toward obstinacy and constipation. "Let it go—don't take anything personally," Finn often told her. All right, she'd try, even if she didn't want to.

She picked up a knife and slit open the box on the counter. The scent of the oils instantly permeated the kitchen. It felt like her mother had just walked into the room. Tears filled Kate's eyes and spilled down her cheeks. She didn't care if the tears were from the oils or from letting go of her hurt and anger; they were welcome. After unwrapping and setting each little brown glass bottle on the counter, she dug around in the box to make sure she hadn't missed anything.

Ah, a CD called *QiGong for Pregnancy*, and there was a card as well. One of the little bottles of oil was called Serenity. Kate drew a bath and sprinkled in four drops. An hour later when Finn got home, he found her drying off, wearing nothing but a big smile. "This place smells like your mother. Come here and kiss me before I pass out from these oils."

After, when they were lying in bed, Kate showed him the card Georgina had sent. It was a picture of a baby's feet with little toes like corn nibblets. Finn turned on his side to face her. "Kate, I was scared when you told me you were pregnant, scared that being pregnant would make you hurt all over again about being adopted when you see how close you are to our baby, how intimate the relationship is."

"So that's what made you hesitant and weird when I told you I was pregnant?"

"I'm not hesitant about this baby."

"I was hurt at your subdued response."

"I was anxious for you. Think about it—carrying a baby for nine months, feeling it growing all safe inside you. I was afraid you'd think, How could my birth mother have been this close to me, with me all snug in her womb, listening to the woosh of her heartbeat, hearing her voice every day—and then suddenly they cut her open, and I'm ripped out and in this big cold, bright, exposed open space, and I never hear her heart again, never hear her voice again? I don't want all these thoughts to make you sad and ruin your happiness about our baby."

Kate softened her voice at his words. "Nothing's going to ruin my happiness about this baby, as long as it's what you want too." She snuggled close to him and kissed his earlobe. "And I'm okay about the adoption thing. This new life beginning is a chance for me to heal all those old feelings about being given away."

He was so different about his adoption from how she was. To him his birth mother was a portal he'd passed through, and he didn't look back. His adoptive parents were his parents. Even though they'd pissed him off, he still considered them his only parents. There were no phantom birth parents that he wondered about. He never asked himself what his birth parents would make of his life or if they remembered his existence, let alone his birthday. They didn't really exist for him. Kate wasn't completely sure she believed this, though he had given her no reason not to. Being adopted, being unwanted, having been given away at birth didn't seem to be an issue for him.

Kate couldn't say this for herself. Adoption and abandonment had always been issues for her despite all the therapy. But it wasn't going to get in the way of her happiness about their baby. Their baby would be the first blood relative she'd ever seen, the first person in her family who might look like her. That thought filled her with gratitude, which spread out from her heart and warmed every cell in her body.

She felt her eyelids grow heavy. Maybe those oils had helped them both open up after all. "Essential oils don't do the work for you," her mother had once explained to her, "but they do prepare the emotional soil so that trapped negative feelings are easier to release, allowing you to feel the positive feelings that have been covered over." She hadn't wanted to let go of her hurt and anger at Finn, so she hadn't even opened the box. Now her resistance seemed silly. She was obstinate. Maybe it had to do with having been a C-section baby. They didn't wait until she was ready to be born; instead, they scheduled her birth for their convenience. The doctor and the hospital chose her birthdate. Ready or not, they just cut her out of her birth mother. Kate felt herself shudder. Finn turned to her with a dreamy, half-asleep, velvety voice and asked her if she was cold. "I'm good," she said. Had her birth mother ever seen her or held her, or was she out cold when Kate was lifted out of her womb like stolen goods?

There would be no C-section for Kate's baby. He or she would choose the moment of its birth. And she wanted a midwife to assist her in giving birth in the ocean. She'd read a lot about that. Having women lie on their backs on a table was all for the doctor's convenience. Nature and gravity helped, if the mother assumed a squatting position. More and more women were giving birth squatting in warm oceans so there was less shock for the newborn baby. The baby could drop from its cozy womb into warm, salty sea water and be caught by its father or the midwife and handed to its mother before the umbilical cord was cut. Hospitals rushed everything, smelled bad, and were full of germs, to say nothing of the garish lighting. Finn might argue with some of her ideas, but she knew Georgina would be on her side.

When her stepmother gave birth in a New York hospital, Kate swore she would never do it like that. Kate was nineteen when Cyrus told her that his wife was pregnant. The news crushed her. He would have a biological child, and he wouldn't love her anymore. He'd abandon her. Her stepmother's pregnancy ripped open Kate's adoption wound. Once again she felt like the deformed outsider who didn't look like any of them and came from a different bloodline. Why couldn't they have adopted? Then both of Cyrus's children would have been equal. She angrily told Cyrus at the time, "Don't expect me to babysit for free."

"Good," he said, "we'll keep the money in the family."

Now it was her turn to be pregnant and have a baby. She'd wanted this for as long as she could remember. "I'm having a baby," she whispered to herself. This thought was like light flung across a dark field, warming it and stirring the waiting life beneath the soil. Kate rested her hands on her belly and fell asleep.

IF YOU TAKE IT PERSONALLY, YOU'LL FEEL LIKE ROADKILL

"You won't have to waste time thinking about it, Georgina," her grandmother told her when she was a little girl, "if you just choose a day of the week for each task and stick to it." Mondays were her grandmother's laundry days, Tuesdays were for sprinkling and ironing the clothes, Wednesdays for visiting her butcher and vegetable man, Thursdays for major cooking, and Fridays for a thorough cleaning of the house. Every day she baked fresh bread and brought in the milk and butter from the front stoop, supervised her five children, and helped her husband with his business. She was quiet and humble and good. *I should be more like her*, Georgina thought.

Georgina also did her laundry on Mondays, but she never ironed anything on Tuesday or any other day, and she never brought in milk from the front porch. She lived in an apartment building, and sadly, there were no milkmen anymore, bringing you milk from their own cows that you could see in the pasture not far from your house. Growing up, Georgina had known their milkman. His name was Art Short, and he delivered the milk to the whole town. She often thought she'd be happier if she'd lived back in her grandmother's day or even in the days of her own childhood. Back then it was easier to feel close to the source of things. Back then there was always the comfort of bread rising in a pottery bowl under a white cotton dish towel.

Georgina folded the last of her soft, white T-shirts, put them in her top drawer and resisted picking up the phone to call Kate. "Leave them alone. Let this big event be just theirs for a time," Cyrus had told her. He was probably right. So instead of calling Kate, Georgina called Selma. "Meet me under the Arch in fifteen minutes. We'll take a turn or two around the park to celebrate this baby news," Selma said. How unlike Selma to be this spontaneous. Making plans with Selma was usually impossible except in an emergency. If there was a reason, she magically appeared, and on time too. Otherwise she was elusive and chronically late. Georgina tied her running shoes while she waited for the elevator. Selma was stretching near the Washington Square Arch when Georgina got to the park. "You're looking good, girlfriend, like you had a massage on your face," Selma said.

"You always say that when I'm happy. It's more like a massage on my heart," Georgina said. "But I hope all the hormonal changes don't set off anything in Kate or make her vulnerable to something weird."

"Don't let fear get ahold of your throat. People who obsess over their children make poor company for them."

"Jung said that too. Let them grow free like trees, I think is how he put it."

"Now tell me, when is this new person due to arrive on the planet?" Selma offered Georgina walnuts and apricots from the baggie she was carrying. "Have some. Then we'll circle around this park a few times and tear up the sidewalk."

Untying her sneakers on the way up in the elevator so she could slip them off at the front door, Georgina could sense the restlessness moving through her. Unable to concentrate on the article she was writing, she checked her email. Up popped her divorce lawyer's name. The name smacked her in the head like she'd banged it on the sharp edge of the counter while standing up. She felt herself stop breathing and tense up. *What now?* That business had finally finished after huge expense and three years of delays and wrangling. And in the end she hadn't gotten a dime from Colin. So what was this? The process had been worse than she'd anticipated. Not like with Cyrus, where it had been amiable. She and Cyrus had used one lawyer, and it was done in a couple of months without dispute even though they had a child to consider.

With Colin, it was entirely different. She suggested they use a mediator since they had no children and no property. He refused and insisted on lawyers. She didn't want lawyers or contention or pain, but he apparently did—for her at least. The pain came in two tidal waves, each accompanied by that unpleasant duo: low self-esteem and massive self-doubt.

The first shock was when her life took a sharp left turn she hadn't seen coming, and she went right off the cliff into a cavern of worthlessness. The gut wrenching and inability to metabolize what was happening were as bad as the heartache. But the insidious feeling of being garbage—or worse, fresh roadkill—caught her off guard, surprising and paralyzing her.

Not long after Colin left her, Cyrus came over one evening to be with Kate and sent Georgina out with Emma to a wine bar in the West Village. "Buy a new dress or a Chanel lipstick," Emma advised. "It'll make you feel better."

"I can't go shopping. No one would even wait on me."

"That's crazy talk. Why do you think that?"

"Salespeople will see I'm an old reject. And why would they wait on an old reject when every other woman in the store is younger and better dressed and has a life? Even the greeter at Madewell looks at me as if he's wondering what I'm doing there. I almost feel compelled to explain to him, 'I'm just here to buy a birthday present for my daughter.' How ridiculous is that?"

"Very."

"I wish I could be invisible. When I try to go out shopping, I end up running home to hide. Each step down the sidewalk hurts. I don't even feel okay when I'm back inside my apartment."

"Why? What happens when you get back inside your apartment?"

"I slip off my shoes and coat at the front door. I always hang up my coat no matter how bad I feel."

"That's because you were trained to be a 'good girl,' and you never got over it."

"And good girls are neat, no matter how bad they feel."

"I hope hanging up your coat does something for you." Emma tried to tease.

"It just keeps the guilt at bay. Then I get into bed and let the tears come to release the humiliation. At least I feel safe in bed, even if it is four in the afternoon." Emma stared at her friend. Georgina said, "At least there, under the covers no one can see my rejected, worthless self. I'd crawl in between the mattress and the box springs if I could."

Emma sipped her wine. "Let me get this straight. You feel humiliated because Colin, an ass if ever there was one, rejected you? In my opinion it was a lucky escape. Time to move on, Georgina."

The wine bar's lights dimmed. It was that time of the evening. Georgina relaxed a little in the darkened room.

"I can't move on. I'm flattened roadkill."

"You're letting yourself be defeated."

"Maybe it was my fault. Maybe I was too complacent in our marriage. Maybe I needed to be shaken up a bit. I thought we were solid, that we'd stand together for our whole lives. Our marriage felt like a big white house with wraparound verandas, surrounded by white fences and tall, thick hedgerows. It was meant to go on and on and weather even the pesky Lars and Alexandra. I didn't know Colin was a man of weak and lightly broken ties."

"Save all that veranda talk for Carrie. I can't listen to it. The man was cruel. Have you forgotten how he tried to destroy Kate?"

"You're right. That was a deal breaker."

"Everything ends. It's just a question of when. Drink your wine." Then Emma did something so uncharacteristic of her. She reached out and covered Georgina's hand with her own for just a moment. "I get that his treatment of Kate, topped off by his affair, was a devastating betrayal. And seeing his obsession with another woman written in his handwriting in that little notebook left no room for letting the blow fall by degrees." Emma's voice was softer than Georgina had ever heard it.

"I dread summer coming," Georgina said. "I can't bear to think of having my skin uncovered, exposed so everyone can see me. And the days will be so long. I need the darkness to hibernate in until I heal. I'm such a self-centered coward. I can't believe I let a man leaving me get me into this state."

"You lost your way of being in the world, but you'll find it again."

"Summer days have too many hours for my mauled flesh to be exposed to the world."

"Autumn will follow summer, and by then your ego will have begun to recover. It is only your ego, Georgina, that's been wounded," Emma reminded her. "The soul doesn't suffer these rejections. Maybe it even arranges them to make us grow. Isn't that what you believe?"

Georgina looked at Emma and smiled. "And I always thought you weren't listening."

Emma smiled back, just fleetingly, before saying, "And Kate needs you. She's only seventeen and still recovering, so pull yourself together. It's enough licking of your wounds."

"I wish I could skip spring this year, and summer and fall, and go right back to winter. It's a relief to cover up and hide inside, watching *Desperate Housewives* with Kate or sitting and staring into the fire."

"You're not watching that ridiculous show!"

"We are. It's a mindless distraction. And I like Gabby and Brie."

"For God's sake, at least watch some old Bette Davis movies if you need a distraction."

"I need more than a distraction. I need endless winter. The short dark days match my mood better. Sweaters and tights and coats make a good protection when you're raw. I haven't even begun to struggle through the exposure of summer yet, and I'm already longing for the early nightfall of winter when the sky grows dark at four thirty."

Emma could feel herself starting to get impatient with Georgina again. Maybe she should try to rough her up a bit to shake her out of her depression. "Don't be so weak and self-indulgent. You sound like such a victim, and it's not who you are. Don't peddle your wounds around me, looking for sympathy. You can't stay stuck in being wounded. Don't make a life out of that."

"You're right. It's not who I want to be."

"Remember all the things you love—the early morning light in late August, the scent of deep purple irises in spring, a crescent moon, reading by the fire, hanging with Kate, a perfect summer dress, horses, newly fallen snow on a woodland pond looking like glazed sugar."

"Really, Emma," Georgina smiled. "'Newly fallen snow on a woodland pond looking like glazed sugar'?"

"At least I got a smile out of you."

"And I will get back in sync with nature. The world is being reborn. The magnolias across from my building are blossoming. I don't want to be crumbling down."

"Good. What's that line you love? 'Some people feel the rain. Others just get wet.'"

"Maybe people suffering from broken hearts should just move to Iceland where it's dark all day for six months, so they can hibernate and feel protected and in harmony with the darkness inside. Then when they can feel the rain again, they can come back out of hiding into the light," Georgina said.

"What? I thought we settled that. No more hiding. You can't lick your wounds forever if you want to be the heroine of your own life." Emma motioned for the waiter and asked for two more glasses of Cabernet. "But blows happen for a reason, at least according to you."

"I know that."

"Then use this adversity. Make it a catalyst to set yourself on your journey of self-discovery again. You have a choice—you can hide or grow from this experience."

"I don't have your strength, Emma. I'm wrecked. Even my doormen see I'm blown apart. I feel embarrassed and ashamed about being dumped. I know I shouldn't care. I sound so stupid and shallow."

"Yes, you do."

The waiter set down the wine without a word and withdrew. Emma studied Georgina's face. It looked caved in on itself, full of shame. "There's nothing to be ashamed about," Emma said. She lifted her glass to her lips. "What you need is to continue your story without him. Stories are the foundation of our identity. You have to write your life forward. You had a life before Colin. And there's Kate. Continue on from there. Let your accomplishments be a foundation for the next part of your journey."

"I don't know, Emma, maybe I should use this loss as an opportunity to forget myself completely, drop all those patterns of behavior that I thought were me, reinvent myself."

Walking home through the Village from the wine bar on that now long ago night, Georgina looked up at the moon. It was a lovely crescent. Tomorrow it would be larger, and in a week it would be full. *You will be full again too*, she told herself. *And this is your opportunity to remember that your "little self" doesn't exist as something separate from everything in existence. You are not only connected to everything, you are everything—you're part of the whole. This is just a stupid little ego blow. Get over it. Be the light being that you are, that we all are. Remember that. Stop wallowing in self-pity. Get a grip. Use this pain as a catalyst to grow. Take stock of yourself. You're a compassionate, honest person who loves easily and forgives quickly. You try to do unto others as you would have them do unto you. You raised an amazing daughter who's braver than you could ever have imagined. You have good work. And try to remember how you have loved this life on earth and the beauty of this planet. Remember how grateful you are for your eyes and hands and the feet that carry you forward each day into the world. You can breathe and walk and see. The gift of Kate alone is more love than your heart can bear without cracking open. Clean water flows right into your apartment. You sleep in a bed. You are more fortunate than ninety percent of people on earth.*

Even at the mundane levels you've done okay. You worked hard to get a PhD and build a private practice. You know how to listen, when to make an observation, and when to be quiet. You've had more than your share of joy. You were your high school homecoming queen. You've been a car salesperson at Berkeley Datsun, a waitress at Windows on the World, an exchange student in Japan. You've taught at two major universities. Once, a man bumping into you leaving the post office apologized, saying, "I'm sorry, I just got so confused looking at you." But that was twenty years ago. So let the winds of change blow. Stand strong inside them. Why make such a big deal of being dumped? You can't let yourself fall permanently into the grip of an inferiority complex. There's nothing to feel inferior about. You're not separate. We're all part of the same whole, each of us a different face of God.

When Georgina got home that night, Kate was asleep, mercifully, and Cyrus was reading. He told Georgina he'd found Kate less depressed and jumpy. She smiled. He said good-night and left. He probably saw from her face that the she'd been struggling with something. She wasn't his problem. He had a wife at home.

Georgina walked into her bedroom and stared at herself in the mirror. Just a few months before, she'd felt loved, secure, a part of the ebb and flow of life. She'd been someone entitled to go shopping. *I have to shake this off,* she thought, *and let being dumped become an opportunity to strip away my identity and my old patterns. I have to step into a new consciousness, using this pain as a catalyst. Isn't that the point of suffering? So what if the Madewell greeter scanned me and found me wanting? Is he the judge of my worth? I'm being an idiot. Emma's right, I have a choice. Think how remarkable it is that we exist at all.*

With that last thought, she set her moisturizer down on her dresser, walked to her closet door and opened it, and pulled out all the dresses she'd worn during her saddest days when Colin first left. She made a pile on her bed and called it "dresses steeped in sorrow." They had to go. And even though there was one she had particularly loved, into the pile for the Salvation Army it went with the rest. *I hope I'm not doing this just because I've had too much wine tonight,* she thought. Then she carried them out into the living room.

It was now six years since she got rid of those dresses, and she hadn't missed any of them once.

If it had been true heartbreak over Colin, there would have been the sweetness of the pain to console her. To be helpless in the face of love would have driven her to that sharp edge of her humanness. There had been the sweetness of melting together in the early days. Deep inside herself, she knew even now that what they shared had been a form of divine eros. Still, there was no beauty in this heartbreak. There had been the months of hiding from everything except work and taking care of Kate. *Only your ego has been hurt,* she'd reminded herself over and over again. At first, the only places she had felt all right were sitting in bed holding Kate and in her office seeing clients. She was a mother with a suffering child. She was a psychologist. In her office, only the client's world existed for that hour. She became a field of consciousness, facilitating their journey. Work and motherhood were her whole world.

Even as she'd wrestled her inferiority complex to the ground and struggled to pull Kate through the last dregs of her depression, there had been another horror going on. "Well, what did you expect?" Emma asked her. "The process of divorce, using lawyers, is not for the faint of heart, the poor, the impatient, or anyone who wishes to maintain a shred of privacy. If you're not broke when you start the process, you will be by the end." Emma sounded like a lecturer in a woman's counseling group, and Georgina smiled in spite of herself.

"You might remember, Emma, that I had no choice. Colin refused mediation." It was the first time Georgina had been uptown since Kate had gotten sick. She'd been down about the divorce proceedings. So Emma lured her up to the Plaza with the promise of ice cold martinis and oysters on the half shell. "It'll cheer you up, remind you there's a world beyond Greenwich Village." So Georgina went.

Emma slurped an oyster and took a sip of her martini, careful to first remove the toothpick holding the three olives. Emma loved martinis straight up. "Now isn't this nicer than a paleo dinner or a vegan dessert in some Village dive catering to millennials?" Emma said.

Georgina agreed. "To sophisticated haunts." And she clinked Emma's martini glass.

"You know, Georgina, in a court of law, Colin's considered the breadwinner. He would have done better without lawyers, just by dealing with you."

Georgina looked doubtful. "Why do you say that?"

"Because you're a pushover."

"I don't agree!"

"Oh, don't get your knickers in a twist. I'm only saying he's been a bad boy. All those years, you supported him through his emotional upheavals. Then you need support, and he not only rages at you and attacks your child instead of helping you, but he goes off and has an affair." Emma summoned the waiter and ordered more oysters. "Another martini?" She asked Georgina.

"Why not." The oysters looked beautiful on the half shell, arranged on a bed of shimmering ice in a silver dish shaped like a giant seashell. The heavy dish tilted a little as the waiter set it down, spilling a bit of water and oyster juice on Emma's lap. She brushed it off.

"I hate dealing with lawyers, and he knows it. And there are only two questions: How much spousal support he should pay per month and for how many months? Two questions we could have agreed on between ourselves. We both know he makes three times what I do. But he prefers for our business to be conducted by two paid strangers."

"Get ready," Emma said, "because these two paid strangers will be picking through your lives to create the financial disclosure documents his lawyer is demanding." Emma squeezed lemon on her oyster. "Every financial pore will be exposed. How much do you have in savings? What do you earn each month? How much is your rent? Your Con Ed, your phone? Your dental bills? How many times a year do you see your gynecologist, and what is your copay? How much did you pay for your reading glasses? How much do you give your doormen at Christmas? How often do you visit the hairdresser, and what does it cost? Is that including tip? What is the exact balance in your checking account? How many times per week do you order in? How much do you spend per month on groceries? Do you dine out? How often? What do you pay your therapist? How much do you spend on clothes, toilet paper, toothpaste, tampons?"

"Sounds like financial rape," Georgina said. She picked up her glass by the long cool stem and rolled it between her fingers.

"You will feel raped before you're done, not only by Colin's lawyer but by your own. Do you want the last oyster?" Emma asked. Georgina shook her head no.

And Emma was right. Colin was "tricksy" too. He started by claiming expenses that were ludicrous. Georgina felt like calling him up and saying, "Have you forgotten we've met? I've seen you squeeze a nickel till the buffalo hollers, so I know you're not spending six hundred a month on cabs and two hundred a month on dry cleaning or eighteen thousand a year on furniture." Emma, Selma, Kate, and Georgina had sat at the dining room table, eating pasta Bolognese one evening and gone over the copy of Colin's financial disclosure statement that Georgina's lawyer had sent her. Georgina imagined Colin and his girlfriend reading through hers, lying in bed together. He read everything in bed.

"When did Colin ever take a cab!" said Kate as they read through the document. "And he has insurance—how can he be claiming four thousand a month in unreimbursed medical?"

"I hope that means he's getting a lot of root canals and colonoscopies," Emma said. At that, Georgina heard Kate laugh for the first time in two years. Selma, Emma and Georgina all turned to look at her. "What?" Kate said. The fifteen hundred a month on books they all believed was true. "He just forgot to mention that they're comic books," Kate piped in. Then Kate made them laugh when she pointed out that Colin said he was living in a studio, but his household staff expense was $2,800 a month. "Really, Colin, household staff?" They supposed he meant a cleaning lady. "He wouldn't pay half that. He'd clean the place himself first," said Kate. When Georgina's lawyer had questioned these expenses, Colin's lawyer explained they were his "expected, likely expenses" when the divorce was settled. "Oh, his expenses for his theoretical future life, the one where he has household staff?" Georgina said.

She didn't want to have a pissing contest with him about whose expenses were higher. "But it does seem strange," her lawyer said to her, "that his expenses are more for just him than yours are for yourself, your daughter, and your dog." In the end Georgina told her lawyer to let the expenses stand. She didn't want to feel like she was raping him. Kate, using language uncharacteristic for her, said to Georgina, "You don't want to rape him, but I guess it's okay for him to fuck you over. I hope you're not still in love with that wanker."

She wasn't still in love with him, but she did feel for him, despite everything. What evoked her compassion for him was Kate joking about his monthly food expense. "This can't be right," Kate said. "Colin'll eat anything. The man could survive being a Dumpster diver. Plus, I thought he told you he was so wrecked that all he could eat was Ensure and mint tea. Three thousand dollars' worth of Ensure a month? Mom, I think I better talk to your lawyer." Kate reminding her that Colin literally would eat anything made Georgina feel sad for him. It made her remember the way he'd been treated as a child by his self-involved, explosive father and his fearful mother, and she didn't want to take anything away from him. She wanted to protect him. "Call me crazy," she said.

"I will if you don't stick up for yourself," Kate said. "He walked out on you. And he started this thing with lawyers." Selma smiled at Kate's strength as she thought to herself, as she often did about Colin, *That boy's lower than a snake.*

Their divorce was now long settled. In the end she'd gotten nothing from him but her freedom. And she'd wasted $8,000 on a lawyer. So why was her lawyer emailing? And why was Colin contacting Kate? Georgina's adrenaline spiked at the memory of the way he'd harried her with the divorce. "I want to be fair," he said, while he was secretly hiring a lawyer and secretly ferreting away money in Scotland. Did he seriously think his secret account would keep him safe or answer the call of his soul? Would the profits of his deceit and unscrupulous accounting be worth the sacrifice of his integrity? *His behavior is a measure of his fear*, she told herself when she discovered his hidden accounts. She left them hidden.

His lawyer tried to claim that their assets were equal, to make sure that Georgina would get no help while she rebuilt her practice. They wanted the fact that Colin earned three times what she did left out of the negotiation. This process made her feel like an unworthy beggar. "Don't be ridiculous. Where's your self-worth?" Emma said. "Stop acting like this is a bad thing—you're rid of a self-centered ass. And don't take any of this gamesmanship personally. It's what lawyers do." Emma never missed an opportunity to call Colin an ass. Georgina tried to take Emma's advice, but nevertheless, it felt personal. *This is a chance to grow*, she reminded herself each day during the divorce process. Thank God it was done now.

So why did just seeing her lawyer's name in her in-box still traumatize her? What did she want after all this time?

WOLVES AT THE DOOR

"I had another nightmare about wild animals," Lydia said. Kate looked up from tying her Converses after their Qigong class. It had been a stretch to get Lydia interested in Qigong, but now she was hooked. "I was alone inside a cabin in a snowy woods full of tall trees. Somehow I knew a pack of wolves was running through the forest in the deep snow toward my cabin. I felt them coming closer and closer. Then they were on the porch at the door. I was behind it, and it was giving way. I woke up drenched in sweat."

"These nightmares are becoming a regular thing with you." Kate double knotted her lace. "What do you think's causing them?"

"I don't know. Does something have to be causing them?"

"Probably, if you keep on having them."

"Something's always after me in my dreams, something wild and ferocious and irrational. Last night it was wolves wanting to break the door down. Sometimes it's a bear going berserk or a wild boar. Stuff like that." Up until now Kate had just listened to Lydia's dreams without commenting much. She knew from Georgina that dreams could be understood to a certain degree without interpretation. But now she went a little further. "A lot of your dreams lately seem to have wild animals in them."

"Wild animals that are out to get me." Lydia picked up her bag, walked through the door, and stopped in the parking lot to take out her phone.

167

Kate waited while Lydia checked her messages. "I don't know what's going on with me," she said as they walked toward the car.

"Your unconscious seems riled up. It could be warning you about something pretty imminent, since the wolves are already at the door." Kate buckled her seat belt.

"You really think the dream is warning me about something? We don't have wolves on Okinawa."

"I didn't mean wolves literally."

"But you think the door is important?" Lydia looked over her shoulder as she backed out of her parking spot.

"That's for you to say. It's your dream. But it does seem like there are wild, irrational feelings trying to break through somewhere."

Lydia shifted out of reverse and into drive. "Are you saying the wolves are my wild, irrational feelings? But why are they at the door?"

"Maybe they want your attention. Maybe they feel unheard and want to be acknowledged. And the door could be the passage between what you're conscious of and what's in your unconscious."

"But why wolves? And why are they so angry and vicious?"

"When someone is ignored too long, they finally get angry. Maybe these feelings are like that too, furious because they've been ignored."

"But why wolves?" Lydia asked.

"Wild animals can represent our own irrational impulses, according to Jung, anyway. But I don't know why your unconscious chose wolves. It's something for you to wonder about."

"Maybe I'd better listen before they break the door down," Lydia laughed.

Kate wasn't sure if Lydia was making a joke or being serious. "Keeping a dream journal could let your unconscious know you're listening."

"Spencer would flip out if he knew I was keeping a dream journal."

"You're kidding." Kate said before she thought better of it.

"He thinks dreams are meaningless, just the result of the sausage you ate for dinner." Lydia glanced at Kate.

"To each his own." Kate smiled. She wasn't going near that. Spencer was entitled to his opinion. But this last dream made Kate worry for her friend. The door between a safe, reasonable, conscious world and an unconscious, wild, dangerous irrational world was giving way. If and when it did, the feelings could tear Lydia apart. "Lunch?" Lydia asked.

"Not today. I've got a date with a graphic novel."

That afternoon as she bent over her work, Kate found herself thinking again about Lydia's dream. She pushed it out of her mind and refocused on her main character, who was, like her, newly pregnant. That's where the similarity ended. Her character was a hypochondriac who created problem after problem for herself and never recognized that her problems were the result of the choices she herself had made. She identified too much with her wounded self, which left her stuck. But her saving grace was that she was funny, and she could at times inspire compassion despite herself.

Finn got a kick out of the way Kate drew her. "Really dope, Kate," he told her. When Kate repeated Finn's comment to Lydia, she'd been mystified. "'Really dope'?"

"He means it's so good it makes you high." After that, Lydia had tried to work the expression into her conversation whenever she was around the younger officers.

Kate stood up and rubbed her palms together to build up some heat, then placed them over her kidneys as she surveyed her afternoon's work. Both her skills and her sense of humor were evolving. It was fun to write a humorous character so different from herself. Her other graphic novel about her breakdown as a teen was pretty dark at points. This one brought balance to her creative expression. Georgina would say together they made a whole. They were dark and light, shadow and persona, conscious and unconscious. As she massaged her kidneys, her mind again turned to her friend. Lydia's unconscious was riled up and banging on the door of her conscious mind. Something wild had been unleashed in her psyche, and it wanted to communicate with her. Was this the result of all the Body Talk? Or something else? Georgina had warned Kate that Body Talk could open up emotional issues that wanted to be healed. Kate rubbed her head and rolled it around on her shoulders. She was pleased with her day's drawings.

Finn would be home any minute. Digging around in the fridge, she found some leftover steak and cut it into bite-size pieces. Then she heated up Cuban black beans, grated some Mexican cheese over them, added rice with salsa, cilantro, and lime, rolled the mixture up in soft sun-dried tomato tortillas, and placed the tray in the oven. A piña colada would be a heavenly addition, but she didn't want a drunk baby trying to grow lungs. She reached into the cupboard for her large, oval, hand-painted Italian platter and set it on the stove to warm.

Half an hour later, Finn was draped over a stool at the counter, squeezing a lime into his Mexican beer. Kate liked the sound of a beer bottle being opened. It meant the end of a work day, a family picnic, a baseball game. But especially, it reminded her of her grandfather's garden. As a little girl, she'd weeded and planted and watered it with him. Together they staked up tomatoes and peonies, measured the height of the sunflowers, counted the morning glories, and tried to keep the mint and strawberries from overrunning everything else. When their work was done, they sat on the glider swing and surveyed it all, Grandpa with a beer, Kate with a lemonade. Usually, about then, her grandmother would call down to them, asking for basil or chives or a cucumber, which Kate would pick and run up to hand to her. She loved her grandmother. Her mother was always tense around her, but Kate wasn't sure why. For Kate, visiting Georgina's parents was like entering a safe world close to a tame nature, not like Lydia's wild nature where hungry wolves hurled themselves at the door.

"Yo, earth to Kate. Pass the guacamole and chips. You're off in Kateland."

"Sorry. Ready for a hot steak burrito?" When they'd eaten, she told him about Lydia's nightmares. "Should I ask my mother about them?"

"No."

"Really?"

"Let Lydia get her own therapist."

"Have you forgotten who they are? Even if it wasn't too much of a narcissistic injury for Lydia to do therapy, Spencer wouldn't approve."

"Why do I have a feeling your mother is about to be analyzing Lydia's dreams?"

"It's just that Lydia has no dialogue with her unconscious. Something has come loose in there and wants to be heard, but it's like she has no ears to hear the unconscious. This last dream of wolves about to break her door down scares me for her."

"Maybe she should lay off the Body Talk for a while. She may have bitten off more than she can chew."

"But Body Talk helps with emotional overload," Kate said. "It helps the brain, heart, and gut to work in harmony. And it helps the head bow down to the heart, which it should. There are even more neurons in the heart than there are in the brain. Body Talk appreciates this."

"Pass the burritos please," said Finn. Kate handed him the platter.

"Lydia's all torn up about something. Maybe I can help her handle it, help her get a dialogue going between her conscious and unconscious, help her see them like two partners with equal rights but different points of view."

"Quit bugging about Lydia. Let her deal with her own problems."

"But she doesn't get it that her conscious and unconscious need to listen to one another. With them being so dissociated, she's lost a vital source of self-knowledge."

"You sound like you're channeling your mother. Come on, let's go. Lose the dishes and take a walk to the beach with me. I know you've been bent over the computer and the drawing table all day, and that isn't good for my kid."

The evening air was the perfect temperature. Kate felt it wrap around her and caress her face and her bare arms and legs. She slipped her hand into Finn's as they strolled seaward. This early in her pregnancy, she was still wearing shorts with just the top button undone and her blouses left untucked. She'd have to go shopping soon if she didn't plan to spend the next six months in her drawstring pajama bottoms. They walked along in silence through the perfumed air past hundreds of wild roses growing by the roadside. Then Kate broke the silence. "So you really think I shouldn't ask my mother about Lydia's wolf dream?"

"Quit buggin', girl."

A car gave a short honk at them, and Lydia and Spencer pulled over to the side of the road. Finn smelled Lydia's perfume through the open window and took a step back. "Hey, you two, want to join us for a drink at the club?" Spencer leaned across Lydia and looked up at them. *He probably doesn't even realize pregnant women can't drink*, Kate thought.

"Another time—we're on our way to the beach," Finn told him.

"Sure thing." The BMW pulled away.

"Synchronicity," said Kate. "Just as I was mentioning her, they pulled up."

"It was a coincidence, an accidental meeting. It's a small island, not a sign that you and Georgina should take responsibility for Lydia's breakdown."

"So you agree she's about to have a breakdown."

"I don't know. Maybe she needs a breakdown. People usually get what they need. Let's keep out of it."

As the bath filled with hot water, Kate sprinkled in serenity oil and dropped her blouse and shorts on the floor. She could hear Finn in the kitchen, putting his Oreos in a small bowl to take to bed. It had been a nightly habit of his ever since they'd lived together. She'd long since given up telling him to eat his cookies before brushing his teeth. "But that defeats the pleasure of it," he'd explained. The last thing she wanted to be was his mother. Wives who did that killed their sex lives. She climbed into the bath. The hot fragrant water felt delicious. She slid down lower in the tub until the water touched her earlobes. She closed her eyes. A few years ago, she couldn't have imagined any of this. Back then she hadn't even been able to conceive of making it to age seventeen alive, let alone having this feeling of being divinely, exquisitely, serenely happy.

She stepped out of the bath and reached for her towel. As she bent over to dry her feet a droplet of water formed on the tip of her nipple and dropped down onto her toes. *I love what a drop of water and gravity can do*, she thought.

Finn was asleep with the little empty cookie bowl on his chest. Kate picked it up and turned off the light. She was about to get in beside him when she heard her email ding. If it was her mother, she'd take it as a sign to ask about Lydia's dreams. If it wasn't, she'd turn off the sound and go to sleep. It was Amazon—who else? As she was closing it, her computer dinged again. Georgina. Kate carried her laptop into the living room and started typing. "Mom, what do wild animals signify in dreams?"

"Are you dreaming of wild animals?" Georgina asked.

"Not me. Lydia."

"Wild animals can represent our own primitive unconscious impulses." Georgina typed back.

"But why would a person keep dreaming of being pursued by dangerous animals?"

"Usually, because some feelings that have been repressed are breaking through. Feelings that want to be recognized."

"You mean the person has ignored them, and now they're becoming insistent?"

"Yes. Aspects of the self that haven't been heard and integrated into the psyche as a whole can stage a kind of rebellion. Once aroused, they can push our rational self off the stage and into the pit, and take command, wreaking havoc on our outer world."

"You mean like causing a nervous breakdown?"

"In some cases. Or sometimes dreams can be about an impersonal archetypal force that has just pushed its way through the collective unconscious to the personal unconscious where it finds an opening, a weakness in the psyche."

"So some unconscious force may have found Lydia vulnerable and grabbed hold of her?"

"Possibly, but you have to consider the external situation of the dreamer in order to determine the nature of the message the dream is trying to convey. The same dream dreamed by two different people can have very different meanings."

"How do you mean?"

"Jung gave the example of two men jumping over a ditch on horseback. A young man dreaming he is riding a horse and jumping over a ditch has a very different meaning for the dreamer from an old man dreaming he is on horseback and jumping over a ditch."

"So what message do you think Lydia's unconscious is trying to give her?"

"I don't know enough about Lydia's psyche to answer that, but since it keeps repeating itself, her unconscious definitely wants to be heard."

"Thanks, Mom."

173

"Love you, sweet-pea girl."

Kate made herself some Sleepytime tea and sat holding the warm cup, wondering if Lydia would be able to relate to any of this, or if she should even tell her she'd asked Georgina. What primitive destructive impulses in Lydia were awakening and forcing their way into her consciousness? And would they overwhelm her before she could either push them back down and secure the door, or better still, invite them in and hear what they had to say? Why was this happening now? Kate's hand went involuntarily to her abdomen. Could Lydia be freaking out over her pregnancy? She had often said her one regret was never having had children. Then there were those memories Body Talk had brought to the surface from Lydia's childhood. And Lydia had no real way to work them through except talking to Kate. She wasn't in therapy, she didn't keep a journal, and she couldn't talk to Spencer about this kind of thing. Maybe it was all overwhelming her. Kate finished her tea and set the cup in the sink. She slipped into bed beside Finn, closed her eyes, and fell asleep to the sound of his steady breathing and the silky rustle of the palm trees outside her window, imagining them as elegant ladies in floor-length gowns crossing a ball room.

SAILING INWARD

When Julia got cancer, Georgina began to face the fact that her own ship was no longer sailing out into the world but was now sailing inward toward death. *This isn't news*, she thought. *Death is with us from the moment of birth and takes the whole journey with us. We just pretend not to see her as she walks beside us. Death has always been my companion, and together we pull the oars, rowing toward the unseen world. It's the same for each of us. Julia isn't the only one who could die. We all will. She may just die sooner, or not.* Georgina pressed her fingerprint on the little machine at the desk that recognized her as a gym member and allowed her to enter.

The elliptical she liked was free, and she climbed on, took hold of the handles, and closed her eyes. The gym was her thinking place. *If I were to die now, what would I regret? Maybe that I've never experienced true love with a partner?* As a little girl, she imagined true love to be like what inspired Emperor Shah Jahan to build the Taj Mahal for his wife. Her mother, a cooler heart, was quick to point out that the Taj Mahal was a mausoleum. Georgina remained a romantic. For a while she believed Colin was that true love. Then in a single moment, a dividing line in time, he became a stranger. Had she locked her own door against true love? Was there some flaw or fear she hadn't faced in herself that had denied her this experience? She opened her eyes for a moment to look at the elliptical and check the elapsed time. Why had she ever thought Colin was her true love? She got off the ellipti-

175

cal, took a long cool drink from her water bottle, and walked over to the bikes. She set the resistance to four, closed her eyes again, began pedaling, and let her mind roam back to Colin.

One morning a couple of months after Colin moved out, she and Kate were walking along Fourteenth Street on their way to Trader Joe's when Kate said, "There's Colin." He passed within three feet of them, walking in the opposite direction, and didn't even notice them. That wasn't unusual for him. He rarely noticed anything because he was usually involved with his own thoughts. Seeing him shook them up. It was incontrovertible proof that their worlds no longer intersected. And he looked so different seen this way, as a stranger. He looked so humorless and geeky and not as handsome. He wasn't compelling at all.

A few months after the Trader Joe's sighting, she and Colin had met to sign their taxes, which that first year they still filed as married since their divorce was dragging on. Georgina debated about where they should meet and what she should wear and whether she should have her hair high-lighted. "Are you kidding?" Kate said. "It isn't a date, Mom."

"You're right."

"And remember, he's the useless tosser in this story."

Georgina took another sip from her water bottle and walked over to the treadmills that offered a view up Fifth Avenue. She missed going to the gym with Kate. It had been comforting to glance up and see Kate across the room, running on the treadmill or using the chest press; the gym felt lonely without her. Georgina had tried to get Selma to come with her, but Selma loved the Y and didn't want to change gyms. Emma didn't exercise, and Carrie had moved to Rhode Island. She missed roaming the Village with Carrie, wandering into little shops, drinking cappuccino. People moved around too much. Why couldn't they just stay put?

Back when she and Colin were still together, before Kate had gotten sick, Georgina had gone to visit Carrie in Rhode Island one weekend. They spent the whole morning at the barn with Carrie's horses. Then in the afternoon, hot and spent, they showered and changed into sundresses to sit outside in the garden. Carrie brought a tray of lemonade and cookies out and set it on the old-fashioned wrought iron table standing among the wildflowers.

Georgina was already lying in the hammock, talking on her cell phone, so Carrie took the chaise. Georgina said good-bye to Colin and dropped her phone in the grass.

"It's dangerous, the way Colin still seems to worship you after all this time," Carrie told Georgina, catching her off guard.

Carrie was the softest of all Georgina's friends and had the most natural access to the unconscious. Her usually gentle manner reminded Georgina of her sister, Julia. Julia's softness was the deep quiet of the forest, shades of green; Carrie's was the silver blue of inlet water. Georgina loved visiting Carrie's lilac-surrounded cottage, hanging out with her horses, and feeding the swans who came close to the shore, swimming through the tall grass.

"Why dangerous?" Georgina asked, sitting up to take a sip of her lemonade.

"Because Colin resents everybody else in your life, anyone you put your attention on. You still wear the face of the goddess for him, but can that last? His inner, ideal image of a woman could so easily be shifted onto someone else if he feels you aren't completely attuned to his needs."

"Do you feel he resents you?" Georgina asked. She set her lemonade down in the grass beside the hammock.

"Yes, but that's almost beside the point. It's more perilous than that. His idealization of you feels wonderful now—you're perfection to him. But the more he idealizes you, the farther the fall will be if it comes." Carrie picked a sprig of mint growing near her chaise and dropped it in her lemonade. Georgina watched her.

"I know you're right. It's just that when he focuses his extravagant attention on me, it feels like being wrapped in a garment woven of warm gold. Besides, aren't all experiences of falling in love the projection of our own idealized image onto the beloved?" Georgina got up and walked over to the little table holding the plate of homemade chocolate chip cookies. She picked one up and took a bite. Then she lay back down in the hammock and rocked herself with one foot.

"Falling in love is a projection, but you and Colin are way past the falling in love part. What worries me for you is that you don't seem to acknowledge his underbelly. You don't see Colin as others see him. He's not as nice as you think."

"What are you talking about? Why are you telling me this now?" Georgina asked.

"I couldn't fall asleep last night after you told me how Colin is getting more and more jealous of Kate. That set off alarm bells in me," Carrie said.

"Alarm bells about what?"

"Colin is sexy, too sexy for anybody's good, but there's something missing in him. There's a cold selfishness at the center of his appeal. It feels ruthless. And I fear for you and Kate if he ever turns against you."

"But why would he turn against us? You're starting to sound like Emma."

"Don't be naïve, Georgina. You know if Colin feels his needs aren't being met, he'll go where he can meet them. I guess what I'm saying is that I don't sense any loyalty in Colin. And his recent jealousy of Kate is troubling. She's the child. He's supposed to be the adult."

"I know what you mean about the cold ruthlessness at his center. Sometimes when he comes home and someone's there and he wants to have all my attention, he freezes the person out. It's embarrassing."

"Why do you tolerate that? Is the sex still that good?"

"No, sex isn't what I'd like it to be, not anymore. Colin's more into role playing than into the numinous aspects of sex that I appreciate."

"You mean the spiritual aspect of sex is too intimate for him," Carrie said.

"I guess. That much connection makes him uncomfortable. He prefers the blindfold and the furry handcuffs–type of sex."

"That way he doesn't have to meet you heart to heart."

"He wasn't like that in the beginning. In those early months, I felt I could unfold to him completely."

"What happened?"

"Maybe partly, it happened during sex one night. We started to approach that wild jungle at the center of our entwined bodies. Invisible energies bound together our mouths, our hearts, our navels. All our chakras were connecting energetically. The fire was building up between us. Searing and reckless, it consumed me, and I thought him too. I felt his fire warm my inner waters and imagined that my watery insides were tempering his fiery rage. For me it was alchemy. I felt free like an animal—free of my thoughts, my fears, free of everything but the moment. Then he stopped moving and he said in a displeased, half-frightened voice, 'You're like a wild animal, Georgina.'"

"Were you making growling noises or something?"

"I don't think so. I was just being a human animal enjoying our bodies. I should have said that to him. But I didn't. Instead I felt humiliated, pierced in the deepest heart of my passion for him. My sexuality wasn't a delight to him. It frightened him. He didn't want the revelation that comes with complete surrender, just the blindfold and the handcuffs. The healing alchemy of sex ended for us that night in my humiliation. I was alone and naked crouching in a jungle, ashamed of my body and my passion."

"But you still have a sex life?"

"It's technical—a weak substitute for making love. That's what we've settled for."

"You sound like you're bored by it."

"It's a pale imitation of where I hoped we could go. There've been no further refinements of passion since his wild-animal comment."

"And you've never talked to him about what he said?"

"Never. It was so humiliating unfolding myself and being rejected, realizing I frightened him. I couldn't talk about it."

"Let's walk down to the water and visit the swans," Carrie said. She reached for Georgina's hands and pulled her up out of the hammock.

Georgina had thought about their conversation all the way back to New York on the train the next day as she stared out the window at the passing scenery. But once home again in their apartment, greeted by Colin's kiss, she'd filed it away—until now. She didn't have the sundress she'd been wearing that day with Carrie anymore. It had gone into the pile of dresses to be gotten rid of after Colin left. And it had been such a beautiful dress, with a heart-shaped top that tied behind her neck and a full skirt that floated around her legs in the breeze by the water that day with Carrie as they fed bread crumbs to the swans.

After twenty minutes on the treadmill, Georgina was sweating. She reached for her towel and water bottle, picked up a mat, and found a

179

space to stretch on the wooden floor. She lay back and closed her eyes to calm her breathing.

So in truth, Georgina thought as she recalled telling Carrie about that jungle night, *I lost Colin long before he left*. In the end losing him had been good for her. The loss of him led her back to herself. *It's facing the worst moments in our lives that makes us who we are*, she reminded herself. The challenge is to see the gift in the hard times. But she hadn't known that yet when she and Colin met to sign their taxes. Georgina stretched her legs and back, then lay still on her mat and did a few sweeping breaths. The sounds of the gym dropped into the background. The day they met to sign their taxes was the last time she saw Colin.

She was standing in the entrance of French Roast on the corner of Sixth Avenue and Eleventh Street when she saw him approaching. In a second he was beside her. "You've had your hair done. It looks good." She hadn't, but she didn't mention it. He looked thin. She asked for the just-vacated table in the window and sat facing him. He was still so familiar, wearing the navy cashmere V-neck sweater she'd bought him at J. Crew two years earlier. But then, he probably didn't own a sweater, a shirt, or a pair of pants she hadn't bought him. When he'd left, he asked her, "Where do you buy my clothes?" He'd cared so little what he wore.

"Just peppermint tea for me," he told the waiter. "Let's sign the taxes first," he said to her.

"So how are you?" she asked him. He dove right in.

"I'm seeing a therapist, an old Greek woman, for anxiety and agoraphobia, except all she wants to talk about is my parents."

"Is she helping?" Georgina asked.

"Yes, more than the Ativan. I could barely get from my apartment to the subway, and then I'd be claustrophobic in the train. Once I got to the office, I couldn't leave even to go downstairs for coffee or lunch. And I've had bad stomach trouble too."

"Can you eat?" Georgina asked him.

"Nothing but mint tea and Ensure."

Georgina had to pull back on the reins on her heart. Without her, he had no legs—he'd come apart. She remembered once, years ago, when his parents came to visit. She had to walk him to work the second day after their arrival because he'd fallen down in the street the first day. His legs just crumpled under him. His parents undid him. The strength drained out of him when they were around. He wouldn't be alone with them even for a few minutes. Either Kate or Georgina always had to be present as a buffer and protector. It was hard to see what they did except through his reactions. He just kept unraveling in response to their presence like a man reacting to the behavior of two ghosts only he could see. To Kate and Georgina, they appeared pleasant and helpful, even interesting and fun. But Colin refused to ever invite them again. Now without her, he'd lost his legs and crumpled down again.

Everything in her melted toward him as she looked across the table into his face. Though she hadn't seen him in a year, other than the Trader Joe's sighting, it seemed so normal, sitting across from him, drinking her coffee, talking about him. The tears built up behind her eyes. This wasn't the haughty Colin who'd dumped her. That Colin had been full of rage and ego. In this moment his vulnerability was visible. She'd always loved him most achingly when he was hurt. How much she wanted to tell him of her journey the past year, her experiences with Body Talk, Radiant Heart Meditation, Language of the Light Meditation, Life Between Life Journeying. How much she wanted to wrap him in the insulation of her love. The temptation was strong, but she stopped herself. He was no longer her one.

Instead she asked about his family and told him a recent dream she'd had about his father. "I came upon two men digging a grave and asked them who they were digging it for. 'Henry,' they said. The only Henry I know is your dad. The earth looked dry, not freshly turned. I wondered if it meant your dad was going to physically die soon or if it meant that I'm killing him off in my psyche and laying that relationship to rest." Colin said his dad was fine as far as he knew. Then he told her his dream of seeing Olive lying at the bottom of a gully, not moving, curled up near a pool of water. Was Olive representing his physical, animal being, his body? Georgina wondered. Was his illness serious? He was very thin. Or had he picked up on Olive's grief over him? Crying inside her head so he wouldn't see, she changed the subject. "Is your sister still living in your parents' mews house?"

181

"Yes, she's sitting there in Notting Hill Gate atop her treasure, guarding it like a dragon. My mother went to London to stay for a month, but she felt so uncomfortable in her own house that she left after two weeks."

Georgina could see it was still a sore subject. "How's your novel coming?" she asked.

"It isn't. I've been too ill to do any writing except for work."

Despite herself Georgina felt for him. Kate would say she was a sap. She knew she'd pay for this indulgence of being with Colin, opening herself up to him. He had broken her heart and torn her guts out, and she still couldn't hate him. He hadn't asked a single question about her life. They left the restaurant together, and he walked her to the post office on Tenth Street. She could see it was hard for him to part from her. Leaving him at the door, she went in and mailed their taxes. Then for some reason, she bought fifty dollars' worth of Forever stamps. Several years had passed since that meeting, but it felt like it could have been this morning.

Georgina sat up, looked around the gym, and folded forward over her thighs, reaching toward her toes for one last stretch. The pounding music of a Zumba class was beginning. She put her mat back on the stack, picked up her water bottle, and headed for the exit.

Her computer dinged as she entered her apartment. She kicked off her sneakers at the front door. It was Kate forwarding her just-composed answer to Colin's email.

Hey Colin,

Sorry it's taken me so long to respond. I wasn't sure what I wanted to say to you. I'm not in NYC, so I can't meet up.

What did you want to talk about? You can write if you like. I won't guarantee an answer, but I will listen.

Kate

Georgina closed her computer and picked up her phone to text Kate. "If it feels right—send it."

"Done." Kate replied a few minutes later.

"How are you feeling honey?"

"Terrific. I can even fly if I want."

"Are you and Finn thinking of flying home for his mother's wedding?"

"Maybe, if he can get leave. She's sent two first-class round-trip tickets as a lure."

"Lure or no lure, I would love to fold you in my arms, my darling girl. I've just come in from the gym. I always miss you when I'm there."

"Yes, your thinking place."

"If you and Finn do come, I'd like to run up and visit Julia with you. But don't try to influence Finn. It's his mother, so it has to be his call."

"He said if he takes the tickets, he'll feel he's in her debt."

"But how hard will that be with him stationed in Okinawa?"

"Mom, you're the psychologist with quantum physics leanings—you know distance doesn't matter. Finn's just coming in now, and the potatoes are boiling over." Kate texted.

Finn dropped his keys on the counter and read Kate's phone over her shoulder. Kate handed him the phone and went to the stove to turn off the potatoes.

"How about we take the tickets and skip the wedding?" Finn typed.

"Don't underestimate your mother," Georgina typed back.

"I never do." Finn typed. "How's Julia?"

"She can't seem to gain any weight. I'm worried about her."

"Wasn't her last scan clear?"

"It was. But cancer is a tricky disease. I have to go, my darlings. I have to shower before I meet my web designer. Bye you two."

Georgina turned on the water and waited for it to warm up for her shower. Leaning toward the bathroom mirror, she surveyed her face. Not too bad for someone sailing inward. She couldn't be too far gone if she was getting her first-ever website. Maybe Kate would design a mandala for it. To Georgina, mandalas represented the self and were therefore the crown jewel of all symbols. Just looking at a mandala restored her inner peace. She'd been sending mandala cards to Julia every week for a couple of months now. Above all she wished her sister a peaceful heart. She stepped into the shower and felt the warmth of the water on her head, washing away all her old memories of Colin.

A SUPERFICIAL CORK BOBBING
ON THE SURFACE OF LIFE

"Your mother has a web designer? That's not her speed. She's more adapted to life in the last century than she is to life in this one. How many times has she told us she'd prefer a horse and buggy to an automobile?"

"She's a bit machine phobic, that's all. She hates the noise machines make, especially food processors and vacuums. But her mind is far ahead, even of the present."

"You mean all her tap-tap juju stuff?" Finn said.

"If you're referring to her mystical side, you can knock it off."

"I love your mother, but she could be the female counterpart of that crazy scientist on *Fringe*."

"Hey, Walter's one of my all-time favorite characters. Come on, he even grooms his pet cow."

"And your mother is one of my all-time favorite people. But she's out there. She's so completely different from my mother. I can't imagine our two mothers being friends."

"Since they inhabit two entirely different universes, I don't see that happening," Kate said.

"You mean that your mom is a Democrat and mine was a Republican fund-raiser for Dubya and vice president Darth Vader?"

"Not just that. How would they even have a conversation? They live in alternate realities."

"True. After 'Hi, Georgina' and 'Hello, Bunny,' they'd have nowhere to go."

"Where did your mom get that name, Bunny?"

"A childhood nickname, I guess."

"How about mashing the potatoes?" Kate said. He loved the way she smiled at him, the way it made him feel.

Finn took the potato masher Kate was pressing into his chest. "I'm becoming more forgiving toward everyone since we're having our own kid," he said. A soft smile started at the edges of his lips and crept up to his eyes as he looked at Kate. She put down the pot holders. He set the potato masher on the counter. He covered her mouth with his lips.

Later, lying in silence beside Finn on their Persian rug, Kate thought about sex. A lot of her friends in college had repressed their sexuality, buried it in their unconscious where their shadow got it or their inner masculine ate it up. "Fear of sex is fear of life," she'd once told Finn. "And I never want to fear life again." He knew he was one lucky guy. Kate sat up. "Shall I see if I can salvage our dinner?" she asked.

"Man does not live by bread alone," Finn said, reaching for her again and then letting her go. "But a bit of bread now and then is good too."

"I'm worried about Lydia," Kate said. She added butter and warm milk to the potatoes and handed the pan to Finn.

"Come on, Kate, don't make me think about her now."

"Why don't you like her?"

"Because it's always the Lydia show. She laps up compliments like a starving kitten lapping up milk. And what does she contribute?"

"That's not fair."

"Why not? She's never sweat for anything in her life."

"Does everyone have to sweat for things?"

"Yes, if they want to be a serious person. She's like a raw egg. You need a friend who's more cooked, someone with a bit of ballast. Lydia's a superficial cork bobbing on the surface of life."

"But I like Lydia," said Kate.

"Okay, like her. Just never be like her."

Finn's cell phone interrupted their conversation. "Hey Spencer, what's up?"

"Lydia's hysterical. She's locked herself in the bathroom. Neither Myrna nor I can get through to her, and there are razor blades in there. Maybe I'm being paranoid. I thought Kate might try talking to her. I'd rather not have to call the MPs."

Kate sank down to the floor outside the bathroom door and told Lydia she was there. In the car on the way over, she'd texted Georgina for advice. "You can't do therapy on a drowning woman—just try to keep up her courage at first. Tell her she's doing well to bear her suffering. Encourage her to hold on so she doesn't have a complete breakdown. Just get her through this moment," Georgina advised.

Kate sat on the floor on one side of the bathroom door while Lydia sat on the other. She spoke softly to her friend. "I know you're suffering, Lydia." There was only silence from Lydia. "Sometimes you just have to allow yourself to sit still and suffer in order to find a way through a situation." Silence. "Endure it, and it may begin to change." Silence. Kate leaned her head on the door and listened. She could hear Lydia sniffling.

Then something loosened in Lydia, and she spoke through her tears. "I don't think I can soldier on anymore. I hate myself. I hate Spencer. I hate our meaningless, barren life. I hate being reminded of things from my childhood. I'm never going back to Body Talk again. It's too fast, too brutal. I'm all torn up. And I'm so jealous that you're young and creative and pregnant. And I hate myself for feeling that too."

Kate could feel Lydia's despair seeping under the door. She wanted to comfort and reassure her friend, but she didn't know what to say, what would help. "Pain is a big part of life, Lydia. Nobody prepares you for that reality, but it is. I've found that if you can acknowledge it rather than close off what's unbearable, you'll slowly metabolize it." Through the door, Kate could hear Lydia weeping. She tried again to comfort her friend. "Whenever anything went wrong, my grandmother used to say, 'Hard times are part of every life, but there's a blessing in them somewhere.'" Lydia was still sniffling. "It's good you're weeping. It means something is getting unstuck. Your pain isn't cut off from you, compartmentalized and frozen anymore." Kate fell silent, hoping Lydia could hear her.

After a few minutes, Lydia said, "Spencer and I half tried to have children in the early years of our marriage but never sought medical help. He wouldn't even get a sperm count. To this day I don't know if the problem was him or me. You being pregnant makes me feel like a loser who's run out of time."

"Oh, Lydia."

"I was mostly controlling my feelings until tonight when I slipped and fell on the stairs," Lydia said. "That pushed me over the edge. Down on my hands and knees, I started to cry and couldn't stop. I hate admitting that I'm jealous of you, just like I used to hate seeing women with baby carriages when I was younger. And now, after tonight, how will I even face you?"

"Try to accept your feelings without judging them. That way you learn to live what you are."

"I'm nothing. What do I do? Every time Spencer looks at me, I know that's what he's thinking."

"Maybe you don't know what he's thinking. You could be far from the mark in your imaginings. Don't hurt yourself this way by telling yourself the worst."

"I hate myself, and I don't even know who myself is."

"Then let that be your task, to find out who you are and live that. I believe that's what life is for—to figure out who we are and what we're called on to do. My mother told me Jung used to tell his patients: 'If you're a sausage, don't make yourself up to look like a pheasant.' Just live what you are. Be natural and real."

"I don't think I ever learned to do that. It was all about appearances, growing up with my family."

"You don't have to live with your family anymore. Maybe it's time to commit psychological matricide and patricide so you can live by your own values."

"I wouldn't know where to begin killing off my parents' judgments and values inside me." Kate could hear Lydia blowing her nose. "I feel hopeless."

"Start there. Accept that you feel hopeless. Don't push the feelings away. Let that be what it is."

"How will that help?"

"I don't know exactly how it helps, but it does. It takes a lot of energy to keep pushing painful stuff away. Then one day you can't keep it locked up, or you fall down, and then the feelings burst on you. Once they're out, you may as well acknowledge them as try to lock them up again. Accepting my feelings, however awful they were, helped me when I was at my worst."

"It's hard to imagine you at your worst," Lydia said.

"Sometimes it's the worst moments in our lives that help us to discover who we are," Kate said.

"All I can see is my worthlessness."

"Then start by accepting that feeling, and it may start to release you."

"Accept that I feel worthless?"

"It's a place to start. And you don't have to figure it all out tonight, Lydia. Myrna's made some tea. Come out and have some."

On the drive home, Kate fell asleep with her head on Finn's shoulder. He breathed in the scent of her hair and pitied Spencer. Kate didn't try to impress anybody. She was simple and real. He killed the engine and sat still, looking up at the night sky through the skylight in the car roof. Kate whimpered in her sleep. He suddenly felt so much rage at Lydia he wanted to burn her house to the ground. How could she dump her craziness on Kate, who'd already suffered enough? Kissing the top of her head to wake her, he asked her what she was dreaming. "Two guys stole Olive by drugging her, but I tracked them down and got her back."

"Come, sleepyhead, let's go in. I know you miss Olive. You're going to see her soon. Time for bed."

Finn was gone when Kate woke up. *Damn.* She made some jasmine tea and was sipping it when Lydia called. "I'm so ashamed about last night."

"Last night was a breakthrough. You admitted your true feelings to yourself, all those things you've been repressing that have been giving you nightmares. I say bravo."

"You think I was having nightmares because of all those angry feelings I let out last night?"

"Yes."

"It did feel good to finally admit those feelings to myself, but I wish I hadn't thrown such a show that Spencer called you and Finn. I'm so ashamed."

"Let it go, Lydia. Shame just gets in the way of healing."

"I don't understand."

"When we're stuck in guilt or shame, we can't forge meaning from our suffering."

"I never considered that there could be meaning to be had from suffering," Lydia said. "And it's true—I didn't have a nightmare last night for the first time in weeks. But Spencer could hardly look at me during breakfast."

"Maybe he didn't know what to say. Maybe he felt helpless."

"I never thought of it that way," Lydia said.

"This is your opportunity to meet yourself in a new way. Your suffering is part of what makes you you." Kate shifted the phone to her other ear and poured herself more tea. They were both quiet, then Lydia said, "Thank you for last night, Kate."

An hour later Kate was in the middle of drawing the heads of two people sitting on a couch. The view was from behind, with the girl's long hair hanging down over the back of the couch. A banging on the door interrupted her. When she opened it, she couldn't even see the person because the flower arrangement he was carrying was so big. He turned sideways and thrust a delivery slip out for her to sign. "Would you mind putting it on the counter for me? Watch the step." She smiled to herself, imagining Finn's reaction when he saw it. "Is that monstrosity courtesy of Lydia's nervous breakdown? Or is my mother reaching her long fingers into our kitchen?"

JULIA, SWEET JULIA

"I'm in the hospital," Julia said. "My small intestine has a blockage, and my right kidney is swelling." Even though Georgina knew something like this could happen, the news stunned her.

"I'm on my way."

"No, Georgina, wait till we know more. It could be scar tissue from when they removed my bladder, or it could be a return of the cancer. We don't know yet. And Rob is with me. It hurts to talk. The tubes in my nose, going down into my intestines make speaking painful."

"Oh, my darling, I want to help. I want to be with you. You're my baby sister."

"Georgina, I'm fifty-two."

"That's beside the point."

"I have to hang up—the doctor's coming in to do something."

"I love you, Julia."

"Love you too."

Georgina sank down onto the floor. This couldn't be. They'd removed Julia's bladder, and in another surgery, just a few months ago, her uterus and ovaries so this wouldn't happen. *Please let it be scar tissue.*

Julia was the sweetest, most gentle of their mother's four children. She was the doe standing in the forest, knowing, tentative, light footed, lovely in a mantle of streaming red-gold hair reaching down to her waist, with eyes the same

190

color. She'd had two daughters with her first husband. Then after he smashed a rocking chair and beat her with a piece of it while their three-year-old and one-year-old daughters watched, she left him. Somehow, he got shared custody anyway for half of each week. After their divorce he moved back into the big Victorian house with the gingerbread gazebo on the rolling green lawn where he'd grown up. He stayed there, living with his father and older, unmarried sister, until he died the previous year when their daughters were twenty-eight and thirty. Once Julia left him, the rage seemed to go out of him. Maybe the loss of her so devastated him that he got control of his temper. He never looked at another woman for the rest of his life. Though he was mostly kind to his daughters, he took out his moods in a quiet way on his long-suffering sister. Until he died, he never missed giving Julia a Mother's Day present.

Julia married Rob five years after that beating with the rocking chair.

Rob and Georgina didn't like each other. Things got worse between them when he forbade anyone to come to the hospital after Julia had her bladder removed. Fury and helplessness collided in Georgina. She had been with her sister for the first two surgeries before Rob got militant. Julia had asked her to just accept his ban on visitors as it was how he could cope. "He believes it's his job to protect me. That's how he expresses love."

"He's very controlling, and to me it looks more like ego than love," Georgina said.

"Let him be the way he needs to be. I know he loves me, and I know he has control issues, but it's okay." So Georgina let it be, but she hated thinking of her gentle, sociable sister alone in a faraway hospital with only Rob for a whole week and none of her friends and family to support and comfort her while she endured God knows what. Georgina's insides churned with fear.

She called Selma, who was home for once. "He thinks he knows Julia so well," she said to Selma, "but I know what it's like to be a child with her, laughing and hiding from our parents in the garden, crouching behind the wheelbarrow, excited and afraid because we'd dumped out all six big bags of raked-up leaves and jumped in them and rolled over and over as the autumn breeze blew them around us in swirls. I know what it's like to listen to Rubber Soul with her for the first time, sitting on the floor in our bedroom in front of our record player."

"Let it go now," Selma advised. "Don't put your anger at Rob on her plate."

Julia's daughter Sara told Georgina not even to send flowers, because they made Julia sneeze. They both knew this was a lie. Nothing of Georgina was to be allowed near her sister because it bothered Rob. Her pain and anger blazed. But she'd stayed away and gone up only when Julia was home again and Rob went out. All Julia's scans had been clean since that third surgery that removed her bladder, but now she was back in the hospital with something choking her intestines and making her kidneys swell. What was this new devil? She couldn't even ask Rob what the doctors said. He was incommunicado.

Rob had been an interrogator during the Vietnam War. Julia didn't know him then—she'd still been in elementary school when Rob was in Vietnam. "How could it not have affected him?" Julia told Georgina. Although Rob had a few close friends, even they were rarely invited to the quiet house built in the 1700s, sitting atop the hill overlooking a green valley. Rob's home was his private castle. Since she couldn't easily entertain at home, early in her marriage, Julia's private place became her car. As long as she could drive the back roads listening to Bob Dylan and Neil Young, Springsteen and the Beatles, she was content. Dusk was her favorite time of day on the country roads she traveled. Her daily trapline had a circumference of less than twenty miles. Her younger daughter, Sara, got both a morning and an afternoon drop-in to check on the kids' doings, see if they needed anything from the store. Her older daughter, Charlotte, was more independent and lived beyond the circumference of Julia's trapline. Both of Julia's brothers were on it, though. Edward got the five o'clock visit on his porch, where they'd have a drink, sharing their latest musical discoveries accompanied by the brook singing beside his house. Then it was over to their brother Stan's for a chat before she swung by her friend Sandy's and then made her last stop back again at Sara's.

But after twenty years on Julia's trapline, Sandy and her husband moved back to Pennsylvania, and that relished moment in Julia's day was no more. Then her older brother, Stan, and his wife moved to New York City. For months Julia couldn't even drive by his house. How could a new family be taking showers in his bathroom, cooking on his stove, mowing his lawn, looking at the deer drinking water in his stream? Multiple, daily visits to her parents had also been part of her routine for years and years—all her adult life, really. Now they were dead. A quiet social butterfly, Julia would land on your doorstep softly, like a whisper or a snowflake, alighting awhile, sharing a coffee, a beer, a glass of wine, lending a hand with whatever you were doing, smiling, always smiling, then moving on. She would have liked for people to come to her house, but that wasn't on. Even talking on the phone if Rob was home elicited his criticism. Before bed when she thought Rob was asleep, Julia would sit outside on the steps with a cigarette and her cell phone, looking at the stars and talking to Georgina. If Rob came downstairs and caught her, he'd say something like, "Who are you torturing now?" Usually, Julia would then say to Georgina, "I love you. Talk to you later," and hang up. Later could mean days.

Because Georgina lived in New York City, she'd never had the pleasure of a daily visit from her sister; but whenever she'd needed her, Julia came without being asked. It was Julia who'd taught her how to bathe newborn Kate and how to burp and change her. Julia liked babies, but she really loved old people. She'd been a country nurse for years, going from home to home, caring for the elderly, changing dressings after surgeries, drawing blood, administering pain medication, giving them their shots, organizing their pills, and listening to their concerns—mostly listening to their concerns and hearing their stories. Because she loved those stories, she tucked them into her heart in that special place reserved for old people. When the township did away with the traveling nurse service, the old people still called her, and she still went to them. They were her first trapline.

Now it was Julia who needed help, and Rob was again keeping everyone who loved her away. "For God's sake, her intestines are shut down. What is he thinking?" Georgina cried to Selma.

"He's probably thinking he's protecting her," Selma said.

"It's not fair, Selma. This blackout of information is an agony when Julia needs all our love."

"But she doesn't need the stress of you fighting with her husband."

"It's so hard not to go to her, be near her, see with my own eyes what state she's in, tell her I love her. It's awful to be kept away."

"You have to bear it. This is about what she needs, and she doesn't need her husband to stress her out because you're fighting with him."

"I know you're right, but I hate it."

Georgina hung up the phone, then reached for it again to call Julia's daughters. But she couldn't do it yet. It made this too real. Instead she got in the shower. Standing still under the hot water, she remembered how Kate, during the bad times, would get in the shower, sometimes with all her clothes on, and just stand and let the water run over her, washing off whatever pain it could. Georgina stood under the falling water wondering why this was happening to her gentle sister. Their mother had never tired of telling Georgina that Julia was the brilliant one with the highest IQ of her four children. Maybe that's why Georgina had to get a PhD, to prove to her mother she too had brains. If so, it didn't work. But at least it didn't make Georgina love Julia any less or be jealous of her. And even though their mother preferred Julia to Georgina, that didn't spare Julia their mother's judgment and criticism. No matter what Julia did, their mother dowsed her in toxic, negative comments, especially in the last years of her life when Julia tried so hard to care for her.

Now Julia was lying in a hospital bed, with tubes in her nose and her life uncertain. Selma was right: Georgina resenting Rob would only hurt Julia. Those feelings had to be crushed. Secretly, she believed that if her sister died, it would be to escape Rob's daily, little cruelties. *That's a mean thought*, she told herself. Her brother Edward disagreed with her about Rob. "Julia knows another Rob from the one you see."

"Maybe," said Georgina.

Julia had absorbed years of Rob's negativity and bitterness, without a word. She'd pushed all her tears down into her bladder and her intestines. Maybe Julia's intestines and ureter were blocked because she just couldn't digest any more meanness and controlling behavior, and it was backing up on her, and she didn't know how else to get away. It wasn't like Rob beat her with a rocking chair. His was a subtle and constant disapproval that ate at a person. At least that's how Georgina saw it. Probably her brother Edward was right, and there was another side to Rob.

Georgina stepped out of the shower. *Stop it*, she told herself. *You know that's not how it works. People make agreements before they incarnate about what challenges they're going to take on, what catalysts for growth they'll face. Maybe Julia's soul chose to be with Rob to help him evolve. That would be like her.* Georgina rubbed herself hard with her towel. *I'm not going to be passive about this. Maybe I can't be at Julia's bedside, but I can be proactive.* She'd call the energy healer and ask her to resume the remote healing sessions on her sister. They already had Julia's permission to work on her from the previous surgeries. And if Georgina couldn't be there, at least she could stay in touch with Julia over the phone. A momentary paranoia swept through her that Rob would have control of Julia's phone now too. She'd check with her nieces.

Georgina knew there was still another piece of work she had to do. It was on herself. Blaming Rob was foolish and possibly unfair—no, definitely unfair. She needed a spiritual makeover to be less judgmental, more forgiving. And she needed to look at the ways she had hurt and judged her sister. Rob wasn't the only one at fault. It was time to stand in the humility of her own heart and take ownership of her part.

And Julia's daughters must break through Rob's barricade. Julia adored them; they were her comfort and joy. To get through this and help her sister and her nieces and her brothers, Georgina would need an energetic field without the negativity of hatred, anger, or judgment. She would have to transform her energy field to be a better person. She knew that who you are inwardly, how conscious you are as a being, provides the energy field for how you interact with others. "Think of Rob as a gift to you," Carrie advised. "Imagine he's what challenges you to be better than you think you can be."

Georgina was a more conscious being than she had been twenty years ago, but not conscious enough to stop judging and blaming Rob. But that's what she had to do. Even Emma agreed with Selma and Carrie that Georgina needed to let go of her judgment and look at her own part. All right then, she would shine light on the dark places in her own psyche, starting with her judgment of her sister's husband. If Georgina disliked Rob less, maybe he'd dislike her less. Her own humility of heart might touch off a healing in his heart.

195

Aside from making inner peace with Rob and doing healing sessions, what else would help Julia? When she first got sick, Georgina sought out a shaman from Peru who channeled a group of archangels. What was it exactly the archangels had advised her? She'd have to go over the transcript of that session with the shaman or listen to the recording. Before the session, she'd wondered what it would be like to speak with archangels: how could it be possible? William Blake had spoken with angels. If he did it, why couldn't she? And she did, even if it was with the help of a channel. And it was the most natural thing.

Georgina took down the little red suitcase with the sturdy clear plastic handle that she'd had since childhood. It was covered in fake red snakeskin that was worn through in lots of places. She'd packed it with her small clothes and stuffed toy kitten to run away more than once when she was a little girl. Third grade was especially hard, and her mother was especially unforgiving that year. This child's suitcase, that now lived in the top of her closet, was where she kept all her readings with healers and intuitives and past life regression therapists and the archangel channel. She found the archangel CD and slipped it into her computer. The reading had been done about six months ago, around the time of the first attempts to remove Julia's cancer surgically. She pressed play and lay down on her bed to listen.

Using the vocal chords of the shaman, the archangel spoke in a funny, clipped, high-pitched voice. "You are worried about your sister, Julia, sweet Julia, dear Julia."

"Yes," Georgina heard herself answer.

"She has taken a hard course with her physicality in this lifetime. It's too much brutality. She's tired of people touching her body in harsh ways. You must remove that sensation of brutality from her energy field. Her body believes it's being tortured by all these medical procedures, so it cannot heal."

"How do I do that?"

"You will help her see the procedures as helpful rather than as torture. In past lives she has been cut, lamed, persecuted, and destroyed as a woman—back when women were treated like no more than cattle. Even in this life, she has known harshness from men and taken it without defending herself. Her body cannot go on with the brutality. It is linked to an old

196

belief system, an old matrix of the past trauma of torture. You must change your sister's belief system from torture to healing."

"If I can do this, will she heal?"

"Perhaps she will go on. We shall see. There are many facets to her choice."

"Tell me how, please."

"You must enter a meditative state. In that altered state, you will feel into her vibrational field. Imagine her sitting before you. Her presence and her vibrational field become very real to you. Call down the shard of light, as you have been taught by the shaman. Surround both your energy fields with it. Center yourself in the light. Align with your soul and with us in the angelic realm. Feel into your sister's field with your hands. Feel in her field where this memory of torture is. She does not need to know this. Go into her field to release this memory of torture. Take down the story on a piece of paper. The story needs to be heard so it can leave. You release the torture through communication. You know from your work as a psychologist that this is true. Is that not what psychologists do, listen with their hearts to stories so the stories can leave? This has to be removed from your sister's field so her body can restore. Her body does not understand restoration with this memory in her field. Destroy the story you've written. Rip it, burn it. It will release very quickly because you are blood in this lifetime. Seal the area in her field that held the trauma. Then we shall see. There may have been agreements to serve others by her early death. And there are the catalysts she chose for her own growth. But she may yet restore. We shall see. We shall see."

Tears streamed down Georgina's face as she listened to the instructions.

"You hold the space of understanding, the space of healing, for many people, dear one. But you too need restoration. Take time every day for this. You will become magnetized again. Take ownership of that divinity within you, within each of us. It has been a great pleasure talking to you. If you need us, call us. We come. Good-bye dear one."

She recalled how the reading had made her panic. In the pouring rain, she had left the session and hurried home to do this assignment on her sister's vibrational field. Would she be able to find the story and remove it in time? Could she face seeing her sister tortured and write down the story? She had to. When she got home Georgina threw herself down on her back, breathed into her heart field, imagined Julia in front of her, and called down the shard of light. Aligning herself with the archangels, she prayed for the visions of Julia's past-life tortures to come. She reached out her hands as if Julia's energy field were right before her, and she felt through the field as she'd been instructed to do. Horrors passed before her eyes. She recoiled, then forced herself again to see. Which was the torture that needed to be written and burned? Then she felt it, and she knew. When she opened her eyes to write, she shuddered. Then she sealed Julia's energy field and walked into the living room to the fireplace. She ripped the story into little pieces and burned it.

But now Julia was back in the hospital. Had Georgina failed in her attempt to remove the trauma, or had Julia's higher self chosen a different path, a path that Georgina was forbidden to alter? She sat up, ejected the CD, and closed her computer. Listening to that archangel session again had left her jumping out of her skin. Even when she'd first burned the story of Julia's torture, she didn't trust her own power; she called her energy healer, told her everything the archangels had advised, and asked her to work on Julia. She had to remind herself that energy healing doesn't subscribe to the limitations of time and space. And it doesn't require the active participation of the person to be healed. It's a system that believes the practitioner can use her intuition to communicate across distance to heal her clients. "Please God, let it help Julia." But now Julia was sick again, very sick. She put the CD back in her little red suitcase, put two twenties in her jeans pocket, and headed for the front door.

Selma and Emma were already seated at a round table in the corner when Georgina walked into French Roast.

"How's Julia?" Selma asked.

"Not good." Georgina dropped into her chair. "There are too many varieties of heartbreak in this world for it to be an easy place to live."

"Earth is a tough school," Selma agreed.

"Do you want to share a turkey sandwich, Georgina?" Emma asked.

"I'm not hungry. You go ahead," Georgina said.

"You've got to eat," Selma told her. "Sorrow robs your strength."

"It's a good thing earth is so beautiful. Otherwise no one would agree to incarnate here," Georgina said.

Selma nodded in agreement. "This is the plane of sorrow. But don't forget, it's also the plane of learning about love."

"So the mystics say." Georgina's voice was almost inaudible. "So it'd better be true that heartbreak is the path to compassion. Because what other justification could there be for all the suffering on this planet?"

"You've got to endure," Emma told her. "And somehow fold the worst moments of your life into a narrative that makes a triumph from your suffering."

"Aren't you always telling us that it's our worst times that make us who we are?" Selma added.

"I'm in a dark wood. All I see is suffering everywhere," Georgina said.

"Don't focus on it so much," Emma told her.

"Did you see that photo of the little Syrian girl, two years old, holding her hands up over her head, surrendering to a camera? She doesn't yet know the difference between a camera and a gun, but she knows how to surrender. That shouldn't be your world when you're two years old. And people are starving, without even clean water to drink. Then there's rape and genocide, beheadings and disease and dead children, dead husbands, dead wives, dead sisters, dead parents, dead friends and animals. These losses rip your heart out and suck all light and innocence from the world." *I'm ranting*, Georgina thought, and stopped. Emma lifted her glass to take a sip of her coffee, and her gold bangles jingled on her wrist. Then she spoke, looking straight at Georgina. "We each have to use our pain and suffering to grow." Was this Emma speaking? Had Georgina won her over, at some point, on the value of suffering, and not noticed? There must have been surprise on Georgina's face, because Emma said, "What?"

"Nothing," Georgina said. Emma sipped her coffee and looked out the window at the fire truck speeding up Sixth Avenue. The waiter put the turkey sandwich down in front of her.

"We know you're hurting for your baby sister," Selma said. Georgina was grateful for Selma's homey words.

"Heartbreak is my whole essence, my every breath," Georgina said.

"My thighs feel as though they're made of cement. I can hardly move them to walk my body around."

"You're depressed," Emma told her. "But you'll come through it."

"I'm terrified for Julia, terrified that they'll cut her to pieces, bit by bit, as they try to remove the cancer winding through her body. Soon, there'll be nothing left to remove. She must be empty inside by now. But she never complains. If only she would." Georgina looked down at her hands in her lap. They were helpless and still, like two bony, plucked chickens.

"It just knocks you down, girl," Selma told her. "It knocks you to the ground." Selma's words comforted Georgina's ragged heart. "Sorry I'm such a drag," she told them as they left the restaurant.

On the walk home, Georgina said to herself, *I'm like a caged animal pacing back and forth, dragging my cement thighs, waiting for news. I see Julia everywhere I look. Now she's holding her first doll—Sally, she named her. And there she is on stage giving her speech as valedictorian of her elementary school. Then we're sleigh riding on Sister's Hill. That sky-blue dress she wore as my maid of honor was the perfect shade for her. No, not the memory of her wedding day and how, as she walked in her white satin gown toward the entrance of the church on our father's arm, the breeze lifted her long, trailing, gauzy veil, swirling it about her slender figure. I smoothed her long red hair and straightened her veil before walking up the aisle ahead of her. I can hear her laughter and study the look on her young face just after she had given birth to Charlotte. The sight of her kneeling with her dog Maybelle makes me catch my breath. Will she ever kneel again to caress a dog she loves? Oh, how she loved the vanilla-coconut cake shaped liked a bunny that our mother made each Easter of our childhood. If only, if only . . .*

Georgina looked both ways before crossing Fifth Avenue. When she entered her apartment, she buried her face in Olive's neck. "I wait, expecting that the burning pain in my chest will surely set my shirt on fire. And I fall to my knees to pray, but tears are my only prayer, and they can't quench this pain. Don't die, Julia, that's all the prayer I can speak." Olive licked her face and tears. Then Georgina heard Selma's voice in her head: *You got to pull up your socks, girl, and help her children. People have born this before and you will too.*

"But I'm such a coward," she said. *Don't give in to it*, she told herself. *Be as you would like to be, brave and strong. Remember how you got through the pain with Kate. You had no voice even, but you never gave up. Please don't die, Julia.*

ELECTRIC TRAIN

Finn lathered his face with shaving cream and debated about going to his mother's wedding. Kate stood leaning against the bathroom doorframe, listening to him.

"I just don't want to be that mean guy who doesn't go to his mother's wedding even if it means fighting for leave and flying halfway around the world." His towel hung around his neck as he leaned in toward the bathroom mirror and bent his head sideways to shave above his upper lip. Kate had watched him do this countless times, and she still enjoyed it.

"Okay," she said.

"Okay? That's all you can come up with? You're supposed to play devil's advocate, Kate." Finn checked to make sure he hadn't missed a spot, then rinsed his face with cool water, and patted it dry. "And you know this wedding is going to be chock-full of dickwad Republicans."

"You might want to keep the name calling on the down low if you have any hope of getting along there. And your story about your mom destroying your family, giving your dog to strangers, and telling lies about you to your aunts and uncles and cousins—that scenario will have to be revised."

"Hmmm, so I'll have to rewrite history with her as a good guy," Finn said. He rubbed his towel though his hair like he was roughing up his thoughts.

Kate smiled. "So with all that bending out of shape, why would you want to go to her wedding?"

"Right. That's more like it, Kate." Finn hung his towel over the hook on the back of the bathroom door. "Here's the thing—I don't want to go. But I don't want to be the jerk who doesn't show up at his mother's wedding, either."

"Sorry, babe, it's one or the other."

Finn buttoned up his shirt and tucked it into his trousers. Kate studied him as he tied his military tie. She liked the way he looked in his uniform. "Maybe it's time to let go of my anger about the past, burn the old story, write a new chapter."

"I could get on board with that, if you mean it. It's generally better all around to let go of anger once it's served its purpose," she said. Finn pulled Kate close to him and kissed her on the nose.

"Maybe something's shifting in me toward my mother. I was never as angry at my father. I felt he was more or less her victim too."

"Wait a minute," Kate said. "You were angry that he let her use him as the muscle against you. You were angry that he took her side without getting your story, even though she'd dumped him."

"True. I hated that he let himself be used by her. He was such a pussy."

"Are you ready to let that go too?" Kate asked.

"I think I am." Finn picked his keys up off the dresser, put his wallet in his back pocket, and gave it a pat.

"Good, if you really mean it." Kate followed him to the front door and down the steps. She stood under the palm trees and waved as he drove away.

Then she went back inside, made a cup of tea, and checked her email. There was one from Georgina in her in-box. Julia was in the hospital again. The news hit Kate in the heart. This couldn't be. They'd already removed Julia's bladder, her ovaries, her uterus. Kate sat there letting the news sink in before calling her mother.

It surprised her how weak Georgina's voice sounded over the phone. "She's only fifty-two," Georgina half mumbled. Georgina wasn't a mumbler. Kate managed to get the facts they knew. Something had wrapped around Julia's intestines, allowing nothing to pass out. It had also squeezed shut her right ureter, closing off the right kidney, which was swelling up. They were moving her to a big teaching hospital that day to open her up and see what it was. Hopefully, it was just scar tissue and not cancer winding around everywhere. Whatever it was, they'd try to remove it.

Surgery was scheduled for the following day. If it turned out to be inoperable they'd at least cut around the choked part of her intestines and splice together two pieces to make a passageway. Then they'd put a stent in the ureter so the kidney could empty into the bag she'd worn at her side ever since they'd removed her bladder a few months earlier. All this information had come to Georgina through Charlotte. Thank God. Bad as it was, it was better to know. Julia was down to eighty pounds now, but she had roused her fighting spirit.

Julia and Georgina had more or less identical bodies. They were both five feet six and never varied much from 125 pounds their entire adulthood.

Julia was already down to 110 when she was first diagnosed with bladder cancer. No one had noticed her weight loss because of her style of dressing, those loose flower-child garments. Last summer when she fell in Sara's yard, her legs giving out, she must have already had cancer. No one realized. How had they not questioned that collapse?

"But eighty pounds, Mom? How did she get down to eighty pounds?"

"She lost weight each time they did surgery, but this last bit has been the worst. She's gone from a hundred pounds to eighty pounds in less than two weeks."

"Why does that happen? Is it cancer eating all her food?"

"Maybe something like that, what little food she eats—a banana, a piece of toast, some yogurt. At this point, between the pain and fear, she hasn't much appetite. It's gonna take a miracle, Kate."

"But you believe in miracles, Mom."

After they hung up, Kate sank into a chair to think. Maybe they should use those first-class tickets and go to the wedding. She needed to see her mom and her aunt. It was too much loss, and she was afraid for Georgina's health, and her aunt's life. Georgina had been to hell with her, then she'd lost her father and her mother, and now, Julia could be dying? And in the middle of it all, Colin had walked out to be with his young mistress and created a huge ruckus of a divorce. That was a lot to metabolize, even for someone with Georgina's outlook on life. Kate picked up her tea. It was cold. The day passed in a haze. Would this be the final blow that sank her mother?

Finally, it was time to start dinner.

"Homemade pizza with artichokes on it, Kate? And a warm chocolate cake? What do you want?" Finn kissed her and dropped onto a stool at the kitchen counter. "Out with it, girl."

"I want to use those tickets and go to your mother's wedding. My aunt Julia is back in the hospital, and my mother's wrecked. I need to see her."

"You're in luck, then, because by coincidence, my leave was granted today." She threw her arms around his neck, smiling to herself. It wasn't by coincidence. It was the universe at work. She wouldn't tell Finn that the universe had picked up on her decision of that morning to go to New York, and that by afternoon had arranged his leave. But that is what she believed. When something was a right action, the universe facilitated it. So many years with Georgina made it hard to see it any other way.

After dinner they sat with their heads leaning in together at the computer and booked their flights. Two weeks from tonight, they'd be sleeping in Georgina's Fifth Avenue apartment in their old bedroom. Kate felt like purring. "You know that wedding is going to be worse than the Tom DeLay episode of *Dancing with the Stars*?" Finn said.

"I don't care. It's one day."

"Wrong. It'll be the whole shebang, the form-without-content rehearsal dinner and the gloating morning-after brunch."

"At their age, are they going to do all that?"

"Come here and kiss me," Finn said, grabbing her.

"Wait, I just thought . . . your mom doesn't know I'm pregnant. Should we tell her before we see her?"

"Now it begins. We have to think about her reactions and worry she'll think we're stealing her thunder. It's enough to make a guy lose his erection."

"Hey, part of letting go of the past is accepting people as they are."

"Got it. Now kiss me before I change my mind." The evening passed with more ease and sweetness than the day had offered.

Kate sat up in bed with a shiver and looked at the floor to see if the electric train was still there. It was dark out. The dream had been so real she thought for sure the train must still be running along on its tracks through their bedroom. There was no sign of it. Of course it had been a dream. It had to have been, because their cat, Dwight, whom Georgina had nicknamed Buddha, was in the dream, and he'd been dead since before they got Olive. The train was long, with many cars, a fancy child's toy or something that would have belonged to a collector. Somehow, she'd known that it came into their room every night at regular intervals and circled around before going back out to the living room. That was its nightly route.

Was it pugged in somewhere out in the living room? In the dream, she'd been sitting up on a wooden stool in the corner of their bedroom, watching the train, marveling that she'd never stepped on it when she got up to pee each night since becoming pregnant. Involuntarily, she glanced toward the corner of the room where the stool had been in her dream, half-afraid she'd see it there. There was no stool. She'd never even seen this train before, yet she knew it came every night. Then Dwight had suddenly appeared in their bedroom, and as she watched, he'd lifted his paw and knocked the train off its track. Then he reached into an open boxcar and lifted out some gold.

Was this a toy-train robbery performed by a deceased spiritual cat? No. It had a more ominous feel than that. It wasn't exactly a robbery. True, the train was stopped dead in its tracks, and the gold removed by a cat, their cat, Dwight, who'd been dead more than ten years. In the dream, Kate felt as though she should go into the living room and unplug the train, if there was a plug. Is that how toy trains even worked? Maybe you just wound them up. She didn't know. Although it was the size of a toy train, it seemed to have power and meaning far beyond a toy. She had been afraid of it, even. Could a derailed train mean a derailed life? Could this be about Julia? Would she be stopped dead in her tracks? But what was Dwight doing in the dream? He'd been Georgina's cat, not Julia's.

Kate lay back down shivering and tried to fall asleep. *Think of mundane things*, she told herself. *What can I wear to this wedding? Nothing fits my waist.* Train thoughts kept intruding. She remembered that Georgina had once written a paper on death dreams. Three of the dreams she'd analyzed in the paper had been train dreams. The train tracks had run out in one. In another, everyone but the dreamer could get on the train to travel farther on. Each time he tried, the doors shut on him before he could enter. In the third, the person was on a train, but everyone else on it was dead in real life. The three people who reported these dreams to Georgina had all died within a month of having the dream. Could her train dream be a death dream? Could the gold be a soul being lifted from the material plane? Could it be Julia's soul? Kate shuddered and snuggled closer to Finn.

REMOTE HEALING

"This time the healer is going to use my body as a surrogate to do a remote healing on your mom. It'll be more effective than using her photograph, because we're blood," Georgina explained to Charlotte. "But we need a new permission from her to work in this way. Can you text me a little video of your mom giving permission or just nodding yes if it's too painful for her to speak?"

"Yes. I'm almost at the hospital. Sara's meeting me there," Charlotte said.

"The healer will try to shift any belief systems your mom may have that are in the way of her body's ability to heal itself. She can see me at three." Georgina knew that energy healers could eliminate many of the accumulated stressors responsible for disease in the body. Working on the meridians and chakras, healers reset the body's energy pathways so the body can heal itself. But it didn't always work. There could be overriding karmic factors.

Not wanting to give her nieces false hope, Georgina told Charlotte, "Some things can't be healed, like things that have to do with agreements a soul makes before incarnating."

"What kind of agreements?"

"Agreeing to help another soul to grow, by being a catalyst to awaken them to their true nature, even if it involves your own suffering. For example, a soul might take an early death, even as a young child, to awaken the parents to a spiritual life. And there can be lessons the soul itself wants to learn. We have a different perspective in between lives than we do while we're incarnated."

"Do you think Mom made those kinds of agreements?"

"We all choose the lessons we want to work on in each lifetime. I don't know if we're in the realm of your mother's soul's prior agreement to die from this disease or if she can rebalance to heal from this cancer."

"But we'll hold the space for healing, right?" Charlotte said.

"Yes, we'll hold the space for healing as long as her soul remains in her body."

Secretly, Georgina worried that maybe Julia had agreed to die young and in this horrible way, being chopped up bit by bit, to be of service to someone or even to several people. The news from the surgeon was bad, the worst case. When he'd opened Julia up, he'd found the cancer winding around everywhere like a climbing plant spreading its tentacles, inoperable beyond his attempt to temporarily restore bladder and bowel function. He had nothing to recommend but palliative care at home, once she recovered from the surgery. They were definitely in the realm of miracles now.

Georgina wished she had a partner to help her through this: not Colin—he would have created additional burdens—but a compassionate partner just to tell it all to, to walk beside. At times like this, it was a relief Colin was gone. He'd have been jealous and scornful of her attempts to help her sister. "Pathological jealousy," Emma had called Colin's reaction whenever Georgina reached out to help another, especially if that other was Kate. Since he wasn't around for this struggle for Julia's life, Georgina wouldn't have to feel torn and guilty. But was it even a struggle, or was it already a done deal, decided long ago before Julia came to earth?

The surgery had been brutal. Julia nearly died on the operating table. The doctors had given up on her recovery, but she would hold the place of healing for her sister. *Please let today's healing session begin to turn things around*, she prayed as she entered the healer's building.

Georgina pushed the elevator button for the twelfth floor and waited with a mixture of anxiety and hope. As she lay on the massage table in the sun-filled room with its crystals, essential oils, and orange salt lamp, Georgina envisioned her sister's energy field covering her own. Using Georgina's body as a surrogate, the healer brought Julia out of the state of fight or flight that had been caused by the trauma of the surgery. She calmed Julia's shock response, then worked on Julia's kidney meridians and her spleen Qi. She balanced the left and right sides of her body, and her upper body to her lower body. She also linked Julia's small intestines to her heart and all her chakras, through the crossroads of her gall bladder.

Everything went smoothly until she tried to remove a cord that their mother had placed in Julia's intestines. "Your mother's not having it," she told Georgina.

"But can she do that—keep a cord in Julia even when she's dead?"

"Your mother hasn't completely left the earth plane. She's in a kind of halfway zone where she's being shown the error of her ways. She was a slave owner in several past lives and still doesn't know how to relate to people except by owning them. She even believes she owns her children. They are her possessions. We'll have to try another way to get her to release your sister."

Anger toward her mother welled up in Georgina. Was her mother dragging her sister into death? She'd managed to die on Julia's birthday, after all.

"I'll work on the family matrix to release all four of your mother's children. She has the remnants of a grip on each of you. She never allowed any of you to relate to one another except through her. She doesn't want to let go of that power, but she must for her own healing."

After the session Georgina walked from Forty-Fourth Street down to Ninth Street, without realizing what she was doing. Exhausted, she fell on her bed and let her mind drift. Even in death her mother had a grip on her sister's intestines. Her beliefs about who she owned had kept her mother bound to the earth plane. In order to release Julia, they had worked on her mother's consciousness. Hopefully, now she'd leave the earth plane and move the rest of the way into the light.

Georgina heard the phone ringing, but she couldn't move. A cup of strong tea would be good. After a few minutes, she dragged herself up. The voice mail was from Kate. They were coming. Just to see those two would lift her heart. She'd buy all their favorite foods and fill the house with flowers. Georgina drank her tea gratefully and lay down again. Still spent, she slipped into a dream.

In the dream, she and her brother Stan were children in elementary school. They stopped off on their way to school at their grandmother Anastasia's house to have breakfast with her. There were so many good things to eat that Georgina was afraid they'd be late for school. Stan was a bit of a chowhound. "If Stan won't eat the school lunch," his first grade teacher told their parents, "I don't make any of the kids eat it." The light in the dream was filtered and hazy, otherworldly. Their grandmother, their father's mother, had died of intestinal cancer over forty years ago, so this couldn't be her earthly house they were visiting. Georgina hadn't dreamed of her grandmother in years. *Was this good, kind, humble woman coming now for Julia? No, Julia wasn't even in the dream,* Georgina rationalized. It couldn't be about her death. Both of her grandmothers had died of intestinal blockages, Anastasia at seventy-two and Maud at thirty-one. Julia, now fifty-two, was right between their ages. Georgina shuddered. She'd booked nine sessions with the healer to work on Julia. Tomorrow she would go again and take on Julia's blueprint to attempt more rebalancing. They would then collapse the new, healthy blueprint into Julia's physical body to alter her cells. Georgina couldn't afford to doubt this method. It was all they had now.

Her mind went back to her dream. *Was her grandmother Anastasia offering nurturing in the form of food in the dream at this sad time, or was she preparing for Julia? Or both?* To push away her thoughts, Georgina made herself get up. Gathering up her bills and another cup of tea, she sat down at her round clay dining table with her checkbook. After she wrote all the checks and stamped all the envelopes, she noticed she'd written her sister's return address instead of her own on every one. She set the envelopes on Kate's baby grand piano to mail in the morning anyway. She was a mess, but Kate and Finn were coming. *Think about that,* she told herself. But her mind kept jumping the fence. *Is Julia dying? The only thing this bad in my whole life was when Kate was struggling to live.* Bad thoughts tumbled over one another. *I wasn't a good enough sister, not loving or understanding or helpful enough. I was too judgmental.* Every unconscious, selfish, mean thing she'd ever done to Julia jumped out at her like a ghoul from behind a tree in a graveyard. She vowed never to be unkind to anyone for the rest of her life if only Julia could live. Guilt over every time she'd ever hurt Julia's feelings or criticized her, even in her own mind, tied her intestines into a pretzel of gut-wrenching regret. She doubled over in pain. She couldn't stomach the thought of losing Julia or the idea that she had ever been unkind to her—which she had. *I must be kind always now and keep my end up. That's all.*

SILENT DELTA

"I love your feet. They're perfect. That's how I knew you were my guy," said Kate. They'd spent the day lying in bed; lazing around; watching documentaries on the laptop; munching on carrots, cherry tomatoes, and slivers of Parmesan cheese on rosemary crackers; taking naps and cuddling. It was dinnertime before they finally got up. "Come on. I'm taking you out," Finn said.

"We leave in five days. Shouldn't we eat what's in the fridge to use it up?"

"Forget the fridge and put on some clothes." Half an hour later, Finn pulled into the parking lot by the beach.

"This rock is still warm from the afternoon sun," Kate said, stretching her legs out on it. "I can feel its life, and it makes me happy. It's been sitting here so long on the edge the sea."

"Eat before it gets cold, my little poet." He unwrapped a burger and handed it to her. Kate took a bite.

"Delicious."

"I've been thinking about something. My mom emailed a couple days ago asking me to give her away at the wedding."

"And?"

"I'm not ready for that." Finn munched a few fries at once.

"Have you told her?"

"Not yet." He cast his eyes down at the ripples left in the sand by the retreating sea. Kate followed his eyes. "It looks like a pleated skirt," she said. Finn nodded. His mouth was full. The evening light and the soft ruffled waves lulled them into a state of somnolence. They finished eating without speaking, watching the sky turn a deeper shade of lavender. Kate shivered.

Finn gathered up their garbage and pulled Kate to her feet. "Let's go home. How about *Family Guy*, the episode with that girl you like from *Downton Abbey*? What's her name?"

"Michelle Dockery. Not tonight. I want to draw for an hour before bed. I've a lot to do before I see my editor in New York next week." Neither her new graphic novel nor the one about surviving her teenage suicidal depression was where she wanted it to be for the coming meetings. And once the baby was born, she'd have even less time. One hour turned into three before she slipped into the warmth beside her sleeping husband.

Kate awoke next morning to find a blue sticky note on her pillow with a bunch of *x*'s and *o*'s scribbled on it. She turned over and felt the baby move. After a cup of tea, she looked at her work from the night before. Not too shabby. Then she checked her email. Georgina and the usual thousand emails from Amazon.

Georgina's email was full of excitement about their visit, but it was obvious to Kate from the one sentence about her aunt that her mother was wrecked. She didn't know what to say to her about Julia. Julia and Georgina's relationship was multifaceted. They had disagreed on how to care for their parents near the end of their lives when they were failing. Kate knew Georgina would now be wishing she'd done more to support Julia, who'd been the one on the front line. She hadn't understood how hard their parents' passing had been on her sister. She'd be wishing she'd been less judgmental and more loving. Kate knew, too, that Georgina would be beating herself up big time about all this. What a heavy burden of guilt and regret her mother must be carrying now as she feared for her sister's life! At the very least, she knew Georgina would be cataloging all the ways she could have been a better sister. Unlike Colin, who was unacquainted with remorse, Georgina was an expert on it.

Kate hit reply and tried to tell her mother not to indulge in too much self-recrimination. Then she hit send and turned to her work, but she couldn't concentrate. Her mind held her too tightly. Thoughts of her aunt and her mother pinged around inside her skull, her brain a locked crypt with beams of light bouncing off the inside walls, playing silent home movies, illuminating the two sisters.

Julia was a silent delta, deep and peaceful. She drove the quiet pictur-esque country roads, thinking her private thoughts. She never hurried. Once, she'd told Kate, "I can only be myself when I'm completely alone and it's dusk—my favorite time." Julia was always home in her house overlooking the valley by the time the sky turned a silty dark. Her husband went to bed early. That's when Julia would sit out under the starlight and moonlight, gazing at the dark outlines of the surrounding meadows and smoking the last cigarette of the day.

Georgina, on the other hand, hated cigarette smoke—it made her cough. And although she longed for one, she had no porch to sit on in the starlight, and no one would describe her as a silent, peaceful delta. Whereas Julia was parsimony itself, Georgina was usually too much sand for most people's trucks. Julia accepted people as they were and stayed centered in herself. A small stone on her dresser was engraved with "Let It Be."

Georgina meant to be accepting, but she couldn't leave things alone. And she had an irresistible attraction to genius that often pulled her off track. Colin, that cold scimitar, had been the worst detour of her life. Yet, though not powerful and accepting in her sister's silent way, Georgina also had an inner landscape with fields of jubilance and rivers of grace. And Kate had known her to stand with the strength of a mountain in the very center of her life in the worst of times. "You have to have dragons to fight in order to be a heroine." That's what she told Kate when Colin left her. Then she quoted Jung. What was it? Something about not taking the sure road. Colin had certainly knocked Georgina off the sure road.

Julia's cancer was another journey off the sure road, an even worse battle for Georgina than her father's death had been. Kate remembered her the morning after her father died, sipping her coffee and quoting Jung. "Life is a brief sojourn between two great mysteries which are one." Then she'd kissed her on the top of the head and gone to rinse out her bone china cup and saucer just as she did each morning. Her mother knew that life and death were one inextricable unity, that death could not be separated from life, that it walks beside us always, taking each step with us. That knowledge had given her strength. You would have never known by looking at her that morning that her heart was torn in a thousand pieces by the loss of her beloved father. Kate had watched her breathe her way forward into that day and through that heartbreak, one breath at a time. *But would her strength hold now if Julia died?* Kate ran her hands through her hair.

It shook her when Georgina told her what Julia had said on the phone the previous day. Julia's bed, which had been moved downstairs since she was too weak to walk up to her bedroom, was placed so she could look out over the deck and down the valley covered in buttercups. The hummingbird feeder hung outside in the breeze. Julia and Georgina were talking of their daughters when suddenly Julia broke in. "Oh, a hummingbird. I guess I'm not going to die today."

Kate was startled out of her reverie by Lydia calling through the screen door: "Hey, darlin', are you ready to go shopping for some clothes that will fit your new body?"

"Ugh, shopping—and for maternity clothes. Let's just go to lunch instead."

"But you'll need some things to wear in New York. You can't walk around the streets there with Finn's shirts stretched over your belly."

"Lydia, you'd be surprised by what you can walk around wearing on the streets of New York."

"Have you had bad news? You look wrung out." Lydia directed Kate toward the door and handed her handbag to her. "Is your credit card in there?" Kate nodded.

Lydia started the engine. Kate was staring straight ahead. "How's your aunt doing?"

"Not good."

"And your mom?"

"She feels she let her sister down in some way, added to her stress, that she's somehow responsible for this cancer."

"How?" They pulled out of the palm grove, and Lydia stopped at the corner to look both ways.

216

"She was critical of Julia's care of their father in the last year of his life. Their mother was impatient and cruel to him when his eyesight and hearing and short-term memory started going. She was vicious, really, and my mother wanted Julia to protect him. Julia lived close by." Lydia still had her foot on the brake at the stop sign when a car behind them honked.

"I'm distracting you from driving," said Kate.

"No, I want to hear." Lydia eased onto the main road.

"No one could control my grandmother. She was a beautiful, wild creature, exciting and brilliant. What we didn't realize at the time was that her mind was going too, because she made up things to cover over what she couldn't remember. My mother expected too much of her sister and regretted afterward how judgmental she'd been. When their parents started failing, it was way harder on Julia than my mom understood."

Lydia clicked on her turn signal and waited for a break in the traffic to pull into the mall. She got a parking spot right near the maternity shop. "But I don't see why your mom blames herself for her sister's cancer."

"She thinks every ailment has its origin in the emotional self, in the belief that we aren't loved or are in some way not good enough."

"Did she make her sister feel bad or unloved?"

"She thinks she did. And since she believes that all disease is caused by stress that gets downloaded into the body, she blames herself. My mother sees the body as a healing machine, but if it gets overloaded with too much stress, it can't process it fast enough, and the stress goes into the tissue and causes imbalances that result in disease. She thinks the stress she caused Julia was the tipping point that set off the cancer."

"But she didn't cause all the stress in her sister's life."

"True, but she's not thinking rationally now."

"Will she at some point?" Lydia asked. She turned off the motor, and they got out of the car. Lydia pointed to the window of the maternity store, which was displaying skinny jeans with expandable waists.

"Eventually she'll see reason, after she digests it all, and if Julia lives. My mom says she grows the most when she's in pain because suffering breaks her heart open and forces her look at her own shadow." Kate's voice trailed off. She could see Lydia was intent on shopping now. Lydia directed Kate's attention to some shelves along the wall. "Here they are. They look just like regular skinny jeans, except the waistband is this wide elastic all the way around."

"They are good," Kate said. She bought three pairs and declared the shopping expedition over. "Let's get lobster rolls."

They were seated at an outdoor umbrella table next to the water when Lydia picked up the thread of their conversation. "Do you believe the same as your mom, that we grow most when our hearts get broken?"

Kate swallowed a bite of her lobster roll. "In a way, I guess. Suffering and loss do break your heart open."

Lydia finished her crab cake and wiped her lips. "I don't see the value in heartbreak. It's just pain."

"Not if you let your heart keep on breaking until you break through to some new understanding of yourself, meet yourself in a new way," said Kate.

Lydia considered this. "So you believe the purpose of suffering is to help us to break through to greater self-knowledge?"

"That's one purpose of suffering," Kate said.

"What else does it achieve?"

"Maybe suffering makes us more compassionate."

"I'd like to believe that," Lydia said. She added sugar and lemon to her iced tea and stirred. "Why else is there so much pain in the world?"

Kate didn't have an answer. She just looked back at Lydia.

"I feel such shame and guilt about that night I fell apart," Lydia said. "I'd like to think I can grow by understanding the meaning of that pain and humiliation."

"Then do think it and believe it."

"I can't. I'm too selfish and stupid," said Lydia.

Kate looked into Lydia's eyes and told her, "Don't do this to yourself. It's dangerous."

Lydia pulled her eyes away from Kate and sipped her iced tea. "How is it dangerous?"

"Because you'll make yourself sick. Negative thoughts create disease. Positive thoughts create healing. Didn't your Body Talk person tell you that? Try thinking of your thoughts as food. Would you give yourself poison?

Negative thoughts are like poison. They make you feel bad, depressed, angry, sad—and eventually you get sick if they're your steady diet."

"I don't even know what thoughts I'm feeding myself most of the time," Lydia said.

"Maybe we could take a meditation class. Then you'd see what thoughts you're eating."

"I'll have to work at wrapping my head around that idea," said Lydia.

"Want to share a dessert?" Kate asked.

"Sure, you choose."

"Hot apple pie with caramel ice cream?"

"Perfect."

TWO SOULS COMMUNING

Georgina uncapped her pen and opened her journal.

Where else can I pour out the ugliest truths about myself but to you? I'm lost. Emma just called to meet up for lunch, but can I even do lunch? I'm an empty vessel. I have nothing to offer. All my thoughts are with my sister as I rake over our whole life together, looking for ways I could have been more present, less judgmental. The more narrow the boundary between life and death becomes, the more desperate I am for her to know how much I love her. There's such an awful feeling of having missed out on connecting with her more completely, and blaming myself for it. Julia, please don't leave. I have never known you until now. The nearness of your death stirs in me an impatient hunger for communion with you.

Georgina put her pen down and got up to open the window. Her restless thoughts stirred, and she picked up her pen again.

This desire to commune with Julia has eclipsed all other reality for me. How can I tell her how much I treasure her? How can I ask her to forgive all my foolish judgments and little criticisms? Why was I thoughtless and cruel at times? I am engaged in an

220

incessant, internal dialogue with her, begging her forgiveness. Her body is vanishing. At less than seventy pounds, her spirit is more present than her physical form. Her Soul is becoming even more visible now as her body falls away. There is no ego left, only the pureness of her Being. Those youthful days of her wildness, her waist-long hair flying behind her, are gone entirely. Once, maybe her ego had one idea and her Soul another. Now they live in harmony. Her Soul's presence is all I sense. There is no other running counter to the Divine in her. She accepts everything with calm. I cannot. Tears overflow the rims of my eyes and sting my cheeks.

It may be foolish of me to hope her body will resurrect and carry her through another twenty or thirty earthly years, but I do hope. I hope, and then I see her lying in Perkins Funeral Home, and I jump back from the image in horror. Not yet, not yet. Subliminally, this image haunts the corners of my consciousness even though I know she'll never be laid out. She will be cremated if she dies. But her earthly life can't be over yet. Her daughters, her husband, our brothers, her friends, me—she can't leave us yet.

All my running to healers to work on her—is it just an ancillary gesture, a balm for my conscience? Was I cowardly and selfish in expecting Julia to manage our mother and protect our father? Did I not see how it all affected her? Why did I focus only on her failings? Was this judgment of mine the final pain that broke her body and started this cancer on its path? There, I've written the worst. I am in hell when I think this. I curse myself for my judgment and lack of understanding, for the pain I caused her. I know others are far more central to her life than I, but if only I could undo the extra pain I added to her life. Now my efforts are for love of her. Am I too late? In the end I will submit to her Soul's will with reverence. It will choose life or death. I can't write anymore. My feelings won't be compressed into this journal. I'll let myself cry, and then go to work.

Two cancellations. The workday would be light. Good. It would give her more time to focus on her family as they accompanied Julia on her journey. To where? Julia stood between two worlds. Which way would she turn as she gazed at the inextricable oneness of life and death? It was difficult for Georgina to control her self-criticism as she compared herself to her sister. Her mind was thin soil compared to Julia's. She had a superficial smartness only, and Julia, a deep well of knowledge and feeling. Julia could be ribald and witty too, and she had succeeded at marriage where Georgina had failed, repeatedly. With Georgina love for a man was always castrated. Though she had longed for true love, she'd never found it.

Tomorrow she would travel up to see her sister for a few days before Kate and Finn arrived. How would she find her this time, her sixth trip there in three months? More wasted or maybe beginning to gain weight and turning toward life again? People were vague on the phone about how she was doing, and Julia said nothing at all about her state of well-being. All their adult lives, they'd always been the same weight. Now Julia weighed fifty pounds less than she did. Georgina imagined a fifty-pound bag of potatoes.

The next morning Georgina boarded the bus at the Cornell Club on Forty-Fourth Street just off Madison Avenue. Its next stop would be Oxley Equestrian Center on the Cornell campus in Ithaca. It was June. She had forgotten that. The greenness of the trees and fields reminded her that it was the beginning of summer. The verdant vision soothed her eyes and heart as the bus ferried her westward. Her brother Edward was at Oxley to meet her and drive her to their sister, who lay in her big four-poster bed in the living room that overlooked soft green pastures and rolling hills.

When they arrived at Julia's door, Georgina pushed Edward in front of her. "You go in first. I'm afraid of my face showing too much before I get it under control." Ever gentle like their father had been, Edward obliged her. It had only been ten days since Georgina had seen Julia, but she wasn't prepared for this. Julia was a skeleton with skin drawn over it. Her jaw and teeth were the most frightening. But as the two sisters and their brother sat and talked, Julia assumed a kind of otherworldly beauty. She was already half in a distant land. Would she keep going or come back to them? One got used to the skeletal look because she was still so Julia. Her essence wasn't in her flesh but in her spirit. And she was now more spirit than body. Yet how one loved her familiar earthly form and wished it back.

A body is such a generous thing. It gives its all for us, and then, in the end, we leave this home of flesh and bone, and someone burns it up or buries it, and our soul moves on to be received by death, the midwife who will birth us into the next world. The body can't come along. It gets left behind. Dumped in the fire, a bag of skin and bones. It doesn't seem fair to part from this old, familiar friend and just throw it into the fire, never to be of use again. *I'll be sad to be separated from my arms and hands, my legs and knees and feet, my face, shoulders, my eyes,* Georgina thought. *How lonely to think of never seeing them again. They won't be mine anymore, not even my heart. They won't even be at all, and after all they've given to allow me to walk on the earth, I'll discard them as I depart for the next world. I must be grateful to this body while I live in it. And I am grateful, too, for Julia's body, which allowed her to walk the earth and be among us. How I will miss her familiar lovely form if she rows across the river to that other world. Even now she sits in the boat, oars ready but not moving, her direction still uncertain.*

Julia was dozing. Georgina and Edward sat nearby. Julia's husband was saying something. His question pulled Georgina out of her thoughts. Did she want coffee? "No thanks, Rob."

Georgina reached into her bag and pulled out the flowing top from Anthropologie she had brought for Julia. Julia opened her eyes. "What's that? It's so lovely and floaty."

"A blouse for you." Georgina carried the top over to Julia and watched Julia's hands feel the smoothness of the garment. Her own hands were a copy of Julia's, but she moved them in a slightly different manner. *I love Julia's hands. Her hands break my heart. They're so slender, so tentative and gentle.*

"Should I take it upstairs and hang it in your closet?" Georgina asked.

"No. Prop it on the couch so I can look at it," Julia told her. Was she thinking her goal would be to get well enough to wear it out somewhere to meet a friend? Or maybe just, *I'll wear it at home, sitting up in bed?* Or even, *I'll never live to wear this garment, this last gift from my sister, in a line of so many over our lives together. But let me look at it, this graceful, whimsical top I might have worn with pleasure if I had lived?* Was it just one more thing she would have to leave behind if she was really leaving everything to journey to the next world?

This moment hung on Georgina for days. Julia asked for so little—just to look at a thing. Her words crushed Georgina's heart. At the same time, the moment felt sublime. As she fell asleep that night at Julia's daughter's house, she knew she couldn't give up believing Julia would recover, that somehow her body would be called back into being. She had to hold the space of healing. She had to believe. The more she held open her heart to the possibility of Julia's resurrection, the more Julia herself would believe in it. The best gift she could give her sister was her own heart energy. She'd keep sending love straight into Julia's heart. Let it be like sunlight sinking softly into a spring field.

In the morning she took Julia's two-year-old grandson Jack to see her. If ever there was an angelic child, he was it. It wasn't just that he looked like a golden cherub with his clear blue eyes and white-blond hair; it was his entire essence of gentle knowing, his soft touch, his mindfulness as he stood by Julia's bed and bent his face close to hers. With difficulty, Julia rolled on her side to look at his face. Neither said a word. They gazed into one another's eyes, two souls communing. What were they seeing and thinking? Did Julia think, *Oh, my darling boy, I don't want to leave you. Let me drink in your being and wrap you in my love for a whole lifetime?* Was Jack looking through her eyes at eternity or just marveling at the visible bones beneath her translucent skin? He was less afraid of Julia's altered form than Georgina was. They opened the double doors to the deck. Three hummingbirds flew in and landed on Julia's bed near where Jack rested his tiny fingers. He didn't move them. He and Julia smiled together at the birds and then at each other. Georgina stood apart watching them.

Julia's friend Kathy came in. She was married to the town funeral director. Five minutes later Julia's friend Joan arrived, followed by Linda, who'd come all the way from Hawaii to be with Julia. Another day was under way. Georgina took Jack out to the garden as the women gathered around Julia, like priestesses of the temple, to bathe her. The men stood or sat outside, talking about what men in the country talk about. Georgina heard the funeral director say to a neighboring farmer, "It's the calm before the storm. If you think otherwise, you're fooling yourself."

"Hornswoggle," said the farmer, "Julia's as tough as they come. She'll pull through."

"Do you think that rose there, its petals soft as velvet, brushing against your overalls, can shut and be a bud again?" the funeral director asked the farmer. Rob approached and their conversation was reduced to shrugs and sighs. Georgina's thoughts turned inward.

When you have a body, you can look in the mirror and see your reflection. When you leave your body, can you still see your reflection in a mirror? Georgina thought not. One is no longer then in the third dimension but in some other intersecting plane. When they were little girls someone had told them that you could see your soul shining if you looked in the mirror at the whites of your eyes. So Georgina and Julia had sat on the floor before the big mirror in their bedroom, staring into the whites of their eyes and saying hello to their souls. Would Julia soon no longer be able to see her own reflection? Nothing could prepare Georgina for that. And nothing could prepare her brothers or her sister's daughters or her husband. And protection wasn't wanted. Let the full weight fall and bow them to the ground if it was to go that way. Let this great mystery of life and death do its worst before it passed over, if that was the will of Julia's soul.

Julia's friend Sandy pulled into the semicircular drive in front to the house and got out of her car. Georgina and Jack walked over to greet her. There was a rhythm around Julia. People came and went, came and stayed minutes or hours or whole days. Julia slept and woke and socialized and inquired about this and that in her visitors' lives. "Have you sold that land yet?" "How's the new pickup?" "Will you march in the Dairy Day parade?" Each question would blossom into a conversation, creating a little world with her visitor, a world to which Julia attended with her heart and mind, putting the other at ease, forgetting herself. She'd always been like that.

In the afternoon Julia's daughters arrived, and the threads of conversation wove in new directions. "Aunt Georgina, tell us something we don't know about Mom as a girl." Georgina thought, then she said, "There was just one time in all the years I can remember from when we were kids that your mother was ever even a little mean to me, and it might not even count because she was only about twelve years old at the time. I came home from a date with my boyfriend. It was our two-year anniversary. And he'd just broken up with me. I threw myself down on the living room couch to cry my heart out. Your mother came in, and I looked up at her and said: 'Julia, don't ever fall in love—it hurts too much.' And she laughed."

"Mom. You didn't!" Charlotte said turning to Julia.

"Yes, she did. I must have looked a real teenage drama queen to a twelve-year-old, because she proceeded to imitate me sobbing on the couch for anyone who would listen for the next three weeks."

"I don't remember doing that." Julia smiled.

The June days lengthened. The garden grew. One thing blossomed and ripened and then another. Everyone had memories to share and facts to check with Julia as she lay like a wounded queen in their midst, suspended in time and space, holding on. Was she withering or had she maybe gained a little weight? No one wanted to face the miserable necessity of living on without her if the worst came. The peonies were gone, but the sweet scent of roses and lilies filled the air. Charlotte placed a bouquet of pale-pink, wild roses at her mother's bedside table. She had to live. No one should die while the world was blossoming.

HOME

"Lydia will be here in five minutes," Kate said. "I hope we haven't forgotten anything."

"Here's a package of tissue paper you didn't manage to use," said Finn.

"Things travel better when you use tissue paper," Kate told him.

"I know your rationale, and I know it comes from your grandmother, who drummed it into your head when you were a little girl packing for camp. But I bet none of the other little girls had their bathing suits wrapped in tissue paper."

"Mornin', darlins, are you ready to fly off this God forsaken island?" Lydia called from the front door. Kate noted how strong Lydia's accent sounded this morning. It was like that when Lydia got anxious. All Kate said was, "No, we're busy discussing the merits of tissue paper."

Lydia walked into the bedroom and smiled at them. "Y'all are so cute. Kate, let Finn get that."

"I'm not an invalid, Lydia, just pregnant."

"Any news on your aunt?" Lydia asked, once they were all settled in her BMW.

"Not any good news. She's skin and bones but completely with it."

"So will you stay on?"

"I don't know—it depends," said Kate. They each fell silent the for the rest of the ride to the airport.

"I'm going to be lost without you, Kate." Lydia kissed Kate on both cheeks.

As they disappeared behind the gate, Lydia called after them. "Try to enjoy the wedding a little, Finn."

"I'll pretend I didn't hear that," Finn said. How unlike Lydia to toss a parting barb at Finn. She must be hurt about something or angry at their going. Usually, she was too polished a specimen to show such a lack of consideration for someone else's feelings.

The flight was long but uneventful. Nick was at the door when their cab pulled up to the front of Georgina's building. "Your mother told me you two were arriving today," Nick greeted them, reaching for Kate's bag. It was all so familiar and comforting: the dark-green awning leading up to the front door, the cool marble floor of the lobby, the painting hanging over the fireplace behind the concierge's desk.

Georgina and Olive were standing in front of the elevator when it opened on the seventh floor. Kate felt herself encircled by her mother's arms, and Olive danced around them and licked Finn everywhere she could find bare skin. With licks and hugs, they were swept through the front door and into the foyer. It was unchanged: the table for keys and packages, the Moroccan lamp with the red shade, the umbrella stand, and the lovely small Oriental rug. Kate had known these things all her life in just these same places they still occupied. Her eyes ran over each thing as if to say hello again.

Georgina stepped back and gazed at the two of them. Kate glowed with new life, and Finn was strong and fit. Kate headed for the bathroom. Finn carried their luggage into their old room. It was just as they'd left it with its two comfy chairs and the oval table in front of them. The collage on canvas Kate had made of Finn extreme roller skating still hung on the wall. Their blue-and-white striped duvet cover and curtains were the ones they'd gotten when Finn first moved in. All their books, CDs, DVDs, and video games sat quietly on the shelves as if waiting for them to return. Home. It hadn't changed. And it felt great, like going back in time. It was all still here, bathing in the late afternoon sunlight.

Neither Kate nor Finn could sit down yet. They wandered around from room to room. Olive followed one then the other as each breathed in home and touched this or that object. Kate looked out the windows at the familiar sight of Fifth Avenue. She picked up a small Buddha that lived on Georgina's desk. Finn wandered into the bathroom and ran his finger over the place where the wallpaper had been coming unglued for years. Georgina observed them in silence as they absorbed their old home. She released the tears that had been dammed up within her in quiet gratitude.

Finn opened the wine. "To homecomings," he toasted. They gathered around the table laden with summer berries and roses. When the buzzer announced the arrival of their sushi appetizer, Olive was the first one to the door. "Stay," Finn commanded, and Olive obeyed. While they ate, Finn told them about his favorite sushi maker, Jiro. "He has a tiny restaurant in Tokyo that's booked up months in advance. To work with him, you have to have extreme patience and dedication because the training takes a lifetime. You don't get to even make a piece of sushi for the first ten years. You have to learn all about the rice and fish first."

When the buzzer sounded again to announce their main course, Olive, with her eyes on Finn, obediently sat ten feet from the front door while Georgina paid the delivery man. Kate handed Finn his steak burrito and Georgina her guacamole enchilada before opening her chicken quesadilla. And there were cinnamon and chocolate churros for them all to share. Olive, as in times past, took up her position between Georgina and Kate so she could apply the maximum pressure to each of them. She had made begging into a fine art over the years. Even Finn succumbed to her charm at times.

"So what's the wedding schedule for the weekend?" Georgina asked.

"I'm not sure. And we haven't told my mom that Kate's pregnant."

"Why not?"

"We didn't want to steal her thunder," said Finn.

"She's going to know the minute she sees Kate," said Georgina.

"I'm showing all that much?"

"Maybe you could start just by texting her that you've arrived," Georgina suggested.

Finn fished his phone out of his pocket. Instead of texting, he laid it on the table.

"What?" Kate looked at him.

But almost immediately, Finn's phone lit up. "Have you arrived? Can you and Kate do lunch tomorrow?" His mother texted.

"How can she be free for lunch tomorrow? Won't she be getting filed and buffed and waxed and polished before her rehearsal dinner?" Kate said. Finn shrugged.

"Ask her where and what time. Then after lunch, I have to find a dress for the wedding."

Kate asked her mother about Julia while they cleared up after dinner. "She's so herself—smart, funny, connected, loving. All she needs is a new body. She told me on the phone today that cancer is a humbling experience that is burnishing her soul." Georgina was trying to speak without emotion, but she could feel her heartbeat rising like thunder as she talked about her sister. It was getting harder to see a way for Julia to turn this around, resurrect her body. It was unthinkable that Julia might not live on earth much longer. Then where would she be? How do the spheres of the living and the dead intersect? Would her sister peek out at her from behind the stars if she no longer walked the earth?

Georgina kept these thoughts inside as she asked Kate where she wanted to look for a dress. "Ugh, shopping. No maternity stores. I'd like to dig around in some East Village boutiques, but there isn't time. I guess it's Macy's. It's less awful than Saks or Bloomingdale's. Something flowing—she's having a Grecian theme. It was going to be either nymphs frolicking in a wild garden or a Grecian temple."

"Maybe she'll rise up out of the sea like Aphrodite on a giant scallop shell to meet her groom," Georgina said.

Kate looked at her mother in horror.

"People have a right to enact their fantasies as long as they don't hurt anyone else," Georgina told her.

"Does making the servers dress as slaves count as hurting anyone else?" Kate looked at her mother and hung the dish towel on the rack to dry.

Georgina started to leash up Olive for her evening walk. "We'll take her," Finn said. "We can sniff around the old neighborhood too. Is the gluten free cupcake place on Eighth Street still open?"

"Yes, if you want to spend a small fortune. But I was planning to put some cookies in the oven."

Half an hour later, they walked into the apartment to the smell of warm chocolate chip cookies. "They're cooling so you can take them to bed, Finn," Georgina said. Finn hung up Olive's leash and slipped off his shoes. Kate collapsed onto the couch. "You must both be exhausted," said Georgina. Finn asked Kate if she wanted one, two, or three cookies. "I'll pass," she said, struggling to get up. He pulled her to her feet, left her where she stood, and went to get his cookies. "I left a little bowl on the counter for you," Georgina called after him. Kate looked as if she was going to sink back down onto the couch again, so Georgina guided her toward the bathroom, with Olive trotting after them.

Georgina kissed them both good-night, went to her own room, and took her white, silk pajamas out of her second drawer. Then, still holding them, she sat down on the edge of her bed. It wasn't quiet tonight. The sound of Kate and Finn's voices talking and laughing across the hall drifted under the closed door into her room. She sat there tasting the happiness of it. These were the moments of life she loved most of all.

The day dawned clear and sunny with a soft summer breeze. Georgina strolled up to Macy's to meet Kate. "I'd like a lipstick I can wear to work and not look too made up," she was explaining to the saleslady when Kate and Finn walked up. "How was lunch?"

"They tried to have their wedding on the Acropolis, but they couldn't get permission from the Greek government," Finn told Georgina.

"Every woman should feel like a goddess on her wedding day," Georgina said. "Will they honeymoon in Greece then, so they can at least visit the Acropolis?"

"Finn's mom says Greece is too run down now. And their honeymoon destination is a big secret," said Kate.

"They can fly to Mars for all I care. I don't give a fat rat's ass where they go."

"Finn's kind of upset that his mom invited his dad to her wedding—and he's coming," Kate said.

"The guy doesn't know what's good for him," said Finn. "How could she invite him to watch her marry another man? He's just her whipping boy showing up to be humiliated again."

"He doesn't have to come," said Georgina. "It's his choice."

"No, it isn't. He's still enslaved by her. He can't stay away, and she knows it. She wants it to appear like everyone's all one big happy family," Finn said. Georgina kept silent.

"Give me a kiss and go meet your skating buddies so I can find something to dazzle you at this Grecian idyll."

IT'S LIKE SHE'S PART OF THE TREES AND AIR

"Hi, sweetheart," Julia called out as Kate entered the living room where Julia lay enthroned in her hospital bed. Only the day before, the bed had been delivered and placed next to her own so she could still look out over the green valley. Kate started at the sight of her aunt. Julia looked like a skeleton with skin, but her smile was radiant as she welcomed Kate. *How can she be so upbeat and loving? How can she speak with so much heart?* Kate wondered as she bent to kiss Julia's forehead and then sat down at her bedside. "Do you know if you're having a boy or girl?" Julia asked.

"We're waiting till the baby's born to find out," Kate told her.

"There is something special in not knowing until the baby's born. I didn't know with either of my babies," Julia said. "And it was magical."

"So when is the baby due?"

"The end of January," Kate said.

"An Aquarius. That was your grandfather's sign," Julia said. From across the room, Georgina sat and watched these two people she loved with a love stronger than death, and she prayed, begged really, for Julia to live. After twenty minutes or so, Julia looked spent, and Georgina drew Kate away over Julia's protests. She knew Julia would doze a bit.

Outside they found Rob alone for once. Kate's phone rang, and she moved deeper into the garden to answer it. Rob asked Georgina to walk with him. "I want you to know something," he said. "I'm madly in love with your sister." In twenty-five years Rob had never spoken so openly or passionately to her about anything, let alone his feelings for her sister. "I know I was born to do this, to take care of her—whichever way it goes. When Julia found out she had cancer, she offered me an out. She told me, 'You don't have to go through this with me.' 'I'm all in,' I told her. Crazy girl. It's always been her. I've always been in love with her. I just wanted to tell you that." For the first time in her life, Georgina put her arms around Rob and held him close. To watch someone you love suffer and die was hard enough, but to still be madly in love with them and have to lose them—Georgina shuddered. She left Rob in the garden.

Julia was gazing straight ahead with a faraway look in her eyes when Georgina went back inside the house. "What were you thinking? You look so far away."

"I was just thinking about my life," Julia said.

"What about it?"

"I don't want to have regrets if I die, that I didn't do all I could for the people I love and even for everybody I know, really."

"Oh, Julia, my darling, you found what you were made for early in your life, and you have lived it. Don't you know that? You've cared for others, and that's what all your life has been about. And it's been hard at times. You absorbed so much negativity doing it. There's nothing for you to regret."

"I don't want to die now," Julia said. "I'm not ready to let go. I don't know how."

"Are you afraid?" Georgina asked.

"Sometimes."

"If you feel it happening, look for Dad. He'll be the one to come for you," Georgina said. "He was always telling us to spread our wings and fly."

"He'll be my Peter Pan," said Julia. "The day he died, I remember him talking to his mother. None of us could see her, but he said she'd come. He wasn't afraid."

"He'd lived out his life," Georgina said. "It's different for you." Julia listened to Georgina and made the slightest nod with her head.

"You've endured so much brutality. If it's more than you can bear . . ."

"I'm tougher than I thought," Julia said. "I know that now."

Before Georgina could answer, Kathy and Joan came in. Julia's temple goddesses, Georgina called them. "Your neighbor just handed me a mac and cheese casserole out in the driveway. She said she didn't want to disturb you," Kathy told Julia.

"So many people are bringing food. Everyone's so thoughtful," Julia said.

"I wish you'd eat a little of it," Joan urged.

"Maybe later." That's what Julia always answered now. But later never came. She couldn't eat. She barely had the strength to sip through a straw and swallow liquid, so several times a day they poured some mixture into her feeding tube. It horrified Georgina to see the tube sticking into her sister. More people came in: friends Julia worked with at the hospital. She broke into a big smile at the sight of them. Rob had shifted, loosened his control. The gates to his kingdom were wide open now. Anyone who wanted or needed to see Julia was welcome.

Georgina went out in search of Kate and instead found her brother Edward sitting on a stump, breaking a slender stick into small pieces. He winced when Georgina said, "It's like she's having calling hours while she's still alive."

"She's been my best friend forever," he said. "She's woven through my heart." Edward didn't cry, but Georgina knew he wished he could. He was so like their father, steady and gentle, but tough too. In their world men didn't cry. Georgina sat down next to him. "She's part of the fabric of this town," he said. "I see her everywhere. Driving down Main Street, stopping at the only red light in town, giving shots to the old people at the church hall, chatting with Mary as she buys stamps at the post office, asking after her mother. I see her laughing with George as she fills her gas tank at the Mobil station, inquiring about his upcoming surgery, visiting Betsey to comfort her after Peter died, picking up milk at Clark's and dropping it at Sara's before swinging by my place to have a drink on the porch with me before heading home. She's imprinted on this town and its inhabitants." Georgina sat on the grass with her arms wrapped around her knees and looked up at her brother.

"And then there's Rob," Edward said. "I've gotten to know him better this past month, sitting on this stump every day, than I ever did in the past twenty-five years."

"This experience is changing him," Georgina said. "It's breaking his heart open."

"He sleeps downstairs with Julia. After everyone leaves for the day, he pushes their four-poster bed right next to her hospital bed and puts his pillow on her bed so his head can be right next to hers, and that's how they sleep," Edward told her.

"I've seen Sara do that in the day," Georgina said. "She lies there for hours, staring at her mother, and then she falls asleep herself and wakes to look into her mother's eyes again, those soft doe eyes. Not Charlotte, though, she stands strong and plays Julia's favorite music and brings her flowers and coaxes her to drink a little juice. Each is accompanying their mother on this journey in her own way. Each knows it is a sacred time, a privilege to be this close to the invisible."

Julia's hospital coworkers were leaving. All five of them piled into one car. Georgina waved when they honked going down the hill. As she and Edward watched the car drive away, she knew that Edward was thinking the same thing she was. "What do you think happens when we die?" Georgina asked him.

"I don't know. Maybe we go through a tunnel of light. Isn't that what people who have near-death experiences say?"

"But after the tunnel of light? Do you think someone comes for us, our parents or guides or angels?"

"I don't believe physical death is the end, if that's what you're asking. I believe the soul carries on," he said.

"But what do you think the point of it all is—this being born and dying and being reborn?" Georgina asked.

"I don't know . . . some kind of learning, new lessons each lifetime to help us in our struggle to awaken. What do you think?" Edward asked.

"I believe each of us is a spark of the Divine, that in all our hearts, there's a light that is a piece of Source. And not just on earth but in every galaxy. And that light never goes out. It keeps trying to awaken us to the knowledge of who we truly are—divine light beings."

"It must be comforting to think that way," he said. "So Julia will see who she really is, if she dies—a little replica of the Divine. It's easy to believe that about her." Edward looked away, up into the treetops and the sky above.

Georgina pressed his shoulder with her palm and went back inside. Julia's cheeks were hollow. There was no flesh anywhere on her body. Her entire skeleton was visible through her luminous skin. But she was still Julia. Only twice in all these weeks had she mentioned seeing people Georgina couldn't see. "Who are those people in the corner?" she asked. "I know they're friends of Mom and Dad's, but I can't think of their names."

"The Gordons?" Georgina asked her.

"No, not them."

"The Frances?"

"No."

"The Bellingers?"

"No, never mind, Georgina. It'll come to me."

The other time was one morning when Georgina and Joan had been bathing Julia, and she asked: "Who are all these people in cloaks and hoods?"

"They're monks," Joan was quick to respond.

"Oh, all right," Julia said. The visible and invisible swirled through one another, and Julia now apprehended both worlds. Later that day, sitting by Julia's bed, Georgina was reading Michael Newton's book *Destiny of Souls* when she came across a passage describing a group of hooded monks called the Keepers. The Keepers are a subgroup of the Restoration Masters. They work in a sanctuary restoring energy to souls who return back to the spirit world after a death in which they have been ravaged by illness. Had Julia seen through the veil? Would these monks be among those who cared for her if she crossed over? Or maybe they would restore her here on earth, so she could go on living. Georgina just could not let go of hope. To sit near her sister was to be enveloped in a field of grace. Julia was aligned to her primordial innocence. Everyone could see. Would she turn around and come back to them? People did. Was Georgina the only one who believed this possible?

All were welcome now. Rob barred no one who wanted to participate in the sacrament as Julia waited on the precipice. High up, near to some other world, right on the edge of a cliff, she stood. *If she leaned forward, even a little, toward death, would she fall downward, but only for a second before she spread her wings? Oh, to see her wings unfurl and catch the swift uplifting current, to watch her soar. It would be an end to this horror of her earthly suffering. But none of us wants to let her go*, thought Georgina. Rob seemed to get it: that this time with her was Julia's gift to each of them. She wasn't his to possess, but only to give thanks for. The threshold was near, but she hadn't crossed it. There was still a chance she could turn back and restore her body, and she was still so Julia. *But monks have come*, thought Georgina. *What other archetypes of the world will show up?* Georgina kept vigilance at her sister's bedside. Julia opened her eyes. "I'd really like a burger and fries," she said.

"I'll run into town for it," Kathy offered.

"Maybe she'll take a bite or two," said Rob. Kate left with Kathy to drive the three miles into town for Julia's burger. Their brother Stan arrived from New York during the burger run. Edward and Georgina sat with him when he went into see Julia. The others drifted out onto the deck or into the garden, and the four siblings were left alone. The sadness was so heavy no one could speak.

Then Julia knit them together. "I loved growing up with you guys and Mom and Dad, especially that trip to Canada where we stayed in that cabin on a lake and had a boat and Mom washed the dishes outside in hot soapy water. I can still see her hands in the dishpan on the end of a picnic table." Georgina's throat tightened as she listened to Julia. Neither of her brothers spoke. "Do you remember the star Mom and Dad always put on the top of the Christmas tree when we were kids?" Julia asked. "I found it a couple months ago while going through some boxes. I hadn't seen it in years." The little stick Edward was holding snapped in his hands. Stan found his voice. "We had a great childhood. Do you remember sleigh riding in Phoenicia on Sister's Hill? And ice skating on Kincade's pond?" he asked.

"I remember sleigh riding with Mom one evening at suppertime on the hill in front of our house," Georgina said. "Mom was pregnant with Edward. You were only about three, Julia. The street light came on and the falling snow glistened under it. Mom had been cooking dinner and waiting for Dad to come home, and suddenly she was outside with us, catching snowflakes on her tongue, laughing and pulling you back up the hill on that sleigh with a back on it."

"I remember that sleigh." Julia smiled.

No one had noticed, but Sara had been asleep on the couch across the room. She sat up suddenly and burst into tears. "I was dreaming I heard you coming into the room, Mom, wearing your flip-flops like you've done a thousand times."

"Oh, sweetheart, it's all right," Julia told her daughter. Edward walked outside.

Kate and Kathy returned with the burger and fries and a milkshake. "Thank you. I'll have it later. You can leave it on the kitchen counter."

"Sure you don't want a bite while it's hot?" Kathy urged her.

"Not now, thanks." Rob took the bag from Kate.

"She thinks she's hungry, and her body is starving, but when it comes to it, she can't eat," he told Kate. "But we get her what she asks for just in case, and sometimes she manages to have a little. Charlotte makes her smoothies, and sometimes she drinks them."

Julia's older daughter, Charlotte, also cleaned out the refrigerator and swept the kitchen floor and put away all the food from neighbors and friends who kept showing up at the door. She wasn't one to lie down or gaze into her mother's eyes. She took action, got things done. Kathy did the laundry, and Georgina folded it. The day moved along hour by uncertain hour. By six or so everyone withdrew, and Rob came in from the garden to spend the night alone with Julia. At that hour the house was wrapped in a silent, grateful peace. Julia had lived another day. Maybe things could still turn around.

Georgina and Kate shared Sara's upstairs guest room and slept in the twin, four-poster beds with the carved wooden pineapples on each corner. Sara had inherited theses beds and the matching nightstands. They had been Julia and Georgina's growing up. Kate watched as her mother climbed into the old familiar bed of her childhood and turned off her bedside lamp. A gentle breeze blew through the screen and drifted across her body as she listened in the darkness to her mother's soft breathing. She knew Georgina was praying for Julia. She imagined the prayers on her mother's lips, mingling with her breath until her every breath became a prayer.

During the day Kate took charge of Julia's two grandsons. Two-year-old Jack grew especially attached to her. They'd lie together in the grass and stare up at the clouds, making up stories about the shapes they saw.

"Dragon," Jack told her. "I have a dragon in here." Jack pointed to his tummy. "He tickles me."

"Like this?" Kate said nuzzling his belly with her face while he laughed.

"There's a sailing ship," Kate pointed out. "It's loaded with cargo from India."

"Cargo?"

Kate explained the word to him. Julia was pleased by the connection between Kate and Jack, as she had been by Georgina's connection to him. He was her beloved baby grandson. Did she know she might not have the joy of being this angel-child's grandmother much longer? Kate couldn't stand the unfairness of it and shoved the thought away. How did Julia have her finger on the pulse of these connections, when she couldn't even move? Somehow she knew when people were connected, and it made her happy. "Please let her live and see this angel-child grow into a boy and then a man," Kate prayed to the sailing ship from India. "Don't make her give this away too."

It was harder for Jack's eight-year-old brother, who understood what was going on, and who shouldn't have had his innocence ripped from him so young. No one at eight should know death. Julia was more a second mother to him than a grandmother. His fear and grief made him angry, and he got in trouble, which was the last thing he needed.

Another day passed in its now familiar rhythm, with one change. Rob drove the 1956 Chevy Nomad he'd bought Julia for her birthday right up onto the side lawn near the deck so she could see it from her bed. She struggled to sit up. There it was, the car of her dreams. Rob's twin brother had finally located one in mint condition, and Rob had bought it as a surprise for Julia. She was too weak to sit in it or even get close to it, but she could see it from her bed. "Have you seen my car?" She asked Georgina.

"It's a beauty."

"Rob'll take you for a ride if you like," Julia offered. Her nomad soul at last had a mascot. Georgina knew Rob still hoped that Julia would recover and be able to drive her Nomad on the back roads she loved, the windows down and her red hair blowing as she sailed along to the sound of Dylan's "Forever Young."

But Julia could no longer sit up or even turn on her side. "If I don't recover," she told her daughters, "I'd like a party, no funeral, just a celebration where nobody steps on anybody's toes." To Georgina she said: "I want to be cremated and for my ashes to be buried near Mom and Dad." Georgina nodded.

"I love you, Georgina," Julia told her sister every day.

Julia told everyone of her love for them again and again during those last weeks. She was breathing her way toward death. As she breathed, Georgina thought she saw a violet light shining from her mouth and nostrils. "If you feel you are leaving and letting go of this world," Georgina told Julia, "fly toward the light."

"Yes," Julia promised.

The rhythm slowed around the house and the hillside. Julia had spent her life showing others how to understand the giving and receiving of love. Now she was letting go of her life publicly, in full view of whoever wanted to participate, and she was doing it with grace, teaching everyone around her how to die. She'd allowed everyone who wanted to share in it, to witness the hard road she'd taken with her physicality. She permitted all to watch her endure the pain and indignity and the sublime aspects of encroaching death. Death was the midwife who would birth her into the next world. So many were traveling this path with her, and none was turned away or shut out. Each received a gift of knowledge, of awakening. Those last days each found his or her place in the rhythm that everyone was beginning to accept as the quiet advancing of death into their realm. It was Julia's old friend Sandy who told Rob, "It's time to stop the feeding tube because nothing is staying in." It was her longtime and fearless friend Joan who offered to administer the morphine every four hours. "Let me give her the medicine, Rob. I'll do just enough to ease the pain, but not so much she'll be out of it." It was her devoted friend Kathy who gently bathed her each morning. "I hope the water isn't too hot. Just tell me if it is, Julia." And it was her daughters, husband, brothers, sister, and niece who encircled her in a ring of love. They all knew now she was most likely leaving them.

On her last morning but one, Georgina bent to brush the hair from her sister's eyes and kiss her forehead. "You smell good," Julia said, opening her eyes.

"I was afraid I had coffee breath," Georgina answered.

"No, your hair smells good," Julia said.

"It's Kate's shampoo," Georgina told her.

"Nice, but I do love coffee."

"Would you like some coffee?" Georgina asked.

"What I'd really like is a coke with ice." Julia tried to sip the coke through a straw, but she had no strength.

"What time is it?" she asked.

"It's about nine in the morning," Georgina told her.

"Oh good lord. I have to get up, but I'm so tired."

"Rest my darling, no need to get up."

"I love you, Georgina."

"I love you too, Julia."

Never in her life had Georgina heard Julia use the phrase "Oh good lord." That wasn't her style of speech at all. Where had that come from? That was the last conversation between the sisters. Georgina had wanted to talk more to Julia of the spirit world and her spirit guides and their past and future lives together, of Spinoza and of Kant. Like a big sister, she'd wanted to arm Julia with knowledge for the journey ahead. Julia didn't need it. She had begun crossing back over the River of Forgetfulness. Perhaps their father or their grandmother was already preparing to receive her. At the thought of her father, Georgina let out an involuntary moan. She would never stop missing his goodness. Or Julia's. It was to herself she must read Spinoza: "All the cosmos is a single substance of which we are a part." Georgina had thought she and Julia would grow old together, taking walks and talking, looking back over their lives, rocking in their chairs, gazing over the green valley, discussing their children and grandchildren and loves and losses. "But you're leaving," Georgina said out loud to the air above her sleeping sister, "and that will never happen now."

Early the next morning, Julia woke Rob. They were alone. "I feel like I'm about to die, and I'm a little frightened." He got into her bed with her and took her in his arms. Julia left her body looking into his eyes on a summer morning. A mighty oak had been uprooted and turned into starlight. Her doe eyes were still open when Sara and Charlotte arrived a few minutes later. Sara couldn't look at her mother, but Charlotte sat and stared into Julia's now lifeless eyes for what seemed to Sara a long time.

"Her soul is now uncaged," Georgina told them.

"I still feel her near, but I can't see her. Where is she now? Where has my mama gone?" Sara sobbed.

"I feel like she's in the ether around us," Charlotte said.

"She is," Georgina told them. "And angels are applauding her for her strength in learning to let go when she didn't want to leave us at all."

"I want another life where my mama is alive and my heart isn't broken," Sara said.

Rob called the funeral home that would cremate Julia's body. Charlotte arranged the catering for her mother's last party on earth. Sara wrote her mother's obituary. Together with Rob they chose a white marble urn for Julia's ashes. They didn't want to know which day Julia's skin and bones and organs and hands and eyes and hair would be put in the fire and turned to ash. They had served her while she needed a body, and now she'd left them, all the parts of her physical body, abandoned after years of service. They couldn't make the journey with her. The thought made Georgina want to cry.

Joan offered her field for the celebration, and a large white tent was ordered. A week later, amid wildflowers, grass, sky, and the sound of Bob Dylan's "Forever Young," friends, siblings, children, cousins, neighbors, townspeople, coworkers, all celebrated Julia's life. And nobody stepped on anybody's toes.

Georgina and Kate strolled away from the group toward a pond in the meadow. They stood by the water's edge. Out of nowhere came a flock of birds. It circled above them in a swift, uplifting rush. Georgina followed them with her eyes.

Alone after the party, Rob drove Julia's Chevy Nomad home to their house on the hill overlooking the valley. Later that night Julia's daughters sent giant colored candle lanterns drifting up into the heavens. Georgina imagined Julia, far above them, moving in rivers of golden light. Now they would meet her only in their dreams. She had crossed back over the River of Forgetfulness, the River Lethe, and once more knew her true nature as an eternal being of light.

"I feel her calming, watchful presence everywhere," their brother Stan said to Georgina. "It's like she's part of the trees and air."

BUT NOT TONIGHT

"My mother won't submit to her grief until I leave," Kate told Finn on the phone. "Only when she's alone, will she live in the middle of it, endure it, and find her way to the other side. As long as I'm here, she thinks she has to be protective and hide her devastation."

Even though time slowed down and seemed to stop at the ending, Julia's death had still been too sudden for Georgina to metabolize. It caught her heart off guard and blew it open. "She's run through, impoverished with Julia gone from the world," Kate told Finn.

"Your mom's had a lot of loss this last couple of years. But how are you?"

"Okay. In a bit of shock myself over Julia," Kate replied. "At Easter she was helping friends and living her life. Then she was dead before summer's end. The cancer gained momentum so fast, it was like an avalanche in Julia's body." She knew she and her mother would have to face their heartbreak in private, find their own path through grief, and eventually to peace inside themselves. There was nothing to do but meet their grief with everything they had to give until it shaped them into someone better than they ever thought they could be.

"Are you really okay?" Finn asked.

"It's hard to see my mother so sad, but I know she'll come through it." Kate knew once she was gone, Georgina would open up to her grief and allow herself to dissolve in it. In the end she'd discover a greater strength. She knew too that her mother understood that mourning and death are as integral to life as love.

"So then, are you ready to come home?" Finn asked.

"I'll go online tonight and book my ticket."

"Make it soon, baby. I'm panting for you."

"I love you, Finn."

Even though Kate knew her mother would cope when she left, it was hard to pull away from her. She'd watched her grieve for her parents and over the loss of Colin, but this had bowed her lower even than all that. Kate gave an involuntary shudder as she recalled the image of Julia's gaunt physical body and the beauty of her endurance. There had been horror, but there had also been love, so much love, in Julia's dying. Somehow, in dying she had opened them up to the meaning of what it means to be human, to have a human body and lose it. So many friends and all of Julia's family had pulled together and wrapped her in love for the journey. And they had cared for one another as they all struggled forward to the final gateway. If death can be beautiful, it had been a beautiful death.

Kate left and allowed her mother to succumb to grief. She knew physical reality would be eclipsed for Georgina as she lived with the images of her sister's dying body, taking them out one by one, turning them over, looking under them. Julia's forehead, her eyes, her long thin fingers, her slender feet, the prominence of her jaw and teeth at the end, her spine covered only by a thin layer of skin, each vertebra visible, her shoulders and hip bones completely articulated through her skin, the tubes hanging from her, the sound of her laugh, her voice—all these images would remain for a long, long time in Georgina's mind, just under the roof of consciousness, waiting their turn on stage.

As she flew across the world, Kate pictured her mother lying on her back in the cool temple of her bedroom, hour upon hour, meditating and remembering and meditating some more. There would be the memories of her whole life with Julia to sort through. Grieving, it was called. But it was so much more as she metabolized the lesson of this loss. Her mother would need extra patience for the bad days when she would blame herself for not having been kinder, more loving, more understanding during all the years she had had with her sister. Regret would drag her into hell. But Kate also knew that Georgina would call on help from the invisible world, and that thought comforted her.

After falling completely into her grief and living it fully, Georgina would pull back and return to live life more deeply, with more compassion, her psyche enriched immeasurably by having accompanied her sister toward death, one of the troupe of saltimbanques who'd come together to receive Julia's gift and journey with her as far as they could go. Still, a big corner of Georgina's foundation had been blown away by Julia's death. She'd have to rebuild, create a new blueprint to accommodate this loss. She'd done it before when her father died, when Colin left. Kate thought about all this as she traveled back to Finn. Her mother would struggle with her grief and self-recrimination until she could make sense of the suffering and turn it into gold, like the alchemist she was.

Finn was at the gate to meet her when she landed. From a distance he could see she was edged about with sorrow. Kate melted into him as he encircled her in his arms. "I don't like our house when you're not there," he whispered into her hair.

There was a bouquet of multicolored roses on the counter when they walked in. "Oh Finn, you—"

"I didn't."

"Lydia?"

"She's desperate for you."

"Well, I guess I can wait to thank her until tomorrow."

"Damn right," he said, pulling her toward him. Kate was grateful to feel all the warmth of Finn. His flesh was firm, and no bones were poking out anywhere, and his cheeks glowed with youth and health. The muscles under his skin were taut, and the skin itself was smooth with palpable strength. She wanted to memorize him as he was at this moment. One day they would grow old and weak and die, but not tonight. Tonight they were full to overflowing with health and life and love and passion. Finally Kate fell asleep wrapped in the shelter of Finn's body.

The morning light was soft. It touched the walls here and there in gentle patterns like an accompanying friend. Kate studied it as she padded into her kitchen, picked up the kettle, and filled it with just the right amount of water. She was grateful to be home in her own house with her own husband where nobody was dying, even if bravely. A quiet happiness settled over her as she set the kettle on the burner and adjusted the flame. She had almost forgotten happiness in the midst of so much grief. As she sat in the morning sun, she felt the events of the past several weeks melt off her. It had been more traumatic than she'd realized, witnessing Julia's final days. There had been no drama. Everyone had cooperated. And the closer Julia's death came, the more a feeling of peace had spread over the house and out under the trees and down the hill into the valley. But it had been a sorrowful peace. Julia's soul had vacated a body no longer able to sustain it. Kate was growing a body for a new soul to inhabit.

Finn came up behind her and kissed the top of her head. "You're far away."

"I was just thinking about the way Julia's house was wrapped in this feeling the last days of her life, this feeling of timelessness. Peace settled in the trees around her house, in the air itself, maybe because she was so calm and accepting. Maybe it emanated from her."

"How about scrambled eggs with sour cream and chives?" Finn asked, calling her back to the here and now. Kate watched Finn crack the eggs into a bowl and whisk them into a froth. His hands were so fine. Each time she'd tried to draw them, she'd missed some aspect, some little elegance about a finger or a sweeping curve near the mound where the thumb joined his palm. The kettle boiled, and Kate turned off the flame.

The morning sun moved through the kitchen and lit up Lydia's flowers. Finn swallowed the last of his eggs and nodded at the bouquet. "I'll call her," Kate said.

Finn bent to kiss her good-bye. "I'm off. Love you."

Before Kate could call, the phone rang. Lydia suggested they go for hot stone massages, then have lunch and talk. "It'll do you good after all the tension and the long flight."

"Shall I book them or will you?" Kate asked.

"I've already booked for us at eleven."

"All right. I'll meet you there then." So much for getting any work done this morning. Kate washed the breakfast dishes and debated working for an hour, but instead she just sat still and did nothing.

Lydia was right: the hot stones felt amazing gliding over her skin and unwinding all the kinks in her back. The stones fit perfectly into the arch of each foot. As she lay enjoying the heat of the stones moving over her body, a memory flickered across the front of her mind. Her cousin Charlotte had taken Julia to have her first and only facial just six months ago, and Julia had said she loved it. Julia would never have another facial. She no longer had a physical body. A small moan escaped Kate's lips at that thought and made her feel grateful for her own body.

While they were getting dressed, Lydia suggested a small seaside restaurant run by a family originally from Barcelona. Strange that she didn't want to lunch at the club; that was usually her first choice. Why was she forsaking its colonial ambiance today? "Tell me how your mother's doing and all about that glamorous wedding, and then I'll tell you my news," Lydia said as they finished dressing.

"Oh no, you can't say you have news and expect me to wait and digress across two continents to tell you things that have already happened." As a kind of compromise, they drove in silence the few miles to the restaurant.

But before they even reached the restaurant door, Lydia burst forth. "I'm leaving Spencer."

"What? Why? What does he say about it?" Kate stood still at the entrance.

"I haven't told him yet. I want to be sure."

"Shall we take one of the umbrella tables in the back overlooking the water?" Kate asked. Lydia nodded. It was a casual place, and they seated themselves. Kate set her bag on the empty chair next to her. "So what's going on, Lydia?"

"I don't like who I've become with Spencer." Lydia opened her napkin across her lap. "He'd soldier on with me forever, but I just can't anymore. I'm dependent, useless, silly, and self-involved." It was like she had rehearsed these words.

"That sounds awfully hard, Lydia." Kate glanced up as the waiter dropped off the menus and two glasses of water.

"I want to do something meaningful with my life."

"How will leaving Spencer help with that?" Kate asked. She took a sip of her water.

"It's about how he views me. I'm locked into this persona with him where I can't value myself because he doesn't value me."

Lydia was close to tears already, so Kate hesitated before asking, "Is that fair? He appears to value you a great deal. Maybe it's you who undervalues yourself?"

"I've already admitted to you that I don't value myself." There was anger in Lydia's voice. "But it's because of how he feels about me that I hate myself."

"Don't let your self-worth be regulated by Spencer or anyone. Each of us is accountable for the choices we make."

"So you think I'm blaming everything on Spencer." Lydia summoned the waiter and ordered a glass of white wine. Then she turned to Kate. "It's easy for you with an adoring hunk for a husband." Kate ignored the aggression in Lydia's voice and spoke gently to her friend.

"Finn adds to my joy, but he's not responsible for my happiness or for creating meaning in my life. It's my own job to plant and cultivate those seeds." Lydia made no answer.

The waiter took advantage of the pause to ask if they'd like to know the special. They both ordered it. He took the unopened menus away.

"I thought you'd understand and be on my side," Lydia said.

"I am on your side, Lydia. I'm just not so sure throwing Spencer overboard is the solution. It seems very drastic."

"Why do you say that?" Lydia asked. Kate had to think. The waiter brought Lydia's white wine and Kate's lemonade, set them down with care, and withdrew. "Because relationships are the best opportunity we have to grow—even though we may not always like the mirror the other person is giving us."

"The mirror I get from Spencer is that I'm a spoiled, useless, shallow bore."

"Have you ever asked him if that's what he thinks?"

"God, no."

"Even if that is his projection onto you, which I doubt, you don't have to wear it," Kate said.

Lydia started to cry. "I feel like you're blaming me and putting it all on me."

"I'm not blaming anyone. I just don't think walking out on your marriage will suddenly make you love and value yourself."

"I can't see the point in carrying on." Lydia took a tissue from her bag and blotted around her eyes. "What's the point of marriage with no children?"

"The point is that relationships are the best opportunity we have to grow and heal from all our wounds. It's in relationships that we have an opportunity to meet ourselves in a new way."

The waiter approached and set steaming bowls of linguine and cockles down in front of them. Kate picked up her fork and wound a few strands around it. Lydia sipped her wine.

"So children are irrelevant?" There was sarcasm in Lydia's question, but Kate ignored it. "Not irrelevant, just a different kind of challenge and joy." Lydia ignored her food and nursed her grievances. She was oblivious to the beauty around them, the birds along the shore, playing in the water, the open blue sky, the red and pink hibiscus covering the hedges. *We're sitting in paradise*, Kate thought. *The earth is so beautiful, so bountiful. How can there be so much human misery here in the midst of all this beauty?*

As she set her wine glass down, Lydia said almost as a challenge, "So what should I do then?"

"Sometimes if one bears a feeling, a situation, sees it right through, it begins to transform. What you thought was a giant sea monster turns out to be just the foam upon the waves."

"Marriage isn't a shape shifter, Kate."

"Things can transform, Lydia."

"I'm gorged with this marriage, and you're asking me to eat more. Spencer and I are like two old cabbages rotting in the garden." Lydia clawed at the white table cloth. Kate reached out and covered Lydia's hand with her own.

"I'm not saying you two will turn into pear trees laden with golden fruit,

251

but if you bear a situation, sometimes things simplify themselves." Kate had the feeling she wasn't being at all helpful. Coming off as critical was making Lydia shut down. Who was she to tell Lydia to bear her suffering so she could learn from it, even if she believed that was the purpose of human suffering? So she fell silent and waited. Lydia was looking out across the water. Above their heads the breeze ruffled the blue umbrella. Finally, Lydia picked up her fork and rolled some linguine around it. They ate in silence for a while before Kate spoke.

"You're right, Lydia. It can be a violation of your individuality to be in an intimate relationship. One can start to feel defined by one's partner."

"That's what I'm trying to tell you," Lydia said. "I feel defined by Spencer and I don't know what to do."

"Can you talk to him about the way you feel?" Kate asked.

"That would lead to an argument."

"But arguments are important in a marriage," said Kate. Lydia looked baffled.

"Because we naturally build up a resistance to the other person in a close relationship and that leads to disappointments and fights. But that doesn't mean the relationship is over."

"I don't see you and Finn fighting and having scenes and resistances."

"We did, and we still do. We nearly broke up a dozen times the first couple of years. In order to be conscious of himself, Finn had to distinguish himself from me, so he tried to push me away. When he wasn't doing that, I was. We had to learn that for our relationship to continue, we had to be two separate individuals in relationship to one another. Sometimes that involved suffering."

"I don't know what you mean," said Lydia. Kate wondered if Lydia was being deliberately obtuse, or if this really was an alien way of looking at relationships for her. Kate gave her friend the benefit of the doubt and tried again. "Your relationship with Spencer is an opportunity for each of you to grow by rubbing up against your differences and weaknesses and wounds, so you can learn from them. Marriage is an alchemical vessel where you meet yourself in a new way, if you stay in the vessel and let the alchemy happen." Lydia seemed to shift and drop her defenses a little. Or maybe it was the wine

252

working. Kate felt a bit like a parrot. *Oh God, am I turning into my mother, talking about marriage as an alchemical vessel?*

Lydia swallowed before she said, "I don't know if I feel better or worse thinking about relationships that way. Part of me doesn't want to listen to you. I'd rather stay angry at Spencer. I was almost sure I wanted out of this airless marriage. Now you're telling me that working on my relationship with Spencer is the way for us to grow."

After Lydia dropped her off, Kate breathed in relief. Lydia had seemed more at peace by the end of lunch. Somehow they'd made it through the rocky terrain by the time the check came.

"I'll give her two rotting cabbages. She's a reckless, fucking drama queen," Finn said. He was watching Kate chop up cilantro. "What does she think, that her life should be wrapped in an endless mantle of joy where she's worshipped like the Queen of Sheba? She's not going to have Spencer for-ever—anything can happen at any time. He could have a heart attack or an accident, or she could. And she makes such fusses."

"Hand me that lime, please," Kate said. "Lydia's in a lot of pain, Finn, and she knows so little about what happens in relationships. I doubt her parents ever talked to her about them, and Spencer is her first and only love."

"Then she should treat him like he's her love, not go whining all over the place about him." Kate handed the two halves of the squeezed lime to Finn, who tossed each one, basketball style, into the garbage pail behind him. Kate knew he had no patience for the subject, but she wanted to defend her friend. "Lydia's just beginning now, in midlife, to understand how love leads to wild hatred and back again to love."

"Oh, boo hoo. I'm not an empath like you. She's an unscrupulous toad to blame Spencer for her unhappiness. It's time she developed some humanity and learned the value of suffering. I hope she's not going to horn her misery all over the base and humiliate Spencer."

"Are you done ranting, Finn?" Kate handed him a platter of sole broiled in lemon and butter and sprinkled with almond slivers, served over cilantro and lime rice.

"No, but let's eat anyway." Then seeing the platter in his hands, he said, "This looks great."

253

THE COAL BOX

Olive was asleep on Kate and Finn's old bed. Georgina lay down beside her and touched her silky ears. The feel of them calmed Georgina's ragged heart, and gratitude welled up inside her, gratitude not only for Olive's jungle presence but also for Kate and Finn, and this apartment, and for work she loved, and for Washington Square Park, especially the trees, and for having had Julia as her sister. A tear slid out of the corner of her eye and rolled down into the shell of her ear. "Oh, Julia, this world resounds with your absent presence. Are you moving through a field of golden light? Something broke in me when you died. Without your fearless and determined heart to count on, my own is broken, and I don't know how I'll ever be whole again."

Julia had been dead for more than four months. Somehow Georgina had lived through autumn. It was nearly Thanksgiving, and she still couldn't believe that she'd never see Julia's familiar form again or hear her voice or kiss her hello or laugh with her over some silly thing or seek her wisdom and comfort in times of need. *Over there is really right here*, she told herself. *It's just that Julia is invisible to me now. But she's alive within me, in a chamber of my heart.*

Georgina kissed the top of Olive's head, got off the bed, and went to take a shower. Maybe the steam would help her breathing, which had been labored since Julia's death. She knew the lungs hold sorrow and grief. But this pain was like stabbing knives in the bottom part of her lungs. Some nights she had to sleep propped up in order to breathe at all. Since childhood her lungs had been her weak spot. Several healers over the years told her she had been exposed to some environmental toxin as a little girl, but she insisted she hadn't, that she'd grown up in the fresh country air.

The crystals on the bathroom windowsill broke the sunlight up, casting dozens of tiny rainbows all over the walls and on her arms and legs as she stepped under the falling water. These rainbows would be invisible if the crystals didn't separate the light waves. So much went unseen in the world, but it was there all the same. Were spirits on other planes visible if only one had the right prism? *Julia, are you near only I can't see you?*

As she washed her hair, Georgina went over her client schedule for the day: a lot of heartache was coming in. Sometimes after a day's work, she imagined she'd have to wade through a pool of salty tears two or three inches deep to get from her chair to her office door. People hurt each other unwittingly, through callousness and tiny cruelties. She knew they were only protecting their own hearts, keeping their distance and shoving their partners away through unconscious maneuvers, or worse, scorching the whole landscape in a violent affair. She turned off the shower. It gave her pleasure to rub her skin dry with a clean, rough towel. *Did I protect my own heart too much? Was it fear that kept me from finding true love? What am I afraid of?* Though in fact she secretly hoped there would be another chance at love, she wouldn't acknowledge it even to herself. *But what am I afraid of? Besides my mother?* she asked herself again as she buttoned her blue silk blouse, tucked it in her skirt, and ran her fingers through her hair.

All her life she had been afraid of her mother. No one else, really. And no one else had shared this feeling about her beautiful but devastating mother, with her cornflower-blue eyes and long, dark hair.

Georgina remembered sitting on the floor as a little girl, playing with her doll and looking up to see her mother skipping down the staircase above her. She looked like a princess in the long, pink circle skirt that floated up around her like a ball gown as she descended the stairs. Georgina had wanted so much for this fairy princess to love her, or at least be kind to her.

Julia had always been an apologist for their mother, as had her brothers and their father. Only her aunt, her father's sister, had dared to ask her mother once, when Georgina was only about four, "Why are you so cruel to that child?" The question enraged her mother. The bond of love had never formed between Georgina and the woman who had given birth to her. Georgina was perpetually anxious around her, even to the last day of her mother's life. Maybe that was why she'd settled for Colin, because she believed she was unlovable. Even now as she walked to work, she wondered about how love happened or didn't.

It was true for many people, her clients and her friends, that love started out rich and full, so sure of itself. Then along the way, it got choked off, and the lover disappeared to be replaced by this stranger who inflicted pain and said mean things. "That looks awful on you. Why are you always rushing? Eating? Sleeping in? Talking on the phone? I don't like the way you dance. No, don't meet me for lunch at my office. I like to keep things separate." Where did the guy who said "No one's hotter than you" go? What happened to swing dancing?

Georgina unlocked her office door and opened the windows. For the next six hours, she would leave her own world and journey with her clients into their psyches. Work brought relief from her own sorrow as she shifted into a state where she was simply a field of consciousness for the other person. Submerging her personal self allowed her to move into a space where her heart and mind listened without judgment.

Later, at the end of the day, she would take out her flattened self, give it a shake, and re-inhabit it. But always she carried home what she'd heard, the pain, the suffering, the confusion, which, somewhere in the night, maybe in her dreams, she would have to metabolize.

At the end of the day, Georgina turned off the lamps and locked her office door. She had to rush a little to get home because tonight was her group meditation via conference call. Samantha, the leader, had the most soothing voice; plus, she was a kind of genius. How could she know so much about physics, the body, the chakras, the meridians, the planets, Western and Eastern medicine, and be psychic too? Georgina had had a stabbing pain in her lungs since Julia's death, a pain which had come and gone all her life in times of stress and sorrow. Massage, acupuncture, Epsom salts baths, magnesium flakes—nothing helped. Georgina hoped tonight's meditation would release something. She'd just have time to feed and walk Olive before the conference call.

She put on her headphones, dialed the number, and entered the six-digit conference code. After greetings, Samantha put them all on mute so they could hear her, but they couldn't be heard. Georgina lay back on her bed and closed her eyes. They began with full-body, sweeping breaths up from beneath the soles of their feet and out through the crown of their heads. After they did the breaths in all four cardinal directions, they entered the heart with the breath and radiated it out to every cell in the body. At that point Samantha instructed them to focus on something for which they felt gratitude, and to hold that vibration of gratitude in their hearts.

That was the moment Georgina's body began to shiver with chills like she was standing in front of a walk-in freezer with the door open. She heard her sister's name in her head, and then she heard her own voice deep inside her telling Julia how grateful she was for all she had given in the manner of her dying, for all she had suffered, the indignity, the pain, the fear, the valor, the sorrow at leaving those she loved as she melted away in front of their eyes, without bitterness or complaint, giving away everything, her future, those she adored, even her own flesh. How much she had taught them about how to die, how to leave the earth plane. She had shown them all how much more we are than just a physical body. There was too much gratitude for Georgina to contain, and her heart began to throb and ache like it would crack open. Frightened by the violence of the feeling in her chest, she thought of getting up to chew an aspirin in case she was having a heart attack. But she didn't get up. *Feel your broken heart,* she told herself. *That's all this is. You can't just stuff it in Pandora's box. Then what a mess there will be when it eventually all spills out anyway, despite how hard you try to keep the lid on.*

Samantha was now telling them to follow whatever feeling they were experiencing, even if it was painful, to the inner planes. Following the trail of the pain, Georgina called Julia's name. She felt herself melting and poured herself out, like liquid pouring from a sacred vessel into a scrying basin. "Forgive me, Julia, for all the hurts I inflicted on you in the life just past. I know I never will forgive myself." And she wept, telling Julia that she had been blind to her strength and beauty until the last weeks of her life when she had witnessed them completely for the first time. In answer, Julia said only one thing, the thing she had so often told Georgina in life. "I love you."

Then it was as if Julia were standing right there beside her and placing her palms over Georgina's chest, sending light into her lungs and showing her an old home movie. The scene was Georgina as a little girl of five or six, standing in the basement of their old childhood two-story house. She could see her child self coughing as she stood next to the coal box in the cellar. The coal was delivered to the cellar through a chute. How could she have forgotten that basement and that coal box? As a small child she had been sent there so often in terror by her mother, to stand alone as punishment for being a bad girl. The memory startled her. It was astonishing that she could have so completely buried it. Was this coal dust the environmental toxin the healers and been referring to? Was this the root of her lung problems?

Samantha was beginning the group healing now, working with the connective tissue from the inside of their ankles, up the legs, around the hips, and further up the lungs and throat, infusing the tissue with the ability to provide protection with each sweeping breath. Georgina floated away again, unable to focus on Samantha's voice. She was still back in the basement, coughing from the coal dust. Julia had sent her this picture, this memory, and shown her the environmental pollutant she'd forgotten. They'd moved out of that house when Georgina was seven, but she'd taken the coal dust with her in the bottom of her lungs. Their new house was a barn that her parents bought and renovated into a modern, light-filled house with oil heat; and the coal box was lost to her memory, buried deeply for all these years. But now Julia had unearthed it and shown it to her.

Samantha was working on various people when Georgina tuned back in. One person's kidney meridians were adjusted so that they passed through the kidneys now instead of taking an alternate path around them. Another person's gall bladder was softened and moved back into place. A third got a past life released through her eighth chakra. Samantha told Georgina that the ground around the tree where she meditated had become sacred. Georgina loved that tree. It wasn't the biggest or the oldest or even the most beautiful tree in Washington Square Park, but it was the one she loved. Standing under it one morning, she'd wondered if it had a name and almost immediately heard the name Thea. In *The Lord of the Rings*, trees walked and talked and had powerful feelings. Trees being human was also a myth Jung had written about. Love between trees and humans was a given for Georgina. Loving Thea and accepting her comfort made the loss of Julia somehow more bearable. Thea was always there, every day.

After they all signed off from the meditation and healing, Georgina lay in the dark, amazed that Julia had sent her the memory of the coal box. How could she have forgotten it? She took a breath. No pain. The stabbing knives were gone. Had Julia healed her by helping her to remember that story and then to let it go? Stories need to be remembered and told, if only to ourselves, before they're willing to leave. She wanted to jump for joy and burst into tears of gratitude at the same time. The universe was miraculous. Her sister had reached into this dimension and placed her healing hands on Georgina's mind and lungs. How else could she explain this? She wanted to call Carrie and tell her about it, but Carrie went to bed early. Emma would scoff, Selma was away at a track meet, and Julia was dead. But she didn't need to call Julia—Julia had been there.

Olive was asleep, making soft dog sounds as she dreamed her own dreams on the love seat at the foot of Georgina's bed. She bent down and kissed her silky ears good-night and then went to look on her bookshelf for some languid, drowsy reading. But even as she perused the shelves, her eyelids grew heavy.

"Good night, Julia," she whispered as she slipped in between the clean white sheets and fell into a grateful sleep.

I'LL PUT HIM IN A COFFIN

If Julia had lived, I would have asked her so many questions about pregnancy, Kate thought. She lay in bed with Finn's palm on her abdomen, feeling as happy as she'd ever felt in her life. Next week they'd begin classes on how to prepare for the birth. Films of actual births and placentas would be on the agenda. Tough guy that he was, Kate wondered how Finn would handle that. There were still things that made him squeamish. Placentas were probably on that list.

"Should we buy some things for the baby? Or think of some names?" Finn asked her.

"We still have time," Kate said.

"You're not superstitious about buying things ahead of time, are you, Kate?"

"No, I just hate shopping."

"Then how about just one of those baskets for next to the bed?" Finn said.

"What baskets?"

"You know, the ones like the infant Moses was in when his mother left him floating in the reeds in the river so he wouldn't be killed."

"A Moses basket?" Kate said.

"Yeah, a Moses basket." A big smile started in Kate's eyes and rolled down her face, turning up the corners of her lips.

"What?"

"You're cute, Finn, the way you say things sometimes. Remember the first time you came to my house for dinner, and we were putting the food away? You asked my mother where the metal paper was?"

"I was so nervous I couldn't think of the words *aluminum foil*."

"It endeared you to her," said Kate.

"It's hard to imagine anyone being nervous around her, now that I know her. Want some cookies?" He asked her.

"No thanks. I already brushed my teeth." Kate closed her eyes and drifted off.

"Wow, do you hear that pounding rain?" Finn asked as he climbed back into bed with his little bowl of cookies. But Kate was already fast asleep.

Next morning they sat outside on the sunny steps in the clean, sweet-smelling air and ate their poached eggs on toast. "I'm going grocery shopping today. Want anything special?" Kate asked.

"Corn dogs, cookies and cream ice cream, caramel sauce, peanut butter cups, Oreos."

Kate smiled at him as she watched him stand up and stretch. "I meant any actual food," she said.

"Okay, I'm out of here, girl." He bent down and kissed her good-bye.

Kate watched him drive off, then picked up their plates from the steps. *I'd better make a list, or I'll forget something*, she thought. *But first I'll see if my editor has emailed the changes she wants.*

Nothing from her editor yet. But there was an unsettling surprise: Colin. The delete button was made for moments like this. But before she realized it, she'd clicked on the message.

Hey Kate,

I contacted you before because I wanted to share something with you. I'd hoped to do it in person. Since that can't be, and I don't even know where you are, I'm writing. You said you'd listen even if you might not respond. So here goes. I'm telling you this because I think this information belongs to you too.

About six months ago, I began having a recurrent nightmare

261

from which I awoke each time, sobbing and thinking of you. I think you know I've never had the experience of sobbing before. (*Right, I do know. You'd have to have a heart to be able to sob,* Kate thought.) My therapist and I worked on this dream, trying to analyze it for weeks, but I still kept having it, which meant we hadn't yet cracked the message my unconscious was trying to communicate to me. (*I know, you ass, what it means when you keep having a recurrent dream. Don't get all pedantic with me. Did you forget what my mother does for a living?*)

In the dream I am overjoyed, holding my infant daughter, who has opened my heart to love. I want to lay the world at her feet. For the first time in my life, I feel joy. We live somewhere in Europe. It is the time of the plague. Then I am bending over a tiny coffin, and I wake up shaking with sobs. Since I kept on having the dream and awakening in sobs with thoughts of you ("Oh, boo hoo," Kate said out loud in imitation of Finn.), I finally went to a past life regression therapist. He regressed me to a life in which many people died of the plague, including my infant daughter. You were my infant daughter in that life. I was your father. And I lost you. (*And you lost me again in this life. You trashed me and threw me in the ditch and ran away.*) The regression therapist said I've never been able to stay connected to anyone since that lifetime.

I am so sorry for hurting you, Kate. Please forgive me.

C.

Kate shut her laptop too hard, grabbed her bag, and went out the door to go grocery shopping. *I'm going to ignore this email like I never got it,* she decided as she backed out of the driveway. *Am I overreacting and being childish?* she wondered as she parked at the PX. *I'll forward it to Finn and Mom and see what they say. I don't want to carry this alone. It may not even be true. Is he trying to push his way back into my life by evoking my pity for his suffering?* She sat in her car in the parking lot, took out her iPhone and forwarded Colin's email.

By the time she got to the checkout, her cart was piled so high, things were falling off in all directions. Twelve grocery bags, the most she'd ever bought at once, and she'd not only forgotten her list but all her reusable bags. Ordinarily, she'd be embarrassed not to have brought them, but she was too shaky even to notice. It pissed her off that Colin could still have any effect on her. She wanted to feel neutral toward him. After struggling to get all the bags into the house, she unpacked them and stuffed everything in the cupboards and refrigerator. At least Finn would be happy she'd bought so much junk food. Because of all the ice cream she'd stuffed in it, she had to tape the freezer door shut to keep it closed.

Kate set the tape down on the kitchen counter and checked her phone in the hope she'd have received some perspective on Colin's email from either her mother or Finn. She didn't want to be alone with it. They'd both written back.

This is a truck load of bullshit sent by a dick. I'll put him in a coffin. Forget you ever got this Kate. He's a pathetic loser sharing his soppy dream with you. I'll give that dickwad something to cry about. xo Finn

Hi Sweet-Pea Girl,
I don't like that Colin is reaching into your world. You don't have to respond to him, you know. He's making an excuse for his behavior to you in this life because of something he claims happened in a past life. But he's also asking to be forgiven. That's something you might want to consider because forgiveness is something we do for ourselves. It's an act of self-love. Then again, you have to be ready. In order to really forgive someone, we have to realize that nothing wrong ever happened. That's a hard perspective to achieve. I do believe things happen mostly as they were meant to happen, and that nothing is ever done to us. It's done for us—so we can grow. At least I try to hold on to that idea. This is a radical take on forgiveness, and I struggle with it myself regarding Colin. But for you to forgive Colin would release any connection to him, and you'd still never have to see him again. Am I making sense?

But don't do anything yet. Step back. Watch your dreams to let your unconscious have a chance to weigh in.

I love you,

Mom

P. S. I hoped you aren't too freaked out by his email.

ZERO-POINT FIELD

"I'm picking you up in an hour, and you're coming with me. You love this kind of thing," Emma said.

"I don't feel like concentrating on a lecture tonight."

"It's not just a lecture. There's wine and cheese afterward, and it's the last one before winter break. Besides, The New School is only three blocks from your house. And maybe Mr. Right will be there sipping a glass of Cabernet."

"What are you talking about, Emma? You don't believe in the idea of Mr. Right. And you've told me often enough that I scare men off because I'm too weird."

"You are weird, but this topic could attract fellow weirdos."

"I'll come, but not to hunt for Mr. Right. I'm used to being on my own now."

Georgina thought about Emma as she ran a bath and sprinkled in three drops of wild-orange essential oil. Emma had never married. When anybody asked her about it, she told them she hadn't gotten around to it yet.

Georgina assumed that the early tragic loss of both parents at once was a big part of the reason Emma had never let herself make a commitment. It was also why, Georgina suspected, she'd chosen to be an obituary writer. People's life stories and how they died fascinated Emma. She claimed that writing about people's deaths gave her some sense of control, as if she could tie up a life in a little package with a neat ending, dated and located in time and space. It was as if, with each obituary she wrote, she worked through a little more of her own loss. *Some losses take a lifetime to metabolize*, Georgina thought as she stepped into the bath.

She was pulling her black cashmere sweater over her head when the buzzer rang to announce Emma. "Hi, I'll be ready in a sec. I just have to run a brush through my hair."

"Don't wear black, and put on some lipstick," Emma said, following her into the bedroom.

"Anything else?"

"A little mascara wouldn't hurt."

"Enough, Emma. This is about the zero-point field not about me snagging a guy."

The auditorium in the new University Center was almost full when they walked in. To find two seats together, they had to sit practically in the front row. The bamboo walls and the soft red leather chairs made this a gorgeous room. "This is the greenest building in New York," Emma told her as they settled themselves. The lights dimmed. The speaker tapped the microphone and began to talk without even being introduced or telling them his name.

"Scientists," Emma quipped.

"Hush," Georgina said.

"The quantum field, which may be thought of as source, or a kind of logos, underlies our entire physical universe."

Emma leaned into Georgina and whispered, "I can see this guy is in your tree." Georgina ignored her.

"At the quantum level, also known as the zero-point field, time and space do not exist. But in three-dimensional reality, we use the concepts of time and space to navigate our lives. In 1905 Einstein observed that time and space cannot be separated but exist together to form the fourth dimension. This observation opened the door for tremendous discoveries in physics." The speaker paused and looked out at his audience as if to gauge their reaction before continuing.

"According to Einstein time is not a constant. It is different for each one of us depending on where we are in space and how fast we're moving."

Emma rummaged in her bag, then dropped it. Georgina gave her a look. When Georgina was able to tune in to the speaker again, he was talking about quanta. "Scientists have also discovered that subatomic particles are not solid objects. They are vibrating packets of energy, which Max Planck named quanta. Physics teaches us that everything is energy. But humans don't experience objects as vibrating bursts of energy. We experience objects, including ourselves, as solid. At the level of the zero-point field, this vibrating energy appears to take shape only if someone observes it. In other words, consciousness affects reality. Einstein also discovered that if you match the frequency of the reality you want, you cannot help but get that reality."

Emma leaned into Georgina: "Just your cup of tea." Georgina stared straight ahead at the speaker.

"Our view of the world dramatically changed in the last century when in 1919 Eddington proved Einstein's theory of general relativity, thereby displacing Newton's theory, which had stood for centuries. Thanks to the work of Einstein and Eddington, we now know that space is curved and that starlight is bent by the gravitational field of the sun. Although Newton had told us that the universe was not static, Einstein showed that it is in fact actually expanding.

"Since the universe is expanding, how did the expansion begin? Was there a singular big bang event? And if the universe did have a beginning, will it have an end? And why did it begin at all, if it did? Recent scientific work suggests that the universe did not have a beginning, that there was no singularity, and that neither will it have an end. If this proves true, it will solve the major problem of the theory of relativity, which breaks down at the point of singularity. Mathematics cannot explain what happens at the point of singularity, or before the event. And this new model proposes that the universe is filled with a quantum fluid, possibly composed of gravitons, which mediate the force of gravity."

"Is he saying the universe may have existed forever, that there was no big bang?" Emma whispered.

"Yes. Hush—we're missing bits."

"Scientists theorize that our own sun has enough fuel to exist for another five thousand million years before it runs out. But our sun is only a tiny part of the universe. What of the whole universe? When it expands to its utmost boundary, will it begin contracting again? This is the old theory. Now scientists are asking if the concept of a boundary even makes sense when talking of the universe. We don't yet have the mathematical models to answer this question."

"Are you following this?" Emma whispered. Georgina nodded.

"Our view of ourselves is evolving along with our view of the universe. We now know, for example, thanks to the work of Bruce Lipton for one, that our genetic makeup can be altered through observation and intention, just as Einstein expected. Lipton's work has demonstrated that we can change our own DNA. His work is consistent with Einstein's physics, which postulate that the act of observing a thing changes it. In other words, all particles that are given attention materialize. The act of focusing our consciousness creates reality. Einstein posed this question: Does the moon actually exist if we don't look at it? This was a startling question for Newtonian physicists. The Danish scientist Niels Bohr went so far as to suggest that anyone who isn't shocked by quantum physics has not understood it."

Emma fidgeted in her bag again. "What are you doing?" Georgina asked her.

"Looking for a Kleenex." Emma blew her nose, and Georgina huffed at her. "What?"

But Georgina had turned back to the speaker. She'd lost the thread of what he was saying by the time Emma was finally still.

"Not only are subatomic particles not solid masses, but rather packets of vibrating energy; but in addition, this vibrating energy, if separated from a part of itself, can remain connected to the separated portion and able to communicate instantaneously with it, even across great distances, because at the quantum level, time and space do not exist. Some of you may be familiar with Gregg Braden's popular book *The Divine Matrix*, which cites multiple studies that demonstrate this phenomenon. Instantaneous communication between particles across great distances can be explained by the zero-point field."

"That's the book you gave me two Christmases ago." Emma said.

"Time is a concept created by our collective nervous system so we don't get overwhelmed by experiencing everything at once. In fact your future has already happened: you just don't remember it. Past, present, and future exist together. Time is simply a mode in which we think in the third dimension."

Emma took out her iPhone and checked her email. Georgina tried to ignore her and tuned back toward the speaker.

"The zero-point field is the vibrating energy that carries the information of the universe. It is a sea of energy, a mesh of light, a matrix that encompasses and underlies all of reality. Scientists have now demonstrated that even our own memories are not stored in our individual brains, but in the zero-point field. Our brains retrieve and download our memories from the field. Anyone can tune in to all memories, theirs or another's, at any time, by vibrating at a frequency in harmony with the zero-point field. This is what meditation attempts to do. And this is what intuitives are able to do. They allow their brains to resonate with the frequency of the zero-point field to gain access to information without the limitation of time. They can tune in through resonance and see the future because it has already happened."

"So Colin was onto something with all those visits to his tarot reader," Emma whispered.

Georgina ignored Emma's comment and stared at the speaker. He looked like he was in his late fifties. She liked his face; its structure was symmetrical, which made him look handsome. And he was so earnest. She turned her attention back to his words.

"One implication of the zero-point field is that we are each capable of creating reality through our intention because this sea of potential is very susceptible to intention. Healers do it. They use their intention to manipulate matter in our bodies. We are capable of making ourselves sick or healing ourselves. It has been repeatedly demonstrated that positive energy and prayer affect the health of those who are recipients of them. Through the sending or receiving of negative or positive energy, we affect one another. What we intend materializes sooner or later. That may be how Jesus multiplied the fish and bread and how he changed water into wine and helped the blind see. He focused the power of his intention. He wasn't distracted by the limitations of the third dimension."

"Is he really talking about Jesus?" Emma said. Georgina kept her focus on the speaker.

"Animals have more access to the zero-point field than humans do. Animals don't second-guess the information they get from the field. When Vesuvius erupted and buried Pompeii, all the animals that weren't tethered ran away and survived. They knew the volcano was about to erupt, because they picked up the information from the field and acted on it. Similarly, dogs are now being used to warn parents when their children who suffer from seizure disorder are about to have a seizure. The dogs wake the parents up in the night before the seizure happens."

"I've read about that," Emma said.

"Through the zero-point field, we are all interconnected in a nonlocal reality that permeates the cosmos. Our intentions matter. They create reality. We are each responsible for the fate of all of us. We can end life on the earth through nuclear war and suffer the fate of the planet Maldek, which once existed between Jupiter and Mars until the consciousness of its inhabitants became so predatory that they blew up their own planet. Its remnants are now an asteroid belt. Our consciousness is responsible for the fate of our planet. The great psychologist Carl Jung once said, 'The world hangs by a single thread. And that thread is the psyche of man.' We are all communicating our intentions continually. They are transmitted instantly, despite the distance, faster than the speed of light. For centuries this was considered to be impossible, as it was believed that nothing could travel faster than the speed of light. But we now know information can travel through the zero-point field—faster than the speed of light. We also know that our intentions create reality. What will we as a species choose to create?"

As Georgina listened to the speaker's closing remarks, she found herself wondering about him. His face looked familiar. How could that be? Did he have children? Was he even married? Maybe he was one of those scientists who had devoted his whole life to his work. No, he seemed too human or well rounded or something for that, like someone who would be in the world as much as the laboratory. And he'd quoted Jung.

The audience was applauding as the host approached the podium to thank the speaker and invite everyone for wine and cheese in the lobby.

"I think you should ask him about dreams." Emma nudged Georgina.

"What about dreams?"

"Whether they're coming from the zero-point field."

"Dreams come from the personal and the collective unconscious," Georgina said.

"But maybe the collective unconscious and the zero-point field are the same thing."

"I could never go up to him. And he's surrounded by people."

"I'm going to the ladies' room," Emma said. "I'll be right back—unless you're coming."

"No, go ahead."

Georgina made her way over to the wine table and picked up a glass of red. Turning around, she found herself face to face with the speaker.

"I loved your talk," she said.

"Human beings can create reality through their intentions, and all time is happening at once—past, present, and future. Not everyone takes those ideas on board easily," he said. He didn't make any effort to move off, but continued to fix his gaze on her face. "I saw you sitting near the front, and you looked familiar. I thought maybe we'd met at a conference. Are you a physicist?"

"A psychologist. I love the quote by Jung you shared." She stood there frozen with shyness, not even taking a sip of her wine or knowing what to do next. He could move away now easily with a "Well, it was nice meeting you." But he didn't.

"Do you work with dreams?" he asked her.

"I love working with dreams."

"Like the zero-point field, they're not bound by the constraints of time and space," he said.

Two women were standing nearby, hoping to catch his eye, and the host was heading across the room toward them, but he kept his attention on Georgina.

"Some people are waiting to talk to you," she said. His eyes released her. The host touched his arm and told him there was someone he wanted him to meet. Georgina took the opportunity to slip through the throng at the wine table and move away. Emma was coming toward her. "I saw you talking to him. You know, he was looking at you during his talk."

"No, Emma, he was looking at his audience."

"Actually, Georgina, although you like to be right even at your own expense, this time you've got the wrong end of the stick. I saw him see you while he was speaking. He gave a little pause as if he knew you."

"Are you ready to go?" Georgina asked her.

"No. Drink your wine and relax while I get myself a glass."

Georgina felt a hand on her elbow. "Have a drink with me after this is over?" It was him.

Without thinking, she agreed.

"Good. I'll come and find you in about half an hour." This would be her first drink with a man in six years. She felt like crying, but she didn't know why.

Emma walked up. "What was that about?"

"He invited me for a drink."

"And?"

"I said yes. But you don't have to smile like a Cheshire cat."

"Oh, I think I do."

THE LAW OF ONE

Kate's skirt flew up as she stepped out of the doctor's office into the windy afternoon. Though she wished Finn had been there, the visit had gone well. The nurse had arranged the camera so Kate could count all ten fingers and toes without being able to see the baby's sex. Seeing each perfect little digit was like slowly unwrapping a gift. Even though she'd stopped her antidepressant medication before trying to get pregnant, fear still lingered around the fringes of her mind that it could hurt her baby. The wind picked up again and blew her hair across her face as she tried to open the car door.

Before she could start the motor, her phone rang. "Hi, Lydia."

"How'd it go?"

"Great."

"What did she say?"

"This last four weeks, the lungs have to fully develop, and the baby should gain about half a pound a week, each week. It's about six pounds now, give or take."

"So everything's on track, and they still say the baby will arrive mid-January?"

"It's hard to get my mind around the fact that I'm going to be somebody's mother in a month."

"I feel as if I'm going to be somebody's aunt in a month. And I think I understand a little of what this means to you to see you first-ever blood relative."

"Do you really, Lydia?"

"I do. And my heart is bursting for you, and I'm grateful you're letting me share it, though I don't know why you wouldn't let me give you a baby shower."

"It's just not me, Lydia. Besides, it's holiday time and there are already so many parties. Anyway, I'm still in the parking lot of the doctor's office. Let's talk later, and you can tell me what you need for Christmas dinner."

"All right, I'm about to leave for therapy anyway; I was only checking in about your visit."

Kate steered the car out into the stream of traffic and headed home. She smiled thinking of Lydia going to therapy. Spencer had been surprisingly easy about it. And Lydia was less tense and more authentic these days. Her therapist had even suggested they do a few sessions of couple work. But Lydia was waiting for the right time to mention that to Spencer.

Kate dropped her bag on the chair by their bed and changed into leggings and one of Finn's shirts. Staring into her closet, she wondered what she could possibly wear to Lydia's fancy Christmas dinner party. Georgina had advised her to add glittery earrings or a shiny necklace as an easy way to make an effort. How would her mother spend Christmas? With Julia dead less than six months, Kate wasn't sure Georgina would even celebrate. But then wouldn't she want to make an effort for Julia's daughters? Besides, she loved Christmas trees, just as Julia had.

Later that evening as she and Finn walked up and down inspecting the evergreen trees all lined up like soldiers along the fence, trying to see which one called out to them, Kate said, "I wish my mother had someone. I don't want her to be alone."

"Why? She seems perfectly happy. And your mom moves to her own beat. Some of her ideas would scare the pants off a lot of guys."

"I know, but it's nearly Christmas, and that's such a romantic time to fall in love."

"How about this one?" Finn pointed to a large tree. "It looks about ten feet tall. Isn't that your criterion?"

"Give it a shake, so we can see it." Georgina's trees were always ten feet high, and Kate wanted to keep up the tradition. Finn lifted the tree and

274

tapped its trunk on the ground a few times. The branches opened up like elegant evergreen arms.

"Perfect," Kate said. Finn paid and tied the tree to the roof of their car.

"I love to watch you do things," she said. "Your competence makes me feel safe."

"Let's hope we have plenty of warning when the baby's about to arrive. I don't want to have to rely on my competence to handle that."

"I should be so lucky as to have a labor so fast we couldn't make it to the birthing center."

"Shall we decorate this beauty tonight or let it open a bit more?" Finn asked. He pulled into their driveway and turned to Kate.

"Let's let it relax for tonight, I think." Before carrying the tree into the house, Finn got a saw and gave the trunk a fresh cut. Kate poured hot water into a pail in front of the window, and Finn rested their tree in it. "Tonight it can drink. Tomorrow we'll put it in the stand," Kate said. Then she sat down in a comfy chair and breathed in the tree. "I love this moment," she said.

"Shall we toast our tree?" He asked. "Or as your mom would say, 'offer it our gratitude.'"

Kate nodded and started to get up.

"Stay put—I got it. Sit and commune with your tree."

"Ah yes, the tree and I are both part of the oneness of life," Kate said smiling over her shoulder at him. But she did want to talk to him about the oneness, about how to raise their baby spiritually. What would they teach it when it started asking questions about how we got here and what our purpose was? How would they instill the idea of oneness and of love for all beings, the idea that the whole universe was one being.

"For you, girl." Finn handed her a mug of tea and sat down with his wine.

"Finn, what will we teach our kids about how to live in the most enlightened way?"

"Whoa, baby. I haven't worried about that yet. I'm still at the stage of letting it be born with all its fingers and toes and various parts in good working order. I think we can worry about that other stuff further down the road."

"But I want to know what you think."

275

"About religion?"

"Not religion. I know we won't bring our kids up in any religion, but how will we support their spiritual life? And their understanding of the universe?"

"Are you kidding? Your mother will have that covered. We'll have to rein her in as it is. She'll be telling the kids all kinds of things about how we're all connected, the trees and animals and humans, and how we're all evolving to a consciousness that we're one being. Even that the whole universe is one great big being, and we're each a part of some giant light or infinite intelligence that is knowing itself in different ways through every living thing. And since we're all part of one being, hurting another is hurting yourself, so try to be kind to everyone you meet."

"Wow. I'm impressed you have her beliefs down so well."

"Hey, I had a front row seat all through her *The Law of One* obsession."

"I don't think that period ever ended. It's still her core belief. But never mind what my mother thinks. I want to know what you believe we're doing here on earth."

"You mean what do I think the purpose of life is?" Kate nodded. "I don't know what the purpose of life is, Kate, but I do know that the best thing about life is love. And the more I love people, animals, the earth, even trees, the happier I am. And I feel lighter having forgiven my mother. And my father. I guess I loved them all along even when I felt abandoned, misunderstood, and controlled." Finn sipped his wine. "Maybe love is always there between people, only we forget it sometimes in our anger. We get afraid we're not loved. Then we hold grudges and hurt ourselves by refusing to forgive when we should be feeling gratitude for all we have."

"Well said, my little orator." Kate smiled at him—the smile he loved. "I agree. Forgiving is something we do for ourselves, not for the other person. In fact I've even been composing an email to Colin in my head."

"To say what?"

Just that I forgive him for not getting it back then, what I was going through, I mean. And letting him know I'd prefer no further contact, but good luck to him."

"If it makes you feel better, do it, but make sure you tell that dickwad the part about no further contact."

"Hey, wasn't that you who just a minute ago said loving everything and everyone makes you happier?"

"I didn't mean him when I said that. Let him suffer. Isn't suffering supposed to be good for you?"

"If it opens your heart and makes you more compassionate—at least according to my mother."

"So let him suffer, for his own good."

"Forget Colin. The way you described love is exactly what I want our kids to understand."

"What did I say again? Come closer and tell me." Kate snuggled into his lap. "That happiness is created by loving others, by forgiveness, that love is the most important part of life."

"Right." Finn took the cup out of her hand and kissed her. "Now that we've got that solved . . ."

TWIN FLAMES

"So . . . ?" Emma said. Georgina shifted the phone to her other ear.

"He's nice."

"And?"

"We had a glass of wine, and we talked, and then he walked me home and said good-night." Georgina took a bite of her toast while she waited for Emma's cross-examination.

"Well, what did you talk about? Are you going to see him again?"

"Do you remember those books that were channeled in the eighties called *The Law of One*?"

"Tell me you didn't," Emma said. Georgina could hear the concern in Emma's voice.

"We were talking about unity and oneness and how everything's connected, and he asked me if I'd ever read the *Ra Material—The Law of One*."

"He asked you?" Emma sounded like the principal questioning a student suspected of lying.

"That's what I said, Emma. Why so incredulous?"

"I just don't want you turning off a great guy by being too weird, bringing up stuff like *The Law of One*."

"So it's okay if he brought it up? If he finds me too weird, he doesn't have to see me again, but I'm not going to pretend to be different for anyone. I'd rather be alone." Georgina put another piece of bread in the toaster.

"Calm down. I'm just trying to protect you from yourself. Tell me how the conversation went."

"Are you working for the government now, Emma? Because you're seriously intrusive."

"I'm just interested in what a physicist thinks of the *Ra Material*. And even you have to admit it's a heavy topic for a first date."

"Oh, I see, you want to figure out if he's a whack job."

"Georgina, you're forgetting I read those books too. I admit it, at your suggestion, and I believe a lot of what's in them, though they made me uncomfortable."

"Why?"

"Trying to accept that everything that happens to us is a catalyst, accepting that the loss of both my mother and father at age seven was something I chose before incarnating so I could grow spiritually in this lifetime—not an easy sell. So yes, I do think *The Law of One* isn't what would spring to mind as a topic for a first date."

"I disagree. In fact, Emma, it's a perfect topic for a first date. If two people are in agreement that service to others, rather than service to self, is the better path to enlightenment and that our purpose on earth is to wake up and realize we are actually all part of Source and not separate at all, then they have a basis for a relationship. If they disagree about these things, their relationship will necessarily be limited."

"So are you in agreement about the nature of being?"

"He believes that the essential task for humans is to wake up in this third-dimensional heaviness and remember our origins as light beings, and then to awaken this consciousness in the hearts of others so enlightenment will sweep the planet."

"Oh, blah, blah, blah. Didn't you talk about anything personal? Didn't you talk about love? Isn't love the highest consciousness for you?"

"Don't play with me, Emma. You know it is. Love is the driving force toward enlightenment, even if it's only love of self. Even if a person is completely about their own gain. It's still a kind of love. But consciousness grows faster if our love is also for others." Cradling the phone between her ear and shoulder, Georgina buttered her cinnamon-raisin toast.

"So even greedy, selfish billionaire banksters can evolve and are legitimately part of the 'Oneness' because they love themselves? And both you and he believe this?"

"It seems we do. Even though it's hard to think that greed and the destruction or enslavement of others is a sanctioned part of the Oneness, it has to be this way because no one could choose service to others if he wasn't also free to choose service only to himself."

"Now that you've agreed between you on the justification for evil, are you going to have a second date?"

"Yes."

"Good. Then I have another piece of advice for you. Don't groan—you'll thank me. Nowadays women are doing more intimate grooming. I'm not saying get a Brazilian. And electrolysis isn't necessary, but I have a very good wax artist."

"I'm glad to hear electrolysis isn't necessary, Emma, because it won't be happening, nor will waxing."

"You may think it's still cool to be rocking a seventies vibe, Georgina, but most men nowadays aren't used to it."

"Emma, I know you mean to help me, but I don't want your advice on this."

"You can be so pigheaded, Georgina. Well, if you won't wax, you better at least do some vaginal steaming to prepare yourself for sex. It's been six years, hasn't it?"

"I don't even know what vaginal steaming is."

"I'm talking about plumping things up down there by squatting over steaming herbs, which the vaginal walls then absorb. It rejuvenates and strengthens your insides. It only takes twenty minutes. Google it."

"Good-bye, Emma."

Georgina hung up the phone and got back under the covers with her coffee and toast to think privately about this new man in her life. She hadn't told Emma, but she was meeting him for lunch.

Matthew was already seated when Georgina arrived at Gottino, and a bottle of red wine was open on the table. "It's freezing out, so I thought I'd warm us up with a claret." He helped her off with her scarf and coat.

"I think I'll keep my scarf on." Georgina sat down beside him on the bench.

"In case you should want a quick getaway?" In response, she gave him a half smile, the kind where your eyes smile, but you don't show your teeth.

The truth was she felt so shy she wanted to cover up. "It's a good day for wine and soup," she said. Her hand shook as she picked up her wine glass.

"Am I making you nervous, or are you just cold?" He was so earnest. She liked that about him.

"Both, I think. Well, I mean, you're not making me nervous. I mean, I'm just nervous. I don't know how to act on a date anymore." He was looking at her with such openness that it rattled her.

"Can I ask you something?" he said. Georgina nodded. "Last night you said that what you most love about your work as a psychologist is hearing people's dreams and working with them to decipher the message. Where do you believe these messages are coming from?"

"You jump right in at the deep end," she said, secretly grateful that he'd taken charge of the conversation.

"Do you mind talking about dreams?" he asked.

"I love it," she said. It felt exciting to be with a man this direct.

"So where do you believe our dream messages are coming from?"

"From the unconscious, the feminine portion of the mind." *I like him too much already*, she thought.

"You consider the unconscious feminine then?" He asked it like a serious question. She appreciated that. He was looking at her with an intensity she wasn't used to. Then he leaned in closer to hear her.

"Yes, kind of the way I think of the moon as feminine and the sun as masculine," she said. "But I believe we all have both feminine and masculine aspects to our minds." She wondered if she was making any sense. *Never mind.* It felt good to talk to him about anything.

"So then is the conscious mind the masculine aspect?" Matthew asked.

"That's how I think of it," she said. "The vast resources of the unconscious are put at the disposal of the conscious, masculine portion of the mind through dreams." She started to relax into the pleasure of his attention. He poured them more wine and turned to face her.

281

"So you see dreams, then, as a kind of bridge between the unconscious and the conscious aspects of the mind." He seemed to get it so easily.

"Exactly. Dreams contain a great deal of information that the conscious mind has no access to in any other way while we're alive on earth. After death the veil of forgetfulness is lifted."

"Then you believe that dreams can pierce the veil of forgetfulness and communicate information we couldn't otherwise have access to."

"Dreams are one way to receive this information. But the dreamer has to first cultivate a relationship with her unconscious, build a bridge between her conscious mind and her unconscious." He was looking at her with an expression compounded of interest and—was it appreciation? She continued: "Our culture doesn't take dreams seriously enough. Native Americans value their dreams so much that they don't sleep within five feet of another person because they don't want their dreams entwined with someone else's." Then she felt she was talking too much, so she reached for her bag to find her glasses and hid behind the menu.

"Where did you go?" he asked. She peeked over her menu. "Am I so scary?" he said. Then he looked at his menu too.

The waiter stepped toward them. Matthew chose the fettuccine with smoked trout, dill, and pink peppercorns. Georgina asked for the lentil soup and black bread.

"What did you mean, dreams are one way?" he asked.

"You were saying last night that some people, some gurus and enlightened beings and psychics, can pierce the veil of forgetfulness and vibrate with a frequency that allows them to view the future as well as the past, even past lives. Most of us can't do that, but dreams are available to everyone."

"Do most of your patients remember their dreams?"

"Not at first, they don't; but with practice, they all remember them. And the reward for the effort is tremendous."

"You mean in knowledge and enrichment of conscious awareness?" he asked.

"You say that like you don't agree."

"No, it's not that." He turned to face her directly on the bench they were

282

sharing. "I want to tell you something," he said. Her heart beat faster—in a good way. Invisible threads seemed to connect her eyes to his, holding her gaze fixed on him.

"Go on then."

"A few nights before I came to New York, I had a dream in which I met a woman that I felt I knew, but I didn't know how I knew her. I was very drawn to her. At one moment in the dream, her fingers grazed the side of my neck and it was the most exquisite feeling, feeling her touch me. That's all I remember. But when I saw you sitting in the audience, I thought I recognized you from my dream, and I remembered the feeling of that touch."

"What a beautiful dream."

"Yes, but, was it a premonition?" he said.

The waiter set Georgina's soup before her and then put Matthew's plate down and asked if there would be anything else for now. Neither of them appeared to register his question, so he walked away. Georgina tasted her soup, but it was too hot.

"How do you like living in Boston?" she asked him. Her question fell on the table like a stone.

"Do you always change the subject when the conversation gets close to the bone?" His forthrightness excited her.

"I'm sorry—I left you hanging out there. I didn't know how to answer except with a statistic, and that seemed dumb."

"What statistic?"

"Jung said that less than one percent of dreams are premonitions." She was grateful for his smile. They ate in silence, but it was a connected silence. When she finished, Georgina put her spoon down. "Why did you choose to study physics?"

"Galileo."

"He's your hero?"

"I had a book about his life when I was a child. I read it over and over."

"What was it about Galileo that captured you?"

"His questioning of accepted beliefs. His desire to base theory on observations of the real world. He tested theories. That wasn't standard procedure in the Aristotelian world of the sixteen hundreds."

283

"So he pushed the boundaries."

"More than that. His ideas were the beginning of modern science, modern physics."

Snow started to fall as they sipped their coffee. Georgina imagined she was looking at them through the window, watching them sitting side by side in the tiny cozy bistro as if they were in a snow globe scene.

"As much as we've said about the metaphysical, I still don't know anything about your life other than that you're a psychologist and that Jung is your Galileo."

"What would you like to know?"

"Tell me something you've never told anyone. I want to know secret things about you."

My heart must be visible, pounding through my sweater, she thought. And her palms were sweating. Under the table she wiped them on her napkin. All she said was, "We don't even know unsecret things about one another yet."

"All right, we'll stick to the known path and take the long way around. I assume you're single? Any children?" He smiled into her eyes. His own were soft and open.

"I'm on my own now, but I have a daughter and son-in-law in Okinawa who are about to have their first baby."

"And your parents?"

"There were six of us—my parents, two girls, and two boys. Half are dead. Both my parents died in the last couple of years. But I have two brothers living. My only sister, Julia, died a few months ago."

"I'm sorry."

"I think of her a hundred times a day. And I regret things I did and didn't do. I feel shame for ever inflicting even the smallest hurt on her." Georgina looked down at her hands fiddling with her napkin.

His gaze followed hers to her lap. He wanted to rescue her, somehow push her pain away. He spoke to her in a teasing voice. "Anyone can see you're a monster." She looked up into his face. He could feel her gratitude.

"And your family?" she said.

"There are times I'd give anything to speak to Mum again," he said.

"What was she like?"

"Lively and musical. She was a teacher."

"And your dad?"

"A straight-shooting Yorkshireman. I did see them both at the last, and I'm thankful for that. There was love on both sides at the parting."

"Do you ever just speak to your mum in your head?" Georgina asked.

"No. Do you speak to your sister or your parents?"

"It may sound crazy, but there's a tree in Washington Square Park where I walk my dog, Olive, every morning. I call the tree Thea because I heard that name in my head when I wondered once if she wanted me to call her something. As soon as I am near Thea, I start to feel connected to her. When I stand under her and breathe, I immediately think of Julia. Sometimes music she loved runs through my head. Sometimes I think of advice I imagine she would have given me if she were here. Thoughts come to me that I interpret as messages from her. It's as if I'm having a little morning visit with her. After I speak with Julia, I say hello to my parents and my guides and my soul. Then I give love to Thea and thank her for connecting us." Georgina looked at him cautiously. Had she said too much? The words had just kept tumbling out. "You must think I'm off the deep end," she said.

"You mistake me if you believe that."

"Tell me about you. I know you grew up in Yorkshire and that you're in the States for a year as a visiting professor at MIT on loan from Cambridge. But I don't know anything about your personal life."

"For the past five years, I've been with a woman. Last night after I left you, I decided to end it. I called her this morning."

"Just like that?"

"Yes, just like that."

"Where is she? How did she take it?"

"She took it well. It wasn't a big surprise. She's in the UK. Our break had been coming since we decided she wouldn't come to the States with me for the year. She's a painter, and her studio is over there, so she chose to stay and work."

"So it's over, with a phone call?"

"I had to do it. I was compelled. I'm under your spell." He was looking directly into her eyes, smiling.

"Someone once told me to beware of charming men."

"Then I shall endeavor to be less charming. Shall I get the check?"

"Yes, let's walk in the snow." These moments with him felt brand new and achingly familiar at the same time. She wrapped her scarf more tightly about her neck, and they stepped out into the falling snow.

Though it wasn't quite four o'clock when they left the restaurant, it was already growing dark. At Jefferson Market Garden, they stopped to watch the snowflakes accumulating on the shrubs and evergreen trees. Georgina turned to him. His face was very close to hers. The fields around their bodies seemed to be moving into one another, connecting them in one consciousness.

A thought moved through her mind. She'd read once about the concept of twin flames: two souls that were really one soul, one spark that split into two at the moment of flying out from Source. Each half would incarnate in different worlds throughout all the galaxies, again and again, over eons of time. Each of the two sparks were tiny replicas of Source and energetically matched to each other. At the moment of separating from Source, the soul split into the masculine and feminine aspects of the Divine and incarnated in separate bodies. If they incarnated on earth, they would be subject to the law that required souls to pass through the veil of forgetfulness. Souls born on earth no longer remember their divine origins. This has to be in order to see if they can wake up in the third dimension, remember their divine origin, and find their way back to Source.

If twin flames find each other while incarnated on earth, their union can ignite other hearts and light the path back for them as well. Once reunited, twin flames can help others move beyond the duality consciousness of the third dimension toward consciousness of Unity. Experiences of suffering, grief, and loss cause humans to question what they're doing on earth and to seek answers. It's the same for twin flames. Life after life each half of the soul suffers, learns its lessons, and evolves in consciousness. Each half develops its own talents for spiritual work and, through this work, serves others. But in the higher frequencies of light, beyond the dualistic conditions on earth, the two halves of the twin flame are never separate, but function as a single unit with a unified field of energy. On earth they function separately until each has achieved Unity consciousness. When each half becomes conscious that it is not separate from Source but part of the Unity, the two meet on the physical plane and recognition is immediate. Their coming together in the third dimension is for the purpose of service to others. Their union creates a unified field of energy between them and is a bridge to the higher-dimensional frequencies of light beyond duality. Once this happens, the twin flames function as a single consciousness. But before this can take place, each half has to transcend the limitations of ego and be able to vibrate in harmony with Source. Each twin must have circled the sun, so to speak, cleared all the cycles around pain, and dealt with all its karma. Twin flames cannot come together if either has avoided dealing with its pain or failed to live a life of service to others.

"You're very quiet," he said. "Are you communing with the trees?"

She glanced up at the evergreens surrounding them with their snow-laden branches. *Slow down*, she told herself. But he had raided her heart. It was already too late. Then she surprised herself by slipping her hand into his. He squeezed her fingers. A frozen spring inside her breast began to bubble forth like a small fountain. He stood still and silent beside her. A momentary vision of her sister and little Jack gazing at one another flashed before her. Two souls communing, she'd called it. How alike dying and falling in love are. Both transform you into something more than your small self.

He walked her home through the falling snow. She invited him in. They shook the snow off in her foyer, and she watched him gaze into her apartment. "This is a beautiful room," he said.

"Come in. I'll light the fire."

"No, I'll do it," he said.

"The matches are on the mantle."

In the kitchen she took out two glasses and a bottle of wine. Should she put on some music? But what music? What did he like? Steely Dan, Bob Marley, Pink Floyd, Dylan, the Beatles, the Goldberg Variations, Schubert, Marvin Gaye, Prince, Stevie Wonder, Miles Davis? She fumbled in the drawer for the wine opener, pulled it out, and walked back to the living room.

He was looking at her CDs. "Bob Marley?" he asked, turning around to face her.

A spark flew out of the fireplace and burned a tiny hole in the ivory-and-red killim that covered her living room floor. She watched him staring into the fire as they listened to Bob Marley sing, "I wanna love ya and treat ya right, I wanna love ya, every day and every night." Georgina felt the walls around her body coming down, a long forgotten self, buried deep inside her, awakening. "I wanna know ya. We'll be together, we'll share the shelter, of my single bed, we'll share the same room. Is this love, is this love, is this love that I'm feelin'?" Georgina's skin grew porous. "Oh yes, I know now. I'm willing and able, so I throw my cards on your table. We'll share the same room." A flame rose up in her heart. She had no insulation against him. "Everything's gonna be all right," Marley sang.

ROLLER SKATES AND A MOSES BASKET

"Merry Christmas, baby," Finn said, kissing her awake. "Come on, get up. The pancake batter is ready to go." Kate reached for her kimono and tied it where her waist would have been if she weren't nearly nine months pregnant. The scent of evergreen filled the whole house. Finn had lit the tree and set two places and a small pitcher of real maple syrup on the floor in front of it. The tiny golden-and-white lights shimmered through the orange slices hung on the branches. She'd only finished stringing the popcorn the night before. It looked like lace or snow lying on the evergreen branches in swooping loops of white. "Coffee or tea?" he asked her.

"Coffee please," she said, carefully lowering herself down onto the Persian carpet her father had given them for their first anniversary.

"We agreed, breakfast and presents together, right?" Finn called from the kitchen. Kate sat on the floor breathing in the tree. Finn handed her a warm cup. She smelled the coffee before taking a sip. He went back to the kitchen and returned with two plates of piping hot pancakes, very thin, the way she liked them. "What do you want to open first, your mom's, your dad's, or my mom's? Because I want you to open mine last." he said beaming at her.

"I'll go for your mom's first," Kate said. He handed her a package with fancy gold-and-silver wrapping.

She read out loud. "The card says, to Kate, Finn, and baby."

289

"Never mind the card. Get to the good stuff." Kate carefully undid the ribbon and opened the box. It contained pictures of a white crib, a white changing table, a white rocking chair and footstool, and a note that said, "If you like these, they'll be on their way. If not, look through the enclosed catalogs and choose ones you prefer. Love and Merry Christmas, Mom."

Kate looked up at Finn to see his reaction before saying, "Wow. Your mom's really gone all out. And I like her choices." Kate took a bite of her pancakes.

"I guess this means we have to call her and wish her a Merry Christmas?" Kate's mouth was full, but she gave him a look. "Just joking. It's only Christmas Eve in the States now, anyway."

"I want to thank her, and I want to see if she likes the books we sent her, especially *Thrive* and *The Heart Aroused*. I already know she'll love *All the Light We Cannot See*," Kate said.

"My mom doesn't read. Have you ever seen a book anywhere in her house?"

"When I asked her what she wanted for Christmas, she told me to choose some things for her to read on her vacation to Lamu. I tried to pick books that would meet her where her thinking is and move her a little beyond it. That's what I like a book to do for me."

"You really think she's going to read a book by Arianna Huffington?"

"*Thrive* isn't political in the narrow sense. It's a breakthrough lifestyle book. It suggests that companies have things like nap rooms and meditation classes for their employees."

"A breakthrough lifestyle book. That is a good idea for her. Next year maybe you can get her the complete overhaul lifestyle book. The one that includes the fact that twenty-six thousand children in New York City sleep in homeless shelters every night while rich Republicans suck down two-hundred-dollar bottles of wine with their escargot." Kate tossed a scrunched up ball of wrapping paper at him. He ducked. "Democrats drink wine too, and if Arianna isn't to her taste, she should like the other one at least."

"Really? The one about how to help corporations become more human friendly?"

"Come on, aren't you touched just a little by her thoughtfulness? She didn't have to do anything for us." Kate handed him a box. "This is from me." Finn set his fork down.

"Hmmm, it's heavy." He broke into a big smile as he opened the box and saw roller skates. "Whoa! Damn, girl!"

"I didn't want you to think all your fun is over just because we're having a baby." Finn pulled on one skate, then the other. Kate smiled at him. He looked like a happy child on Christmas morning.

"Okay, time for your mother's." He pulled a big box out from under the tree. It held their Christmas stockings, the same ones Georgina had filled for them every year. Finn's had a chocolate Santa and a large candy cane sticking out of the top, socks to go with his skates, new headphones by Dr. Dre, and under them a couple of baby pacifiers with a little note that said, "If all else fails." Kate got the tinted moisturizer she loved, B. J. Novak's new book of short stories, a set of watercolors, several styles of paint brushes, and a card telling them an ox had been given to a family through Heifer in their name. Kate smiled at this. It had been her job since childhood to choose the animal they would give to a family in some far-off country each year. "There's a card in the bottom of the box, Finn."

Finn opened it. "It's photos of three car seats and four strollers, and it says, 'Choose one of each, and they're yours. Love, Mom, Selma, Emma, and Carrie.' This kid is almost set."

"What do you mean, almost?" But Finn was on his way out the door. Kate heard his car trunk open and shut, and then he appeared carrying his gift all tied up with a red bow. It was a Moses basket overflowing with wrapped presents. He'd bought newborn diapers and onesies and receiving blankets and a baby towel with a hood that looked like a duckling and a baby bathtub in the shape of a whale.

"You wouldn't let Lydia give you a baby shower, so I went shopping myself." He grinned.

"I love it. I didn't know you knew about all this baby stuff."

"Hey, don't underestimate me. I know how to Google what newborns need."

"That's my phone ringing. Can you grab it? I can't get off the floor."

"Your mom," Finn said, tossing it to her.

"Merry Christmas, Mom. We just opened our presents. Thank you for everything. You even sent our stockings." Kate shifted her position, straightening her legs out in front of her on the floor. "What are your Christmas plans? Is that Marvin Gaye in the background I hear singing 'Sexual Healing'?"

"Matthew's here. We're sitting in front of the fire, sipping cognac and admiring the beautiful mandala painting you did for me. I don't know how you had time to create it with all your other work. I love it. Thank you, my darling."

"Hold on a minute, Mom."

"Kate, tell Finn I've already opened his chocolate-covered, salted caramels. Selma and I dug into them when she came by to say happy Christmas before leaving for Georgia."

"Wait, Mom, you mean Matthew, the physicist you met when he gave a talk at the New School, is there now, on Christmas Eve with you, and you're listening to—what is it I'm hearing—'Let's Get It On'?"

"Yes. We had an afternoon of Schubert, and now we're coming back down to earth."

"Is he spending the night?"

"Yes," Georgina said rushing ahead. "And Emma and some friends of Matthew's, who are in town from London, are coming over tomorrow at five for champagne, and then we're all going to Morandi for Christmas dinner. Mathew wants one of his friends to meet Emma."

"So it's serious?" Kate could hear "If This World Were Mine" coming over the phone.

"Yes."

"And you've been keeping this a secret?"

"I told you I met him. And I've only known him for two weeks."

"Well you certainly downplayed it, Mom."

"This is your time, Kate. You're about to have a baby. How are you feeling?" Kate didn't want to change the subject, but she answered the question: "Like a beached whale."

"Let me wish Finn a Merry Christmas. I love you, sweet-pea girl."

"Wait, Mom, I want to hear more about you and Matthew." She could hear Marvin Gaye singing in the background: "If you wanted the moonlight I'd give you that too."

"We'll talk about it next time. Now put Finn on."

"Mom, wait."

"Sweetheart, this is a good thing. It feels right. I love you." Kate handed Finn the phone.

❧

"So your mom's new guy is spending Christmas Eve with her in front of the fire, drinking cognac, and listening to Marvin Gaye. Good for her."

"I'm glad she's met someone who's in her tree. But I don't want her to get hurt."

"From the sound of things, she's having a very good time," Finn said.

"Maybe too good."

"She's an adult, Kate. Stop worrying and hand me your plate."

"She is and she isn't. She's too innocent. After his talk at the New School, she was so excited that he had so many of the same ideas about things as she does. But does he really?"

"Even if it flames out, she's having fun now," Finn said.

"I don't want him to break her heart."

"Life breaks your heart, Kate. That's part of the deal. Didn't she always tell us that?"

"But I hear something in her voice. Like she's got more ballast. And Matthew seems inclusive. They're having friends over."

"So stop worrying." He carried their plates into the kitchen. "Hey, we missed your father's package," Finn said, coming back into the room. He pulled it out from under the tree.

"Go for it." Finn tore off the shiny red wrapping and pulled out a snuggly with a check for a thousand dollars tucked in it. "This will completely cover the midwife. Thank you, Cyrus." Finn kissed the check.

"What does the card say?" Kate asked.

"Here's something for my first grandchild. Love you to the moon and back."

"That's what he used to say when he tucked me in at night," Kate said. "Before the divorce." She suddenly felt like crying but pushed the feeling away. "Can you help me off the floor? I've got a few dozen reindeer, Santas,

293

bells, angels, and Christmas trees to bake to take to Lydia and Spencer's. But let's call your mom to thank her first. Then we'll call my dad."

Finn pulled her to her feet and kissed the tip of her nose. "Merry Christmas, baby."

"Merry Christmas, Finn."

WINTER HARVEST

"You've been holding out on me, Georgina," Emma said. They were walking under the arch at the entrance to Washington Square Park on their way to the movies. "And you're going to make a mess of things without my help." Georgina picked up her pace as they neared the fountain. "Don't stalk off. I want to talk to you about Matthew."

"Emma, I appreciate your concern, but . . ."

"No, what you mean is, you don't appreciate my concern. But I have to tell you, as well as you've done in your work life, your Achilles heel has always been your relationships with men." Emma stopped and stood still by the fountain, even though it was turned off this time of year.

"Why are you stopping?" Georgina asked.

"To get your attention. Do you want to be alone, Georgina? Because you're not cut out for the single life. And you've already had enough relationship failures."

"Ouch."

"I meant it to sting, to bring you to your senses. You're going to put Matthew off, with crazy talk about the earth moving into the fourth dimension, the veil of forgetting, and extraterrestrials coming to our aid. Save that stuff for your conversations with Carrie."

Georgina smoothed her hair back as if to calm her mind, wipe away her reaction. Then she chose her words carefully. "I want to be with someone who is struggling with the same questions as I am, or else alone."

"Well, you will be alone if you keep on about negative entities from Orion battling positive entities from the Confederation. You sound like an episode of *Star Trek*." Georgina let Emma's comment go. Emma continued. "And what are these consuming questions you insist on struggling with?"

"It's too cold to stand here arguing, Emma."

"Well, I told you to wear a hat."

"It hurts that you can ask me what I struggle with, after all these years."

"Oh, don't get your knickers in a twist. I understand what drives you. You've told me enough times that it's your soul that compels you in your search to understand the purpose of suffering."

"Emma, it may surprise you that Matthew is as interested as I am in the purpose for incarnating and the reason for suffering."

"Well, good then, but why not keep some of your wackier ideas on the down low for a while so you don't blow it with him? That's all I'm saying."

"That's not all you're saying. You're saying: be somebody different."

"No, I'm saying: don't show all of yourself at once. Unfold a little at a time."

"But keep hidden all the questions that are most important to me?"

"I didn't say that."

"Well, what then?"

"Just stick to your main stuff, like: What are we doing here? Where did we come from? Where are we going? Leave the negative beings from Orion and the war in the fourth dimension stuff out of it."

"You think you can conduct my life better than I can. That's it, isn't it?"

Emma ignored her. "Are we going to see this movie or not? Selma's probably there already, pacing up and down," Emma said.

"Unlikely, as she's always late," Georgina said.

Lights all over the park twinkled on, revealing oak and sycamore branches dressed in snow. "What did you think of Matthew's friend Peter?" Georgina asked. "You never said."

"I like him, but he lives in London."

"So that's that then?" asked Georgina.

"We've been emailing."

Georgina stopped and gave Emma a look. "It's just emailing, Georgina."

"London could be a good change for you. Besides, you've written enough obituaries for one life. And you don't need the money."

"There's Selma," Emma said.

When she got home that night, Georgina slipped off her boots in the foyer and hung up her coat. Then she put the kettle on for tea and opened her laptop. In a week she would fly to Okinawa for the baby's birth. Her plan was to stay until Kate felt comfortable at home on her own. Knowing Kate's serenity around babies, that could be instantly. In that case Georgina would stay two weeks and leave the new family on its own. She was curious to meet Lydia and Spencer and Myrna too.

Georgina pressed "Command R" and up came three emails from Matthew. That was unusual. He nearly always waited for a reply before writing again.

I've been invited to speak at a conference in Tokyo the first week in February. Someone dropped out, and they need a replacement. I'll accept if you'll meet me there on your way home from Okinawa. What do you think? M.

I don't want to interfere with your time with Kate, Finn, and baby. Just thought if the timing works out, it might be a little fun to be in Japan together for a few days. M.

I won't give them an answer until I hear from you. M.

Japan. Georgina hadn't been there since she was an exchange student her junior year of college. Japan with Matthew? This trip to the Far East was about Kate and Finn and the baby. What if she wasn't ready to leave Kate until after Matthew's conference had come and gone? *Am I looking for excuses not to do it? Maybe I am afraid. Maybe I do ruin all my relationships out of fear. Not this time. Okay, into the breach.* She hit "Reply."

Matthew, it's a lovely idea, but I don't want you to accept unless you would even if we weren't meeting there. And the baby could be late, so the timing might not work out.

Georgina reread her answer before hitting send. She'd only hedged a little. His reply was immediate.

But if the timing does work out, will you stop in Japan and meet me? M.

Yes. But if it doesn't, will you mind all the flying just for the conference? Is it something you're interested in? G.

The conference is on sources of energy that various governments may be keeping secret and the possible physics of these energy sources. It does interest me. M.

Okay then, you're on. And, there's a remote Japanese hamlet, a little spot on a mountaintop that time forgot. I'd like to visit it with you. You leave your car at the bottom of the mountain and hike for several hours up a winding spiral path that encircles the mountain to reach the ancient village at the top. We can spend the night up there, back in time, in a small guest house, all in Japanese style with tatami floors and futons, sliding rice paper doors opening onto the quiet of the mountainside, our own private Japanese bath. G.

Perfect. M.

Their emails were so minimal, so restrained. But then there were those moments of melting in the fierce heat of the magnetism between them. It felt like hooking into the electric current of the universe. She hadn't expected to fall in love, especially not into a love this staggering and ferocious, but love had found her. It wasn't the subversive act that the falling in love of youth can be, but it had altered her as much as if two chemicals had been mixed in a beaker and created a new substance. And he knew things about her she'd never told him—like her favorite lines from Yeats, whom she'd first read as a teenager. Out of the blue one evening, unknowingly, he'd quoted them to her:

> *But one man loved the pilgrim soul in you,*
> *And loved the sorrows of your changing face.*

Still, she'd gotten used to walking alone since Colin's departure, used to the freedom of her aloneness. Was it the sense memory of Colin's demand that she submit to his will that made her fearful of a new relationship? Was that trauma not completely wrung from her flesh? *Let go of the fear*, she told herself as she lay in bed, unable to fall asleep. Maybe Emma was right, and she was too weird. And how about Emma, anyway, writing her secret emails. Maybe she'd finally worked through the trauma of her parents' deaths and could give up writing obituaries. Emma and Peter? Maybe.

Georgina got up, walked to the window, and pulled back the curtain. *The moon rose like a white fruit*, she heard in her head. Had she read that somewhere or just made it up? She knelt on the love seat under the window and gazed up at the moon. Olive banged her tail up and down a few times in greeting before settling to sleep again. *The fact is, I do feel an emotional harmony when I'm alone letting the moonlight wash over me. This moon bath is a note perfectly hit, a note speaking to my soul in a language so direct it hurts.* For years she'd had a relationship with the moon, always searching the night sky for it on her walk home from work, following its phases, mindful of its cool feminine beauty. Gazing up, searching for the moon, was an old habit of seeking nurturing from the Divine Feminine. Tonight, staring up at its silent, white face, she offered gratitude for its faithful presence in her life. The moon was a completely feminine being to Georgina. She wondered what kind of relationship Matthew had with the moon. He had come into her life like a meteor. Holding on to her own center of gravity had been difficult at first. His directness was more like bright sunlight. "I think about you a thousand times a day," he told her the first week they met.

As she sat bathing in the moonlight, Georgina remembered this same moon shining down on her when she lived in Japan at age nineteen during her junior year abroad. As she walked home from the Japanese bath, she looked in the sky for it. She went to the bath each evening to warm her blood before going back to her room to study in bed under the covers. Entering on the women's side of the bathhouse, she'd pick up a wicker basket, a small wooden bucket, a little bar of jasmine soap, a washcloth, and a towel. Then she'd remove her clothes and drop them in the basket. Naked, holding her small wooden bucket, she'd slide back the rice paper doors and walk onto the tiled floor of the bath, breathing in the scent of the deep pools of scalding water. She could picture it so vividly that she could almost smell it.

At each of the twelve sets of spigots along the tiled walls squatted a naked Japanese woman washing herself and rinsing off with water from her wooden bucket. Georgina kept her eyes down as she made her way to the "before" pool and slipped in to soak. Always the only Westerner, she'd sit on the ledge that lined the inside of the pool and feel the hot water cover her body up to her earlobes. Sometimes a young woman already seated in the pool, her black hair piled high on top of her head and held in place with two lacquer sticks, would watch discretely as a teenage Georgina entered through the mist rising off the water. Before closing her eyes to soak away the cares of the day, Georgina would offer a smile to the other girl, which would be returned with discreet shyness. After a delicious soak, she'd climb out and carry her wooden bucket and cloth to a free spigot, and squatting, she'd imitate the Japanese women by washing each finger and toe and every inch of herself before pouring buckets of hot water over herself and watching it stream down her body to rinse off the soap. Once all the soapy water had flowed in rivulets down one of the many drains in the tiled floor, she'd stand and walk over to the "after" pool for a final soak in the steaming water. Then once again she'd emerge, her flesh pink and warm, and walk over to the rice paper doors, slide them open, and slip through, feeling a sudden chill before wrapping up in her towel. On the way home after the bathhouse, she'd stop at the small shop next door for tangerines to eat in bed while she studied. That had been her nightly ritual in Japan at age nineteen. And she still cherished the memory of it.

From the first moment she landed for her junior year abroad, Japan felt familiar. It was like coming home. Kimonos, lacquer rice bowls, wood block prints of young geishas, the sweet scent of straw sandals, people bowing to one another, shopkeepers exercising in front of their stores each morning, and the lovely, meticulous way they wrapped each package, *The Tale of Genji*: all these had captivated her. One of things she'd treasured most was the simplicity of haiku.

> *The little fish*
> *Carried backwards*
> *In the clear water.*
> —Takai Kito
>   (R. H. Blyth)

That was all long ago now, and so much had changed. Georgina looked up at the New York moon outside her window, but her heart and mind were in Japan.

The present merged with the past as Georgina unloosened her mind in the moonlight. So much had happened since her nightly ritual Japanese baths at age nineteen. Julia was still in high school when Georgina first went to Japan to study. Her brother Edward had not yet even begun high school. Stan had just graduated. Her parents were still young. Georgina hadn't yet sold cars in Berkeley or waitressed at the Gaslight Club or Windows on the World or even met Cyrus or Colin. She hadn't even thought of becoming a psychologist. It was all about literature and writing back then. Her grandmother Anastasia was still alive. And Kate, of course, hadn't yet been born. There was no Internet, and computers were so big, they took up an entire room. Women still dreamed of having mink coats, cooked with Crisco, and served their families iceberg lettuce and Wonder Bread. Department stores still sold rubber girdles, and bras with pointy cups. TVs were bulky and

Cadillacs looked like rocket ships. Telephones in bright yellow or red or beige hung on kitchen walls. Teenage girls coveted pink Princess phones.

Georgina had turned from child to teenager in the sixties. She could still see the brown album cover of *Rubber Soul* propped up on the record player in the bedroom she shared with Julia. *How I would love to be back in that room for just a moment*, she thought, *saying good-night to my sister before we climb into our twin four-poster beds with their matching bedspreads, turn off our matching bedside lamps, and lie in the dark listening to Bob Dylan sing us to sleep*. Her life had held so many treasures, so many moments of joy and grace and pain. A feeling of gratitude swept through her as she leaned her head back in the moonlight and gazed starward. And now there was Matthew. At the thought of him, a shiver ran through her body.

NOTHING, THEN E.T.

While Georgina unpacked, Kate and Finn sat on the floor surrounded by the sides of the white crib. Kate read the assembly instructions out loud. Though Finn was the muscle, Kate was better at making sure they did things in the right order so they wouldn't need to take everything apart and start over. So far their teamwork had managed the changing table and the rocking chair without a hitch. Picking up a wooden hanger from the new rocking chair and stowing it in the closet, Georgina announced she was going to start dinner.

"Mom, the skirt steak is marinating in the fridge. Just take it out and put the water on for the pasta. The pesto sauce is already in a bowl." Georgina opened the bottle of red wine on the counter and poured two glasses. It was easy to find things in Kate's kitchen. She'd pictured this house a hundred times as she'd imagined Kate and Finn's life in Okinawa. But it was even quirkier and more charming than she'd expected. The tatami floors in the bedrooms smelled fresh and delicious, and the stone floor in the kitchen made you feel you were cooking back in time, in some rustic setting. Kate's workspace, in a corner of the living room between two large windows overlooking palm trees, held her computer, piles of books, and jars of paintbrushes. Watercolors and sketches were tacked all over two walls. Georgina sipped her wine and drank in her daughter's home. Kate came in to ask her to make salad dressing and then went back to her task. The water boiled, and Georgina added salt before stirring in the spaghetti. She poured olive oil into the bottom of a bowl and picked up the scissors to cut off a few pieces of scallion to flavor the oil. She squeezed in half a lemon, added some fresh crushed garlic, and salt and pepper. Then she rolled the whole mixture around in the large bowl to cover the sides before dropping in the arugula and tossing it. Pesto pasta with small pieces of skirt steak mixed in was a dinner Kate and Finn had often made back in New York when they were still teenagers living with Georgina. Tonight they would gather around their own table in this far-off island and share the familiar meal. Georgina carried her wine into the baby's room to check on the progress with the crib. It was standing, and Finn was tightening the screws. "The pasta's about ready to be drained."

"My job," said Finn, heading to the kitchen. Seeing Kate grimace, Georgina asked her, "Are you all right?"

"I thought I felt something, but it's gone."

"Come sit down at the table, and I'll bring you some water," Georgina said.

Finn placed the steaming platter in the center of the table. Georgina held her palms over it for a few brief seconds and whispered a blessing. Kate and Finn exchanged smiles. Finn toasted her presence in their home and then served them. They all dropped into silence to enjoy their food.

After dinner and a soak in Kate's big, deep, squarish bathtub to wash off the plane, Georgina lay in bed and marveled at her daughter's life. How close they'd come to the end those years ago when Kate's life hung by a thread. And now, Kate was about to be a mother. "Thank God. Thank God," Georgina said almost out loud in the dark in what would soon be the baby's room. Then Kate would know the joy and pain of attempting to secure safety for her child—a sacred and impossible task. With this thought, Georgina fell asleep.

"Are you awake, Mom?" Kate said, sticking her head in the door. "My water broke a few hours ago, and I've been having contractions since right after we went to bed."

"Oh, my darling," Georgina said waking herself up. "What time is it?"

"It's almost six. I've called the midwife—she's on her way here now."

Georgina counted on her fingers. "You've been in labor eight hours. What can I do for you, my sweet-pea girl?"

"Walk around the house with me. Finn's finally fallen asleep after being awake all night, holding me up through the contractions." Georgina got out of bed and went to her daughter's side. "After dinner I thought I was having indigestion. Finn had to tell me I might be in labor. I guess I was more afraid of the labor and birth than I expected. I didn't even recognize it when it started."

"It's okay, my darling; everything's going to be fine."

"Let's keep walking, Mom. If I can stay upright, maybe gravity will help the baby to come."

"Good thinking, my little physicist."

"Tell me something to distract me, Mom, something Matthew's said to you."

Georgina rifled through her mind. "He explained to me that gravity isn't a force like other forces because it's always attractive and because it's curved by objects. The sun, for instance, causes gravity to curve."

"This is what you and Matthew talk about? I meant something personal he's said to you."

"You mean about love?"

"For instance," Kate said.

"He said he thinks of me a thousand times a day."

"That's pretty romantic."

"And he believes that in some plane of existence, long ago, we made a plan to meet."

"And you believe that too, don't you," Kate said. Georgina nodded.

Together they padded down the hall, out to the living room, and into the kitchen, and then back into the living room, and back again into the baby's room, waiting for the midwife. Georgina watched the light come into the rooms, making invisible things visible, a prayer on her lips all the while.

"I wanted the baby to be born in the ocean, but the water temperature is only about sixty degrees this time of year," Kate said. "But there's a small round saltwater pool about eight feet in diameter at the birthing center where I'll give birth—unless there are complications." Kate was breathing with effort. "The pool is big enough for me, Finn, the midwife, and you, Mom, if you want to get in with us."

There was a tap at the door, and the midwife came in. An hour later they were entering the birthing center, Finn supporting Kate, Georgina following with Kate's bag. Typical of Kate, she had preregistered online sometime during the night. The whole place reminded Georgina of a temple or a patrician home in Pompeii. There was a central courtyard open to the sky and surrounded by palm trees. In the center of the courtyard were four circular saltwater pools fed by a central fountain. Around the courtyard were four sets of tall pillars with long, sheer flowing curtains on either side of each column. On each side of the courtyard, between a set of pillars, was a spacious room with low tables and daybeds draped in softly colored fabric and pillows. Each room had a marble bath with a large sunken tub adjoining it. "This place is like a temple," Georgina said. "It'll be like giving birth in a pool in a palace garden."

"That's what it's supposed to feel like. It was donated by an Okinawan billionaire who believes women should be honored for giving birth," Kate explained. "Treated like goddesses."

"Is it open to all women?" Georgina asked.

"Yes. And it costs less than giving birth in a hospital. You're only here until shortly after the baby is born, and then you go home," Kate explained. Finn continued walking Kate around the garden circling the gurgling fountain, one strong arm supporting her back, the other under her elbow. "There's also a wonderful kitchen with delicious, healthy food," Kate said.

The midwife came out to the garden to see how Kate was doing. She had been in labor twelve hours already. "Keep walking with her as long as she has the strength," the midwife said. Kate paused to suck on some ice chips. The midwife noted the time between contractions. Georgina ordered coffee, fruit, and omelets for herself and Finn. Kate and Finn kept walking. A lovely young woman in a flowing dress left bathing garments, robes, and large fluffy towels for them.

After three more hours of walking, the midwife finally told Finn and Georgina to change while she shepherded Kate into the birthing pool. Georgina and Finn followed. As she walked down the steps into the warm saltwater, Georgina heard church bells in the distance and realized it must be Sunday. "This water feels so good," Kate said before another contraction seized her. Georgina looked from Kate's face to Finn's. They wore the same expression of exhaustion, pain, fear, and anticipation. The four of them sat in the gurgling pool and waited. Kate breathed and watched the fountain flow down into the pool. "A few more contractions," the midwife finally said, "and the baby will be here."

And he was. It had been just the four of them, and then suddenly it was as if E.T. was in the pool with them, having arrived from some distant land. The midwife directed Finn to catch the baby as it shot forward into the saltwater, and Finn caught him and held him in his strong hands for only a few seconds before placing him in Kate's arms. "It's a boy," he said, as he gave the baby up to her, his eyes not moving from her face. Georgina's heart was bursting in her body. Her eyes overflowed as they moved from the baby's face to Kate's to Finn's and back again to the baby's. He had the same tiny round face and dark hair that Kate had had as an infant. The memory took her breath away, and tears rolled down her cheeks. A newborn person had come among them, fully visible and whole. But the most arresting sight for Georgina was not the baby but the beauty of Kate's expression as she gazed at her child. Her eyes were soft with love for her son, and light seemed to pour out of them and from her whole face. Finn was staring at her too. Nobody had words for this moment.

Georgina climbed out of the pool and left the new family to themselves. She walked to the dressing room to change and felt suddenly aware of being surrounded by many invisible beings—her grandmother Anastasia, her parents, her sister, Julia. Had they come for the birth? The strongest presence was Julia. Naturally she had come, as she had for every birth and death and illness in the whole family while she walked on earth. Had she accompanied Kate's son to the threshold and lingered near them to share their joy?

Georgina sank down on the bench in the dressing room to absorb what had just happened. Though it was a miracle all humans experienced, it never lost its majesty.

Desiring to hold on to this moment, unable even to take off her wet bathing suit, Georgina shivered and pulled the soft robe around her. *New-born*: how much this word meant if you let yourself feel it. The first newborn person she'd ever seen was Julia. Georgina had been four when her father took her and her brother Stan up to the hospital to stand outside in the falling snow under the window of their mother's hospital room. Her mother held newborn Julia up to the window so they could see her, a tiny being in her arms. Georgina could see the scene as if she were looking down at it from a tree. A handsome man standing between a little girl and a little boy, holding each child by the hand. All three gazing up in the direction of a window where a beautiful woman with long dark hair and cornflower-blue eyes held a newborn baby girl. Her mother was twenty-seven when Julia was born, so young and already the mother of three children. Now the handsome man, the beautiful woman, and the new baby were all gone, back to some other world whence they'd come. How quickly the time had gone from that moment to this.

"Thank you for guiding this child safely to us," Georgina said to the invisible trio. And she sat there in her wet bathing suit and wept, her heart overflowing and spilling out of her eyes for the living and the dead.

Kate was sitting in bed, holding the baby when Georgina finally came out of the dressing room. "We've decided to name him Leo," Finn told her. Georgina moved closer to have a good look at her grandson. Kate held him out to her mother, and Georgina took him in her arms and held him to her heart. He seemed a tiny replica of Kate except with Finn's forehead and hands. "What joy you bring, Leo, what great joy," she whispered to him.

"Lydia, Spencer, and Myrna are on their way to our house with dinner. I told her we wouldn't be released for another hour. I hope you're hungry, Mom. If I know them, it's likely to be a five-course meal, complete with champagne and cigars," Kate said.

"Kate, are you up for that? You've been walking around and having contractions for hours and hours, and you've just given birth," Georgina said. "You must be exhausted."

"I'll sleep later. Anyway, there's no stopping them, Mom."

Georgina handed Leo to Finn and checked her phone for the first time since arriving in Okinawa. Cyrus, Matthew, Emma, Selma, Carrie, Sara,

Charlotte, Stan, Edward—all had texted for news. Many beloved people were dead, but there were still many alive, she reminded herself. "Everyone wants news," she said to Kate and Finn.

"Hand me your phone, Mom, I'll send a group text. I want to let Bunny know too."

Georgina handed her phone to Kate. "They'll all be more thrilled to have the news directly from you."

Finn sat holding Leo, beaming while Kate snapped a photo to send.

A little while later, the midwife came in and released them. They headed home, with Leo safely buckled into his car seat, his mother beside him and Georgina up-front with Finn. Lydia, Spencer, and Myrna had already arrived when Finn pulled into the driveway. Dozens of blue balloons were tied to the palm trees in the yard, and floating above their front door, was a banner saying only "Leo." *How did they make that so fast?* Georgina wondered.

Inside a feast was in preparation. Lydia and Myrna bustled about Kate's kitchen, and Spencer popped the cork on a bottle of champagne, then handed Finn and Georgina cigars. "I'll save this for Matthew," Georgina told Spencer. "Do you want to get into bed, Kate, or settle here on the couch?" Georgina asked.

"The couch for now."

After much passing around to receive the admiration due him, Leo nursed and fell asleep on Kate's heart. Finn took him when Lydia handed Kate a plate. Later, after they'd all cleaned up and put the leftovers in the fridge and Lydia, Spencer, and Myrna had left, Kate nursed Leo again and then settled him in his Moses basket on the floor next to their futon. Finn turned out all the lights and said good-night to Georgina. Then he climbed into bed next to Kate. "Now we're three. Well done, my darling." He kissed her forehead and then her lips before leaning over her for a last look at their sleeping baby.

Georgina lay on her futon across the hall in Leo's room, trying to fall asleep. But sleep wouldn't come: too much gratitude for this day and this new life, and too many thoughts rolling around in her head. It was like she was watching her life from a long way off. *I'm not the same person I was twenty years ago, or even five years ago. I've been transformed by each thing that has happened. I'm less afraid to trust love, even though I know deep in my bones that loving will always break your heart, one way or another. Loving Kate and nearly losing her, her failed life with Colin, Julia's death, Leo's headfirst dive into the saltwater and Finn's waiting arms, Matthew's sudden appearance—each was a gift, even if it didn't always look like one at first. My arms are full of the gifts of my life. No one will ever again make a victim of me or send me to the cellar to stand by the coal bin. That's done and forgiven. Everything is forgiven, even myself.*

You just have to bear the things that come to you, she told herself, *and then an opening occurs and life transforms, the circle comes together, the meaning becomes clear, if only for the moment, until the next transformation*—which was already unfolding inside her as she began to let her dreams live in Matthew. Feelings that had lain hidden in her were blossoming again, as if the sun had unexpectedly fallen on a cold flower bed, warming and awakening it. This was the wonderment Jung must have felt when Toni Wolff entered his life and he described her as a gift—"dropped from heaven, unasked."

Two weeks later when Georgina left for Japan, Leo was still sleeping in his Moses basket next to Kate and Finn's bed, just as Kate had slept in her bassinet beside Georgina and Cyrus in the first months of her life. And when Georgina landed in Tokyo, Matthew stood on the other side of the rope, beaming like a lighthouse. *I was a lost ship,* she thought as she smiled back at him. *A ship that has finally found the light it has been seeking with an infinite ache for longer than memory.* With her heart full of infinite gratitude, she walked into his arms.